PLAYING GOD

Also by Barbara Whitehead:

Ramillies

Quicksilver Lady

The Caretaker Wife

BARBARA WHITEHEAD

Playing God

St. Martin's Press
New York

This book is lovingly dedicated to my aunt
Muriel Kathleen Garner
whose delight in books, history,
and the Derbyshire countryside,
has always been an inspiration.

The places in this book are real places, the plays are real plays. All the characters, however, are completely imaginary.

 For information, address St. Martin's Press, 175 Fifth Avenue, New York, N.Y. 10010.

Library of Congress Cataloging-in-Publication Data

Whitehead, Barbara.
Playing God / Barbara Whitehead.
p. cm.
ISBN 0-312-03910-7
I. Title.
PR6073.H543P55 1989 89-27094
823'.914—dc20 CIP

First published in Great Britain by Quartet Books Limited.

First U.S. Edition

10 9 8 7 6 5 4 3 2 1

1

I am gracious and great, God without a beginning.
I am maker unmade, and all might is in me.
The Barkers' Play

It was the last concert of the tour. The hall was hot and full. Dark except where the coloured lights probed across it, playing with the blackness but always returning to concentrate on the gyrating figure on the stage. Sound rocked the auditorium, vibrating the walls, drowning the screams of the girls. Poison Peters was working up to a crescendo to beat the crescendo his whole performance had been. They saw him in the flesh, yet through their memories of his videos, his record sleeves, his TV appearances. At last it ended. He left the stage. They let him go slowly, as though they would drag the flesh from his bones.

In a quiet road in the ancient city of York, Tom Churchyard had parked his bicycle. Sydney Absolom came by at that moment and together they walked past the pale stone walls of the city towards Monk Bar.

'There'll be the devil to pay over this,' said Absolom.

He was an oldish man with hair which seemed to have settled on his head like a small inconsequent cloud. He looked very like the painting of a saint on the fourteenth-century glass of the window of the north choir aisle of All Saints Church. They were going to a meeting of the Medieval Reconstruction Society (known as MRS) in an old stone cell of a room slung high over one of the busy streets which led into the heart of the congested town.

'I can't believe it. They wouldn't choose *him* as Christ,'

replied Thomas.

They arrived at the meeting; the speaker was already there; nothing more was said between them until afterwards, when the time arrived for coffee and biscuits.

'There'll be the devil to pay over this,' said Mr Absolom again.

'What's the matter?' asked Julia Bransby, who had been giving them a lecture on early woven fabrics. She had turned to Thomas Churchyard, the chairman, beside her.

'You haven't heard? It was in the Press. I can hardly believe it myself.'

'I've only just got back from Manchester. I haven't even been home. Adam had to get his own tea.'

'Bruce Exelby has named his Christ.'

'At last! You've been rehearsing for weeks, haven't you? What's taken him so long? There's only one professional actor in the cast, you wouldn't think he would leave the choice until the last minute like this.'

'They stir up a lot of publicity about it these days. It all helps to remind people that we have a festival, that they can see a performance of medieval drama without going to Oberammergau, that each time there is this search for the Christ.'

'Well, and who's he ended up with?'

'You won't guess.' Thomas Churchyard took a mouthful of his powdered coffee and hot water in its expanded polystyrene beaker. He seemed reluctant to tell her. Then at last he said, 'He's chosen Poison Peters.'

'Poison Peters? You've got to be joking.'

'No, unfortunately.'

'Not Poison Peters that ghastly pop singer?'

'Afraid so.'

'Not to play Christ in the mystery plays?'

'Yes.'

Now the name was actually spoken among them, the enormity of the producer's action seemed to grow and glower in the still air of that medieval room, poised over the thoroughfare, held in quietness over the busy cars and people.

'Well!' Julia drank her coffee, unable to say anything else. Absolom looked at them, went over to his raincoat (he was never without it, even in May), pulled a newspaper out of the pocket and came over. He had been listening to their conversation. 'POISON CAST AS CHRIST' screamed the headline, and below it was a large photograph of the pop star looking as though he was about to take a bite out of a microphone, face distorted and deathly pale, hair in a sort of aureole of blond spikes.

Absolom looked heavily at Julia, and repeated his words.

'There'll be the devil to pay over this.'

'I should just think there will! The whole city will be up in arms. It's a desecration. What a person to choose. Drugs, orgies, smashing up hotel rooms, you name it . . .'

They all remembered the reports of occasions when Poison had been disgracefully sick in public; the damage done by his band; the hotel carpets ruined; the trans-dressing, being refused entry to a prudish Catholic country because he was dressed as a woman; the stark white make-up in the daytime; the hair in a variety of fluorescent colours; the groupies thrown out by hotel managements . . .

'There is a feeling of outrage through the city. You'll see. There'll be letters in the Press about it tomorrow. More than that,' said Absolom darkly. 'There'll be *something done*. It won't be allowed to go through. There'll be a stop put to it.'

'I should think there might well,' replied Thomas.

'It's an insult. What does he think he's doing? It's shaming that such a man should be given the role of Christ. Man? He doesn't deserve the name of *man* – filthy creature.'

'It is a surprise, certainly.'

'A surprise?'

'A shock, if you like.'

Sydney Absolom's face was flushed under the small round-edged cloud of hair.

'I think it's disgusting,' added the secretary, Sally Vause, a plump, lively woman, catching hold of the plate of biscuits as though she was fielding a cricket ball.

'I'd better go.' Julia put down her beaker. 'Thanks.'

'We'd like you to accept a small token of our gratitude,' said the treasurer, Velvet Smith, coming up with a white envelope.

'You shouldn't have,' said Julia. 'I didn't expect anything.

You're such a small society, I'm sure you're short of funds.'

'Yes. But not so short that we can't acknowledge an excellent lecture like yours, Mrs Bransby.'

The pleasantries went on.

Julia had not lived in the city very long, but as she looked round the room she found she knew, at least vaguely, most of the people in it. Apart from herself there were eleven – four men and seven women.

The chairman, Thomas Churchyard, struck her as one of those big dependable men who were nice to have around. Sydney Absolom was so earnest about everything that he could be amusing. George Grindal, a dear old man, she had met when she had been called in to advise on a textile in the Minster. Then there was a roly-poly couple, Mr and Mrs Moore, who were always together like Tweedledum and Tweedledee. The women she knew less well. The secretary had arranged the talk; she was the retired head of an office department. Velvet Smith, about forty, did the society's typing and looked as though she worked in an office. The newsletter editor was a rather aristocratic type of middle-aged housewife who probably had not worked for money since her marriage. Then there was a university student, rather quiet and mousy. The other two were friends in their thirties whom Julia seemed to see wherever she went, difficult to place, slightly arty. In fact Betty and Sandra Tweddle ran a flower shop together and were cousins.

Thomas smiled in the direction of Velvet Smith a little apologetically. She was an insignificant person and when she was not in his line of vision he always forgot her. So he made up for it with his smile. Then he took both his beaker and Julia's over to where the secretary and newsletter editor were beginning to tidy up in the corner.

The society had its meetings in different places throughout the city, as varied as possible. This room had been loaned them for one night only by the Boy Scouts. It was in one of the barrier entrances to the city, and the stir of traffic could hardly be heard through the thick chilly stone walls; really an ideal place for a meeting of the MRS.

Somehow the women members had managed to bring up a supply of water and a camping Gaz stove, and refreshments had appeared as usual. Now they were rinsing things in a bucket which was later to be carried down the steep, narrow stone stairs into the street.

You couldn't find anything more ersatz and modern than the coffee they'd drunk, Thomas thought, not for the first time; home-brewed ale out of horn beakers would be more authentic and not as much trouble.

If only this wretched news had not come to spoil a very pleasant evening.

'I'll see you out,' Thomas said to Julia as she put on her coat.

'There's no need, really.'

'We're all going, anyway. At present we see one another so often there's no need for our usual business discussion.'

'You're all in the mystery plays, I suppose?'

'We're all involved, one way or another. What would you expect of a medieval reconstruction society?'

'Of course.'

They went down the stairs. Outside, the tender dusk of late spring was gathering.

'I'm on my moped, actually,' Julia Bransby said. 'It's parked across the road.'

'Cheers, then.' Thomas Churchyard nodded. He watched her slim figure in a neat grey coat vanish. He went for his bicycle. It was always good to see that it was still there. No wonder the city had a road called Thief Lane and one called Bad Bargain – no bicycle was safe. And it was a relief to get away from the explosive feeling which had arisen when Sydney Absolom had raised the matter of the Christ. Here out in the street Thomas breathed deeply. He liked Julia Bransby, and wondered vaguely when he would see her again. They did meet from time to time. In a city like York people with similar interests could not help bumping into one another, for all the different societies were like the interlocking Olympic circles. The Georgians, the Philosophical, the YA-YAS, the MRS, the Victorians, the Dickens Society, the Thirties, the Family History, the After Eights, you name it . . . .

Looking not like a pea on a drum but like a drum on a pea, Churchyard mounted his bicycle. He was a big man and bulky, with a large head and impressive though scarcely handsome features, and riding he gave something of the impression of a circus elephant balancing on a ball – the combination of size and dainty precision. Silent and non-polluting, he slid into the stream of vehicles and became part of it.

Goodramgate was narrow and turned at angles which made it impossible to see ahead. The bright mixture of cars jerked forward, played follow-my-leader round a parked van, moved slowly past the colossal side of the Minster, was held up by a stream of pedestrians at the zebra crossing. Churchyard could move more freely than most. He travelled steadily up the gutter, looking round, glancing at shop windows where some lights were now burning, admiring the pretty girl tourists in their summer clothes, noticing how the soft dusk caressed the bronze-green of the Henry Moore statue in its grove of trees at the east end of the Minster, lifting his eyes for a split second to the darkness of the Minster itself. Soon surely they would be turning on the floodlights, so that it could be seen clearly again, unshadowed, creamy and proud over the city.

A sudden gust of dry dusty air caught him as he passed St Michael le Belfrey. Ahead there was a dapple of colour as a group of American tourists crossed the road. Churchyard moved steadily past the gables of the Dean Court Hotel – once a row of prebends' houses – to the traffic lights and the screaming bed of shocking pink geraniums – turned right – moved into the left lane past the twinkle of gilt on the black ironwork of the Georgian crescent of St Leonard's – went with the green filter light into Bootham – passed Alexa's Tasty Nibbles Sandwich Bar in its Tudor-looking frontage – and, leaving the core of the ancient city behind him, moved out into the suburbs.

A few minutes later he turned left into a road which had been built across the centre of the grounds of what had once been a gentleman's residence. Now it was a modern small estate. Ahead he could see a removal van; his new neighbours must have arrived.

As Thomas spun silently down the road towards the Harrogate van, he saw that the moving-in process was nearly complete. The men were handing back tea mugs to a slim young woman and climbing into their cab. As he reached the van its engine started.

Turning into his own drive Thomas felt a twinge of conscience. OK, it was late – after nine o'clock. But he felt he ought to give the newcomers a word of welcome. There wouldn't be time in the morning, and it was the kind of thing the sooner done the better. He put the bicycle into the garage beside his car, locked up, and wandered back indecisively to the front of the house.

The houses had been built around 1960, and were semi-detached. He had become used to living on the other side of the wall to an old couple, and now he could see it was all going to be different. An upstairs light was on and he could hear sounds of children preparing for bed. The young woman had vanished. Then he saw her through the uncurtained window of the children's room.

'She won't want me butting in at present,' he thought, and went back again, into the garden at the rear. Here it was different. There was no light from the house, but a dim glow from a newly-lit pipe, and the scent of Holland House, told him that one at least of his new neighbours was available. Thomas moved towards the irregular line of shrubs and small trees which hid the posts and wire separating the two gardens.

'Evening,' said his new neighbour, taking the pipe from his mouth. 'Robert Southwell.' And, coming close to a gap in the shrubs, he extended a hand dimly seen in the gathering darkness.

'Thomas Churchyard,' – taking the hand.

'Bob,' amended Robert Southwell.

'And Tom, of course. Welcome to York and to Ouse Avenue.'

'We've come from Harrogate.'

'I noticed Harrogate on the van.'

'We think we're lucky to have got a move to York. We're looking forward to living here.'

'Can I offer you and your wife coffee – can I help at all?'

'Linda's got it all under control.'

In a few minutes Bob discovered that Tom was a bachelor (and Tom, remembering Julia Bransby, wondered why he was). Tom found out that the Southwells' two children were called

Susan and Paul.

'Have you come to join a York company?' Tom felt he was making the inquiry about as delicately as a bull in a china shop but it helped to get the basic facts about people straight at the outset, then you knew where you were with them.

'Not exactly. I'm CID – Detective Chief Inspector. Transferred to York on promotion.'

'I'm British Telecom myself. Engineering. I should have thought we were a pretty quiet place from your point of view,' said Thomas.

'Oh, I don't know. The city seems to be crowded with people at the moment, many of them foreigners. I might uncover the odd international diamond-smuggling ring or two,' said Bob.

After a slight pause, Tom said, 'You'll find there are several different cities in one. There's the tourists' York; the one you know already, the one everybody sees before they come to live here. Then there's the in-comers' York; that's the one you and I belong to. Most of the societies in the city are full of ex-pats.'

Thomas had been thinking about this as he rode home. He went on. 'Then there's the native York; people who were born here of York families; you don't get many of them in the societies. Their view of the place is quite different. Most of the time they aren't interested in the antiquities and think it would be just as useful if the Minster were pulled down to make more parking space. They see a side of the place I never see at all. It is as if separate worlds exist in parallel. They can't see mine and I can't see theirs, yet we're physically in the same place living and working together.'

'You're very involved in local voluntary activities, then?' asked Bob.

'I suppose I am . . . I've just come back from a meeting of the one I'm chairman of and I've been thinking how odd it is that we only have three members who were born in York.'

'Linda's very interested in the mystery plays,' said Bob. 'She's thrilled to bits because we'll be able to go for once.'

'Now that's something quite a lot of the real Yorkists are involved in, as well as ex-pats.'

'Are *you?*'

'Oh, yes. In fact I'm acting this year.'

Summing him up through the gathering darkness Bob said, 'You don't look the type.'

'I'm playing God,' Tom replied in suitably modest tones.

'You don't mean to tell me we've come to live next door to God?'

'Well, yes.'

'I can see you in that part. Large and impressive. And your voice fits.'

'Thank you for those few kind words.'

'Good Lord!' Bob drew in his breath. Tom looked at him sharply. Bob was not making uncalled-for jokes. Thomas could see that the pale egg-shape of his face had become a half-moon profile with inquiring nose. Turning to look in the same direction Thomas saw that the Minster floodlighting had been turned on, and the great building hung suspended against the night sky like a vision.

'Yes . . . I suppose I've got used to it . . . even blasé about living where it can be seen like this . . .'

'How could anyone ever become blasé about something like that?' asked Bob.

'Wait five years.'

'If I waited fifty I could never get over it.'

They stood in silence for a while, and Bob let his pipe go out. Linda came out of the house to join them, and her perfume replaced the smell of Holland House. At last she broke the spell by inviting Thomas to come in for a coffee.

'I came into the garden with the intention of asking you the same thing.'

'All right then,' said Bob, 'we will. But only for half an hour. The kids are asleep in a strange place, and we're pretty ready for bed ourselves.'

'You can step across the wire near the house.'

Bob and Linda looked around them with interest. The house was a duplicate of their own. The small hall had three doors and the stairway opening off it and a cupboard for coats, so there was virtually no wall-space; a smallish mirror framed with dull carved gilt hung on the only bit of wall; they stood on a thick plain carpet of welcoming crimson. They followed Thomas into his kitchen and perched on a couple of stout ash stools. In a few minutes he had a percolator bubbling on the stove. The floor was crimson linoleum which exactly matched the colour of the hall carpet.

'Lived here long?' asked Linda.

'Five years. I took over the carpets, curtains and decorations from the previous owners.' He had noticed her look around. 'Afraid I'm always too busy to get round to altering things.'

'I like it the way it is. Tell me something about the mystery plays,' said Linda. 'I love anything from the Middle Ages. It's really my favourite period.'

'Oh, yes.' At first Thomas looked at her blankly, as if he didn't know where to start. 'Well, they were suppressed in 1572 and not performed again until 1951.'

'And then they became an annual event?'

'Not annual. Every three years or so. There's a lot of work involved.' He found a leaflet on the shelf and handed it to her.

'"The plays performed by the craft guilds of the city,"' read Linda. 'Were they like trade unions?'

'More or less.'

'On the Feast of Corpus Christi which falls in May or June . . .'

'The Body of Christ.'

'The Feast of the Body of Christ!' repeated Bob. 'Sounds rather gruesome.'

'The Middle Ages often were,' Thomas turned to him seriously. 'Think of the plague. Think of the charnel houses. Gruesomeness was definitely part of their lives much more than it is of ours, don't you think so?'

'I hadn't thought about it,' replied Bob.

Linda was still looking at the leaflet. 'Originally forty-eight plays! They must have taken a while to get through!'

'All day, dawn to dusk. They show first God and heaven, then the fall of Lucifer and the angels, the creation of man (and woman of course),' he added hastily to Linda. 'All that part shows the need for man's redemption. Then the story of the life of Christ, the redeemer, from the birth right through to the resurrection and ascension. The epilogue shows the end of the world.'

'Gosh,' said Bob comprehensively.

'The forty-eight plays have been amalgamated so that they flow together into one long one.'

'I should hope so.'

Thomas turned round with the mugs of coffee. He was glad to have the chance to study his new neighbours in the light. Linda was dark-haired, young, pleasant-looking, dressed in pale grey and remarkably clean-looking when you remembered that they'd been moving house all day. Bob was tall – nearly as tall as Thomas – and reminded him of Fred Astaire with glasses. He looked bright, alert, perceptive, even though he was perched, temporarily at rest, on the ash stool.

'Just reading that booklet can't give you any idea of what a performance is like – the drama, beauty and majesty of the whole thing – the way the audience and cast are all bound up together in seeing the great story through . . .' Thomas produced a plate of garibaldi biscuits. 'I hope you like these.'

'I do,' said Linda, taking three.

'In 1951 the whole thing was done with great reverence, as a religious experience. You can see how things have changed.'

'Yes. Loads of adverts. Potted biographies. The plays themselves take rather a back seat.'

'It was inevitable I suppose when they became a tourist attraction. But there's a furore in the town tonight.'

'What about?' A look of keenness crossed Bob's face.

'We always have a professional director nowadays, and a professional actor as Christ. It's become something of an excitement every time to see who the director chooses as his Christ. This time Bruce Exelby is directing – have you heard of him? He works a lot in London – and he's chosen Poison Peters.'

'I can't believe it,' said Linda.

'Neither can anyone.'

'It's sacrilege!'

'That's what the city thinks. There is fury over it.'

'But his whole life-style . . .'

'It's nothing but a publicity gimmick. The decision has been spun out until the last possible moment – we've been rehearsing weeks and there's only a fortnight to go before production. When Peters arrives he'll be lucky if he isn't greeted with rotten eggs or something worse.'

'We'll have to provide a police escort,' smiled Bob.

'I expect you'd do that anyway. He had one when he gave a pop concert at the university. That was nearly a riot. Thousands of pounds worth of damage.'

'Is his career slipping a bit? Whatever could make him accept the part of Christ? He's not an actor.'

'I don't know.'

'Bob, you'll be here all night.' Linda got up. 'Early start in the morning. Good of you to ask us round, Tom. I'm thrilled to bits about the mystery plays. You'll have to meet the children tomorrow. I'll be telling them all about it.'

'Anything you want to know? The dustmen collect on Fridays and two milkmen deliver down this road. Northern Dairies at seven o'clock and the Co-op a bit later.'

'What time is the post?' asked Bob.

'About eight.'

'Thanks for the welcome. It's taken our minds off the traumas of the day. We're really looking forward to living here.'

'Great to have you as neighbours.'

Linda lightly clasped Thomas's outstretched hand. 'Thanks for the coffee and the garibaldi biscuits.'

Left alone, Thomas felt pleased. He hoped he hadn't bored them about the mystery plays, but they had seemed interested . . . and the plays filled his own life just now.

If they were going to live in York they would have to get used to the fact that the past might be dead but it wouldn't lie down – it was all around and among present-day living, giving it a dimension in time. He felt it was an enrichment, and couldn't imagine how people could live in new towns, where there was no ancient heart still beating.

2

Hail, doomsman dread that all shall doom!
Hail, that all quick and dead shall lout!
Hail, whom worship shall most beseem!
Hail, whom all things shall dread and doubt!
  We welcome thee
  Hail and welcome, of all about
  To our city!

The Skynners' Play

The first outrage over the appointment of Poison Peters had hardly died down before a second wave began, because having accepted the role he seemed in no hurry to play it.

The director, Bruce Exelby, had arrived. He had been to the city several times since his appointment the previous September. He always left York shaking as though it had been visited by a whirlwind, and the work he organized other people to do kept them fully occupied until his next descent.

In January the casting for the major amateur parts had been carried out, in February the crowds had been cast. There was the perennial shortage of men coming forward to act. The male sex was happier fiddling with the scenery or fixing wires for the lighting, or passing its opinion on the design of the set.

On Shakespeare's birthday, rehearsals had begun. The flying visits of Bruce Exelby became more frequent. Christ had been named in late May, the three weeks of performances were to begin in the first week of June. Exelby took up residence in the flat on the top floor of St Mary's Lodge, and moved into the last two weeks of rehearsal, where the crowd joined the principals of the cast.

It was as well that police crowd control had been provided for Poison Peters when at long last he arrived at York station. Sergeant Smith and a couple of constables were in readiness. A large crowd began to gather. There were Poison Peters's ardent fans, mostly dressed in black but with multicoloured hair, like a carnival of crows. The media were there in force; the ITV unit was over from Leeds, with brilliant lights and a loud-hailer blaring; Radio York was there with a van and microphone; the reporters from the *York Evening Press* and the *Yorkshire Post* both had their notebooks and attendant photographers. Even the national dailies were interested. A freelance journalist was there with a commission from several of them for a report if there was anything worth reporting.

Bruce Exelby had insisted on the leading members of the cast going down with him to meet the pop star, so Thomas Churchyard had had to ask for time off work.

'You realize you're going to be away for three full weeks for this damn pantomime of yours,' said the executive engineer heavily.

'Yes.'

'That takes every shred of what's left of your leave for the rest of this leave year, Tom. It'll be no use you saying you want any more time off.'

'*I* don't want to go to meet the wretched man. It looks as if I'm condoning his appointment, and I don't, none of those involved in the plays do.'

'You don't?'

'No, I don't,' repeated Tom heatedly. 'He's quite unsuitable. This sort of thing brings into disrepute a fine and precious part of our heritage. Something that means a lot to me personally. When the committee appoint a director they give him a free hand; that's fair enough; how else could he operate? And you've got to trust him. OK, so this time Bruce Exelby's gone and done this. It's only fair to say that otherwise he's good; the whole production's shaping up well. It's really developing a terrific feeling. That's why it's so sad this is happening. But we've just got to weather it and make the best we can of it. It's no use Sydney Absolom and the rest kicking up a stink. They may as well grin and bear it.'

'So you're going to grin and bear it at the station at eleven o'clock, are you? What, in costume? Have you got your nightie with you?'

'If you let me have the time off. And no, I'm going as I am.'

'Go on, then. Don't be away longer than you have to. I'll see if I can put it down as a public relations exercise. If the press are there make sure they know that you're there by kind courtesy of British Telecom.'

In the end, the police had to put a cordon across the narrow part of the entrance to the station. 'I need help to deal with this lot,' Sergeant Smith had radioed to his station. 'There's crowds arriving with banners . . .'

A group of constables came in support, and the duty inspector arrived to take overall control.

Thomas stood waiting near the barrier as part of a line-up which included the Lord Mayor (wearing his chain of office), the Lady Mayoress, the Sheriff (wearing his chain of office) and the Sheriff's Lady; Clare Black, a prefect at Queen Elizabeth's School, who was playing the Virgin Mary; James Bowes, who was Lucifer – a large and important part with a real opportunity for character acting – and Humphrey Hale, a local solicitor, who was the Archangel Gabriel.

Bruce Exelby arrived. He was dressed up for the occasion, in a black soft leather bomber jacket over a fawn shirt and cream jumper, and fawn cord casual trousers. Giving Clare, the Virgin, a charming smile, he lounged over to her.

'Big chance coming up,' he said caressingly. 'Next stop RADA and then the West End, name in lights!'

'You're teasing me, Mr Exelby,' Clare dropped her eyelashes and blushed.

'Not me, I'm renowned for my talent spotting.' His voice dropped and, lips close to her ear, he murmured something more. Thomas could not hear him, but could see the effect on Clare. He felt irritated; the director often irritated him. Why did Exelby have to go turning the girl's head? She was a good actress, of course, but she was a good all-rounder and Thomas happened to know that she had done exceptionally well in her O levels and, like her boyfriend the Youngest Shepherd, was hoping to go to Cambridge. The career of an actress was glamorous but it could also be a worrying one, largely spent 'resting'. Weren't women scientists and engineers and statesmen (he hesitated to include politicians) just as useful?

He had plenty of time to think of these things, for the train was late.

The police could not stop the missiles which hurtled through the air at the waiting group. Two squashy tomatoes found their mark, one among the elaborately-worked links of the mayoral chain and the other in the hat of the Sheriff's Lady. Thomas fidgeted, glowered at the noisy crowd, and was sure he glimpsed some familiar faces, including that of Sydney Absolom.

At last the train pulled into the vibrating station. After the tomato-throwing the police had cleared the crowd from the area of the ivory-coloured terrazzo tiles of the entrance back to the grey drab flooring of pavement and covered roadway. The only people allowed through were *bona fide* travellers who passed the line-up of notables with a furtive and apologetic air. Bruce Exelby had gone onto the platform and soon could be seen walking over the bridge talking animatedly to two other men; one undistinguished, slightly above middle height, weighed down with suitcases; the other was undoubtedly Poison Peters. A porter followed behind with a loaded trolly.

Those who had only seen Poison on the television and video might have been surprised how small and slim he was; five foot five in his socks; even with built-up heels he was barely five seven. His tight trousers and built-up jacket were of silver lamé, and worn over a sweat shirt of black fabric as light-absorbing as velvet, embroidered across the chest with a broad silver star. But after the first glance no one noticed his clothes. It was that dead-white face with its rouged lips, the great aureole of spikes of hair bleached until it was almost white, the busy gesturing hands, which riveted attention.

Catching sight of the media persons Poison carried out what Thomas could only call a cavort. He leapt into the air, punching high with his right fist, mouth wide open in a Comanche yell. Flash bulbs spurted light from the cameras of the waiting media men. One of them caught the shot which, blown up and used a thousand times over, was to become the symbol of the year's mystery plays – Poison, against the dark shadows of the background in which you could just pick out Bruce Exelby, the road manager and the porter, exploding in energy and light, for he had leaped into a shaft of sun and looked in the photograph as though he was ten feet above the ground, more demonic than Christ-like.

Tom thought of the ordinary people of the city, thought of Sydney Absolom, shut his eyes and shuddered. Outside, the teenage fans in the crowd set up a wail that sounded like the cry of lost souls.

There were at least three groups from the university. There were students among the fans; then there was the group from the students' Christian Union who had a large red banner proclaiming 'WE WILL NOT HAVE A DEVIL TO PLAY CHRIST,' and a third group containing several lecturers under a board on a pole proclaiming 'FREE SPEECH AND FREE DRAMA'; no one was quite sure what they stood for. Another section of the crowd was from the Church and had a large proportion of dog collars. They were making a dignified silent protest and Sergeant Black had no need to worry about them. Their placard, neatly lettered, read 'WHAT THINK YE OF CHRIST? Matt. 22.42.' There was also a noisy group of fundamentalists. They began to shout 'Out with Poison!' and unrolled their banner which said 'NO BLASPHEMY', while other parts of the crowd had placards reading, 'GO HOME PETERS,' and 'KEEP YORK CLEAN – BAN POISON.'

After that much photographed leap into the air Poison Peters had walked down the remaining steps, through the barrier, and up to the line of the reception quite calmly and in an ordinary way. In a minute Thomas found his hand being shaken, and looked down into a pair of heavily mascara-ed golden brown eyes.

'We'll get to know one another real well, I expect,' said Poison.

'I'm sure,' said Tom. 'Not too well, I hope,' he added hastily to himself. His hand tingled from the quick bony grip. In a few seconds Poison moved on to greet the next in line; seconds later he passed through the foyer with the official party quickly bunching together at his heels.

As he appeared there was a scuffle as the police pounced on someone in the crowd and confiscated a quantity of rotten tomatoes. The fans screamed and sobbed for joy. Poison grabbed a sparkling guitar from his road manager, posed with it held across his loins, and then held it in the air as he stretched out his arms to his fans as if to embrace them.

A tomato missed him and took the mayoral Rolls Royce full in the bumper. An egg dashed itself to pieces at his feet. The TV cameras rolled. The man from Radio York advanced with his microphone. The reporters broke into a volley of questions.

'Have you ever acted in a play before, Mr Peters?'

'There's no other play like this one, yeah?'

'Do you know that there is opposition in the city to your playing the part of Christ?'

'I have been chosen, yeah?'

A tomato sliced itself on the strings of his guitar.

'Have you ever been to York before?'

'This is like my first trip to your beautiful city, yeah?'

'We'll have a press conference in the Mansion House,' interposed the Lord Mayor. The car doors swung open. With a last open-armed gesture to his fans, Poison bent and manoeuvred his head into the long black limo without damaging a single spike of hair. The civic party hastily climbed into the official cars, made sure the windows were wound up, and sat back with sighs of relief.

Poison kept up an interplay with his fans through his closed window. The sleek cars, now well spattered with tomatoes, glided slowly away from the station, the city's arms on a tiny flag fluttering from the nose of the first.

'I'll get back to work,' said Tom Churchyard with an air of relief.

'You won't,' replied Bruce Exelby. 'There's a civic reception and lunch at the Mansion House. Get in.' The assistant director had brought Exelby's Porsche up, next in line.

Tom found the civic lunch an agony. Fortunately he was not near Poison, except for one moment when they were jostled close in the crowd as trays of drinks were passed round.

'Got my own, yeah?' said Poison, bringing out a vodka bottle from his pocket and taking a noisy swig. 'I don't drink any sort of rubbish.'

Tom was grateful that it was a buffet lunch. He grabbed a few shrimp vol-au-vents and decided he could sustain himself until the tea-trolley came round in the afternoon at work. He would just have time to pop into St Olave's parish room, where the wardrobe people were working, and have the last-minute fitting he had promised Sally Vause.

'He'll barely have time to learn his lines,' said Sally, secretary of MRS, and wardrobe mistress to the plays. 'Have you seen this?' She flapped a tabloid newspaper in Tom's face and it fell open at a montage of images of Poison Peters. Spiky eyelashes, bleached white hair, pale face, great lips open wide in a spongy mouthing of sound. 'He must finish these concerts exhausted, then go to bed with half a dozen groupies.'

'Not if he's that exhausted.'

'Well! He'll be high on adrenalin if not heroin or coke – probably runs through a few groupies instead of taking sleeping pills. How's he going to find time to learn to give full quality to medieval verse?'

'He'll be here full time. We all have to fit it in round normal work.'

'Humph,' said Sally. Her needle made vicious darts at the cloth of Tom's costume, short stabbing movements leaving a trail of thread. Tom flinched and looked at the ceiling and thought of England.

Julia Bransby entered the parish hall.

'How's it going?'

'Very well, really,' answered Sally.

'Everything's looking super. Where's Velvet?'

'Oh, she's around somewhere. No, she's gone.'

Tom didn't like standing there like a dressmaker's lay figure and not being spoken to.

'She's such a self-effacing person,' he put in. 'One doesn't always notice her.'

'I don't think she's really self-effacing,' answered Julia. 'I think there's something very strange and deep in her, she makes me feel she is waiting for someone or something . . .'

'Oh Julia!' exclaimed Sally Vause. 'How you love dramatizing people! Even dull predictable women like Velvet. All she's waiting for is the next bus.'

They dissolved into laughter.

'I'm ravenous,' said Tom. 'All I've had for lunch is three shrimp vol-au-vents. Would you like to join me for a sandwich and a beer, Julia? There's a pub in Marygate.' Work can wait, he thought.

'I'd like that.'

It was the first time Poison Peters had seen the place where the mystery plays were to be performed. He was part of the informal procession walking the short distance from the Mansion House, along Lendal, across busy Museum Street and in through the gates of the Museum Gardens. The crowds had mostly grown tired of waiting outside the Mansion House for the civic lunch to be over. Anyway, lunch hour was up and many of them, even on flexitime, had had to go back to work. The streets were full, but with summer tourists who were not really aware of Poison's presence in the city, or of its significance.

Once in the Gardens the group with Poison at their centre moved in a phalanx through the undulating, sloping, glancing landscape; the great trees made grateful with their summer shade the parched grass; men in shirtsleeves and girls with bare midriffs lay around, some eating, some studying guide books about York.

Ahead was the unlovely back of a stand of seats; the area was partitioned off; a few of the people concerned with the plays were around.

It was not until Poison had been admitted through the barrier and had passed through the grandstand, that he could take in the ruins of St Mary's Abbey, in front of and around which the set had been built. The row of stone arches rose against a warm blue sky, lovely, serene, and breathtaking. In front of them and up to them lay the centre stage, but there were slopes, and steps, and holes through which one could see other things.

Poison had just finished a gruelling concert tour. His thin body was taut with nervous energy, his face expressionless.

'Show me my pad, yeah?' he said to Bruce Exelby. Turning to those of the civic party who had come to the Museum Gardens with him he said, 'Be seeing ya, right?' He raised his hand in farewell.

With director and road manager he walked round the end of the ruins.

'You're not suggesting he sleeps in a graveyard?' The road manager was aghast.

'The caravan's right here.'

It was. Tucked away round the end of the set, next to but not in the graveyard, in a quiet spot near a bowling green, was the silver-grey caravan with its wide bright silver streak along the side.

'Right,' said Poison.

'You're sleeping in my flat,' Exelby said to the road manager. 'You did want to be isolated, Poison, isn't that right?'

'Yeah. Where I can do my own thing.'

'Here's the key of the set. It's all locked when we aren't here. You're inside the enclosure, quite private. The whole gardens are locked up at night of course – we'll have to see about access for you. You can probably have the spare key to the gates on to Marygate. I use that entrance to reach my flat.'

'Right,' said Poison.

Bruce Exelby's head was full of images of what might happen at night in the caravan. 'What do you want to do for the rest of the day?' he asked. 'I'd suggest you do a bit of sightseeing but if the antis catch sight of you you would get mobbed.'

'I'll disguise myself, right?'

The thin garish figure went into the caravan. The key clicked in the lock. The blinds went down.

Later in the day, after work, Thomas Churchyard went back to St Olave's parish room. He walked through the Museum Gardens and out through the Marygate entrance, then down Almery Lane.

Ahead of him a group of Devils in scarlet and black burst out of the room door, and came screaming and tumbling down the lane. They wore masks like the sanctuary knocker of Durham Cathedral – great beaky frightening things of papier-mâché, with horns; they carried forks, or tridents; an old lady ahead of Thomas shrank against the wall in fright.

'Behave yourselves, lads!' cried Tom, but was only answered by waving tridents and hands waggling defiantly at ears.

'You wouldn't think they're nicely brought up lads from a public school,' said Tom to the old lady, who looked as if she might never recover.

'Oh. Are they the seven boys from St Giles? I heard about them on Radio York.'

'You know what they're like at that age.'

'Oh yes.' The old lady looked brighter. 'I've had boys myself, you know.'

Thomas nodded at her and went into the dusty, crowded parish room.

'I see the little Devils are ready.'

'Little Devils is right. Velvet, fetch that costume for God.'

Thomas looked at Velvet with more interest than usual as she helped him on with the costume. She had some redeeming features, after all. Her teeth were very good, he noticed when she smiled at him. He shook out the folds of fabric.

'That's much better.'

'Do you think it's quite full enough?' came a strong penetrating voice; Tom knew without turning that it was Jane Bugg, thankfully not one of MRS, but very much one of the mystery-play scene.

'Quite full enough, thank you, Jane,' said Sally Vause, with exaggerated patience.

'The medieval cloak was cut on a full circle,' went on Jane, 'hence the flowing folds. Julia Bransby would tell you.'

'She already has, thank you very much.'

'As I was saying to *Bruce* –' went on Jane.

As if on cue Bruce Exelby swaggered into the room. Since the reception he had changed back into his more normal clothing. Although he must be, Tom thought, about forty, Exelby still wore the kind of things he had worn for the last twenty-five years – today it was his usual, a checked lumberjack shirt and faded jeans. He combed his curly black hair carefully forward and his shoes were handmade, his huge metal wristwatch gold. Otherwise the years had changed him little, only adding a stone to his weight, rounding out all his contours.

'How's it going?'

'I think the cloak should be *fuller*, don't you, dear *Bruce*?' asked Jane Bugg. Sally Vause cut in with, 'All this re-dying and making new costumes has meant a lot of work.'

'You've got the effect I wanted. Subtlety. Harmonies of colour are important to me. I speak to the audience not only through groupings and disposition of actors but through the audience's subconscious appreciation of the colours I use.'

Thomas looked around hastily to see what gallery Exelby was playing to, apart from Jane Bugg who was looking adoring and gathering up his every syllable. Nearly everyone had stopped to listen and there were at least a dozen figures in the room, busy among the host of garments in colours from white to black, brilliant yellow to russet and deep brown, pale to deepest blue, with flashes of scarlet and purple.

'These vegetable dyes took no end of researching,' grumbled Sally. 'They are messy and time-consuming and will fade. The Burco boiler is practically worn out and so is the spin-dryer. If it hadn't been for Julia Bransby's advice and research I don't know how we'd have done it.'

Exelby did not care how people did things as long as they were done.

'The quality is incomparable.'

Thomas felt bound to agree. The colours were a triumph. They had the curious quality of not clashing; of looking rich and varied and yet all of a piece. Exelby turned to Jane Bugg.

'And how is my Porteress today?' he asked, giving her a brief hug. The word of praise given, Exelby went. Glowing, Jane trailed out after him.

'He was always the same,' muttered Sally Vause, helping Thomas off with his costume, now completely ready.

'Always?'

'Oh! He's no stranger to York, you know, though I notice he doesn't publicize it. It's all his past triumphs, for the media, but himself he never looks back. Always what he's doing next, that's our Bruce. But I remember. He came to the York Rep as a young actor. I believe he'd been in the Sheffield Playhouse company. He was here for a couple of seasons and then went off somewhere else. The next we heard he had gone into directing. Just as well. He was no sort of an actor. Took what he wanted in the way of stage experience and when he might have been expected to be a mainstay for a year or two, off.'

'Do you remember all the small-time actors we've had here?'

'No. His name struck a bell and I got out my old theatre programmes. Then they reminded me.' Sally stitched vigorously at a length of woollen cloth.

'He wasn't much good, then?'

'I only actually remember him as Mole in *The Wind in The Willows*. He was wooden. Good-looking but no use as an actor at all. Top of the tree as a director though, I'll grant him that. I've grumbled about these costumes but they'll look terrific on set.'

In another part of the parish room were the Angels.

'I tell you he's wet,' said the plump blonde Angel sulkily. "Call yourself a Devil," I said, "you ought to be one of those boring blessed Souls," I –'

'We all know what you said.' A thin dark Angel in glasses raised her head from Chaucer's *Canterbury Tales* which she was swallowing in much larger chunks than next year's O levels required. 'What we want to know is, why you said it?'

'I had an absolutely super idea to sabotage one of these boring rehearsals. I'd got one of Poison's tapes, the one the BBC banned because it's supposed to be all about drugs.'

'"Angels on a Trip", you mean?'

'That's it. Very appropriate, isn't it?' the blonde Angel giggled. 'I know he's pally with one of the music people and I told him to substitute the tape for one of theirs, wouldn't it have been a shriek? But he wouldn't do it. Said it wasn't worth being chucked out of the plays for.'

'It's you that's wet,' replied her friend. 'It would never have worked, they have all the tapes marked and numbered, and they'd spot it at once. It wasn't worth the row.'

'Who cares about the beastly plays anyway?'

'We do, and if you don't it's only because you were turned down for the BVM because you were too young,' said her friend with devastating candour.

The blonde Angel said two very rude unangelic words and took her mug for a refill of coffee.

'Don't drink too much,' warned Velvet.

As the director strode back to the set he saw Clare, the Virgin Mary, walking slowly with her script in her hand, folded open. She was looking first up and then down and muttering. Exelby stopped, which gave Jane Bugg the opportunity to catch up with him.

'You go on, Jane,' he said genially. 'See how everyone is getting on for me, will you?'

Then he moved to the Virgin's side.

'Problems?' His voice was gentle and understanding.

She blushed. 'Not really problems, Mr Exelby. I want to do credit to everyone who has faith in me for the part. I suppose I'm a little nervous, that's all.'

He took the book from her hands, his fingers brushing lightly over hers.

'Let me hear you.'

'Oh no, I couldn't possibly take up your time . . .'

'Please, Clare.'

She spoke some of her words nervously to his intent ear.

'Yes. Could be better. You seem a little lacking in self-confidence, my dear. After all you've been rehearsing some time now and all this should be perfect. I thought you knew your lines.'

'I do know them, Mr Exelby. I'm word-perfect. It's just nerves, and I'm worried over some of the emphasis.'

'A few of the cast go to have a drink after the rehearsal, don't they?'

'Yes.'

'Do you go?'

'Yes. I'm under age but I have an orange juice.'

'I'll join you tonight and we'll have a chat about it.'

With a reassuring smile he left her.

Night fell over the city.

In his caravan Poison Peters was alone. He had washed out his hair and it fell limply on to his shoulders. His face was bare, pallid and slightly pimply. He sat on his bed with his head bowed over the text of the plays, as he had been sitting for the past three hours. Sighing, he got up and went over to the tiny fitted fridge, lifted out the plateful of food he had bought and prepared earlier, and took off the cling film. There were some good cheese and varied salads. He put a carton of natural yoghurt ready on the flap table, and a bottle of untreated orange juice. The vodka bottle full of Malvern water stood on the small draining board.

He switched on the tape recorder to a low volume and the sound of medieval instruments filled the van.

After eating he washed up neatly and raised the blind to see the moonlit wall of the ancient ruins towering outside. He was in a triple-locked enclosure. Turning off the music, he let the silence wash through him. He felt, as he always did – and as an actor playing Christ must always do – completely and utterly alone. He undressed and slid into bed, a thin white radish. Closing his eyes he murmured, 'God, I'm not very good at saying this. But I need your help.' Then he was silent.

3

Mine enemies now will come nigh and draw near,
With all might they may, to mar my manhood.
The Cordwainers' Play

The next morning the hate mail began to arrive. Both the director and the Christ received a pile of it. 'You will burn in Hell,' said one of the letters. As the whole lot was delivered to the festival office, neither of them was as yet aware of the infinite variety of abuse, which was to become a feature of their lives.

For the first time Poison Peters was on the set of the mystery plays. He had been heralded by a little flurry from the wings, otherwise he might hardly have been noticed. The road manager had left York – he had the next tour to arrange – and Bruce Exelby was on one side of Poison, the assistant stage manager on the other; they walked forward into view together.

Exelby was to put Poison through the scenario. The set was quiet, although a dozen people had arrived already. It was half an hour before the technical rehearsal was due to begin. Sydney Absolom was fiddling with the lights. Thomas Churchyard was sitting sharing a flask of coffee with Humphrey Hale. The day was still warm and light, with the sun high.

'You appear here first,' said Exelby. Poison, a small slim figure in jeans, trainers and T-shirt, face devoid of make-up and hair falling limply about his head, climbed up the set after him.

'You wouldn't recognize him,' said Humphrey.

'No.' Thomas could hardly take his eyes from the insignificant figure. 'I didn't think he'd be able to wash all the stuff off his hair as easily as all that.'

'You've been taken in by appearances like everybody else.'

'Have I?' Tom pondered that. 'I wouldn't have said that I could be easily deceived. Of course I suppose I knew that he must look quite ordinary underneath.'

'No you didn't. No one expects a pop star to look ordinary, ever.'

For a while they both looked across at Bruce and Poison in silence. No acting was going on. Poison was only following Bruce from place to place, listening to his instructions, repeating phrases after him, opening and closing his arms, placing his feet, looking around now and again as if to memorize his positions in the complicated set. The younger man looked serious and concentrated, all his force drawn within himself. Thomas had to think a long time before he hit on the right word. Humility. That was it. The last thing one would ever associate with Poison Peters. Well, if he was conscious of his deficiencies, that was a good thing. He had never acted before and had only a few days to acquire what people spent years perfecting.

'When do you want the sound equipment ready?' shouted Sydney Absolom belligerently from the wings.

'As soon as you can, Sydney.'

'None of the others need amplification.'

'Poison is used to it.' There was no irritation on Exelby's part, but a firmness that invited no arguments. Absolom grunted and disappeared again. Bruce Exelby went into the shadow of a piece of mock wall in his wake. Their voices could be heard clearly.

'You've set the amplifier up here?'

'There isn't anywhere else to put it.'

'Hmmm – well, it'll do – but look, I don't want to be able to hear you moving about. I don't want to hear anything. No clicks, no footsteps. Nothing.' There were faint noises as Exelby examined the set-up.

'I'll put down a rubber mat.'

'All right. That should solve the problem. I don't want to hear a sound from you, Sydney.'

'I'll go home and fetch the mat.'

'When will you be ready to turn on? I want Poison to test it.'

'Later this evening.'

'OK.'

'I've got all the other electrics to look after, you know. This is just an extra burden.'

The two men emerged from behind the wall. Bruce clasped Sydney's thin bowed shoulder with a substantial hand.

'You'll do it.' He sounded suddenly jovial. 'I know I can rely on you, Syd.'

'I'll have to hurry or I won't be back for when you want to try the lights.' Absolom sounded reasonably mollified as he hurried off.

This was the night Sydney and his assistant were to give the lights their trial run, synchronized with the action. The technical rehearsal was the one the actors hated most. It dragged on and on while minor adjustments were made. Thomas assumed Syd had arrived back in time with his mat, because on cue the first spotlight lit up, and was followed by all the other lights in their elaborate sequence. The whole thing was jerky, because Absolom and his assistant were having to fit in with the action which was constantly stopping and starting as Exelby interfered, asking for one scene to be repeated, cajoling one actor, yelling at the Crowd, softly coaxing the Virgin Mary, joking with the group of little Devils and cursing the group of unco-operative sheep, who were proving almost as bad as the donkey.

There was no doubt that the director was singling out the Virgin Mary in a most marked way. Thomas wondered how her boyfriend felt about it. Flattery and praise were altering the girl; some of her dignified simplicity was wearing off, and she had taken to simpering at the director and making her gestures more elaborate and stagy. It wasn't an improvement.

The technics themselves seemed to be going rather well. Apart from the wrong spotlight being used in one scene, and trouble getting the right angle for the light beaming on the detached tower of stone on top of which the Archangel Michael made his dramatic appearance, there were no real hitches.

Poison had his script in his hand, but everyone else knew their lines by heart. Because of this perhaps, he seemed different; yet Thomas noticed that the slim pale figure drew the eye. He slid into place in the jigsaw with an ease and lack of commotion that Thomas, standing now in his archway in the sky, found rather surprising.

As the time wore on he noticed that Poison's hesitancy was falling from him. In the big speech in the Taylors' play Poison dropped the hand holding the script to his side, and obviously had the words by heart; his voice rose clearly and Thomas could hear every syllable. Suddenly the attention of the cast focused on their Christ as though a group of iron filings had swung to point at the pole. A power, thin yet and faint, seemed to radiate from him. 'I wonder if Exelby *did* make a mistake, after all? Or if Poison is going to be good?' thought Tom.

At last Exelby called a break.

'Got that amplifier fixed?' he asked Absolom. 'I want Poison to test it before we go any further. Set the mike up where he can use it during the Harrowing of Hell.'

'Right.' Absolom disappeared behind his spur of wall to switch on.

The amplifier and microphone were tested and all functioned perfectly with no problems. Everything else went off without any important hitches. On his high vantage point Thomas Churchyard felt happier and light in spirit, as the whole wonderful wheeling production turned through its sequences.

The only place where there was an uneasy pause came when the Christ had to be fastened to the cross and hang there suspended in centre stage for about twenty minutes, at the end of which the lights snapped off, leaving everything in darkness, while thunder rolled. During this dramatic darkness covering the moment of death the cross was lowered. The whole thing was a gruelling event for any actor. Poison Peters went through it well, considering that it was his first experience of the ordeal. Tom wondered whether he would not find it much worse when he was only dressed in a loin cloth. In that twenty minutes the air – summer though it was – would cool his body unbearably. He would hang almost naked and very uncomfortable, isolated, martyred, with a growing feeling of suffocation and light-headedness, in front of the gaping audience. The actors would be working away at their parts below him, separated from him as if by a void of miles and centuries.

After Poison had been lowered from the cross and was off-stage Thomas, who could see behind the wall of the abbey into the churchyard as well as in front of it on to the stage, noticed him rubbing his wrists and flexing his back and limbs to relieve them of tension.

On the whole it had been an encouraging rehearsal. If only those dratted sheep would behave themselves a bit better.

Sally Vause had been at the front, watching.

'At least there were no tantrums or hysterics,' she said to God as he was about to make his way home. 'He hasn't given much out – but most actors don't on a read-through. He'll have to work hard to learn his lines, but singers have to learn the words of their songs, I suppose, and perhaps the rest of the cast might carry the production.'

Tom looked at her in some surprise. 'I think he might turn out to be good, after all,' he said. 'How long have you been watching?'

'Oh, off and on. Velvet stayed in wardrobe.'

'I might be imagining things. But I think he might just possibly be very good indeed.' Tom put on his bicycle clips.

Sally looked after him indulgently.

It was during Poison's second rehearsal that Bruce Exelby was talking to the Virgin Mary.

'Still feeling unsure, Clare? Why don't I give you a little coaching? Are you free later?'

'Yes . . .'

'It might make all the difference. Contact your parents and tell them you'll be later than usual and we'll fit in an hour's tuition. Don't forget you've a career ahead of you, my girl! A good impression in this part will make all the difference in your student days – may make the difference between acceptance at a drama school and refusal.'

'Oh, Mr Exelby!'

'Bruce, please.' He nodded. 'See you later, then.'

When rehearsal was over, Clare was ready, clutching her lines to her bosom and all starry-eyed. Bruce Exelby came across her as though he had forgotten all about her – put his hand to his forehead – said, 'Yes, of course!' – then added, 'I *will* make time for you, my dear – just give me a minute . . .'

She waited half an hour, while he spoke, it seemed, to everyone else in York. At last he came up to her and, taking her elbow in his hand in an avuncular way, walked along with her, talking.

'Where are we going, Mr Exelby?'

'Bruce, *please*! We theatricals, you know, must stick together . . . the gatehouse seems quite a good place, don't you agree? Quiet and comfortable, which is all that's necessary to let us really concentrate on the words and their interpretation.'

The top floor of the gatehouse, St Mary's Lodge, was the flat which was available to the director of the mystery plays. They went up the stairs to it, Exelby dropping the latch behind them. He walked about switching on a lamp or two to counter the fading light outside, chatting briskly. He could really be very bright and amusing when he tried, telling stories of various productions. In the kitchen he made powdered coffee and brought Clare a mugful. She was on edge, but the casual handing to her of the thick workmanlike mug of hot liquid reassured her.

Exelby at last dropped down with an exhausted sigh in the chair opposite.

'Now to work!' he exclaimed.

She read, and he criticised, for some time. Exelby could be a patient and inspiring teacher, and he was that now. He made her move across the floor as she spoke the lines, and they thrashed out the relationships of words to movements, the thought and inner emotions conveyed.

'There is nothing better I can do than quote to you the words of Stanislavsky,' said Exelby. '"Out of the fusing of elements arises an important inner state which we call the inner creative mood." Once you learn how to achieve that you will be a superb actress. No, my dear, I am not flattering you. I believe it to be true. Now. It is late and I am tired.'

'I'll go at once!'

'No, no. I need a little refreshment. Won't you join me in a light supper?'

'Well . . . it would be a trouble to you . . .' Clare was dazzled by the situation. The director had the power of creating an atmosphere of sophistication, of giving her the feeling of being part of his world.

'I was only thinking of whipping up an omelette – a little French bread – a lettuce leaf or two –'

What could be more innocent, what could there be about that to cause her parents any worry?

'Perhaps your parents will be anxious if you stay out any longer. Give them a ring, the telephone is over there. I will of course take you home in the car.'

'It's only a step,' replied Clare, who lived in a big old house in Bootham Terrace. 'It is very kind of you. I would like an omelette very much. And I'm often out later than this.'

'Talk to me while I make it,' he asked. 'First put on a tape. You'll find them over there. I'll leave the door to the kitchen open and we can talk.'

She selected some softly wistful music and put it on. Now that the slight uneasiness of being alone for so long with a large and dominant male had passed and she felt quite safe, she began to feel a little provocative. The general mood relaxed. From the kitchen came a slight noise of cooking and table laying. Once she offered to help, but a cheerful 'No, no!' reassured her and kept her where she was, sitting by the tape deck and looking dreamily out of the window at the darkening sky.

'Come and get it!' came his voice at last.

On going into the kitchen she was surprised to find it almost in darkness and to see the table lit by two candles stuck on to saucers.

'I love candlelight, don't you?' he asked. 'And I've found a bottle. Do you drink, Clare? Or would you rather have a fruit juice? I find I sleep better after a little alcohol.'

Flattered, she agreed to have a glass of wine. How pleasant it was to be on these easy friendly terms with the great director! He had a way of making her feel part, not of her little provincial world, but of an altogether wider and different one.

It was not until they had enjoyed a long and intimate meal and two glasses of wine each that – as she offered to help clear the table and they were both moving to and fro in the flickering light – he touched her. He slid a powerful arm around her waist and pulled her closer to him. At first Clare was stunned and her initial quiescence was read by Exelby as the assent which he had learned to expect in the women to whom he made his advances.

'Just a little kiss,' he murmured. 'You are so attractive . . .'

As his hands moved downwards over her hips and he bent to kiss her tempting young mouth Exelby was unprepared for the violent reaction which now came.

Clare suddenly realized her position and how carefully she had been manoeuvred into it. Apart from the fact that she was in love with her boyfriend she found the stubbly reddened face of the director repellent at such close quarters.

She jumped back violently, the mood of relaxation and provocation gone. '*No*!' she spat like a wildcat, her eyes suddenly alive and angry. She vibrated with horror and the shock of her awakening from the mood of easy undemanding companionship.

Before Exelby could remonstrate, could try to restore the cosy and propitious atmosphere, Clare had snatched up her play-script and had fled from the room. She stamped down the stairs as if each step was a personal enemy. She listened for hasty footsteps behind her but Exelby contented himself with standing at the top of the staircase and bellowing, 'Clare! Clare! Come back, you little fool!'

She was afraid that it would be impossible to get out of the door without returning and asking for the key, but it was only latched and opened easily. The wrought iron gates on to Marygate of course were closed. She ran back, half sobbing, to the wooden stair-ladder which led up the wall, built for the convenience of the players, chased up it and down the other side into the graveyard of St Olave's, thinking that from there she could get out on to Marygate. But after spending a full minute chasing round the church she realized that she could not.

Up and down the stair-ladder again – terrified that Bruce would come out of his tower-like dwelling and would catch her – she decided that the only way out was over the high gate. Blessing the long hours spent in the school gym, she shinned over the gate at the lowest part, placing her feet neatly between the vertical bars . . . then she was safely outside the gardens and in the road, where she stood for a moment shaken and trembling.

She had not been pursued. Bending her head and crying a little she made her way home and slipped upstairs without seeing her parents, only calling out that she was in and was going straight to bed and had had a hot drink, thank you.

The accident did not happen until Poison's third rehearsal.

The feeling against him in the city was stronger and more vociferous than ever, now that it appeared he had not been frightened away, but was likely to remain and actually act.

Everyone on the set itself had relaxed a little. Poison had stopped carrying his script and hardly ever forgot his lines. Exelby was beginning to work on him to bring out his own unique interpretation of the role. It seemed, after the worries of a week before, almost incredible that the plays were progressing as normally as they were. The sheep were still, at the moment, causing the most problems. The assistant stage manager was tired of clearing up after them, but didn't like to delegate the job to anyone else.

It had been noted as a strange thing that the person playing Christ in some way seemed set apart; it always happened. The rest of the cast were inclined to treat him, as time went on, almost with reverence. It may just have been that after spending so many hours looking up to him on stage, the feeling was hard to dispel. But it is certain that the Christ always acquires authority.

Thomas could not have said that he found the part of God enlivening. It was rather static. He spoke from the archway in the sky which had once been the centre window of the wall of the ancient abbey, and when not speaking was either standing there looking impressive or sitting on the wooden walkway behind the medieval masonry. It did give him a bird's-eye view of the action, and it did give him the chance to sit out of sight and talk in whispers to the Angel Gabriel if enough noise was going on below to drown the sound.

Humphrey Hale always brought up his hip flask of whisky and a good book; the book to while away the time and the whisky to keep him warm. The plays began as the sun started to go down in splendour in the western sky and the arches were outlined black against it; then, as the performance wore on, the time came when the floodlights illuminated the arches and they in turn were light against the blackness of the night sky. By then Humphrey could no longer see to read, and the bottle came into its own.

This was the first of the three dress rehearsals.

All went as well as any rehearsal ever does. Exelby lost his temper rather fewer times than usual. The only unpleasant episode came between the director and the Virgin. After all his buttering up, she had definitely got a little above herself; it had gone to her head and she had begun to behave like the star of the production. But the way he treated her was hardly justified.

'Do you have to behave like that?' he suddenly barked at her, and as she jerked round and looked at him in surprise: 'Heaven save me from amateurs! What the hell do you think you're doing, girl? You're supposed to be the Mother of God, for heaven's sake, not a wooden doll strutting across the stage. You're useless. Absolutely useless. Get off. Is your understudy here? Anyone's performance would be better than this.'

'What's wrong?' faltered Clare.

'Wrong? I can't imagine why you ever thought you could act. What made you come for audition?'

'But you chose me, Mr Exelby – you said – you've said lots of times – RADA – the West End –'

'Never mind what I said.' His voice was a snarl, nothing else. It hissed out so clearly that the most distant person must have heard. One of the gardens' regular inhabitants, a peacock, began to call hoarsely as if in response.

'It's what I'm saying now that matters. As for RADA they'd as soon have a girl from behind a supermarket counter as you. Better in fact. At least she might be able to look intelligent. You either improve in the next two minutes or you're *off* and I mean *off*.'

Thomas heard afterwards that the tears overflowed from Clare's eyes and ran down her cheeks, clear crystal drops, hardly marking the soft pinkness, leaving her eyes unsullied, not reddened, only washed and sparkling. Tears such as only the young can shed. She was shaking. She acted on bravely, commanding her voice and quelling its quavering.

'For God's sake!' Exelby exclaimed irritably, once or twice.

The whole cast had gone quiet. If Clare was in trouble none of them was safe. The director said nothing else about sending her off, but at the end of that part there was no final word of praise, no hastening over to pat her hand. He ignored her, contrary to his recent practice, as she walked off the stage.

The scene had so shaken the rest of the cast that they acted as though mesmerized. For once their thoughts were not centred on Poison Peters. It was with a conscious effort that Thomas turned his thoughts back to Poison, as the time came for Christ's first long speech.

Thomas saw Poison approach the microphone. From his viewpoint he could only see the singer's back. By noticing the movement of his arm, he had no doubt Poison was reaching out, as he usually did, to slightly adjust the mike. He seemed to do it automatically, however recently he had adjusted the mike before.

It was obvious at once that something was wrong. Even from behind and above, Thomas could see that. Poison did not at once drop his hand and launch into the speech. His whole figure went rigid, clenched, and no words came.

Exelby was out front, looking up at the stage and Poison Peters. As Thomas left his high window arch and began to run along the wooden walkway and down the ladder Exelby also moved. The singer appeared to be frozen onto the microphone, still and voiceless.

'I knew he'd be on drugs,' came a disgusted voice from the Crowd.

As Exelby ran across the stage towards the singer he tripped over the microphone cable, almost went sprawling, then recovered himself. Simultaneously Poison Peters's body seemed to give a great jerk like a hooked fish leaping out of the water, and he flew through the air across the stage. He crashed into the stones of the abbey wall and fell down helplessly, sprawling like a rag doll.

'Don't anybody touch anything!' yelled Exelby. He ran to the singer, reaching him at the same time as Thomas Churchyard hurled himself panting from the bottom of the ladder onto the stage near the place where Peters had been thrown.

Exelby bent over Poison Peters. Poison's golden brown eyes

were open and aware.

'I'm all right,' he croaked.

'You're alive. Thank God. I'll kill that electrician.'

Flinging away, Exelby rushed to the hidden place where Absolom was sitting serenely on his rubber mat, adjusting the amplifier. Taking one look at him, Exelby rushed to the plug which connected the amplifier to the mains and threw the switch. Only then did he turn on Sydney Absolom.

'You've done it this time,' he shouted at the top of his voice. Turning to the assistant stage manager who had been running close behind him, he ordered: 'Fetch the police and an ambulance at once.'

'What?' Absolom looked up for the first time from his amplifier. 'What have you turned the juice off for? That drug addict of yours wants the mike. Too weak to make his voice heard without it.' Making a great show of indignation he walked towards the plug.

'Don't you touch that!' shrieked Exelby as he grabbed Absolom's arm. 'It's lethal. Oh, hell,' letting go of the arm – almost throwing it away from him – 'touch it if you want. You're expendable. You do what you want to yourself. But you've just nearly killed Peters. It's no thanks to you that he isn't dead.'

'Nearly killed . . .?'

'Your bloody equipment is live. You've just about killed him!'

Sydney Absolom went white. 'What do you mean? If anything was wrong I would have known. I was handling the stuff.'

'Oh yes, on your little rubber mat! Set it up nicely, haven't you? Well, don't think you're going to get away with it.' Exelby took hold of the older man once more, in a vicious grip. He dragged him out on to the stage, towards the spot where Thomas was standing guard over Poison and waving back the Crowd who had rushed over to see what was going on.

'Good man, Churchyard. Do you think he ought to go to hospital? I've sent the ASM to ring for an ambulance. Have we got a first aider around?'

'I'll be all right,' came a thread of a voice from Poison. 'Just get me back to the caravan to rest a bit.'

'Not a bad idea,' said Tom to Exelby.

'Right. Can you help him? I'm not letting go of this murdering bastard.'

'I'm not a murderer,' said Absolom in a voice almost as faint as the singer's.

'He's been Across,' said Exelby. 'Have *you* ever been Across? Know what it's like? Another few seconds could have killed him. I've never been Across but I know a few who have. Oh yes, it was easy for you to arrange, wasn't it?'

Thomas knelt down by the singer and slid an arm under him. Until now there had been no movement of any part of the thin body except the lips and eyes, since he had flown through the air and crashed against the wall. Thomas eased him upward. Poison's legs seemed too weak to support him, but after a few seconds he was standing, leaning heavily on Thomas.,

'I think you ought to go to hospital.'

'No thanks. The caravan will do. Will you help me there?'

They set off, Tom half carrying the singer, who staggered the few steps off the stage and through the opening in the abbey wall. The caravan was only yards away. Thomas came to a decision. He didn't say anything. He just turned towards Poison and picked him up in his arms. Poison lay passively across his chest, legs and arms dangling, his head bowed on to Thomas's shoulder. They looked like Michelangelo's 'Pieta'.

The actors who saw them drew back, shocked and awe-inspired. Only one person, Sue Brown, the assistant director, rushed ahead to the caravan door. It was locked.

'Pocket,' whispered Poison, and Sue felt in his jeans pocket for the key. It seemed minutes before she managed the lock. Then Thomas climbed the two steps and slid sideways through the door with his load.

Like all caravans there wasn't much room, but what space there was was clean and tidy. A bed with a checked wool cover was made up under the end window.

Lowering Poison's legs to the floor, Thomas flipped back the bedcovers with his left hand and then set the slim body on the edge of the bed. He bent down and unfastened the trainers, slipped them off Poison's feet and then raised the thin legs and slid him into the bed. Poison settled his head on the pillow with a sigh of relief, and Thomas stood erect and looked down at the pale face.

'I'd better get you something.'

'I'll be all right now I'm in bed.'

'You need some kind of stimulant. Brandy or something.'

'A cup of sweet tea,' suggested Poison.

Thomas now had time to look round the caravan. He had pictured it as a den of iniquity and expected it to be stinking and revolting. Instead it was immaculate, and smelled pleasantly of the bunch of culinary herbs stuck in a jam jar on the tiny worktop. He began rapidly to open cupboard doors. There were no bottles of either wine or spirits, certainly no brandy. Remembering the vodka bottle he had seen Poison swig from, Tom looked for that and found it at last, but empty. Perhaps a cup of sweet tea would be as good as anything. He didn't like the look of the closed eyes and the white face on the pillow. He found the kettle, half full of water, and the small stove and a box of matches. In seconds the kettle was on and beginning to sing as Thomas searched for some tea. He found Earl Grey and a small china teapot. Spooning it in lavishly he next looked around for sugar. There was some in a delicate fluted china basin which matched the teapot and cups and saucers.

Stirring the tea madly Thomas wondered how long he dared leave it to brew. Poison had not spoken for what seemed like hours. No doubt the doctor would arrive any minute. Thomas poured a cup of tea, sweetened it, and added skimmed milk from a carton in the fridge. It looked very much as if Poison was on a cure of some kind. He could hardly be slimming.

Raising Poison to a sitting position Tom held the cup to his lips.

'I'm not a baby, you know,' said the singer.

'I couldn't find any spirits,' Tom sounded apologetic.

'You won't. There aren't any.'

'I thought . . . you insisted on being alone in a caravan so that you could behave how you liked.'

'That's right.'

'I don't see . . .'

'Look, for heaven's sake keep quiet about this. How I live is my own affair, right?'

'Right.'

'A word to anybody and you're for it.'

Poison had taken the cup of tea in a trembling hand. 'You've made this strong, haven't you? Don't you know Earl Grey is supposed to be drunk weak without milk and sugar?'

'The sugar is for shock.'

'Well – you didn't have to put milk in – still, I'm grateful. Thanks and all that.'

'I'm just puzzled about the drink.'

'It's none of your business. Well – if you don't let it out! I'll skin you alive if you do and then deny anything you've said. I've never been able to touch alcohol and that's the top and bottom of it. It makes me ill.'

'But all the drunkenness?'

'That's the line, isn't it, yeah?'

'All that being sick on stage?'

Poison grimaced. 'That was the time I did try some, to see if I'd grown out of the reaction. I was as sick as a pig, all over the stage. Aaaah! Still it was good for business and all that.'

'What do you drink, then?'

'Milk – Malvern water – and Earl Grey tea, but weaker than this stuff.' Poison made a face and took a few more sips from the cup. 'Don't you dare tell anyone.'

'My lips are sealed.'

A knock came at the door, then it opened and a man came in, pink-faced, wearing a suit and carrying the kind of briefcase doctors use.

'Dr Belcombe,' he said. 'I'm told Mr Peters has had a powerful electric shock. Been Across, as they say, the main current. He ought to be in hospital.'

'I'm alive,' said Poison, 'and if I was in hospital the place would get besieged. I'll be quieter here. I'll be all right soon.'

It was still a struggle for him to speak, the words came out with an obvious effort, and Thomas regretted talking to him earlier. The singer's forehead was covered with a fine sweat. He fell back on his pillow exhausted.

'You escaped death by seconds.'

'Crashing against that wall didn't half hurt.'

'Let's be sure there's nothing broken.'

'I'm going,' said Thomas. 'Perhaps you could report his condition to Mr Exelby, doctor.'

Thomas walked away slowly, thinking about Poison Peters, the drunken pop star who was made sick by the smallest amount of alcohol. Back on stage he found the place bristling with policemen.

'The rehearsal's off,' Humphrey Hale told him. 'The little Devils and Mary and the sheep have gone home already. Everyone else is going now.'

'They won't want me, then.'

'Oh yes they do. Our Bruce is screaming that this is a case of attempted murder. He and Absolom have gone to Fulford Road police station and you've got to follow them.'

'Why me?'

'Because you were noticing what happened – otherwise you wouldn't have got down that ladder so fast.'

The seven little Devils were supposed to have gone home, but they had other things to do. What was the point of going home tamely when the Angels were still about? On one or two nights they had had quite a good time making frightening ghostly noises around the church and the Angels had responded quite satisfactorily . . .

'I dare you,' one of them said to Christopher, the biggest of the seven.

'All right, I will, then.'

'What's he going to do?' asked Nicholas as Christopher ran off into the dusk.

'Oh, only lever up one of the tops of the tombs. It'll really scare the girls. We've all got to be ready to groan.'

Christopher returned, and set to work on the heavy stone slab, while the others groaned and moaned, and the Angels shrieked and clutched each other nearby.

'What on earth are you doing?' asked a cool voice from the darkness. It was Velvet Smith.

'Just playing . . .'

'Come along this minute and get your costumes off. You'll spoil them.'

The Angels came obediently. The Devils scattered and ran wildly in all directions at once, shouting, rattling sticks, and one of them creating a metallic fusillade on some iron railings . . .

'I don't undersand what all this is about,' said Sydney Absolom. He was sitting miserably in an interview room at the police station.

'It's about this,' said Bob Southwell. The amplifier, microphone, and all the rest of the sound equipment were in the corner, and he pointed graphically to the plug, which had been placed on the table. His glasses flashed with reflected light, as if they too were accusing. 'Do you usually wire things up so that they will electrocute people you don't like?'

'I don't know what you mean.' Defensively.

'You know the actor, Mr Peters, had a near-fatal accident earlier this evening?'

'I've been told so, yes. I wouldn't have known about it otherwise.'

'He reached out to adjust the microphone – apparently it's a habit of his – and was wrapped across the main circuit and unable to tear himself away. Fortunately Mr Exelby, in rushing to his assistance, tripped over the microphone cable and by so doing must have pulled out the microphone plug from the amplifier and broken the current. Mr Peters's muscles then went into spasm, he was hurled back from the microphone and crashed into the stone wall a few feet away.'

Sydney Absolom said nothing, although there was a pause in which he could have interjected some of the mad words which were reeling round in his head.

'So we were called to the scene to investigate the cause of the accident. I came along because we were told it was a case of attempted murder. And we found this' – he gestured again at the plug – 'with the earth wire unconnected and touching the live pin. Who wired this plug, Mr Absolom?'

He gulped. 'I did.'

'Well? Do you want to make a statement?'

Sydney Absolom swallowed again, hard, as if he was trying to digest his Adam's apple. He nodded.

A minute or two later a constable was sitting, ballpoint at the ready, and another constable had brought Sydney Absolom a cup of tea. Bob Southwell had taken pity on his white and horrified face, and began to reconsider his first assumption that this was a deliberate attempt to harm Poison Peters.

'We don't usually have sound amplification in the mystery plays,' began Absolom. 'I've done the lights on the last two plays. So I was chosen to do them on this one again. Everything went all right until Mr Exelby announced his Christ.'

'You were very much against his choice?'

'I was – I am – yes. That doesn't mean I'd try to kill him!'

'You have been heard to make threats, Mr Absolom.'

Sydney bent his head. 'Yes.'

'Go on with your story.'

'Because P – Mr Peters was our Christ, and Mr Exelby wasn't sure about the strength of his voice, he wanted the amplifier and mike. The road manager brought it and the mikes and everything. I was expected to fix it up in a hurry. They wanted to test it straight away and see how it worked in the open air, so I had to connect it up. Then I found it had a modern continental-type plug and the power sockets are an older style. Luckily I had an older-type plug in my odds-and-ends box.' There was a note of pride in his voice, the note common to handymen with odds-and-ends boxes. 'When I tried to fix it to the amplifier there was a slight problem – there were only two retaining screws for the three wires of the main flex. So I used those to fasten down the live and neutral wires, just to get the amplifier working.'

'And what did you do with the earth lead?' asked Bob Southwell in a noncommittal voice.

'Well, that was a problem. I thought I'd have a search for a third screw later. So for the time being I rested it inside the plug top with its bare end near the earth pin.'

'And you think that was safe?'

Absolom spoke to his fingers, which were resting on the edge of the table. 'It was only temporary. I switched on and tested the amplifier and microphone, and everything functioned perfectly. Mr Peters used the microphone that night and all was well.'

'Did you find a third screw?'

Absolom made another remark, very low, to his fingers. 'I forgot all about it.'

'Oh, I see! You forgot all about it. You have a bare wire loose in a plug and forget all about it. This is the perfect murder plot, is it not? You sit secure on your little rubber mat. The play goes on. Inside your safe-looking plug the plastic covering on the earth wire twists and flexes as plastic coverings do. Sooner or later the set-up is going to become lethal and Poison Peters is going to get hold of it. This man you've been making threats against. He's the only one who uses the microphone, isn't he?'

'Anyone might have touched it,' said Absolom.

'True. Every time you switched on it was like a time bomb which might kill someone at any minute. Including you.'

'Yes. It looks like that.'

'Looks like that! It damn well was like that. It was a murder plot aimed at Poison Peters but liable to kill anyone at all at any time.' The large lenses of his glasses were filled with reflections of the lamp on the table and his thoughts could not be read.

'I never wanted to kill anyone,' muttered Absolom.

'You nearly did. A few seconds more and you would have.'

Absolom began to cry, bending his head on to his hands, his narrow shoulders shaking.

'All right,' said Bob Southwell after a few minutes. 'We've had all the equipment and the plug looked at by a local expert in electrical things. He says it was stupidity and inefficiency and that it doesn't look like a murder attempt.'

'You just said it was,' sniffled Absolom.

'It might well have been. If Poison had died do you think I'd be able to let you go?'

'Can I go?'

'Yes.' Tiredly. 'Though Mr Exelby would rather I kept you in irons in a padded cell.'

'I'll get that third screw now.'

'I'm afraid you're off the job. You are not to be allowed on to the set of the plays again, and I must warn you that if you try to go there, or make any contact with the cast, or make any more threats against either Mr Exelby or Mr Peters, then I will have to take a much more serious view of the whole incident than I am doing today.'

The Youngest Shepherd and Clare, the Virgin Mary, were still sitting in a quiet corner of the public house on Marygate. So far all she had done was cry quietly and all he had done was glower at her. Now everyone but them had departed, the landlord was washing the glasses, and casting glances in their direction.

'What was it all about, then?' he said at last.

Very quietly, and with her handkerchief still at her eyes, she told him all about the previous night's happenings.

'I'll kill him,' said the Youngest Shepherd fervently.

'Oh, no, David, you mustn't. Please don't be so angry. Nothing *happened*, you know. I'm still . . . what I'm supposed to be.'

'You'd better be.'

'Oh, yes, David, I'm waiting for . . . us . . . you know . . . when the times comes.'

'I want to marry a virgin,' said David, who liked to dominate exclusively over Clare.

'Oh, yes, David.'

'Come on. I'll walk you home.'

Poison Peters was kneeling by his bed in the caravan. The text of the plays lay near to him. Closed, under his left hand, was a copy of the Bible, which he had read for the first time since arriving in York. He was trying to pray.

'Lord God, I'm not good at this. I can't remember how you're supposed to do it.' Words and phrases from school assemblies ran round his head like half-heard music. 'But like I said before, if I am to carry out this task Thou hast put before me, then I need Thy help. Today I nearly came to You. Bruce Exelby said I'd "been Across". It nearly finished me and I'll never be the same again. It's so close, the dividing line. It's so quick – the time needed to cross it. Death and I have shaken hands.'

He stopped and there was not a sound except the whirling of his thoughts.

His language became more archaic as he remembered words and phrases which seemed the right ones to use.

'I always thought it a great honour, Lord, to be asked to represent Thy Son. Now I have been very close to Thee.

Please let this experience help me to be worthy. I am but a miserable . . . what . . . worm, one of Thy creatures; and if one of Thy creatures, can I be other than part of Thy glory? I pray that this miserable worm be allowed in some sort to figure forth the image of Thy Son . . .'

His little stock of words exhausted, he knelt on with bent head, closed eyes and calm hands, motionless as they lay separately on the coverlet. The night deepened outside. The gates of the Museum Gardens were locked. High in the tower of St Mary's Lodge by the St Olave Gate burned the lights of Bruce Exelby's flat. Above the deep shadows, the heaps of blackness which were the trees, the jet shadows of the walls of St Mary's Abbey, were other gleams of light. The floodlighting which lit up the city, the yellow lights of the roads which ringed it, wove a golden cocoon high in the air, a cocoon of silk-like threads of light as if York were a holy city, and as if the depths of night resting within were a holy sleep – a sleep within which vigils and consecrations might take place.

4

Now raise him nimbly. Heave and Ho!
And set him by this mortice here,
And let him fall down at one blow –
For sure that pain will have no peer,
Heave up – let down! All his bones so
  Are sundered everywhere.

The Pinners' and Painters' Play

Thomas next saw Robert Southwell the following day when he went home after work before attending the second dress rehearsal.

'I was wondering what you're going to do about all the threatening letters,' he said diffidently, not wanting to sound as if he was teaching the police their job.

Bob looked up from his weeding at the sound of the deep, authoritative voice. 'How did you hear about them? I'm doing nothing,' he said, pulling up a dandelion and scrutinizing its root. 'It's all sound and fury.'

'But yesterday?'

'Pure accident.'

'Well, I didn't think poor old Sydney would actually try to harm anyone. He looked very crestfallen when I took him home.' Even Absolom's fluffy cloud of hair had seemed to join in his general dejection, drooping about his ears.

'It's easy to think there is danger when there is none. We're checking the hate mail in case any of the letter-writers really seem serious, and keeping it all for the time being. Exelby and Peters are both getting a fair amount.'

'You aren't putting a guard on Poison Peters?'

'No need.'

Tom felt disappointed. Things to do with the police were not as dramatic as he expected. There was an amused glint in Bob's spectacles.

Thomas put on his costume and make-up in the parish room of St Olave. The next day the props and costumes for the principals were going to be taken up to the superior dignity of the Tempest Anderson Hall, which was much nearer to the place of performance and more private. Only the lesser fry – the Crowd, the Devils and the Soldiers – would remain based in the parish room. This was the only time he would have to take the rather embarrassing walk in full costume up Almery Lane, across Marygate, and in through the St Olave's Gate.

Thomas mounted the set of wooden steps which had been built from the Museum Gardens up the wall which divided the gardens from St Olave's churchyard, and then walked down the corresponding set on the other side of the wall, finding himself in the graveyard. It was shadowed by its beautiful trees and full of medieval people in colourful clothes, sitting or leaning on the tombs, their vast garments draped over the chill stones.

A great deal of cheerfulness was to be sensed, in spite of the tension inseparable from a dress rehearsal. Soldiers and the mothers of the Innocents they were shortly to massacre were fraternizing in a manner which would have worried Herod. Lucifer was offering a cigarette to one of the Crowd whom he was later to drive screaming into Hell. Humphrey Hale, the Archangel Gabriel, had lifted his nose out of his book and was chatting to a scantily dressed Eve. Michael the Archangel was complaining about the weight of his flaming sword to the props mistress, who had a little tent in which all manner of things were being looked after, mended, altered, as the situation demanded. She could hardly move in there for the piles of willow branches which had been freshly cut, ready to serve as palms during the entry into Jerusalem.

It seemed as if the near-accident the evening before had had a cathartic effect; everyone was less nervy than they had been.

'Is Poison all right?' Thomas asked Jane Bugg. 'Has he got over the shock?'

'He seems to be fine. He was here a minute ago with dear *Bruce*. Even *Bruce* looks cheerful.'

Jane, the large medieval lady whom nobody could stand, was one of the clerical staff attached to the engineering division in the office where Tom worked every day. It was a pity she was such a know-all. Underneath he was sure she was all right. She even looked better in a wimple than when one could see her hair strained back over her head to make a minute knob at the top rear of her skull. She went on in her crass voice, 'I don't know if he's planning to let Peters off the Crucifixion tonight, until he's had more time to recover.'

Thomas had hardly looked round for his friends before Bruce Exelby appeared again, purposeful and dominating – even brutal, bull-headed, bruising, in his attitude that day.

'Everyone ready? Good. Musicians, take your places. Everyone else, to your starting positions. Crowd, I don't want to hear you. Of course it isn't much fun to stand and wait but that doesn't mean you've got to rhubarb rhubarb while you're doing it. God, your throne is in position now on the platform centre top. Would you go up there please instead of in the window? You can come down and do what you like when you're not on. I want to know at the end of your first stint whether you're happy with the arrangement.'

The throne, resplendent with gold paint, had been placed on a specially built platform on the very top centre of the remaining abbey wall, on one of the places where it corbelled out to support gothic vaulting which had long since vanished. 'It's lucky I don't mind heights,' thought Thomas as he seated himself high in the sky in front of the sunset. He was aware of majesty descending on him like a mantle.

Feeling strangely remote in his position, Thomas declaimed his great opening speech and then moved into the interplay with Lucifer. The wide set was peopled only by Angels and Seraphs and the Devils, who, led by their infernal Lord, went tumbling down the long slope which had been built on one side of the stage, as in a moment of high drama they were precipitated into the red-lit masonry arch of Hell's mouth.

'You're no bloody good up there for that scene,' Exelby yelled up at Thomas. 'Too far away. Your voice gets lost. Save the throne for the end. Go on using the window arch for the beginning.'

'Right.'

The production moved smoothly into the plays of the Cardmakers, Fullers, and Coopers, which three had been amalgamated in Canon Purvis's modern translation into one play of Adam and Eve and the Fall, indicating the necessity for the Redemption. Among their Eden of stitched felt leaves the slender and beautiful ancestors of man were a pair of delightfully touching young lovers.

To those sitting out front Thomas Churchyard's voice, echoing with its fine resonance, speaking out in love as well as anger the condemnation of Adam and Eve, brought suddenly home the whole allegorical meaning of the Fall of Man.

God now descended from his window arch and went to sit in the front of the stage. It was the only time he was going to have the opportunity of seeing some of the production from the point of view of the audience. He particularly liked the next bit – the Spicers', Pewterers' and Founders', Tile Thatchers', Chandlers', Goldsmiths', and Marshalls' Plays, which took the action through the conception and birth of Christ.

He loved the symbolic birth, where Mary bent over, in the vast circle of her blue cloak, then unfolded herself and lifted up her arms like wings, revealing the infant child in her lap. Then came the Shepherds with their recalcitrant sheep, who seemed to be learning their parts at last, and the pathos of the flight into Egypt.

The time now came for Jesus's baptism, which was Poison's first entrance, and a feeling of heightened expectancy ran through the whole cast and those elsewhere on the set. He came, a figure in a simple white woollen gown which fell into natural medieval folds, and with his first words, 'John, all mankind is frail,' which rang out clear as the voice of a bird, the plays, powerful as they had been before, moved into a wholly greater dimension. Thomas Churchyard, recognizing an extraordinary stage presence, also recognized subconsciously that this man had no need of amplifying equipment to make his voice carry to the farthest seat on the staging.

From this point in the Barbers' Play, the action moved smoothly through the Locksmiths', the Cap Makers', and the Skinners' Plays, before breaking for the interval after the wonderful entry into Jerusalem, the triumphant high point where Christ, on the ass which had earlier taken Mary down the slope on her flight into Egypt, now ascended the same long slope, leading up through flat areas and flights of steps crowded with happy cheering colourful people waving their palm branches.

He thought Bruce Exelby could have nothing but praise for such a first half. But the director, striding on stage and looking out of place in his modern dress, had plenty of faults to find. 'And we'll get it right if we have to stay here all night,' he announced ominously.

Thomas saw the Virgin Mary trembling, and felt that he could not bear to see her publicly disgraced again. Getting up hastily he went round to the back of the set and climbed the ladder on to the walkway which ran behind the window arches. He might be wanted and woe betide anyone who was not ready to jump instantly at the director's word.

After this beginning the fault finding was not all that bad; there were details Exelby didn't like and couldn't think how they had crept in, even if he had ordered them himself the day before. No one was likely to point that out or contradict him. There were faults and hesitancies which were remarked on scathingly. No one was praised. A good many people, including the Virgin Mary, were made to feel that they had got off lightly from heinous sins.

Then suddenly the mood changed; all was sweetness and light. 'Coffee for everyone,' Exelby declared, and happy chattering began. The Soldiers broke ranks and managed to be first in the queue for coffee.

But instead of going better after Exelby's exhortations, everything went worse. The sudden sunniness had only been the smile on the face of the tiger. People forgot their lines and their positions right through the Cutlers' and the Cordwainers' Plays; it was not until the Bowyers' and Fletchers' that they began to get back into the swing they had attained in the first half.

Yet Tom Churchyard, who had again ventured to sit in the front, had to admit that there had been some truth in all Exelby's criticisms, though they would not have occurred to him. But that was what a director was for, after all. That was his job, to see the faults no one else had noticed and do something about them. The Tapestry Makers', the Cooks' and Waterleaders', the Tile Makers', the Shermans' Plays progressed; Christ was condemned.

Now came the Pinners' and Painters' Play, in which Christ is crucified. Exelby had said no word to the contrary, so Thomas supposed he must consider Poison fit enough for the ordeal. Remembering the dead weight of the young man in his arms the previous day – his white face on the pillow – Tom thought he would have got someone else to do that bit today. What were understudies for if they did nothing?

Meanwhile Poison was journeying ever upward to the place of execution, carrying his cross. In this production two crosses were used. The cross on which he was actually crucified was left permanently on the highest stage area. During most of the performance it lay back at an angle, its head resting on a support pole. It was only when Christ was firmly fixed on it that it was raised up to the vertical. It could be seen by the audience, particularly in the highest tiers of seats, but their attention was always on the action, and it was hardly noticed that Poison carried a different and lighter cross, for which he was truly thankful. This lightweight cross was discreetly disposed of by a group of actors before the crucifixion itself, being lowered inconspicuously down the back of the set.

Poison lay down on the cross, which was at an angle of thirty-five degrees. He placed his feet on the footrest, a meagre few inches of wood projecting from the upright. He put his fingers on either side of the bolt projecting from the crossbeam, the bolt which was meant to look as though it penetrated his hand, but which he would have to clutch as time dragged on. Then he did the same with the other hand. He was wearing only a loincloth by this time. Pieces of white cloth were bound strongly round his wrists and angles and hips to help take his weight. Then came the moment for him to be lifted upright.

All the soldiers began to heave, and the cross rose.

'Stop!'

The voice came, it seemed, from the earth, the very ground. The soldiers were still tugging. Their job was almost done.

Another few degrees . . .

'Stop! You must stop!' came again, loud and desperately. The cross shifted in a way no one had expected. It lurched about two feet downwards, and there was a cracking sound.

The soldiers dropped the cords they had been pulling to raise the cross and rushed forward, grabbing at it, two on each side.

'What the hell is happening?' cried Bruce Exelby.

Tom, seeing that something was wrong, jumped up from the front seat he had been occupying and dashed across the grass to where the built-up set began, up one of the flights of stairs, to the base of the upper stage. There were several archways which led underneath the wooden structure, which had been made to look like an extension of the ancient ruined walls themselves. He dived into the nearest arch, at the same time as several other onlookers.

It was dark under the upper stage, but light filtered in through the various openings, and a shaft of light beamed down the hole for the foot of the cross. One plank of the staging, the exact width of the cross, hinged back to allow the movement of the cross. When the cross was raised to the vertical, the plank was lowered to form an additional rear support for it, and to prevent anyone accidentally stepping into the narrow slot. It was through this slot that the desperate voice of the ASM had risen to the soldiers above.

The assistant stage manager had the unenviable task of waiting down here until the moment came for him to fasten the cross firmly in position. A board was locked to the scaffolding under the upper stage, and the foot of the cross was fastened to this with an ordinary half-inch bolt which acted as a pivot. Once the Christ was fastened on to the cross as it lay in the sloped back position, it was raised upright pivoting on this bolt. When the ASM pushed a second, higher, bolt into position through cross and board, it was secure. Last of all the plank on the stage above was lowered.

With upstretched hands which looked tiny and fragile against the thick wood the ASM was trying to support the base of the cross.

'Well?' said Thomas, panting.

'Get Peters off the cross,' cried the ASM. 'The pivot has

given way. The whole thing shot downwards. Look at it now! It's caught on that cross pole of the scaffolding, or it would have crashed down at once.'

Tom could see. One edge of the base of the cross had just come into contact with a round scaffold pole on its lurch downwards, and looked as if the slightest jar would make it slip off the smooth cylindrical surface.

'Can we push something underneath to support it?'

'If someone can fetch a lump of wood or something . . .'

'Is it safe to touch him at all until we've supported the base?'

'No – but he must be got off. And without moving the cross. Another movement however slight and it will come crashing down here out of control, with him on it.'

Sweat broke out on Thomas's forehead and the hairs went up on the back of his neck. He could think of nothing that could be done to stop a tragedy. The slot in the stage was only a few inches wide; if cross and actor came down together, the combined weight and impetus – for it was tall – would break Poison's legs and probably his spine, if it did nothing worse.

'Can you support the cross up there and stop it sliding down? It mustn't move at *all*, not a fraction!' he shouted, hoping that his strong voice would carry up through the hole and the shaft of light to the soldiers clutching the cross. 'Some of you hold it *firmly* and others get Peters off.'

There was a noise from the stage as though the people up there had understood and were acting on his words. Bruce Exelby came charging into the dark crowded space under the stage.

'My God,' he said softly, picking up a piece of the broken bolt from the floor. This isn't an accident. The iron bolt didn't snap. This isn't iron at all. It is a bloody bit of wood, broken in two . . . Get the police.'

'Get Peters off first,' retorted Tom, holding the bottom of the cross as well as he could to help the ASM. Not that their hands could have stopped its downward movement if the whole heavy thing had begun to shift. He looked at the smooth surface of the scaffold pole, and the narrow edge of the cross which had rested on it and stopped the downward progress.

Thomas could see that the thing in the director's hands was

not iron at all but a broken bit of wood. And when he looked at the end of the cross he saw the rest of it protruding from the pivot-hole; a round stick like a branch of willow, only thicker than the willow wands which were used as palms.

'I'll get the police my bloody self,' said Exelby, and went.

It had taken a long time to tie Poison to the cross, and it took longer to get him off, for he was high up now, and the actors hardly dared move for fear of setting the contraption sliding. The soldiers, who had been chosen for their strong and heavy appearance, were trying to hold it firmly on either side, and several of the Crowd had come rushing up and were gingerly pulling at the white cloth strips round Poison's feet.

'We want a step ladder,' someone said.

Poison said nothing.

If he had had any colour in his face to start with it would have gone, but he looked very little different. He was biting his bottom lip and holding on grimly to the two handholds, as if that would have saved him. He himself could not slide through the long narrow opening in the stage. He was going to be banged and shaken if the cross got free of the restraining hands, how badly he could not tell, except that a human body is frail compared to thick wood moving under its own weight.

If he escaped with broken bones he would be lucky.

5

Well, say it no more, that is twice.
The Bowyers' and Fletchers' Play

Bob Southwell arrived on the scene before Poison was released – which showed either how long it took to get Poison off, or how quick Bob had been, whichever way you liked to look at it. The fact was that he had been on his way to the Museum Gardens to see if all was well, and that although it seemed like hours to the actors who were struggling with the cross, it was only minutes until they found a loose set of stage steps which could be carried over and used to stand on to untie Poison Peters.

As soon as Bob stood there looking at them, his eyes stern behind his glasses, everyone felt better. Authority had arrived and authority would not let this thing happen – and indeed a second later they loosened the last band and Poison gingerly moved first one arm and then the other, and as soon as he dared, reached out a foot to touch the steps; then he felt safer. There were hands to hold him and support him.

At this point he released the cross of his weight very slowly and gently, climbed down the steps in a bevy of helping hands, reached the secure stage, stood alone, and then crumpled up and fell at Bob's feet in a dead faint.

'Hospital for him,' said Bob firmly.

'He won't go in because of the fans,' explained one of the actors.

'What about the Retreat?' asked a policeman at Bob's shoulder. Grateful for the bit of local knowledge, Bob looked at him encouragingly, so the man went on.

'It's a private Quaker nursing home near the city mainly for the mentally ill, but they take other cases and they would be able to protect him from fans – I've known them have show-biz personalities before, who needed a rest in private. They're very discreet.'

'Or there's the Purey Cust,' broke in another policeman. 'That's nearer.'

'Go and see what you can fix up, John,' said Bob Southwell. 'That OK by you, Mr Exelby?'

'Yes, of course. Don't worry about the fees. Anything as long as he has the chance to recover in private from this.'

'I'd be happier if he was in hospital, but . . .'

'He'll get good medical attention at either of those,' said someone.

While the talk was going on one of the actors had picked up Christ's garment from the ground and covered him with it.

Bob Southwell asked to see the under-stage fixing arrangements for the cross and vanished below, where he found Tom and the ASM still desperately holding the base of the cross.

'You can let that go now,' Bob said.

'Well, we know he's off, but it still might slide down.'

'I doubt if it will do any damage. Lower it.'

'Is he out of the way, up there?'

The ASM shouted up, and someone shouted down again to say that they had moved Poison and it was all right to lower the cross, no one was in the way.

Once their hands were removed, and the Soldiers up above also let go, the cross finally slipped off the scaffolding pole and thumped down so that its foot rested on the lower stage. The violent crash shocked them even though they were expecting it to happen.

'Let's have a look at this mechanism, then,' said Bob.

Tom tried not to give Bob an 'I-told-you-so' look but could only just resist reminding him that four hours before he had been ridiculing the idea of danger. He had to close his lips firmly together and stop himself speaking. Even so Bob got the message. He didn't say anything but his face was grim. The twinkling humorous expression Tom had liked so much had gone. The wide rounded forehead and thin lower face looked stern and concentrated.

'If it's a practical joke it's a particularly nasty one,' Bob said. 'The branch that was shoved through would hardly retain fingerprints but it's worth trying,' he remarked to one of his men, the one who had suggested the Purey Cust. 'Get someone on to it, and examine anything else that looks likely.'

He could not ignore Tom's silent questioning, and turned to him. 'Oh yes, we'll have to take action,' he said. 'Though I think this might be someone's idea of a joke. Do you have any teenagers in the cast?'

'Only the Devils – the Angels – the Virgin Mary – some of the Crowd – the Youngest Shepherd –'

'It might well be someone's idea of a funny. They might not realize the danger of real harm.'

Tom thought Bob had a touching faith in human nature, but did not like to say so in front of his men. So he smiled and nodded in agreement. The main thing was that the danger to Poison was going to be taken a bit more seriously. Two risks to Poison Peters' life – two near misses – were two too many, however caused, whether by negligence or what. The third one – and Tom was sure there was going to be a third one, didn't things always go in threes? – might succeed. Third time lucky. This time there would be nothing amateur about it.

Bob Southwell was at the police station. 'Get me Detective Chief Superintendent Duncan, please,' he said to the girl on the switchboard.

When she had rung through to Newby Wiske, got the right extension, and said, 'I have Detective Chief Inspector Southwell for you, sir,' she connected Bob with his superior.

'Good morning, sir,' said Bob. 'Yes, it's fine here. Festival weather as they keep telling me. Yes, the festival starts on Saturday. The reason I'm ringing, sir, is this: we've had two rather nasty little incidents on the set of the mystery plays. The second one last evening. How nasty? I'll tell you . . .'

After explaining, he went on: 'I'm inclined to think this was a practical joke that went wrong, but there have been too many unpleasant incidents connected with this production altogether. I wondered if Task Force were busy or if they could spare me a bit of manpower for supervision? . . . I thought they could hang around and see if there are any vandals about and try to trace the focus of trouble – it's probably in the cast . . . Right . . . Yes, sir . . . I'll look forward to hearing from him . . . Yes, the kids seem to be settling very well, thanks . . . Oh, fine! . . . I'll tell Linda, and I know she'll want me to remember her to you.'

A few minutes later his phone rang.

'Southwell.'

'You can't manage without us, then, sir? The DCS says we're to help out, pronto.'

'Diamond! You're quick off the mark.'

'Do you want us today?'

'Yes. The sooner the better. You need to get to know the set-up before this afternoon. What did the boss tell you?'

'Slight problems you can't handle, sir.'

'Get yourself down here, Sergeant Diamond, without the funny stuff, and with as many men as Task Force can spare.'

'Plain clothes?'

'Yes. How many of you will there be?'

'Ten, sir? Is that all right?'

'Yes. Fine. See you here at the station in half an hour.'

Bruce Exelby was asked to come in for consultation.

'Not before time, Mr Southwell,' he said.

'We'll have men here shortly who will spend some hours or days, or however long it takes, on duty,' replied Bob Southwell. 'I want them to mingle with your actors unobtrusively – have you any suggestions as to how we can do that?'

'We could dress them up and they could take part.'

'Have a heart, Mr Exelby, they won't have time to learn any lines.'

'They won't have lines if they are part of the Crowd.' Bruce Exelby was suddenly enthusiastic. 'They can wear costume – we made a few extra sets in case of accidental damage or other contingencies – and the Crowd is always being divided up into groups – they could be in separate groups and listen and watch. One of them could stay under the upper stage near the base of the cross to stop any more murder attempts.'

'Yes. I'd certainly thought of stationing a man there. Not that anyone is likely to try the same trick again. They would know a lookout was being kept. Murder attempts is a bit strong, Mr Exelby.'

'Murder is nearly what it was. I don't mind the people of York trying to scare Poison out of the city – I don't mind them letting off steam and all that – it's just good publicity as far as I'm concerned. What I do mind is them nearly killing him. You were there. You know how close the danger was, how delicate the business of unfastening him and getting him off the cross was. If it had crashed down with him still on it you know he would have been lucky to escape with shattered legs. What are you going to do about tracking the culprit?'

'We didn't find anything which could indicate who did it, but I suggest interviewing the younger members of the cast. To my mind this is a prank and you have quite a lot of youngsters taking part.'

'This idea of a prank is a fixation with you, Mr Southwell.' Exelby's tone was contemptuous. Bob Southwell felt like reminding him that he was a Detective Chief Inspector, not one of the cast, and was not to be spoken to in that tone of voice.

'Well, this afternoon is the photocall,' went on the director. 'The whole cast will be on set and the journalists and photographers will be having their own way. It saves a lot of trouble later. We put on whatever incident they want to photograph. They always want to do the crucifixion, from what I hear of earlier productions.'

'Peters shouldn't be expected to go through that just for the photographers.'

'No. We'll use his understudy. But I want him to do it for the last dress rehearsal, tonight. It's like driving again after an accident. The sooner the better. I want to be sure, too, that the production is right in all details because the first night is tomorrow, and once that's over I shall be leaving York and going on to my next production.'

'So soon?'

'Oh yes. I'm a busy man.'

'I somehow thought the director would be here all the time.'

'For the full three weeks? No thank you. There'd be nothing for me to do. My assistants will manage perfectly well. They can always contact me if anything comes up that really needs my attention.'

'As soon as my men arrive I'll bring them to the Museum Gardens and liaise with you there. Perhaps you'll explain what they are to do, and we'll get them fitted out with costumes. They can practise during the photocall and get used to wearing them, and begin to keep their ears open. With any luck we won't need them for long.'

Sergeant Diamond and his ten men were kitted out by Sally Vause and Velvet Smith in the parish room of St Olave. The two women were used by now to working as a team, and did the job neatly and efficiently. They did not make much impression on the men of the Task Force.

Sally was too old – and she had not aged well; her hair was dyed a suspicious shade of walnut brown, her face covered with pouches, her neck thick, and her clothes were too young for her.

Velvet at forty still had some feminine charm; the good teeth Thomas had noticed, and a brightness sometimes in her quick though subdued movements; but it was not noticeable to the men she was dressing in flowing robes. Like Tom Churchyard, they found her instantly forgettable, with her pinched figure and pale face. Only her name made any impression. Hearing Sally use it, Sergeant Diamond asked, 'How did she get a name like that?'

Sally answered confidentially as she showed him how to tie the tapes which held the costume in place: 'Her mother was very keen on the theatre. She thought the name would look pretty in lights.'

Sergeant Diamond cast an unbelieving glance in Velvet's direction.

'Velvet was never mad on being an actress herself,' went on Sally, 'but she must have a bit of her mother's interest, or she wouldn't be working as she does towards the plays' success – you've no idea how many hours we've put in, and no one thinks of that, they just assume costumes make themselves and look after themselves.'

'I suppose she has to be thankful her mother didn't call her

Satin, Muslin, or Voile,' said the Sergeant, whose wife was keen on dressmaking. 'Well, at least you're in on the action – you have the chance of watching rehearsals and all that.'

'You've got to be joking,' said Sally. 'I haven't seen a thing yet, and Velvet is never away from this place. But I'm going to watch at least some of it in rehearsal, come what may. There's that moment when God calls out to Michael – and suddenly the lights pick him out standing on that high needle of wall – I did manage to see that the other night in plain clothes and I just must see it in costume, it's so dramatic – look out for it, sergeant, don't miss it.'

'I have a job to do. We're not here to watch the plays.'

The sergeant and his men walked rather self-consciously along Almery and across Marygate and in through the St Olave's Gate, up the wooden steps and over the wall into the graveyard. Exelby met them and instantly broke up the group, heading them into different knots of players. Although the cast knew one another well there were a great many of them, and Exelby saw fit just to say things like, 'Adrian will be with you lot today,' or 'Will you have Barry in yours? You look a bit thin as you go up the stairs . . .'

The members of Task Force knew how to melt into backgrounds and as soon as they were with a lot of other people also dressed in medieval costume they stopped feeling self-conscious and began to do their job, chatting and mingling yet keeping their ears open and their every sense alert.

The afternoon was long and dreary. Poison Peters came on set only for a half-hour session with the photographers. He looked drawn, as if he had not slept. Thomas Churchyard got near enough to him to ask how he was, and if he had rested properly at the Retreat.

'Yeah, they were great. I'm going back there straight after this to rest, and overnight tonight. But I want to be on my own again. I can't concentrate on preparation like I can in the caravan.' Poison's voice was low and he spoke simply to Tom. That first incident had made them friends.

'Look, if you want you could stay with me.'

'No. Thanks and all that. I *like* being on my own, particularly when there's this part to prepare for. It's like no other part on earth.'

'Will you pose with John the Baptist, Poison?' called a photographer.

Poison gave Tom an expressive look. Then he turned and in a split second had assumed the role of Christ. His movement, his whole person seemed to change, and he went towards John the Baptist as if this was a living performance.

Soon after, Exelby stopped the star's interviews and poses and sent Poison back to the Retreat in a taxi. The rest of the cast and his understudy carried on for another hour before they were allowed to go. Everyone felt exhausted. It was worse than acting.

'I'd rather be on traffic duty,' was the opinion of Sergeant Diamond.

During the afternoon one of Bob Southwell's detective inspectors was interviewing the younger members of the cast, as they were available, depending on the exigencies of the photocall. Some members of the Crowd were first. They all seemed to have stuck with their groups fairly well throughout their time on the set the previous evening. They were all at school or in work and he took notes of where they had been during the morning and afternoon for later verification.

Next the party who had been responsible for cutting the willow branches was called in. One of them admitted that on the previous day he had brought along the straight branch which had later been used to imitate an iron bolt. It had been lying on the ground among other branches torn off by a storm and he had thought it might come in useful. He had trimmed off the side branches and it had made a rather handsome stave. Claiming to have left it leaning against the back of the props tent, he was very distressed at the idea that he was implicated in the near accident.

The only other youngsters in the cast were Eve, the Virgin Mary, the Angels and the Devils. Mentally dismissing Eve and the Virgin Mary as unlikely to have had anything to do with it, Bob Southwell suggested the Angels, who were all from Queen Elizabeth's, be interviewed next, with the Devils, who were members of the Fourth Forms of the local public school, St Giles, and as full of pranks and tricks as a wagonload of monkeys.

As both Angels and Devils were under the age of seventeen, their mothers had to be present too, and this took some time and trouble to arrange.

'No, of course we aren't accusing them of anything.' Bob Southwell had to soothe a number of parents. 'Only a routine enquiry. There has been a certain amount of – horseplay, perhaps we could say . . .'

Velvet Smith asked to see the detective in charge of the questioning.

'It may not be relevant at all,' she said hesitantly.

'We're always pleased to hear . . .'

'Only that the youngsters were so long reaching the wardrobe to take off their costumes, you know, the night before this dreadful thing happened with the cross, that is, after Mr Peters had that awful accident with the electricity, that I went out to look for them, and saw one of the boys playing about with a bit of iron. It didn't look very thick, but it was metal, I'm sure, by the sound it made.'

'Thank you very much for that information.'

'It was only when I heard the pivot had been taken that I thought it might be relevant.'

'Did you see which of the boys it was?'

'A dark one; he had his headdress off. I said, "What are you playing about at now? Come on, all of you." So they did. I don't know what happened to the rod, or whatever it was.'

It did not take long to break down the resistance of the youngsters. Yes . . . they had been playing about a bit, once the performances were over . . . Yes, the devils had made noises to frighten the girls . . .

The story of the night before the accident with the cross came out.

'I hear one of the boys was trying to open one of the table tombs, and that it was your idea, is that correct?'

'Oh, how mean of him,' said the blonde Angel with brimming eyes. 'It was all his fault. I told him not to do it, I never thought he would, honestly.'

'Really, Inspector, Sergeant,' said the blonde Angel's large and formidable Mum, 'I really can't see the point of all this, my daughter would never be involved in anything . . .'

'It's all right. The attempt to open the tomb did not succeed, I understand. There are some scratches on the stonework, but that is not actually the matter we are investigating, and we do not hold your daughter in any way responsible.'

'I should hope not . . .'

'I'm only trying to get a general picture of this juvenile behaviour . . .'

Sure enough, one of the boys broke down under the penetrating eye of the detective inspector.

He had wanted to open the table tomb to frighten the girls . . . he had tried with the stick he found near the props tent but it wasn't strong enough, he wanted something which made the right kind of noise, too, he wanted to get a creaking . . . he had noticed the pivot bolt through the cross sticking out . . . Nicholas had dared him to take it . . . it seemed quite loose in its hole, and he decided to borrow it, just for a little while. He'd put the stick in its place so that his borrowing it wouldn't be noticed . . . he'd been going to put it back next day, really he had . . .

'Why didn't you?' asked the detective inspector, as mildly as he could make himself.

'Well,' said the Devil, with a glance at his mother, who was speechless, 'I tried to open the tomb but I couldn't. So I rattled the bolt along the railings – that was good – while we were howling . . .'

'And then?'

'And then I rattled it on one of those drains in the road, that was good –'

The DI was able to remember the infinite possibilities drains seemed to offer at one stage in his own life. He nodded, and waited.

'Then it sort of slipped out of my fingers and down the drain . . .'

'It would, wouldn't it?' said the DI.

'And I had to go to take my costume off, and then I went

home. Next day I looked in our garage, and I couldn't find one like it, and I didn't dare tell anybody, and I thought the branch might be strong enough after all, and that in that case it wouldn't matter . . .'

Bob Southwell said nothing for a minute when told this by his DI.

Then, putting aside all the remarks about modern youth and what did parents teach their children these days which whirled through his head, he went in to speak to the boy.

The Devil – who was the largest though not the oldest of the boys – was sent home in disgrace and the school was contacted. Another member of the production was never to be allowed on the set again; they would manage with only six Devils. The headmaster agreed to have a stern word with the villain himself at once if not sooner, dwelling on such things as the honour of the school.

The police sighed breaths of relief that the act, though criminally stupid – and there was debate among the higher echelons as to whether or not the boy should be prosecuted – was at least not a deliberate attempt to injure the pop star; and for that they gave thanks.

Thomas had been told by Poison Peters that policemen were to take part in the performances; and he noticed with some amusement that although in other respects the members of Task Force looked like part of a medieval crowd, instead of sandals or bare feet they were wearing trainers, casuals, and in a few cases highly polished substantial black boots, which showed under their sweeping cloaks or tunics.

At last the final dress rehearsal had arrived. A small audience gathered in the front seats. Wives, husbands and/or parents of the performers, of the electricians, of the stage hands, of the set designer, of the ASM, and of all and sundry connected with the production, had come along.

The photocall and the police between them had thrown the whole cast into a state of the jitters. They had been told not to mention the questioning, or the two incidents which had thrown a shadow over the production.

It was a situation none of them had been in before, and combined with the awe-inspiring plays themselves and the normal tensions of a last dress rehearsal it was almost overwhelming. Most of the cast were busily doing whatever they considered calmed their nerves. Some were watching the unperturbed bowls match which was taking place on the adjoining green; some reclining on the grass of the graveyard with their backs against the stones, smoking cigarettes as if cancer had never been heard of; Humphrey Hale had made inroads already on the contents of his hip flask; Judas Iscariot was desperately peering at his copy of his lines, which had gone out of his head as completely as if an early schoolboy had taken a damp sponge and wiped clean a chalky slate.

Thomas Churchyard, the large and imperturbable, was fidgeting and wandering to and fro. He visited the dark area under the upper stage and inspected the new strong iron bolt for himself. He went up to the box from where the lights were controlled and spoke to the young man – formerly only the assistant – who had taken over the whole job. There was no longer amplification equipment on the set. He went to Poison Peters's caravan and lifted his hand to knock on the door, then changed his mind and went back via the props tent, which he looked over carefully as if it was going to sprout weapons more lethal than the hardboard spears.

At last, with the arrival of the powerful presence of Bruce Exelby from his flat in St Mary's Lodge, everything pulled together. Cigarettes were stubbed out. The hip flask disappeared into an angelic pocket. The Virgin Mary disposed of the mug of coffee she had been nervously drinking. She was standing next to the Youngest Shepherd and before he left her the young man put his arm round her and gave her a hug. God stood behind a bulwark of stone next to his window arch, ready to appear for the opening words. Below him the cast moved into their various opening positions.

Some groups who had an hour to wait before they were needed went into the Tempest Anderson Hall where they could talk and play cards to while away the time, but most of the cast were too keyed up to leave the scene of the action. What untoward thing was going to happen next? What fresh danger threatened Poison Peters? As time went on and they had grown used to him, the cast had stopped thinking of him as a pop star and begun to think of him in his new persona; he was central to their play. He was like the boss of stamens in a rose; they the petals surrounding him, he the embodiment of Christ.

And it went beautifully.

Poison Peters performed as if lifted out of himself – as if this was not Poison Peters the revolting pop star but Christ as he might have been, combining intense humility with dignity and power. The watchers forgot everything else but the mystery plays. The members of the Task Force found themselves caught up in acting out the most vital of all the experiences of mankind. They lived through the story as if it was new to them, as if it was happening at that very moment in time. Against the sky God looked down and was moved by the plight of His people and His Son beneath him.

When the crucifixion approached Thomas Churchyard exercised his prerogative of leaving his throne, which he had been using for some scenes. It was a strain to sit up there, and not necessary again until the Taylors' Play, but he thought he would go up for the start of the Saddlers' Play, the Harrowing of Hell.

He didn't think he could sit above while Poison went through the mental agony of being lifted by the pivoting cross in the Pinners' and Painters' Play, remembering with him the scene of the previous day. Neither did he want to sit up there during the long minutes of Poison's physical and mental anguish during the Butchers' Play. For, with everything that could be done to alleviate it, anguish if not in truth agony it was and must be, to be endured nightly, solitary yet in front of all.

Once Poison was lifted down, then Thomas felt he himself would be able to relax and take part in things again. So while the agony was going on Thomas sat on the wooden walkway along the scaffolding and listened, out of sight behind the abbey masonry.

It was over, and Christ had been taken down from the cross and placed in the tomb. Whatever Poison had thought and felt, Thomas could tell from what he had heard and from the general atmosphere, that Poison had acted supremely well. Thomas himself was shaking. In relief, he thought. The worst was over now.

And sure enough, a minute later Poison came climbing up the ladder to the walkway, freshly dressed in a white robe, and sat down near him out of sight of the stage.

'All right?' asked Tom. Poison nodded. Then he huddled himself within the robe and bent his head, with a gesture of one hand which said plainer than words, 'I'm all right but I want to be left alone.' There would be ten minutes or so rest for him before he had to make his blinding appearance in the archway next to them and confound Lucifer and all his works.

Straightening up, Thomas decided to climb the ladder to his platform and throne. Before doing so he took a leisurely survey of the scene below him. Evening was deepening into night. The lights on the set seemed to make the sky black by contrast. In the distance the bowls players had packed up and gone home, and their green looked grey in the deep shadows. Nearer at hand he had the peaceful scene of the graveyard of St Olave's, and the lovely ancient church of St Olaf himself, both lit by stray beams of light, to look at. It always amused him to see the cast waiting among the gravestones. Now they were silent, listening intently to the play so that they could move into position in good time for their next entrance. They might indeed have been ghosts, medieval ghosts in the graveyard.

Here and there he recognized friends. There was Judas Iscariot, talking to the other Apostles. Then Peter, Thomas, John and James went off, presumably to be ready for the Scriveners' Play, though it was not for a while yet. Judas was left alone and wandered over to talk to a group of the Crowd. The woman who carried a spindle was actually spinning from it, even in the gathering dark, and winding the wool on, in between creating the thread. For centuries women must have used every spare second like that. Glancing down at his feet Thomas saw the shadowy form of one of the Devils running, hips swivelling, towards the east end of the Abbey where the others must be waiting for the cue for their entrance in the Harrowing of Hell.

Everyone was going to be needed at the end for the great crowd scene in the Mercers' Play, the Day of Judgement. Then the Good Souls would mount the steps to the window openings, and line up behind them on the wooden walk along the scaffolding, looking down from their blessed state on to the scene of the Bad Souls being thrown down the long slope to the flames of Hell's Mouth, with Lucifer and the Devils standing by to harry them on their way.

Thomas turned reluctantly and climbed his ladder. He stepped slowly – the drop on to the stage looked like an abyss – in front of the throne, and lowered himself on to it. Once here he had to be careful. He was in view, and must behave like God and not like Thomas Churchyard, telecommunications engineer. All the same, he could move his eyes, and thought it was permissible to incline his head gently as if looking down with interest and compassion on his creatures.

The scene below him was Hell. It was the Saddlers' Play, the Harrowing of Hell. Adam and Eve were sitting in the centre of the lower stage, and Adam was speaking. Isaiah walked across and stood near to them, ready to chime in with his speech. Presently John the Baptist and then Moyses would make their appearance, before the Devils joined the scene.

The set was complex, with two main levels, but with wide staircases joining them and slopes up and down, and it was working very well. It looked so like the ancient stone which backed it that many people were deceived into thinking that ruins and set were all one, all weather-worn limestone, and did not realize that so much of what they saw was wood covered by painted expanded polystyrene.

Directly below Thomas was the cross, now empty, the upper stage on which it was fixed almost level with the bottom of the window archways. In front of it a flight of stairs led down to the flat lower stage where Adam and Eve were sitting and where Isaiah stood. On the left was the long slope downward with its flanking low wall, behind which and out of sight of the audience a narrow ladder led down to the under-stage area. On the right was the flight of steps up to another window, where later the saved souls would climb to Heaven. Further still to the right was the broad stairway leading down under the stage.

Thomas could see the three wide stairways which led down to ground level, but he could not see the lower exits and entrances because of the jut of the wide stage. It was all very familiar to him by now; 'like the back of my hand,' he thought and smiled. Did one really know the back of one's hand? Seeing it among a thousand others would one pick it out through its distinctive bumps and hollows? Then he remembered that God, watching his creatures in Hell, would not smile, and he smoothed out his features. Yet he could not resist taking a look down sideways at the back of his left hand, as it lay calmly on the arm of the throne. His glance passed on below.

A figure was climbing slowly up the narrow ladder behind the long slope. It was the flicker of movement in an unexpected place that caught Thomas's attention. He inclined his head a little more, slowly and graciously. A black curly head was rising into the broad light of the set. Bruce Exelby. Now what was the matter? Trust him to go interrupting the scene just when it was going so well.

Exelby's hand clutched the wide wall between the ladder and the slope and he came gradually into full view. He heaved himself up on to the stage, walked forward, and stood there swaying slightly. Adam had faltered in his speech and fallen silent, looking apprehensive.

Above, it was so quiet that Thomas could hear Exelby's heavy breathing, and the thought flashed through his head that the director must be very out of condition to be winded by the short climb up the ladder. But the loud breathing died away, seemed to become quicker and quieter as the director stumbled forward. He reeled almost into Isaiah, then wavered a couple of steps farther, before collapsing altogether and lying face down.

Red-stained bubbles foamed from his mouth and tinted the dusty dun of the boards of the stage a gentle pink. One of his hands reached forward in front of his head towards the drop on to ground level, touching and almost caressing the edge of the wood.

Sergeant Diamond, dressed in plain clothes, had been sitting with the other people in the audience. He jumped to his feet and ran forward up the flight of steps nearest to him on to the stage level where the action had been taking place, before Thomas had had time to do more than take in that something was very wrong.

Bending over the director, the sergeant took hold of his wrist and felt for his pulse. Straightening, he yelled at Isaiah, 'See if there's a doctor here!' and turning round in a circle, shouted to all and sundry, 'The performance is suspended. Mr Exelby is ill. Clear the stage please. Tell my men to come here.'

Adam and Eve, John the Baptist, Moyses, the little Devils, Belzebub, and Satan, who had all been either on stage or waiting in the wings, obeyed him and made a group on the grass at the front of the seats. Isaiah had gone rushing to find a telephone.

One of Task Force came running from the graveyard and up on to the stage.

Sergeant Diamond was holding Exelby's wrist in one hand and the radio in the other, speaking rapidly to the station. 'Emergency at the mystery plays site, Museum Gardens,' he said. 'Director taken ill. Get an ambulance here. Pulse rapid and weak. Unconscious.' He looked up at his man. 'Get that lot out of here,' with a glance at the spectators.

The man from Task Force gathered up his skirts and left the stage. First he spoke to the audience. 'Would you all go home, please? There will be nothing else to watch tonight.' Then to the group of actors, 'The rehearsal won't go on. Would you change out of costume, please. You schoolboys can go home.'

'Can we all go home?' asked Eve.

'You can, miss.'

'I want to know how he is and what's happening,' said Adam.

'Then perhaps you'd wait after changing.'

The actors went off silently, glancing backward. Even the little Devils seemed subdued as they scampered into the darkness. More Task Force men had arrived and the first one had put them rapidly in the picture. They went back to the rest of the cast to tell them to get out of costume, the play was over. Thomas had come down from his pinnacle and with everyone else trooped off to change. In passing he had spoken briefly to Poison.

'What now?' the singer had asked, lifting his head.

'Exelby is ill. Some sort of collapse.'

Poison had sighed. 'That puts the tin lid on it. There's a jinx on this thing.'

'Come on. Go to the caravan and have a cup of tea.'

Poison had unfolded himself and followed Tom down the scaffolding, drooping wearily and shivering.

'There blows a cold wind today, today,/The wind blows cold today . . .' he murmured as if saying goodbye to Tom. As Tom watched him walk off into the night he thought what a difference adrenalin makes. If he had been going on stage now the man would have been radiant with energy. And in his mind he completed the quotation: 'Christ suffered His passion for mannes salvation. To keep the cold wind away.' The cold wind was blowing with a vengeance.

Getting down from the scaffolding had delayed Thomas and Poison. The others were already walking either towards the Tempest Anderson Hall or through the St Olave's Gate. Poison had vanished in the direction of the caravan as Tom rounded the edge of the masonry, supposedly on his way to the Tempest Anderson Hall, and came briefly in sight of the front of the stage. He knew gawpers were the last thing needed but he could not resist a quick look at the stage where Exelby lay still and Sergeant Diamond knelt beside him. Then the sergeant lifted his head and stood up. In the distance the scream of an approaching ambulance could be heard. The sergeant spoke to one of Task Force.

'I think he's dead.'

By Sergeant Diamond's watch he had been kneeling by Bruce Exelby for exactly two minutes.

6

> Make ready, and ding you him down,
> And deafen us no more with his deeds.
> *The Bowyers' and Fletchers' Play*

DCI Southwell got the message at home. He had been thinking about Task Force and wondering whether to go down to the Museum Gardens to see how they were getting on, but he was not prepared for Sergeant Diamond's urgent voice.

'We've had a death, sir. The DI is on his way but asked me to speak directly to you.'

'Poison Peters?' asked Bob.

'No, sir. The director, Mr Exelby.'

'What the heck . . . How? Where?'

'How – we don't know the cause yet. Could be natural, I suppose, but I don't think so, sir. He had bloody foam coming from his mouth and there's quite a lot of blood now. We're just waiting for a doctor to confirm death but I've no doubt of it. Where – he died at my feet, sir. On the stage.'

'Witnesses?'

'Too many if anything.'

'Hold everyone. Don't let them go home. The best place for them would be the Tempest Anderson Hall, I think. I'm on my way.'

The sergeant coughed. 'Some of them have already gone, sir.'

Bob Southwell swore picturesquely and slammed down the handset.

Detective Inspector Smart had already arrived on the scene

when Bob Southwell got there. He had coincided with the ambulance and the doctor. The doctor had knelt beside Exelby, taking Sergeant Diamond's place, and examined the body. The sergeant explained things rapidly to his superior.

The doctor was about to flip Bruce Exelby onto his back. He had reached forward to take a grip of the shoulder. He lifted him slightly. Then he paused, looked up at DI Smart, and by a glance indicated a small area of blood, hardly more than a spot, dark crimson, on the left side of Exelby's shirt towards the front.

Letting go, the doctor allowed the body to slump forward once more.

'It's pretty obvious he's dead,' he remarked. 'And that looks like a wound to me. I don't think I ought to disturb him further. You are going to want to investigate.'

'You can certify he's dead?'

'Yes.'

'We'll have to treat this as a suspicious death then. Possible murder.'

'You'll only know exactly with a postmortem.'

The blood had been flowing freely from Exelby's mouth and nose. The pool on the boards was no longer that delicate pink of the first touch.

'Diamond, please ask for the scene-of-crime officers to be sent down here. Get someone appointed as coroner's officer and see they send a message to the coroner. There are still a lot of people about. Perhaps you'd better ask for screens and get them put round the body. Tape a path to the body for everyone to use, we don't want any more disturbance of the forensic evidence than we've had already.'

Bob Southwell drove in through the gates of the Museum Gardens. The man on duty at the gates was one of the constables from Task Force. Bob's headlights lit up the curving gravel footpath before him, cutting a swathe of light through black trees and bushes. He drove unceremoniously. The dark back of the grandstand was pierced by cracks of light, the grass and gravel cut up by the wheels of police car and ambulance. Above, the stage lighting irradiated the sky; the arches were glowing white gold; the more distant sky a black backdrop behind them.

As Bob arrived the van from the station came up behind him, and as he reached the stage and stood beside the body of Bruce Exelby, the two constables with the screens were already lifting them from the van and carrying them through the gateway and up the flight of stairs.

It had only been that morning that Exelby had been making a nuisance of himself in the police station, demanding action. Bob could not help thinking that it looked as though his demands had been justified. The big body still looked strong and fit in death. The hair curled as crisply. What could be seen of the face held no look of pain. It had been smoothed out, emptied.

'Is that the way he was?' Bob asked the doctor.

'Yes. I haven't moved him. Well, perhaps a fraction as I was examining him, but it was obvious at first that he must be dead, so I didn't turn him over. I lifted him slightly and then let him drop back again.'

'That's all right, then. We want to know because of the photographs.'

'I don't think we need detain you and the ambulance any further,' the DI said to the doctor. 'We'll almost certainly be calling the Home Office pathologist and a team from the forensic science lab to take tests. Perhaps we can call on you later to give a statement when you are off duty.'

Sergeant Diamond had been busy again with his radio.

The photogaphers arrived and began to use up several rolls of film.

The pathologist and the forensic scientist arrived, and so did an undertaker. As he was a local man, he looked around for someone to talk to, and could only find the members of Task Force. A few at a time they had gone to change out of their costumes, and one of them, now dressed in jeans and anorak, told him a little of what had been happening. The undertaker's habitual look of discretion hid fervent curiosity. There was no way he was going to betray his interest, but this was the vindication of all that the people of the city had thought. The director, responsible for the pollution of the mystery plays by

Poison Peters, had been punished. To the undertaker it seemed as if heaven itself had had a hand in the matter.

The pathologist and the forensic scientist seemed to spend a long time standing at a distance with their hands in their pockets, just looking at Exelby, at the place he was lying, and taking in the surroundings.

Then they moved in on the body. They had worked together before and for anyone who knew what they were watching it was a beautiful bit of teamwork, like a *pas de deux* in a ballet. They exchanged a few words in undertones. Their movements were small-scale but neat and swift. After a few minutes they lifted the shirt and confirmed the thought of the doctor – there was a wound in the left chest, a hardly visible puncture, which had only oozed a little blood. They slid plastic bags over Exelby's head, hands and feet. The crisp curls were crushed down by the translucent film, the hands which had made so many arrogant gestures looked strangely blundering. The two men wrapped Exelby's whole body in a corpse-sheet of plastic. At this point the undertaker went back to his van, and with his assistant, who had been waiting in the passenger seat and listening to his walkman, brought the undertaker's shell, and soon was lifting the director into it and carrying him off the stage which had been his kingdom.

The forensic scientist, whose name was Brian and who had had to leave a wife, kids, and a perfectly good television programme to come down here, took a quick look around.

'He came up those steps at the back,' said Sergeant Diamond, showing him. They went down together. The steps were hardly more than a ladder and narrow for Diamond. Under the stage it was completely dark, but Brian had a powerful torch, and by its light looked intently at every step, then swung the beam on to the grass. Sergeant Diamond knew what was being looked for: blood, drops, splashes, signs of struggle. He felt like saying that there wouldn't be any drops or splashes – that he himself had seen the first blood rise to Exelby's lips, in that dreadful pink foam, as he stumbled across the stage – but he said nothing. In this area the grass had been constantly trampled over the last days as the actors made their way from one part of the set to another, out of sight of the stands.

They went to the entrance through the ancient walls into the graveyard of St Olave's, without seeing anything which seemed significant.

'Have to look with floodlighting,' said Brian as they prepared to go back up the ladder. 'Hopeless now. See if you can get some rigged up before I get back from the mortuary. No trampling about though. You'll be seeing no one comes in here until I've done a proper examination.'

'Yes, sir.'

'Better go to the mortuary, I suppose.'

The pathologist was waiting for him. Bob Southwell was walking back from the Tempest Anderson Hall, and decided to go with them. They set off together, following the undertaker's van.

Earlier, once the pathologist and forensic scientist had arrived, Bob had left the set and gone to the Tempest Anderson Hall, where the actors, subdued, had been waiting for him. Some of course had gone home in the first few minutes after the announcement that Exelby was ill. The others had changed out of their costumes, and were waiting uneasily, not knowing what was happening and what to expect.

Time had dragged; many of them had wondered whether to go home or not. Thomas, from overhearing Sergeant Diamond, knew that the director was dead, but he told no one. Afterwards he wondered why he had said nothing, and decided that it was because he could hardly believe it himself. He could not take in that such a thing could happen so quickly and so mysteriously.

There was talk, of course; general gossip about how things were going, worries about the city's reaction to Poison Peters – most of the cast had stopped resenting him and were now only anxious for the success of the plays; worries about what was wrong with Bruce Exelby; speculation about whether he had recovered consciousness yet, and about the cause of his sudden collapse.

There was a stir among them as though a giant spoon had agitated the air in the hall when Bob Southwell walked through the door, between the two Task Force men. He walked in with that air of authority which is unmistakeable.

Bob had moved on to the platform; whether it was his presence, or the news he had to tell, Thomas could not decide, but they were all in the hollow of the hand of this tall slim man with the large glasses.

He spoke without beating about the bush, without any preliminaries.

'I am very sorry to have to tell you that your director, Mr Bruce Exelby, has died.' There was a stunned murmur during Bob's pause. 'We are unfortunately having to treat the death as suspicious, and we would like to talk to each of you and try to piece together the events of the evening.'

He paused again; this time a profound silence filled the gap.

'We will be setting up an incident room and would like to see you all there individually tomorrow; it will probably be here in the Museum Gardens. Now, we would like all your names and addresses, if you will give them as you go out.'

Everyone seemed to draw breath into their lungs at once. Bob had spoken very slowly, so that every word had time to sink in. Humphrey Hale was the first to gather his wits.

'You tell us he has died,' he said. 'Can you tell us how this has come about?'

Bob answered carefully. 'You are all aware that Mr Exelby collapsed on stage. At that point you were asked to leave the area while efforts were being made to help him. In fact he died. There are indications that there is something suspicious about this unexpected death. We will be making routine inquiries. At the moment we cannot tell you what caused the death, but you will be kept informed. The questions will be normal police procedure in a case like this.'

It appeared as though Bob might have nothing else to say, so Thomas Churchyard got up hastily, with a half-smile and gesture to him, and turned to the cast.

'I'm sure you agree with me, ladies and gentlemen, that we must not let this affect the mystery plays. That is the last thing Bruce Exelby would have wanted. This production is his creation and we owe it to him to give it all we've got and make it the best performance ever, even if he isn't here to get on to our bones and make us do well.'

'The play must go on,' said Lucifer.

'That's right. So are we agreed on that?'

There was a gentle sound of assent.

'Sue,' said Tom, turning to Sue Brown the assistant director, who was sitting among the actors. 'You'll have to take charge.'

She stood up, white-faced. 'Yes, you're right of course, Tom. Everyone – business as usual. The first performance is always the most trying and goodness knows how we're going to get through, but for everybody's sake, including all the people who'll be coming to see us, we've got to. Try to rest well tonight even if you can't sleep. The arrangements already made for tomorrow stand. Now perhaps, since the police say we can go, we should all get home.'

Bob nodded assent. The two detectives were at each side of the door with notebooks. Everyone got up and began crowding towards them, talking furiously. Over the heads of the others Tom's eyes met Bob's and he was given a friendly wave. 'See you later,' said Bob's lips soundlessly. Tom felt himself relax. It looked as though he himself was not regarded with suspicion, which was a relief. It would have been very uncomfortable living next to Bob and Linda if he was regarded as a potential . . . murderer?

For a moment Thomas's mind went blank. Suspicious death, they had said. No word of murder. But he knew instinctively that that was what it must be. It could hardly be a heart attack, with that bloody foam issuing from nose and mouth – he had been near enough to see it, on his walk to the Tempest Anderson Hall. Exelby had always seemed very fit. He couldn't have had an accident, surely? How? Under the stage? No, it must be – if 'suspicious' – it must be murder.

And if Bob had signalled to him, 'See you later,' and Tom had not misread his lips, then he himself was not under suspicion. Though surely everyone must be equally suspect? Then he realized anew what he had been thinking. Murder, the killing of one human being by another . . . someone on the set tonight must have done it. He shivered.

It was then that he realized Poison was not with them in the Hall. He went over to Bob Southwell and said: 'Poison Peters isn't here, he won't know. Is it all right if I go to his caravan and tell him?'

'I'll come with you.'

Once the press of actors at the door had lessened, Bob and Tom went together the few yards to the silver-grey caravan its wide streak of shining silver catching the reflected gleams from the stage lighting. Poison opened the door to them reluctantly. 'Oh, it's you,' he said to Tom.

'Detective Chief Inspector Southwell,' Tom introduced Bob. 'Can we come in?'

'I don't like the look of your arriving here in tandem like this,' said Poison. 'What's been happening? Whenever I get the police to see me they're hunting for drugs, yeah?'

'Not to worry, Mr Peters,' said Bob. 'May we come in?'

Poison let them in, but only just, Tom felt. 'Any tea going?' he asked to break the atmosphere. 'We could use a cup.'

Poison was still quiet and suspicious, but he filled the kettle without comment, gestured them to a seat, and set out fluted cups and saucers on the flap table. Tom felt that Bob must be taking everything in, but the policeman's manner was calm and easy and and betrayed no surprise when he was handed a cup of clear weak Earl Grey tea in delicate china.

'I'm ready for this,' he remarked.

Poison made no move to take his own, but sat facing them and waiting to hear what they had to say. When the words came – however gently put – it could be seen that they were a shock to him, although he barely moved a muscle. At last he said in a forced tone to Tom, 'Told you there was a jinx on this thing, yeah?'

'Performance goes on as usual tomorrow.' Tom's deep voice came comfortingly, reassuringly normal. 'Sue Brown will be in charge.'

'Good girl,' said Poison. At last he picked up his cup. As if to reinforce to Bob an impression of loutishness, to counteract the tea and the almost dainty general aspect of the caravan, he slurped at it loudly. As soon as they had all finished their cupfuls, he rose and said, 'Well, be seeing ya, yeah?' and Bob and Tom gracefully went.

'I'll go home if that's all right,' said Tom when they were

outside the caravan. 'See you when you interview me tomorrow.'

'Don't worry too much,' said Bob.

'You mean I'm not under suspicion?'

'It looks as if you were sitting enthroned in the sky when the deed must have been done.'

'But you don't know.'

'No. And for heaven's sake don't quote me in case you have done it after all,' said Bob in a light manner.

'My God . . . you really think it's murder . . .'

There was a silence for a few seconds. The two men looked at one another in the odd mixture of light and darkness. The electrician up in the lighting box at the top of the stand of seats had been relieved long ago by a detective who knew enough about lighting to be responsible for running it for as long as it was needed. Apart from this the night had deepened. The golden halo of threads of light over the city could be seen faintly, high over their heads.

Then Bob went to join the pathologist and the forensic scientist and Tom went in search of his bicycle.

'I think we're due for a beer,' said the pathologist, straightening his back.

Forensics looked at his watch. 'Just time before they shut,' he remarked.

'I can do with one,' added Bob Southwell.

He hadn't enjoyed the past half-hour or so in the mortuary. These chaps obviously did enjoy the grisly job in a kind of way; dead bodies they were used to; it was the excitement of discovery, detection, which fascinated them. Clothing bagged individually. More photographs. Wound traced to make a 'guesstimate' of size, depth, and direction of weapon. Collect blood, urine, etc. Carry out rest of PM to exclude natural causes. He had hated being there while they did it.

Seeming to divine his thoughts the pathologist said, 'This was a nice one, you know, compared to most. If they've been dead a long time even we find it pretty stomach-turning.'

'Let's have that beer,' replied Bob, and it wasn't until they were in the Angler's Arms, with its curious internal courtyard overlooked on all sides by upper-floor windows, that they went back to the subject. The pub was quiet that night apart from a group of Dutch teenage tourists filling the small bar area. The three men got a corner by the fireplace in one of the small rooms, and although it was too warm for the delights of glowing coals, the shaded lights rid them of the harsh glare of the mortuary and the beer took some of the taste of death out of their mouths.

'Bring us good ale, and bring us good ale / For our Blessed Lady's sake, bring us good ale,' said Brian.

'You've been watching too many mystery plays,' said Bob; then, 'Well?' to the pathologist. There was no one likely to overhear.

'I'll go straight home and type out my report for the coroner.'

'Have a heart! I need to know something now.'

'Right. Just for you.' The pathologist found a notepad in his pocket and began to cover it with his near-indecipherable writing, talking as he did so. 'One blow. A knife of the stiletto type, narrow-bladed. He was stabbed on the level of the nipple on his left side, slightly to the rear. This punctured the aorta and pulmonary artery, small punctures.'

'How long before he died do you think he was knifed?'

'I would guess he would lose consciousness in about forty seconds after the blow, and die in two or not more than three minutes. I *would* have said two, but you told me, Bob, that Sergeant Diamond was standing by him for two minutes, and before that Exelby'd climbed that narrow stair on to the stage. I would guess that he'd been attacked only seconds before that.'

'So it had to be someone in the cast. I think we can exempt Task Force. The audience couldn't have done it either.'

'Surely anyone could have wandered on to the set? Incidentally, there's going to be no help from forensics.'

'Why not?'

Brian was lugubrious. 'He didn't bleed immediately. Therefore, no blood on the culprit. Well – let's qualify that. There might have been the slightest trace on the hand of the assassin, from withdrawing the knife, but it would be very slight indeed; the blood from the wound was very little altogether – the stain on the shirt only an inch across, even after death. The victim seems to have been taken by surprise – there's nothing under his fingernails, for instance; he doesn't seem to have gone for his attacker. I wouldn't mind betting in fact that he never knew what happened.'

'How can you be murdered and not know what's happened?'

'Easily. Someone's coming past – stops to speak to you – makes a lunge at you with a thin knife – you might think at first they're just given you a friendly poke in the ribs, a bit overdone it, perhaps.'

'Oh, come on, Brian,' said the pathologist. 'There'd be a searing pain, surely.'

'There aren't many nerve endings once you've got in through the skin.'

'True. I still think it would feel like a kick in the ribs from a wild horse.'

'You wouldn't necessarily realize you'd been knifed.'

'No, you might not.'

'Then his breathing starts getting difficult; he realizes something is wrong. Wanting to get help he climbs the ladder on to the stage. By now the internal bleeding is really getting under way. He feels dizzy, tries to speak, can't do that. Feels faint. Loses consciousness. Blood coming up in throat. End of stout party.'

Bob drank the last of his beer and tried to erase the picture from his mind. Taking the scribbled notes from the pathologist, he said something about going and got to his feet. 'Give you a lift?' he asked Forensics.

'I think I'd like to walk back. By the time we reach your car and drive there I could have been working ten minutes.'

'Goodnight, then.'

'Are you ringing the detective chief superintendent?' asked Brian.

'Wait till this gets in the papers,' said the pathologist.

Bob Southwell rang Detective Chief Superintendent Duncan from Ouse Avenue. Linda had called downstairs sleepily when he came in. There was no sound from the children. He thought of Thomas Churchyard next door, no doubt also asleep by now. Sitting down in a chair for a moment, Bob almost dropped off himself. To bring his alertness back he went and made himself a powdered coffee and hoped it wouldn't keep him awake all night. Then at last, with a nervous look at the clock, he walked over to the telephone.

'Sorry to disturb you, sir. I hope you weren't asleep.'

'It's quite all right, Southwell,' but the words came over the line one at a time, like small but weighty blocks of ice.

Bob explained briefly.

'My God, the papers will get hold of this.'

'I'm afraid they will.'

'And the radio. And the television. We'll have the whole of the blasted media down on us, Bob.'

'I'll have to tell the assistant chief constable, better ring him now. He won't be very pleased at being disturbed.'

'No, sir.'

'I'd better come down myself tomorrow – organize a press conference, that kind of thing. Perhaps the assistant chief would speak to the press. He's bound to be very concerned. I'll see what he thinks. Leave that to me, Southwell.'

'I wish we could keep it under wraps for a bit. Give us more chance of finding the bastard who's done it.'

'Don't we all! How much easier it would be without blasted reporters! But that's life, Southwell. Ten to one there's been a leak already. In a place like York, and a lot of people involved – how many in the cast alone?' But he did not wait for an answer. 'It'll get out – bound to. You might not have long. Hours, perhaps, before the whole lot are round your neck.'

'We'd better announce it straight away.'

'The morning will be soon enough. Say ten o'clock for the press conference and official announcement. I'll come to see you first thing. Got everything under control?'

'Yes, sir.'

Bob set his alarm for half past five.

Brian, the forensic scientist, had found nothing, although he had been searching carefully with another of his team for half an hour. The area under the stage was not unpleasant in the still watches of the night.

At last, a portable floodlight in his hand, crawling across the crushed grass on all fours with his nose an inch from the ground,

Brian happened to glance sideways; a glint of something under one of the supports caught his eye. He went over at once, and got down again to peer under the horizontal beam of wood. The knife did not look as though it had been deliberately pushed underneath; it looked as though, casually hurled away, it had fallen flat and bounced sideways, as Brian had noticed knives sometimes did when dropped on the kitchen floor, and so hidden itself under the wooden framework. He found a penknife in his pocket and poked delicately, moving one end of the knife out from its hiding place until at last he was able to pick it up with wrapped fingers and drop it into a plastic bag.

His team-mate let out a long gasp of breath.

'I think we'll go home now.' There was undeniable pride in Brian's voice.

'That really looks like a murder weapon,' whispered the other.

'Meant for him, must have been. Even got his initials on it,' said Brian, showing the handle, with two letters inlaid in silver dots: B.E.

7

Haha! This was a merry note,
By the death that I shall die,
I have so croaked in my throat
That my lips are near dry.
The Chaundlers' Play

The dawn of the first day of the festival spread over the city. It was going to be fine and warm – festival weather. The visitors from all over the world were not yet stirring in their beds, the buskers had not yet even thought about taking their varied instruments out into the streets and beginning to spread their web of sound. The sunbeams licked awake the sparkles of gilt embellishing black wrought iron and carven heraldry; the spires and towers of the ancient churches shone cream and rose in the first light. The spire of All Saints North Street in particular was in such a rose glow that the stone seemed incandescent pink. The east end of the Minster glittered dazzling gold, its vast tennis court of a window reflecting ten thousand facets of sunlight.

The incident post had already been set up in the form of a second caravan in the Museum Gardens, for the police force rests not neither does it sleep. The murder room was in the police station itself. Teams of men were being drafted in from North Yorkshire, and eventually gathered fifty strong to set up the murder system, to find and sift information. A computer, its blank, powerful memory ready to be imprinted, was waiting.

At half past seven, when Thomas Churchyard arrived at his office to collect some papers, Bob Southwell had already been in the incident post for over an hour.

'We don't want to disturb the performance at all,' Bob had said. 'So if you forensic people can possibly be finished by then. We really ought to get someone to clean the stage. It's going to be bad enough for them without having to act round the blood.'

There were hundreds of people to interview. A master list was being compiled, teams were being made up, and each man was given his own list of people to see and a number of standard questions. The results would then be fed into the computer. Meanwhile the most obviously important witnesses were going to come one by one into the incident post to see the detectives who would be working there.

Bob Southwell was not meant to be actively investigating in this first stage; he had enough to do seeing that all wheels were set in motion and preparations made for the descent of the assistant chief constable and Detective Chief Superintendent Duncan later in the day. He did not expect them until late morning, by which time he hoped to have the initial work under way. A press-relations man arrived from HQ to liaise with him and organize contacts with the media, and he had to be shown the local ropes before he could be of real use.

Thomas did not usually work on a Saturday, and had officially begun his leave, but a manhole was being enlarged in the middle of one of the narrow medieval streets – the worst possible time of year to carry out such work from a traffic-flow point of view – they would not have done it if an emergency had not arisen. He felt compelled to make sure all was going as smoothly as possible. The contractors were already busy, having, like the police, worked through half the night. Traffic cones, shortly to be knocked over, defined a narrower than ever passage for the cars of residents and visitors alike. Emergency traffic lights were installed and in operation. Tom's second in command was there, looking competent, calm and in control.

Leaving the scene with his conscience a little clearer Tom walked towards the Museum Gardens. Both he and Bob were to meet a pretty girl that morning, and Tom's was walking towards him now.

She looked breathless and helpless, a lot of white-blond hair framing a lovely face with wide blue eyes; she wore a fawn raincoat belted over an hourglass figure.

'Which is ze way to ze railway station?' she asked, looking at Thomas as though her life depended on his reply. He explained carefully, remembering a film he had once seen starring Mai Zetterling. She listened, but the minute he stopped speaking she asked, 'Which is ze way to ze Castle Museum?' So he explained again, then turned to watch her go, thinking that the way she was taking wouldn't lead her to either of them.

Bob's encounter was less light-hearted. He had to meet Bruce Exelby's secretary at the station.

She was a tall girl, self-possessed and beautiful.

'But why should anyone murder Bruce?' she asked. 'Was it in mistake for Poison Peters?'

'That's a possibility.' Not really though, thought Bob. Not in mistake for. Because of, perhaps.

'I suppose it's that Absolom man. He must be a bit unhinged.'

'What do you know about that?'

'Bruce told me on the phone. He was just about steaming.'

'As far as we know Absolom had nothing to do with it.'

Zita was in York to do two things; to make funeral arrangements and to clear the flat, taking Exelby's possessions back with her. The police had already gone through the flat in case there was anything helpful, but Exelby had brought very few things with him and nothing was added to their knowledge.

With the aid of a nice young constable Zita soon packed the clothes into suitcases and papers into a briefcase. The constable, who had been told to help as much as he could, took the cases down to the station while Bob took Zita to make the funeral arrangements. He went with her to the door of the mortuary and watched as she walked forward to the body and stood motionless looking down at the still face. He went out to the car and sat waiting for her.

She was calm, almost rigid in feature, when she came and got in beside him.

'It *was* Absolom, then,' she said bitterly. 'And because of that crackpot I've lost a perfectly good job.'

Bob whipped his head around to look at her. She needed no

encouragement to go on. 'The undertaker told me. He talked to the stage electrician last night, who told him there'd been the father and mother of a row. Absolom had been warned off the place, but he was in the audience at the dress rehearsal and Bruce went absolutely mad.'

'And?' asked Bob.

'And the man went off, but obviously he just concealed himself and waited till he could have a go at Bruce.'

'I'll look into it.' Bob drove her to the station. As they drew up there he decided to do one more thing. He produced the stiletto knife, in its polythene bag. Forensics had already gone over it, and he was taking it to the murder room to be exhibit A. 'Could you just look at this for me? Can you identify it as Exelby's?'

Zita shuddered and refused to take it in her hands. Bob turned it over and round and round for her.

'I've never seen it before in my life.'

'You've never seen it? But these initials on the end – B.E. Perhaps he had it in a drawer or tucked away somewhere at his flat.'

'Look. He worked a lot from home. I was in his flat all the time. What's more I packed his things for him when he came up here – he had an appointment and was going to be rushed. No, I wasn't his mistress if that's what you're thinking. Not that he didn't try it on. But I've a perfectly good boyfriend and we're saving to get married . . . Yes, he must have had things packed away I never saw. I saw all the things he brought with him though, and he was wearing those skin-tight jeans and a T-shirt when he left. If he'd had a thread underneath it would have showed, so he hadn't got a knife stuck in his belt. Why does it have to be his just because it's got B.E. on it? Could be anybody's.'

Bob had no reason to disbelieve her. He put exhibit A away and politely got out of the car and opened the passenger door. The young police constable came forward, carrying the suitcases. She smiled around graciously and departed.

She had made the arrangements with the undertaker. The police had no objection to the funeral taking place as soon as the inquest was over. There was nothing else to learn from the body. Exelby had no near relatives; Zita was acting on behalf of the lawyer who had been Exelby's friend, and was now his executor. 'It gives me a few days more work, tidying up,' she had said. 'Then it'll be back to the agency. Just when I thought that if I played my cards right I'd have a job for as long as I wanted it.'

As Bob parked his car beside the police caravan he saw Thomas Churchyard approaching. He decided to leave the matter of the undertaker's evidence and the row with Absolom for the moment. He attracted Thomas's attention and said, 'Just the man I want.'

'I'm not sure that I like the sound of that.'

'You're here early! The performance isn't until tonight, is it?'

'Half past seven. Finishes about half past eleven or a quarter to twelve.'

'Bit gruelling, surely? Every day for three weeks on top of working for a living?'

'Well, I'm taking annual leave this year. But a lot of people do work and take part as well, that's right. It is exhausting. But there's a group spirit – I can't explain it – it's such a wonderful feeling, taking part. It buoys you up, somehow.'

'And that's why you can't keep away from the place?'

'I'm a bit worried about Poison. He's taken a lot of hammer this last week and he looked worn out to start with. Just thought I'd see how he was, and what was happening generally.'

'Before you go to see that punk you can come and explain what you saw to me.'

Tom discovered that Bob's eyes were like needles, and compelling. He wished he'd stayed talking a bit longer to that nice young tourist. But he did as he was told. Together the two men climbed the scaffolding to where Tom and Poison had been sitting together the previous evening.

'The forensic evidence suggests,' said Bob, 'that he was stabbed; and stabbed in the few seconds before he climbed that ladder to the back of the stage. Come on. Re-enact what you did for me.'

Thomas described carefully the scene as he had looked down from the base of the steps leading to his throne in the sky, and a young detective, who had followed them up at a gesture from

Bob, took down the names and positions of all the cast as far as Thomas could remember them.

'Then you did what?'

'I stood up, climbed on to the throne, looked down, saw him.'

'Do it for me,' said Bob, producing a stopwatch.

'Quite leisurely, you know,' replied Tom, and demonstrated.

'Leisurely, as you say, but it only took ten seconds until you say he reached the top of the ladder. Let me do it . . . Yes. I see. Tom, these seconds are crucial. Go through again exactly what you saw. Tell me every detail, no matter how unimportant. Do it again, this time not worrying about how long it took but talking us through it.'

Tom turned his mind back to the previous evening and stated as well as he could who had been on the stage, where they had been standing, what attracted his attention to Exelby ('I happened to look down at my left hand,' he said, without recounting why) and how he had watched him climb the ladder slowly – cross the stage, reeling a little – apparently speak to one of the actors – then fall.

'And Absolom?' snapped Bob.

'Sydney? He wasn't here!'

'But he was. You didn't see him, then? Didn't witness the quarrel?'

'No.' Thomas was shaken. 'It can't be Sydney.'

'Stranger things have happened. The way I have to hear of things! Exelby's secretary talks to the undertaker who talked to the electrician who told him Absolom was here and that there was a flaming row. You know nothing about it. No one else so far has said a thing about it.'

The matter, though, once known, was soon uncovered. The team of detectives and constables had been telephoning and visiting house to house with a questionnaire. 'Did you witness an altercation between Mr Exelby and Mr Absolom?' was hastily added to it, and the audience was included in the people questioned. Locating the different members of the audience added hours of work for the backroom staff.

What the hell had Sergeant Diamond, sitting there among the audience, been doing not to notice it? was the question Bob Southwell was not so much asking as shouting. Sergeant

Diamond, much shaken, appeared, to say that he had only joined the audience during the interval. Before that he had been patrolling generally; and it turned out that no member of Task Force had been in the audience before the interval, the danger being expected to be to Poison, and among the cast somewhere.

All the members of Task Force had already made statements about where they were and whom they were with, whom they saw, during the vital time. Busily on duty they had all been, there was no doubt about that. It was unfortunate that the five of them – they were working in shifts and only five of the ten had been on duty just then – did not seem to have been anywhere significant or with anyone acting at all out of character.

One had been in the Tempest Anderson Hall, Sergeant Diamond had been walking the bounds of the Gardens, one had been in the props tent, and the remaining two had been in different parts of St Olave's graveyard with the other members of their groups of Crowd.

The assistant chief constable for Yorkshire arrived, together with Detective Chief Superintendent Duncan.

'We'll be swamped by television crews and intrusive journalists as soon as they know about this,' said Duncan. 'It's bedlam anyway when the festival is on. When the journalists get in on the fact that the director's been murdered, bang go our chances of just quietly finding out who did it.'

'It amazes me that they aren't on to it already.'

The first press conference finally took place that morning at eleven forty-five, a quarter of an hour after the ACC had arrived, and was the least gruelling of all the many press conferences that were to be held in the course of the next ten days. Word had gone out that the presence of the gentlemen of the press was requested, and a small number of them had come. Although news of the director's death had spread, the full piquancy of the situation had not yet reached the whole of the British media.

The announcement was simple and factual. Suspicious death, under investigation by the police. Bare details were given. The bare details were, at that point, enough to make a story and to send the reporters rushing to telephones.

'Well, that's that,' said his chief to Southwell. 'Now wait. Or rather, work like mad to do as much as you can before we're inundated.'

'I've started the interviews and questionnaires already, sir. We've been working since six o'clock.'

'Good man. You've arranged police protection for Peters?'

'He didn't want it, sir.'

'Whether he wants it or not he's got to have it. They're aiming at him, aren't they? We don't want his murder on our heads.'

'We aren't positive they'll try for him next, sir.'

'No, but they might. He's exposed on the stage. If the murderer gets a gun they could pick him off. No problem.'

'We'll do our best, sir.'

'Any idea yet?' the DCS asked Bob Southwell.

'The man originally in charge of stage-lighting, Absolom, has behaved and is behaving oddly. If you remember, Chief, he nearly electrocuted Poison Peters,' ('Good riddance if he had,' grunted the assistant chief constable) 'and he came here to watch the dress rehearsal after being warned off both by Exelby and ourselves; stood up to Exelby's browbeating when he was noticed, and was truculent back; then, did he go quietly and chastened away? He did not. We don't know what he did then, as he's flatly refused to tell us. But he certainly hung around the place.'

'Have you arrested him?'

'I could, if I thought he had anything to do with it. Damn him! He's just muddying the water.'

The water, as far as Bob could see it, was very muddy indeed. It was going to be a long slow job eliminating members of the cast. The audience, apart from Sydney, were in the clear. But even when they narrowed down the suspects, there still remained the possibility that someone from outside – quite unconnected with the plays – had found his way in, hidden under the stage, seized his moment to kill Exelby when for once he was alone, and then got away under cover of the subsequent confusion. Where, in the teeming tourist-swelled city, might he be?

As soon as his talk with Bob Southwell was over, Thomas Churchyard had decided to put off his visit to Poison, and had gone round to see Absolom.

'Well, why shouldn't I have gone to the plays?' Sydney asked aggressively.

'The police told you to keep off the set.'

'I've a right to see the mystery plays same as any other member of the public. And why should I pay for a ticket? All the work I've put in? I just asked the Lady Mayoress if I could join her party. We were at school together and she knows how I've worked for the plays so she said yes.'

'You knew Exelby was bound to see you.'

'And didn't he look small! Bouncing up and down foaming at the mouth with anger just because one innocent old-age pensioner was sitting in the audience.'

'Syd, how could you be so silly? You aren't *any* old-age pensioner. You're the man who nearly electrocuted the star in this production. You and I have known one another in MRS for years but I never knew you'd be so out and out provocative.'

'I didn't nearly electrocute him on purpose.'

'You went in the audience on purpose.'

'I've a right to see the mystery plays same as any other citizen of York . . .'

Tom sighed. Somehow this argument seemed to be going in a circle. He got up from the heavily patterned moquette sofa where Sydney had seated him, and put the half drunk cup of thick tea in its fine china cup ornamented by rampant roses down on a French-polished coffee table.

'I can't do anything with you, Syd. You don't even look as though you're sorry.' And indeed the small cloud of fluffy hair was full of bounce, as if about to take off for an unknown destination. As Tom approached the door on his way out, he saw through the panels of ornamental obscured glass a heavy blue shape with a helmet approaching up the narrow concrete path.

Tom set off back to the Museum Gardens in a mood of black introspection. He paused in a group of people to find out what they were looking at and in front of him a great devil's head sprang into the air, an eruption of evil, filling his vision, startling and shaking him. A medieval play was being enacted on a cart; it was an ordinary enough event at festival time, but he was shaken unreasonably and decided to go and have a beer and a sandwich. Evil, surfacing through brightness, erupting into daylight, had become a reality. Curiously spiky and uncomfortable, it had torn into shreds the bright tapestry of the society in which Thomas lived.

In the warm crowded interior of the Punch Bowl on Stonegate he bought a shepherd's pie and a beer with a whisky chaser, and soon began to feel better. If there was evil in the community it must be rooted out. Then the body politic would be healthy again. He wished he could help. The trouble was he didn't know how to begin. If he knew more clearly what had happened he might be able to think of something . . .

Bob Southwell had on his desk a number of accounts from people in the audience who had witnessed the director's angry reaction on catching sight of Absolom, the unparliamentary language, the rush down from the stage to pull Absolom up from his seat by the lapels of his raincoat and shake him.

Was that kind of public humiliation – which Exelby seemed only too good at inflicting – enough to make a man commit murder? A quiet, elderly, respectable man? A man disgraced in front of his friends and the leaders of his little community? Was it enough to make him somehow find his way under the stage and strike at the director with a narrow-bladed knife? Combined – Bob reminded himself – with Absolom's resentment of Exelby's importation of Poison Peters?

He was in the middle of interviewing the man. 'So then what did you do?' he asked.

'Went home,' Absolom answered, with much the same nonchalant bravado he had shown to Thomas Churchyard that morning. Bob sighed. He sent two detectives with a search warrant, who combed the tidy little home from insulated loft to neat workshop without finding anything in the least suspicious.

Thomas knocked at the door of Poison Peters's caravan. Poison opened it and stood there looking at him.

'How are you?' asked Tom politely.

Poison made a gesture with his head and turned away leaving the door open; Tom followed him in.

'How are we all, after last night?' Poison asked in reply, putting the kettle on. 'D'yer want tea? I've been drinking gallons.'

'Fine. But I didn't come to beg a cup of tea. I came to ask if you'd like to have a meal with me before the performance tonight. Do you good to get out of this caravan for a bit.'

'Oh, I've been out.' Poison shot Tom a penetrating look from his golden-brown eyes. 'Had a walk round the city centre before breakfast, and finished by the river, watching the birds. The river's all right. Always something different. Not boring. Know what I mean?'

'Not boring – no. Particularly when it floods. I thought a light meal about four o'clock. Soup, salad, fruit, that sort of thing. Unless you go in for steak and chips before a performance.'

'Walk along?' asked Poison.

'Why not? You could walk along the river path. If you're dressed as you are now you shouldn't be recognized.'

With his hair hanging limply, no make-up, washed-out jeans, Poison could have been anybody. Seemingly unable to feel happy without a large symbol on his chest, he was wearing a scarlet T-shirt printed with a huge devil-like head in black surrounded by the words, 'Eric Blood-Axe Rules OK'. Tom shuddered as he looked at it, reminded of the devil's head which had shot up in front of him so unexpectedly. Even this ornament only made Poison blend into the background in York, where the design sold in its thousands to tourists every year.

'I don't want to be back late, though, 'cus I've got to practise my meditation and relaxation before a performance,' said Poison.

'I'll have you back on time.'

'What are you down for now, then? Apart from asking me to come for a meal?'

'I came originally to check on my work – a manhole we're enlarging. It's fine so I was coming to see you when Detective Chief Inspector Southwell saw me and wanted to ask me questions.'

Poison spat neatly into the sink. 'I've had that bastard too. Nine o'clock this morning. "Just routine, Mr Peters," he mimicked. '"So that we can eliminate you from our enquiries." I gave you as my alibi, and I expect you gave me. Perhaps we stabbed Exelby together and are making the alibi up.'

'Did you want to stab him?' asked Tom, interested.

'Sometimes. Insolent bastard. All smarmy nice with me and then there'd be that superior tone, as if I was too dim to understand anything. I understand a lot more than Mr Superior Exelby, I could have told him that.'

'He did manage to put people's backs up.'

'Didn't he yours?'

'Not particularly. His manner was pretty brusque and abrupt but he's – he was – such a damn good director you put up with that.'

Poison shrugged.

'How did you know he was stabbed?'

'I was having a walk round last thing last night and saw them find it.'

'Find what?'

'The dagger.'

'You mean you were snooping?'

'You could call it that. I went under the stage and stood in a dark corner and watched them. They had floods and didn't see me. You can't, you know.'

'Anybody could hide under that stage. But the way we all walk under it to get to the entrances and exits it's surprising no one saw the killer yesterday. Look, Poison, don't go under the stage any more. You don't need to. You can manage all your entrances and exits without it. Come to think of it, don't come to my house along the river bank either. I'll fetch you in the car.'

'They can get me anyway, can't they? Like the juice, and the tree?'

'I expect so. But don't ask for trouble. Those two things – the first I'm sure was a genuine accident. The second was that stupid schoolboy, not thinking of the possible consequences. Criminal ignorance if you like, but not criminal intent. Now – if they're aiming for you, why kill Exelby?'

'Those two – the old sparks nutter and the lad from that posh school – he told them both off, right? So they'd a motive for hitting at him then. Doesn't mean they won't try again for me.'

'If you're looking for someone who's been humiliated by Exelby it could be any of us. Look at the way he treated the Virgin Mary.'

'I felt sorry for that chick.'

'Her boyfriend wasn't too pleased about it either. And Jane Bugg, who's been pushing herself forward all week. He told her to go and stand at the back of the group, out of his sight.'

As Thomas left Poison's caravan he decided to walk home. By now it was mid-afternoon. His bike was locked up at work and he could get it any time. Quite a few of the cast were drifting around the set. The public, shut out of the plays' enclosure, were strolling round the gardens and eating sandwiches in the sun; the police were still scouring every blade of grass in case they had missed something in the night, and a steady stream of them were arriving at the incident-post caravan to report progress before knocking off at the end of their shift.

Sydney Absolom stumbled out of the police caravan.

'Tom!' he grabbed at Tom's jacket. 'They think I've done it. They suspect me. They're going to arrest me at any minute.'

'I'm sure they're not. You're shaking. I'll take you home. Which seems to be becoming a habit.'

Sydney was still shaking.

'I'm perfectly all right.' The older man straightened his spine. 'I've got my shopping to do. I haven't got the joint yet and it's Saturday. I suppose if they arrest me I won't have to bother. They'll have to feed me in prison. That will serve them right. It will save me money as well.'

'Sydney, how long have you and I known each other?'

'Ten years in June.'

'Is it? Well, it's a long time anyway. I never thought I'd see you behaving like a wet hen.'

Sydney let go of Tom's sleeve, smoothed down his hair with a thin nervous hand, and began to check that he had got everything. Shopping bag, glasses, wallet.

'No need to concern yourself, Mr Churchyard,' he said at last. 'No need at all.'

'Syd!' But like an offended stork Sydney Absolom went alone to the entrance of the partition and was let out by the constable on duty.

Tom went home.

It was a relief to turn into his own quiet avenue. As he walked past the Southwell's new house Linda saw him through the window, and came out to intercept him.

'Tom, can you tell me of a good plumber?'

'What's the matter?'

'Oh, nothing much. Just that there's a stop tap in the bathroom – I'm not sure what it's for – and it keeps dripping. There's quite a wet patch on the carpet and I don't like it. Plumbers aren't busy at this time of year are they? I thought one might look at it.'

'The summer is when they're putting in central heating,' replied Tom. 'Have you pointed it out to Bob?'

'Well I did mention it but he's so busy I don't think he even heard me.'

'Should I have a look?'

'I'd be pleased if you would.'

Tom went up to the bathroom. It was rather small, so Linda had to stand at the door and point the problem out by remote control, as it were. There was a nasty wet patch under the stop tap.

'I know what this stop tap is for – it's for the shower. Mrs Spartan showed me the shower after she'd had it put in and she mentioned it.' He twisted the tap closed. 'There – that stops it dripping, only now you can't use the shower.'

'That's no use,' said Linda. 'It's ideal for this weather. The children are under it every day.'

Thomas was kneeling on the floor peering at the tap. 'I think I have a bit of tow in the garage,' he said. 'That would stop it. It's quite a simple thing. Hardly warrants calling out a plumber. I'll go and fetch it.'

'Thanks,' said Linda.

With a little tow wrapped round inside the tap obligingly stopped dripping.

'That should be all right.' Tom got up, gathered his odds and ends, and prepared to go. 'When you have anything else you want a plumber for, get him to look at it while he's here, but you shouldn't need to send for him specially.'

'It is good of you, Tom. Will you stay for tea?'

'No thanks. I've got a guest for a meal myself – have to go and get something ready towards it.'

During the day reporters of various sorts and kinds descended on York. Camera crews from both BBC and ITV were busy filming the Museum Gardens from every angle. The set was barred to them, as was the Tempest Anderson Hall and the St Olave's parish room. But to be going on with they had plenty of material in St Mary's Lodge and the other buildings, and the place was filled with enthusiastic and personable young men and women speaking earnestly into microphones, the cameras rolling.

The national newspapers had sent up ace reporters, and camera flash bulbs were popping all over the place.

The police investigating team on house-to-house questionnaire duty were only hours ahead of the newshounds who would presently be going over all the same ground again. The city was already full of tourists; now it became impossible to find a hotel bed inside the old city walls.

Tom drove Poison out to Clifton in his vintage Rolls without either of thèm talking. There was too much to think about: fear and horror and sudden death and brightness and sunshine and the pavements busy with people of all colours and from many different countries; the roar of traffic and the quiet of Bruce Exelby as he had lain on the stage; the fact that they were alive and hungry and that somewhere there was a killer, who might not have stopped yet.

Tom left the car parked in the road.

'Nice,' Poison patted the mudguards.

'One has to have one extravagance in life.' Tom sounded defensive.

'Why not? Why stop at one?'

On the doorstep was a packet. Tom unwrapped it and found

an orange cake with icing, and a message, 'Thank you from Linda.' He smiled. The little neighbourly things which make up everyday life in Ouse Avenue were doubly precious in their contrast to the horror of sudden death.

Poison made himself at home. He walked into the sitting-room, and looked round critically. The walls and curtains were all pale grey though of different textures; the walls smooth and semi-gloss, the curtains velvet. Over the fireplace the chimney breast was papered with a large design of bright tulips on a background of grey, with dark grey leaves. The carpet and furniture were old; a patterned square of carpet with a dark-blue ground, an old-fashioned suite in small-patterned blue velvet. There were lots of bookshelves on either side of the fireplace and a bureau bookcase.

'Got any music?' he asked.

Thomas obligingly fished around and found Britten's 'Noe's Fludde', and put it on. 'That sharp enough for you?' he asked.

Poison looked at him. 'You don't like my type of music, then?'

'I don't much like the sort you make, no. I like the medieval stuff you were playing in the caravan.'

'You're another one who didn't want me to come to York.'

'Not at first. But I didn't know you then. That public image you work so hard at is a bit off-putting. Look, come into the kitchen and tell me what you'd like to eat. We can still hear the music in there.'

'We eating here?' asked Poison, lounging into the kitchen.

'If you like. Or in the dining-room.'

'I like it here. I like that lion you've got on the wall.'

'That's left over from the family who used to live here, like a lot of other things. The place felt homely so I left it alone. The children must have put that poster up.'

Poison walked to the stove and inspected the soup. 'It isn't that powdered stuff, is it?' He sounded doubtful. 'What's it got in?'

'Just fresh vegetables. I like making my own soup.'

'That's all right then. Salad's all right too. What's with it?'

'Salami – cheeses – cold roast beef . . .'

'Any cottage cheese?'

'Yes.'

'I'll have that, and the salad, and a glass of water, and wholemeal bread if you've got any.'

'Fussy, aren't you?'

'All right! All right! Only checking. I can't eat additives, you see. Allergic, I am. Have to be careful.'

They ate the simple but satisfying meal and Tom drove Poison back to his caravan in plenty of time for his relaxation and meditation, or whatever.

Tom was still concerned about Poison Peters, worried about his safety, wondering how he would find the courage to act in the plays, knowing that a killer was at large and presumably hated him. But when the time came Poison emerged from his hour's relaxation and contemplation in the caravan pale but composed, and dressed in the Tempest Anderson Hall with the rest of them. Tom spoke, but Poison was now withdrawn; he smiled, close-lipped, and that was that. They were all tense.

In less than quarter of an hour the first performance of the mystery plays would begin. There was a kind of light excitement in the air of the city, an electric sparkle generated by the crowds of brightly dressed tourists, and the office girls in their holiday frocks.

The cast were all assembled on the grass in front of the stage. Another minute and the door would be opened to admit the audience. Bob Southwell stood in front of them, for it was the first opportunity he had had to speak to all of them together.

'The position is this: when Bruce Exelby staggered up those stairs to the stage he had just been stabbed by someone. You were all around at the time. I'm not saying that you are all under suspicion of murder. It could have been an outsider, hiding in a dark corner under the stage and awaiting his opportunity. But for your own sakes, I must eliminate as many as possible of you from suspicion as soon as we can. That's why you've been undergoing all this questioning today, and why it's going to go on tomorrow, and probably every day until we find the murderer. You do understand that, don't you?'

They said they did. Everyone wanted to be cleared of suspicion. At present they were looking round at their neighbours, wondering . . . They didn't know, of course, that they would never be eliminated from suspicion – no matter how good their alibi – until the murderer was found.

'Right,' said Bob. 'The performances are to go on just as if nothing had happened. But for heaven's sake be careful. Be on your guard. The violence might not have ended. Bear with us. We will be as little trouble as we can. Good luck, everyone.' He and the ACC were to sit in the front seats and watch the performance. They were both more nervous than the performers themselves. Would it go through without incident?

The members of the audience came in, carrying their vacuum flasks and their hot-water bottles and their umbrellas and their cushions and their travelling rugs, and settled on the tiered seats. The day was still warm; a perfect June day. Blue sky with small clouds scattered across it as though balls of Sydney Absolom's hair had come adrift and floated into the firmament; a light breeze moving the leaves of the graceful trees in the gardens; flowers in bloom; the stir of the city, the cries of the peacocks, and the lapping of the river in the background.

In spite of rehearsals, tonight was the night. Things could go wrong. The audience out there had paid to see a great theatrical performance and – in spite of everything – that must be what they were to get.

There were many members of the cast who had the greatest possible reluctance to walk under the lower stage, or to approach that strangely clean area on its surface . . .

Tom walked to centre stage before the play began, and held up his hands for silence.

'Ladies and gentlemen! Before we begin, the cast would like you to join with us in one minute's silence in tribute to our director, Bruce Exelby, so abruptly taken from life yesterday. May we keep silence, please.'

Before the silence fell, there were two full seconds of murmuring surprise. Except for a squawk from a child or two ('They shouldn't bring them so young,' thought Thomas) it was then completely quiet. The far shriek of a fire engine hurrying along High Ousegate came clearly.

After the silence Tom left the stage and went up to his niche in the arches; he had decided not to use the gilded throne in the sky except for the Last Judgement. The audience had arranged its rugs and cushions and hot-water bottles about its many persons and now was quiet again for his opening words.

There was that incredible, magical leap. At one moment Thomas was a telephone engineer, dressed in a funny outfit, standing on scaffolding behind some ruined masonry. In the next second he became transformed. He lifted up his arms, and spread them to embrace the world. An imposing figure, he became God; and began, 'I am Maker Unmade, all might is in me . . .'

They stopped being actors. They were the Angels, they were Lucifer, they were Devils, they were Adam and Eve in the world's dawn, they were the People of the City portraying the springs of the world and all of life that was therein. The arches, dark against the gradually glowing beauty of an unearthly sunset, the flights of steps, the flat raised areas, the grass in front, were the Heaven and the Earth.

8

> Keep thy tunge, thy tunge, thy tunge;
> Thy wikked tunge werked me wo.
> There is none goes that groweth on ground
> Satenas ne peny-round,
> Werse than is a wikked tunge
> That speketh bothe evil of friend and fo.
>
> *Medieval English Verse*

It was the day of the second performance.

Jane Bugg had been into the incident room and talked at length.

'I had to tell them about seeing Absolom near the props tent,' she remarked virtuously to Sally Vause, Velvet Smith and an assortment of female Crowd in St Olave's parish room where they were all sitting round having coffee. Although it was Sunday, with a performance to do many of the cast and the supporting team had brought picnic lunches down and were spending the day in town.

'Why did you *have* to tell him? asked Sally. 'No one supposes for a minute that he would commit murder.' She passed her mug to Velvet for a fill-up.

'*You* might not suppose it – all pals together, aren't you – you members of MRS? Wouldn't do for us all to be so cliquey.' Her broad unpleasant face looked around her.

'We're not in MRS,' remarked an Angel.

'You're too young to be in anything, you're still at school.'

'I expect you think we're cliquey too, Miss Bugg,' said one of the Angels cheekily.

'We're not cliquey,' exclaimed the first, and the half-dozen of them began to chase one another around the hall, dodging in and out of the racks of costumes, shouting to one another,

'I'm not cliquey!'

'Yes you are cliquey!'

'Cliquey!'

'Cliquey!' . . . until the row was deafening.

'Ignore them,' yelled Sally Vause. 'We're a very friendly society, MRS, though, Jane. Anyone can join. I've often wondered why you don't. We are the Medieval Reconstruction Society and you enjoy this kind of thing so much.'

'Enjoy it? Well – one feels an obligation, you know – to the community – to take part in these things. If one is capable of serving in a particular way one should not be held back by the fear of putting oneself forward.'

'You haven't been,' said Velvet, *sotto voce*.

'*Bruce* was so keen for me to take part. "What shall I do without you, Jane?" he said to me. Poor innocent Bruce. What animal could kill him?'

'He did put people's back's up,' said Sally. 'Of course, he wasn't alone in doing that.'

'Some people have a gift for it,' agreed Velvet, gazing intently at Jane Bugg.

'He was so flattering,' went on Jane as though no one else had spoken. 'So kind of him to place so much reliance on me. I could only do my best to live up to such trust.'

'Trust can be misplaced,' said Velvet, then got up abruptly and took the mugs over to the sink in the corner and washed them viciously, clashing them together.

Sally reflected that for Jane Bugg her public humiliation at Bruce Exelby's hands might never have happened. He had been annoyed by her constantly pushing herself forward, on a number of occasions; but for her to forget how roughly he had told her to keep out of sight at the back of the crowd – well, Sally couldn't have forgotten and forgiven. She wondered if Velvet could. She doubted it, and turned to ask her. But Velvet was washing up again.

The Angels had calmed down. They came and sat again as part of the circle, but the calm did not last long, because a car drew up outside, driven by a parent, and a group of Devils piled out of it and into the parish room.

They had not yet assumed their Devils' dress, and still looked like typical nicely brought-up English fourth formers, in T-shirts, jeans and trainers.

The effect on the Angels, though, was drastic.

'We're not staying here while you're changing,' said the blond plump Angel, aggressively.

'Wouldn't notice if you were here or not,' retorted one of the boys . . .

There was a general mêlée. One small Angel shrieked. A Devil was jostling a medium-sized Angel with the apparent intention of twisting her arm behind her back. The dark Angel who enjoyed Chaucer and a more serious Devil were standing together, discussing the different chemistry experiments they had been doing.

'Break it up,' said Sally firmly. 'Go on, you Angels, it's not raining. Go along to the graveyard. It's lovely there under the trees, so peaceful and shady. Velvet, come and help me with these Devils. Did you get the damaged mask back?'

The boys liked wearing their masks. They had been built up on a foundation of old motor bike helmets, so were easy to put on. Once on though, vision was restricted to the great long slit eyes, which because down the plastic of the visors, reflected light and darkness so that at times in the production they were black holes and at other times seemed to dance fire. Although they were only supposed to put on these masks at the end of their spectacular tumbling descent down the long slope from Heaven, they liked them so much they wore them whenever they could, with the aim of frightening as many people as possible.

Velvet produced the damaged mask, which she had retrieved from the props tent that morning. The right horn, carelessly banged against a wall, once more curved up bravely.

The female Crowd including Jane Bugg had left the hall upon the advent of the boys, so, used to the presence of Sally and Velvet, they changed noisily into their devilish outfits. Once in, they were completely covered in red and black; but then they put on their white angelic robes. These had been specially made so that they could be shed instantly at the moment of their being cast out from Heaven; the boys emerged from them leaving the robes scattered like split banana skins on the downward slope.

'I say, Miss Smith,' said one. 'Is it true then that old Exelby was murdered?'

'The police are investigating his death,' said Velvet.

'That means he was murdered, doesn't it? We might get murdered as well!'

'I wouldn't be surprised.'

'Who'd want to murder him? Now if it had been old Pikey' – naming their form master as none but they knew him – 'that would be all right –'

'I'd murder Pikey,' said one boy with relish. 'I'd boil him in oil and give him the death of the thousand cuts and blow him up with a car bomb and vaporize him with a laser gun.'

'Take no notice of him,' said a larger Devil patronizingly to Velvet. 'He's only Lower Fourth. Very lower, and very fourth-rate, Jones minor, aren't you? Sound more like a first former. Be your age.'

'Be your age yourself! I saw you talking to Louise.'

The racket was still going on as the group of six Devils pushed out of the door of the parish room. Encumbered by their angel drapings and their padded tails which tended to stick out of the white robes at the back they solved the problem of what to do with their masks by putting them on their heads. Wearing their costumes made them into anonymous creatures and freed their inhibitions, if they had ever had any.

The disgrace of one of their number for his stupid and dangerous escapade with the branch and the bolt from the cross had not quelled them. Even the stately eldest of them revelled in being a child again, skipping, jumping, banging a smaller boy up against the walls of the lane which ran towards Marygate. With a sort of chorus of wild yells they plunged and swooped in a crazy progress.

'Thank goodness they've gone,' said a left-over female Crowd, who had been unnoticed in a corner, getting up and shaking out her long medieval kirtle. 'I should think you're tired out in here when you've got rid of everyone.'

'You've said it,' said Sally.

'That Jane Bugg! Isn't she poisonous?'

'Positively so,' agreed Velvet. 'Some one ought to stick a knife in *her*.'

'Is that what they did to Mr Exelby? At least the weather's fine so far. These woollen things smell sheepy when they're wet. I really feel as if I'm back in the Middle Ages then. Remember the last time the plays were performed, when we kept on getting drenched? And Bruce Exelby hasn't done us any favours, saying we haven't to wear underclothes. Not that I took any notice.'

'What he said was he didn't want any nylon frills peeping out or long thermal underpants.'

'Well, fair enough. But if he thought I'm having wool next to my bare skin he'd another think coming. My skin's very sensitive. I've got bra and panties and vest and tights on.'

'You shouldn't really have a bra,' remonstrated Sally. 'It doesn't give the correct medieval droopy look.'

'You look fine,' Velvet cut in sharply.

This was the lady in the Crowd who carried a spindle and had already during rehearsals spun enough yarn for a woolly hat. She was hoping by the end of the plays to have enough for a matching scarf at least. Although she chatted brightly she always seemed half abstracted as she drew on her thread and watched the descending spindle. Yet it was she who produced the new bit of evidence.

'I saw Mr Absolom that night,' she said now, giving the spindle a twist to set it moving. 'I think it's awful the way Jane Bugg just called him 'Absolom' without the Mr.'

'How do you mean, you saw him?'

'After that row with Bruce Exelby. I saw him hanging around the props tent.'

'You'd better tell the police,' advised Sally.

'Oh, don't worry. I'm going to. As soon as they get round to interviewing me.' She twirled again. The spindle spun round. Everyone's eyes were on her, standing there with that assiduously withdrawn look. Just what, and how much, had she seen?

'Of course, as I said to the police,' Jane Bugg remarked, 'the Virgin Mary was very upset. Are you better now, dear? It must have been dreadful for you, poor Bruce going off at you like that. I did explain it all to that nice detective. "He'd thought she showed such promise," I said, "and had such hopes for her. It was very natural for her to get upset, even if she did go to extremes. Young people are very melodramatic, especially if they imagine they've got theatrical talent. I've seen it so often. As we get older we learn a few lessons. But when we're that age it all means so much to us, we are likely to go off the deep end and do over-dramatic things." That's what I said to them, my dear. I did stick up for you as much as I could.'

The Virgin Mary's mouth had gradually been falling open as she listened.

'What do you mean?' she gasped out at last. 'What were you talking to the police about me for, you old bag?'

'You mustn't be abusive, dear. That won't be for your own good at all. They only asked me if I had seen anyone behaving in a peculiar manner. And you must admit, dear, your behaviour was very peculiar when dear Bruce just said a little word to you.'

It was fortunate that at that moment Mary could not speak at all.

'I did what I could to excuse you, my dear,' ended Jane, smiling beatifically, giving the Virgin Mary's arm a little pat before walking away through the gravestones.

'Pity no one murdered *her*,' murmured a female Crowd, looking anxiously at the Virgin Mary. Suddenly Mary burst out into wild irrepressible laughter. A group gathered round her. The laughter changed to tears, paused, broke, continued.

'She's hysterical,' someone said. 'Somebody do something. Where's a first-aider?'

'She's told them I did it,' sobbed Mary, then laughed in a kind of shriek. 'She must be mad. Stop her somebody. I didn't do it.' She wept. A motherly woman in a russet woollen gown gathered the girl into her arms and for a few seconds she sobbed heartbrokenly on the edges of the cream wimple. Then she broke away and let out a scream. 'She's accused me!' she cried.

'Look, this isn't helping,' said someone.

Thomas Churchyard joined the group – they opened to let him in, looking at him anxiously, sure he could help, relying on his dependable aura. Tom felt far from capable of coping with the situation. He knew hysterical people ought to be slapped. So did everyone else in the group. No one had had the courage to do it.

'Fetch a glass of water,' Tom said sharply to a lad in jerkin and hose who was at his elbow. 'Run to the police caravan, they'll have one.' He turned to Mary. 'This won't do,' he said, but she was wailing wildly.

Tom slapped her twice, lightly but sharply. The noise stopped as if someone had flipped a switch. Her blue eyes looked at him, dazed and blank.

'You're hysterical. No need for that.'

The boy arrived with the water.

'Drink this,' said Thomas, 'and be quiet for a minute.'

The motherly woman took Mary's wrist and felt her pulse.

'You'd better have a hot drink, something warm round you, and be alone for half an hour,' she said.

'There isn't time . . .' the nervous tone rose in Mary's voice.

'There's plenty of time. We can find a side room in the Tempest Anderson.' Mary let herself be led off.

The group who had gathered round her dissolved, either to regroup with others, or to drift away.

Thomas went in search of Jane Bugg.

He did not get the chance to reproach her with upsetting Mary, for she waded into him at once.

'I wanted to have a word with you, dear Thomas. Thank heavens you've come. The police suspect me – I know they do, some of the things they said. Just because dear *Bruce* scolded me a little. As if I minded that! If he needed to let off steam far better on me – his old friend and colleague – than on some of these over-sensitive melodramatic creatures. Still, as I said, they led me to think they suspect me – but I saw Absolom behaving in a very peculiar manner.'

'What was Mr Absolom doing?' Tom couldn't help himself. Defending Mary would have to wait.

'I had to tell the police of course. How could I keep it to myself? I saw him acting in a very peculiar manner, I said to them. But then he's a very peculiar man. His appearance, to start with. That mack he always wears. And that funny hair.

And that nervous way his hands twitch about.'

Thomas thought Jane Bugg's appearance left much to be desired, but he didn't say so. 'I like Mr Absolom's appearance,' he said, 'but of course people's appearance in general one likes or dislikes as a matter of taste. The police are hardly likely to be influenced by your not liking the way Mr Absolom looks.'

'But I saw him acting in a most peculiar manner. It was after the row. He was supposed to leave the place. "*Go*!" dear *Bruce* told him.' She showed how, with theatrically outstretched finger and deepened voice. "*Go*! and don't come near the plays again." But did he go? No, he did not. He lurked. He lurked around the props tent. And where else could he have got that dagger? That was where that wretched Devil found the willow branch. The props tent is full of all sorts of lethal objects.'

'Your tongue will get you into trouble, Jane,' said Thomas. '"Alle bakbiteres hi wendeth to helle."'

He felt infinitely weary. Telling her off seemed like too much effort. He turned and left her, and went over to the props tent.

The props tent had a look of impermanence, a gaiety, missing from the rest of the scene. The willow branches for the day were leaning against one side, the tall spears with their hardboard blades glittering with silver paint leaned against the other.

'Build me a willow cabin at your gate,' thought Thomas. A curtain of large felt leaves strung on strong thread and suspended from a rope between two coat stands obscured the door.

Inside it was dim but light, as it is in tents. There was a table strewn with the materials of the prop-maker's trade – Stanley knives, pots of glues, paintbrushes, aerosol sprays of various substances, scissors and a pincushion full of pins. A crown was in the centre having its topmost jewel re-attached, and one of the Three Kings was standing by looking anxious and filling what empty space there was with his robes of brown and gold.

Behind the tables a calm-looking woman was carefully wiping away surplus glue. She looked up quickly as Thomas entered. She was a small neat person, all rounded shapes in a shirt and jeans and flat sandals.

'I'll wait,' said Thomas. At that she dismissed him from her thoughts and concentrated again completely on the job in hand.

It seemed to take a long time. At last the King departed joyfully and she turned her attention to Thomas. He came to the conclusion that she was a painter. No other people rivet one with that impersonal stare.

'Yes?' she asked.

'Er . . . on the night of the murder . . .' he started, hesitant.

'I was in here. Always am in here. Live in this place. Told the police and the journalists so. Nothing else to say.'

'I hear Sydney Absolom was seen hanging about here after Mr Exelby threw him out of the audience.'

'He may have been. I didn't see him.'

'No chance of him – er – pinching a Stanley knife or –'

'I did go out for a coffee and a break,' admitted the woman, 'during the interval. Told them that. Nothing missing. The dagger wasn't ours. Wouldn't have cut anyone if it had been ours, because if a dagger had been needed we'd have made it of hardboard,' she added with the first touch of humour.

'Oh. Right. Thanks.'

'Anyway it's not me that leaves my post. You want to have a talk to those wardrobe people. Whenever you want them they're never in St Olave's parish room.'

'They have to look after the costumes in the Tempest Anderson as well, you see,' he said defending his members of MRS, Sally Vause and Velvet Smith.

He withdrew. She had already forgotten him. As the felt leaves of the Garden of Eden brushed past his face, he glanced back and saw that she was completely absorbed again, drawing a shape on a piece of paper. He felt that the props tent was as much a bit of another world, dropped down from the sky or somewhere, as was Poison's caravan or the police incident post. Except that the props tent came direct from an older world than anything else – a world before the medieval, when the Little People sang under the Hollow Hills.

It seemed perfectly in keeping that this was the place where silly innocent Sydney Absolom had been seen 'lurking about'.

Somewhere else evil was lurking, hidden under some fair exterior; it was like an abscess, out of sight, poisoning the whole. Would he sense it? He could sense it – running near him; spoiling for him like an underground cesspit the pure pleasure of being involved in the mystery plays.

Sydney Absolom was walking through the Museum Gardens, minding his own business, looking longingly at the tall fence round the play area, when he met Jane Bugg.

'Oh, Sydney!' she said. 'What do you think to all this? It's all very peculiar. You must be glad you were out of the way before it happened.'

He gave her a glum look. 'I was still here. The police suspect me,' he said.

'Nonsense, Sydney. They know you didn't have anything to do with it. Even if you are a member of MRS. They're bound to suspect you all, of course.'

'What do you mean?'

'You're all in it, aren't you? All involved in the plays? And some of you knew dear poor *Bruce* when he was in York many years ago. Don't try to fob *me* off, Sydney. You know jolly well who I mean. Wasn't there someone *rather* close to him? Oh, I was new in York then and of course you were all born here. But I remember the gossip very well. She did nothing but talk about him in those days. It was "Bruce is going to do this and Bruce is going to do that". I can see why you tried to electrocute him, Sydney, wicked though it was of you. I told the police I could see why you'd done it. You were expressing your sympathy for her, weren't you? I didn't tell them that of course. Just that I could see why you'd done it. They didn't ask anything else on that point. But you and I know, don't we, Sydney?'

'You think I really tried to electrocute him, Jane? You haven't been and told them that?'

'I said it was very understandable, Sydney dear. Old loyalties die hard, don't they, dear?'

'Don't you think it's bad enough being suspected, Jane Bugg, without having you push your oar in? And goodness knows what you're talking about or think you've remembered.'

'Well of course I'm not good enough for you. Not a member of your famous MRS, am I? You're too exclusive for that. Well, this is what I think of you all, you superior lot!' And Jane spat on the ground.

'Jane!' Absolom, who was unmarried and had a high ideal of women, looked revolted. 'Jane! You forget yourself. You would have been welcome to join MRS at any time. Tom could have told you that.'

'Do you think I would have wanted to join you, you murdering crew?' cried Jane. '*Bruce* was worth all eleven of you. Bruce knew how to value the help of a lady. Bruce relied on my help. I wish you would explain that to the police, Sydney dear. They seem to think I had a grudge against him. So silly.'

9

> We get no rest until this thing
> Be brought to end.
>
> *The Skynners' Play*

The assistant chief constable was giving a press conference. He hated doing it. His uniform was hot and uncomfortable and middle age was thickening his neck, so that the size sixteen collars were now a little too tight. He could think of things he would rather be doing on a warm June day than facing a ravening horde of journalists and photographers. It wasn't as though he could tell them of any startling progress, or indeed of anything much at all . . .

'Yes, we have found the murder weapon. Yes, you may use the photographs of it which we will be issuing to you. No, there were no fingerprints on it, it has yielded no evidence at all.

'Are we looking for someone showing scratches and with bloodstained clothing? No, we are not. There was no skin under Exelby's fingernails and no sign that he resisted his attacker. We think he was taken by surprise.

'This may indicate that he knew his attacker, yes. It may only indicate that he was just standing there, or walking, and the attack was so swift and unexpected that he did not have time to react. Someone passing stabbed him, withdrew the stiletto, threw it away, left him. It must have been as simple as that.

'Why aren't we expecting bloodstains on the attacker? Well, puncture wounds of this type don't bleed much. In fact it was not until he had collapsed on stage that he really bled.

'As to why Exelby was murdered . . . No, we don't know.

Yes, our first thought was that it must be in connection with his choice of Poison Peters to take the part of Christ.

'We still consider that the strongest possibility.

'Other possibilities we are considering? Exelby was a very dominating personality and caused a certain antagonism wherever he went.

'Whether the antagonisms were a sufficient motive for murder is what we have to find out.

'No, I certainly don't mean that the cast of the mystery plays is riven by dissension, and all at each other's throats. I understand theatrical productions always create a great deal of tension between the various members of the cast. In my judgement the mystery plays have less of this than ordinary performances, because of the whole nature and theme of the plays. As theatre goes they are a remarkably united and harmonious cast.

'A suspect? Until the murderer is found we must suspect everyone who could have been in the right place at the right time.

'You are quite right in your supposition that the director lived for a while after the wound was inflicted. He lived for about two and a half minutes.'

A reporter asked if Exelby had said anything.

'Said anything?' Here the assistant chief constable for Yorkshire paused. He turned to Bob Southwell, who was sitting at his side. 'Did he say anything, Bob?' he asked quietly.

Bob replied just as quietly. 'Yes, he was speaking.'

One of the more intrusive and cheeky of the journalistic bunch shouted out, 'What's that? Speak up! Let us all hear!'

At the request of his superior Bob rose and took the microphone.

'Yes is the answer to your question. As Bruce Exelby crossed the stage he passed close to the actor playing Isaiah, and seemed to be trying to speak to him. The only word the actor could catch appeared to be "father?". He said that Exelby's tone was questioning. That is all he was heard to say. What the significance of it is I only wish *you* could tell *me*.'

At this slight touch of levity the gentlemen of the press shouted with laughter and Bob's popularity soared. He gave the microphone back to the assistant chief constable and sat down again.

Bob's levity had gone when he and the ACC were alone together after the press conference, sharing a percolator-full of rather bitter coffee in the partitioned-off end of the police mobile incident post.

'The opposition to Poison included good and responsible sections of the community,' remarked the ACC. 'Could any of these apparently decent people tip over into fanaticism and actually commit murder?'

'It sounds possible, put like that,' Bob answered. 'It's baffling because there's so little to go on,' he went on. 'No fingerprints, no scratch marks on the assailant, no fibres, and so many people were around the place. It can't have been easy to find him alone and in a secluded spot, actually. The AD was with him most of the time, walking behind taking instructions.'

'AD?'

'Assistant director. Sue Brown. Though she was sent off pretty often to fetch sandwiches and all kinds of other rather trivial jobs. But whoever did it was lucky to find him alone and in a place where they were not observed . . . Exelby spent a lot of time in front watching the action, or charging up on stage saying, "Do it like this". It was his last night but one in York. If they had not struck when they did it might have been much more difficult on the actual first night.'

'Motive,' put in the ACC.

'Motive? – how big a motive does anyone need for murder? Religious fanatacism? The world tells us that can be a motive, though the good burghers of York seem unlikely to be so carried away . . . Is it enough to be slighted and shown up before your fellows in a thing which is, after all, make-believe? No, don't get me wrong. I'm a Christian. But any play must be make-believe, whether or not the events it portrays are true. Is it enough to have someone you disapprove of cast as the living God? Is it enough to have someone make a pass at your girlfriend? Are these big enough motives for taking a life?'

'They might be if the person's mind is unhinged.'

'Unhinged. Or in the heat of temper. Or in cold deliberation of planned purpose.'

There was a pause between the two men. That last had not been spoken before.

'It's a needle in a haystack,' said the assistant chief constable in his weighty voice.

'The only thing is to keep on looking. To sift the haystack until we find the needle.'

'If it's someone unhinged they might do some other mad, useless thing. Have you got that protection on Poison Peters? If it was because of him, he's in danger. Even though nothing was tried last night that could be to put us off our guard.'

'I've got him to have a personal bodyguard. Though it wasn't easy. He isn't persuadable and doesn't like me. He doesn't want his privacy threatened. For my part, I'd just like to know what *does* go on in that caravan of a night.'

'And if it was your second reason, in the heat of temper. Then there must have been something to trigger off the explosion. The person must have seemed agitated either before or after, and surely that would have been noticed. Either agitated or unusually silent and white.'

'It could have been a number of people then. Exelby upset the Virgin Mary, and therefore by implication her boyfriend, the Youngest Shepherd; the Porteress, and others. So far the only person fitting your pattern of agitation is Sydney Absolom.'

'He who muddies the water? Don't reject him out of hand, Bob. The obvious is often the solution.'

'Right.'

'Now we come to your third hypothesis. The cold deliberation of planned purpose. Doesn't that seem the most likely? With no clues left behind? No fingerprints? No carelessness? Above all – the *preparedness*? I think someone was watching for their chance, ready for it, prepared for it.'

'Everyone is careless sooner or later,' muttered Bob Southwell.

'Granted. And that's what we as policemen look out for. The tiny telltale carelessness.'

The ACC often lectured to recruits. The phrases he used to them tended to slip out at less appropriate moments. 'But let's think further about this. Cold deliberation. Planned purpose.

This might have its roots far back in time, long before this performance of the mystery plays, long before Exelby's choice of Poison Peters. Detach someone from the team and set them to finding out about his past life, Bob.'

'I already have done that, sir.'

'He was a man who made enemies, who bear him grudges. The chap you have detached might come up with a lot of possibilities.'

'Not so many when you think the person with a grudge has also got to be here in York now.'

'Could be a contract killing?'

'Contract? He isn't a gangland boss.'

'No. But you don't know what you might uncover. Stage people. Was he involved with drugs for instance?'

'There's one thing,' Bob brightened. 'Fingerprints, none. Either the murderer took time to wipe the weapon clean very carefully, so that not even the tiniest fragment of a print was left anywhere. Or else their hands were covered.'

And the only people with regularly covered hands on the set of the mystery plays were the Devils, the arms of whose costumes ended in grotesque gloves, claw-ended, which they used to maximum effect – spreading their fingers and raking the air, making threatening gestures to the lost souls in their care, pointing and dramatically gesturing. And there was the stupid young Devil who had messed about with the cross. Had he sneaked back into the performance? Once in his costume Bruce Exelby would not have recognized him or realized that he had disobeyed orders. It was unlikely anyone would notice a Devil too many. Yet anyone could have put on gloves.

'The main motives for murder, you know,' remarked the assistant chief constable, 'are sex and greed.'

'I had noticed, sir,' replied Bob, thinking to himself that he didn't see how either fitted in this particular case. Exelby had apparently been trying to make the Virgin Mary, before he gave her a public humiliation; he had several times had a flashily pretty girl in tow for the after-rehearsal drink, but never the same one twice; he had been married briefly for six months, and happily divorced ever since. It all gave the impression that what really made him tick was the theatre.

Greed? Blackmail – inheritance after his death – at first sight both seemed unlikely. There was no doubt Exelby had done well, but he obviously spent heavily; West-end flat, glamorous secretary, beautiful luggage, expensive hand-made shoes and exclusive watch. Bob Southwell doubted if there was much left of his earnings when all that lot was paid for. He remembered the Porsche, and thought some men might kill to own one of those – maybe.

He shook his head. Those deliberations hadn't seemed to get him anywhere.

'There's nothing for it, sir,' he said to the assistant chief constable, as though all this had been spoken instead of revolving internally, 'but to go on working steadily away in the normal police manner. Interview all these hundreds of people, tabulate them, computerize the information – see where it gets us.'

'All this technology! Nothing wrong with a pad and pencil.'

'Nothing, sir. But these new tools exist. May as well use them. Apart from anything else, the media criticise us if we don't. They think we're efficient if we use a computer – inefficient if we don't. The fact that the Yorkshire Ripper was caught by two constables who noticed a wrong number plate and checked up on it, and not by all the computers in the world, doesn't seem to register with them.'

The ACC nodded. 'You go on doing what you're doing, Bob, and I'll try to keep these man-eating media tigers out of your hair. The trouble with computers – I've really nothing against them, mind, we have to move with the times – is that they're still in their infancy and, more to the point, so are we in dealing with them. When all the Force have been using computers since junior school we'll find them a darn sight more useful than we do now, when most of us are only learning the language and what they're capable of. There's never going to be any substitute though for common sense and intelligent observation of trifles. Now – this murder – I'm very much afraid there'll be another attempt, this time on Poison Peters. He's the target, I'm sure of it. *Protect him, Bob.* When did you fix the inquest for?'

'It's to be a week tomorrow, sir. If we're going to get

anywhere with this case we should have an inkling by then.'

'I hope so, because that's the outside limit of time I can let you have all this extra manpower.'

It was on the day of that first press conference and of the discussion in the police caravan, in the midst of all the growing furore, that Linda had a real emergency on Ouse Avenue. Tom was in the garden pottering about, and had been chatting to the children, Susan and Paul, over the low post-and-wire fence. They had chased around on their bicycles until they were exhausted and were now flopped on the grass reading, with a pile of books between them.

'What are you reading?' Tom asked.

'We're going to join the police force when we grow up,' explained Susan, 'so we've got Daddy's books out of the bookcase and we're starting to learn about it. We want to find murderers like Daddy does.'

'Doesn't he mind you getting his books?' asked Tom doubtfully. But he didn't like to interfere and Linda – who was papering Paul's bedroom upstairs with a design of sailing ships on a wavy sea – was nowhere to be seen. So Tom got his shears and went to trim his front hedge, wishing the family who had owned his house before him had not planted privet.

He worked for some time and at last gathered all the trimmings together into the wheelbarrow and went round into the back again. As the privet trimmings were still young and softish he decided they would do perfectly well in the compost heap, and was putting them into it when he heard a kind of gasping sound from the next-door garden. It was Susan, who with her hand to her mouth was looking down at something. In a second she turned and ran into the house, crying, 'Mummy! Mummy!'

Thomas moved over quickly to the divide between the gardens, looked over, and saw Paul lying motionless on the grass. He was no quicker than Linda, who flew out into the garden and over to Paul.

She knelt by him, moved her hand over his forehead and took his wrist.

'What's the trouble?' asked Tom, realizing he might be able

to help.

'He's unconscious. They've been playing some game . . .' Linda's voice could hardly stagger out of her lips.

'Ambulance,' said Tom.

'Yes.'

'I'll phone for it.'

An ambulance was fortunately nearby, returning from taking someone home, and was with them in half a minute. Paul, now moaning a little, was lifted into it, and Linda went with him. Everything happened so quickly it was incredible. Tom stood there holding Susan's hand. 'I'll look after her,' he said.

'Don't tell Bob yet,' said Linda. 'I always try not to bother him at work. Paul doesn't seem as deeply unconscious as he did.'

With that the ambulance was on its way.

Tom looked down at Susan. 'What happened, Sue?' he asked.

'I was learning self-defence,' she answered in a small voice. 'Paul told me to practise pressure points on him so I was. Well, I was trying to. I had my arm round his neck, sort of. Then he went all funny.'

'I thought you shouldn't have been looking at grown-up books.'

Susan began to cry in great torrents, and he put his arm round her. 'There's no point in crying,' he said awkwardly. 'Look, let's go inside and wait in the room with the phone. Mummy will soon be ringing to tell us that everything's all right.'

'I've killed him,' sobbed Susan.

'For heaven's sake don't blame yourself, Susan. All sorts of things happen when you're playing. You didn't mean to hurt him, did you? I'm sure he'll be all right.'

He couldn't bring himself to be severe with her while she was in such misery, though he wished he had drawn Linda's attention earlier to the fact that the children had Bob's books in the garden. Remembering the Virgin Mary's hysterics Tom wondered what he had done to deserve the sole care of weeping females.

'Let's go and fetch your Daddy's books inside,' he said at last. 'We can put things right that much, anyway.'

It seemed a long wait for news. The worst of it was that Bob phoned.

'What are you doing there, Tom?' he asked, surprised. 'Changed your job to switchboard operator?'

'Just holding the fort. Linda's had to take Paul to hospital. Nothing to worry about. Susan and I are tidying books away to pass the time.'

It was not so easy to fob Bob off. His voice hardened to that of a practised interrogator. Tom found himself explaining the whole thing, making as light of it as he could. 'Paul was already beginning to recover consciousness,' he explained. 'But you have to take all possible precautions where a child is concerned. He'll be right as rain.'

Bob was in the middle of dealing with the murder enquiry and with the well known personality who was the representative of the regional TV programme *Almanac*. He had to put down the phone and be on view and in action, however sharp his private worry.

'What significance does the Saddlers' Play have, Mr Southwell?' asked the well groomed and glamorous Hermione. 'Why was it in that particular play that Bruce Exelby was stabbed?'

Bob, thinking of his son lying unconscious and what his wife's agony must have been as she stood beside him, found it was all he could do to answer. But his words came out efficiently and clearly all the same. 'As far as we know it has no significance . . .'

'This is an angle the police enquiries have taken into account?'

'We try to take all angles into account, Miss Hermione.'

She did not look convinced, but took her leave. At once Detective Inspector Smart came in, with sheets of computer printouts to discuss with Bob. Bob thought afterwards that it had been one of the worst half-hours of his life. Ringing in his head were thoughts of the strong manly son he was so proud of and the dainty daughter he cherished. Suppose Paul didn't come round . . . suppose . . . DI Smart thought his new boss very keen and super-efficient, and began to fear as well as to respect him.

As well as featuring an item on *Almanac* about the Saddlers'

Play, Hermione told a journalist friend of her theory about the significance of the play during which the murder was committed. The friend had gone into this in depth, producing a very long and academic article on the hidden meanings of each play and why, in the opinion of a psychologist, the murderer had chosen the one he did.

Thomas found his time of looking after Susan exhausting. He had managed to stop the worst of her crying by making her help him pick the books up from the grass and return them tidily to the glass-fronted cupboard, though he knew they must be all in the wrong order. But every few minutes she was overcome with remorse and began crying again, wanting to know if Paul would die and if it would be all her fault.

When the phone rang again he snatched it up.

'It's all right,' it was Linda's voice. 'He recovered perfectly and we're coming home. He's had four X-rays of his head and neck and they can find nothing wrong. They think it was pressure on the carotid something or other. I feel as if we'd been here hours. They think to be on the safe side he'd better wear a surgical collar for a few days, but there don't seem to be any after-effects.'

'Do talk to Susan and calm her down a bit,' Thomas begged. 'And Bob rang.'

'You didn't tell him?'

'I didn't have much choice. I had no right to keep it from him.'

'I'll ring him as well. Put Susan on. And thank you, Thomas, you've been a brick.'

'It'll cost you,' said Tom. 'Another orange cake will do nicely.'

Over the next few days, the results of the hundreds of interviews poured into the murder room, where two young police personnel, a man and a woman, sat keying them into the computer. At least, as Bob Southwell said, it seemed to eliminate some people from their enquiries. There were quite a lot of convincing alibis, people who corroborated one another, and whom there was no reason to doubt.

Bob had made light of his worry over Paul's accident, and the boy seemed none the worse. He went around rather proud of the thick white collar protecting his neck. It was really unnecessary, but seeing this precaution made everyone feel better except Susan, who could hardly look at Paul without wanting to cry. She decided to be a nurse instead of a policewoman. It was really Bob who came off worst in the end, for, just when his mind should have been entirely free to concentrate on his work, it kept reverting to his son, and to the ease with which he might have lost him for ever.

Bob had the extra manpower for just four days, before an emergency in another area caused them to be drawn off and left him with his usual team.

'You know most murders are detected in the first forty-eight hours or not at all,' said the ACC.

'Well, you've certainly given us all the help you can, sir. We've got masses of information to sort.'

'I have the feeling this one is going to remain unsolved, Bob. Just nothing to go on.'

But Bob was not willing to believe that.

A plan had been made of the abbey ruins, and one by one dots were placed where people were confirmed as being at the beginning of the Saddlers' Play. There were three overlays; one for the main stage, one for the upper stage, and one for the heights above.

So far only three people were marked on the upper levels. Poison Peters, who had been resting with his head sunk in his arms, recuperating from the crucifixion and preparing for his next entrance; Humphrey Hale the Archangel Gabriel, who had been trying to read a book in the peculiar lighting – half dusk and half stage-floods – with the aid of nips from his hip flask; and Thomas Churchyard, playing God, who had risen, surveyed the scene of shadowed grass, trees and tombstones, climbed to his throne in the sky and looked down at the brightly-lit stage below him.

On the second overlay there was nothing; the upper stage where the cross was had been empty at this period in the plays.

On the third overlay, there were six actors on the lower stage.

The ground plan showed a further eight just off-stage in Hell's Mouth, visible to the actors already on set. Also a number – an uncomfortably large number – in among the graves at the back of the set, in the props tent, or in progress from one place to another. They were all wanted for the finale; and, cool though the evenings became as night deepened, they preferred to be there, listening to the sounds from the plays, than to being anywhere else. In front there was the audience.

On the understage area there was so far only one person, Exelby himself.

Bob stood for a long time seriously studying the dots. He looked at the list at the side of persons whose whereabouts were not yet fixed. Only one name now remained on it – Sydney Absolom. Bob Southwell sighed.

'Of course,' Tom said to him later, 'People did drift round to the front and join the audience from time to time.'

'What sort of people?'

'Oh – props – costumes – make-up – backstage people.'

'And drifted away again, do you mean?'

'Yes.'

'I'm only interested in where they were for that few seconds. You mean someone might have been in the act of drifting back to their post, and taken in Bruce Exelby on the way?'

'I hadn't thought it through.'

'It's possible. It's worth getting the audience to remember if they can, anyone who joined them for a short time, whenever it was. And having a close look at the backstage people. I wonder if any of them escaped questioning? We would tend to assume that they stayed put at their posts, well away from the stage area.'

The press had had a field day after the press conference. Photographs appeared in the national dailies – glamorous photographs of Bruce Exelby, many of them from ten years earlier; photographs of the set and the cast, fortunately in good supply from the photo-call session. Poison came in for a lot of publicity and his agent rushed northwards, to act as a buffer between him and the ravening reporters. Poison refused to face the media. He said he felt that his role demanded all his energy, and outside performances he was husbanding his resources.

'Have you seen the article in the *Guardian*?' Bob Southwell asked his second-in-command. 'No? Well, it's worth looking at. *The Times* virtually ignores us, the tabloids shriek the most melodramatic and inaccurate version they can, but the *Guardian* bloke has been doing a bit of research. Did you know that Exelby had been in York before?'

'Didn't know anything about him.'

'He was here for two years at the beginning of his career.'

'Is it important?'

'It might be. Everything's important. Who did we put on to tracing his past? James Jester? Give him this article, will you?'

'The electrician chappie is the murderer, surely.'

'Sydney Absolom is a retired grocer with an interest in everything electrical and in local history. He's a mild, conventional man, rooted in his community.'

'So was Crippen,' retorted the other. 'Perhaps apart from the rooted in the community bit, sir. Well – the same kind of man, anyway.'

'He doesn't seem the one, to me.'

'Then there's the Youngest Shepherd – jealous as hell over the Virgin Mary – no one's quite sure whether he was with them just at the right time or whether he was in transit to another group, or snogging with Mary which is where we've put him, it seems the likeliest . . .'

'I would have agreed with you – that young man is both callow and cocky and I wish I could think that the world would teach him a lesson pretty soon, but somehow I don't think it is going to – until recently the Youngest Shepherd and the Virgin Mary were on the "whereabouts unconfirmed" list, but there were several well attested sightings of them in a remote corner of the graveyard. Whatever they were doing, they were not taking life.'

'Hmm. Then there's that Devil who mucked around with the cross. His parents say he was at home, upstairs doing his homework with the radio full on. There's the roof of an extension outside his bedroom and he could have got out of there and later climbed back again without their knowing.'

'I'm considering him, don't worry. All I'm saying is that sometimes murder comes from way back – from something everyone but the murderer has forgotten. Just give that article to James Jester. And find out from that wretched woman playing the Porteress how it was she knew Exelby so well – to hear her talk you'd think they were blood relations.'

''S all right now, yeah,' said Poison.

He was sitting with Thomas and with Humphrey Hale, the Youngest Shepherd, and the Virgin Mary, round a table in a dark corner in one of the pubs in Marygate. They were a week into the production, with two weeks still to go. 'I've got over the beginning a bit.'

Thomas thought, without saying so, that Poison was more relaxed today than he had ever seen him.

'You had a rough time,' said Humphrey Hale sympathetically.

'Yeah – being called a blasphemer and all that. Folks saying "He thinks he's good enough to play Christ."'

'They don't think what they're saying,' soothed Thomas.

'Too right they don't think about it,' said Poison, fishing the slice of lemon out of his Malvern water. 'If they'd felt like I did going for that audition they'd know. I was shit-scared when I was asked. Then as I went along I felt all this aggro – you know – what the hell are they after? Why me? Are they taking the mick? I nearly turned round and went back.'

'I felt a bit like that,' chipped in the Virgin Mary. 'I'd only gone with Louise – you know she's my young cousin, don't you – and the rest of her gang hoping I'd be an Angel, and they were only going because Louise's sweet on one of the Devils. Then they picked me out to read for Mary. I wanted to find a hole to crawl into. Then I felt honoured, you know, and chosen – it was terrific really, all mixed up with the nerves.' The mauve plastic disk suspended from one ear swung wildly as she shook her head at the memory.

'Go on,' said the Youngest Shepherd. 'You only wanted to be in it because of *me*.'

'It was you that wanted to be in it because of *me*,' protested Mary, giving him a push under the table where their knees and ankles were pressed close together.

'I sing of a maiden / That is makeles,' thought Tom, watching the flutter of Clare/Mary's plastic earring.

'You're both extremely good.' Humphrey Hale was pacific. 'The whole thing gets better each time we do it, in spite of everything.'

'I don't know about it getting better – it changes,' Thomas sounded thoughtful. 'Even the first time – when we were all in a state of shock about poor Exelby – it all just came together, as if we really were medieval people celebrating their view of their world and their God. Each performance since has been different, but there's always something special, isn't there – something which comes off as it never has before.'

'Tell me then,' said Humphrey to Poison, 'when they told you you'd got the role, there wasn't much time to prepare, was there, when you had that concert tour right before?'

'I couldn't have done the gigs if I'd been thinking and preparing for this.'

'No, I see that.'

'Well – when I saw how people felt about it . . . I was more shit-scared than ever . . . nervous of offending people's feelings by seeming to show disrespect . . . that's what everyone was expecting me to do, right?'

'Right,' said the Virgin Mary.

'Yeah,' said Thomas.

'I read the script for the first time my first day here and thought, "How the hell am I going to do justice to this?"'

'Having a Christian upbringing helps,' Humphrey meant to sound comfortable, comforting, understanding. He succeeded in sounding smug.

Poison's thin, bony fingers were fiddling compulsively with his glass, twirling it in jerks. The cubes of ice clattered sharply.

'Sure might have done if I'd had one.'

Everyone looked down at the table.

'Your family atheists then?' asked the Youngest Shepherd.

'If you'd asked me that at one time, I'd have said yeah, before I punched your teeth down your throat. I don't suppose they're anything. Never said anything about it to me.'

'Must have been worse being a pop star,' put in Clare. 'No

experience of acting.'

'I don't agree,' Thomas said heatedly. 'What experience could anyone have brought to the role of Christ? However many RADAs they'd been to and however often they'd played the West End?'

Clare tossed her head and the Youngest Shepherd glared at Thomas. They both had their A levels lined up for the following year and he and Clare had both decided to try for Cambridge, before this damn fool talk of RADA had been started by Bruce Exelby. He had his life mapped out, and she was in it, and he didn't want any more upsets thank you.

'So you started level with everyone else then,' Humphrey said, interested enough to press on with the conversation in the face of antagonism. 'There could be no experience that was helpful with the spiritual aspect of this role.'

'S'right.'

'It seemed to me,' Thomas remarked, 'that you approached the role with a kind of reverent simplicity.'

'What else could I do? You just start in.'

'But if you don't mind me saying so, a kind of spirituality has entered your playing of it,' Humphrey was ignoring the young lovers, who were getting increasingly entwined beside him. His urbane sophisticated voice for once sounded deeply sincere, moved, even.

'Well, that's terrif.' Poison buried his nose in his glass and slurped. The dark lashes dropped over his golden-brown eyes. An air of embarrassed modesty and gratitude passed across him like the shadow of a cloud over a hillside.

Clare disentangled herself from the Youngest Shepherd. 'I've the same problems with my role,' she said perkily. 'But acting is a process of self-awareness, don't you think?'

'Awareness. Do we always have to put the emphasis on self?'

Thomas was irritated by her all of a sudden. Was it just that she was so sure of herself – so confident with the unseeing, selfish confidence of pampered youth? Whatever else he might be and do, Tom was sure Poison's childhood had been anything but pampered. When they were acting, Clare's youth, beauty and innocence brought a lovely radiance to her part; but Poison brought something else again – a growing majesty, spirituality and touching dignity; an authority and compassion, which the previous day had drawn tears from some of the audience. He had grown in stature immensely during the week's performances, startling enough though the first day's rendering had been.

'Don't know about you lot,' Poison rose, 'but I've got to get back. We've a play to put on, yeah?'

He walked out, stiff-legged. The detective who was trying to protect him got up hastily from another table and quietly followed him out.

Clare shoved the rest of her cheese and onion sandwich into her mouth and the Youngest Shepherd drained his beer. Humphrey, as always elegantly suited and immaculate, dusted a crumb from his long trouser leg. Thomas bundled himself to his feet, massively ignoring crumbs, which would not be seen anyway on his slightly hairy tweeds.

Poison was still standing on the edge of the pavement, though he was not looking round or in any obvious way waiting for them. They came up to him and surrounded him. A group united in common purpose, they walked across the road and back towards the Museum Gardens. A summer shimmer hung over everything. The river at the bottom of the road threw flashes of light into the air. A train thundered nearby on its way to Scarborough. The trees of the gardens leaned over the white limestone wall.

A girl in a white dress, looking Scandinavian with her blonde hair, singled out Thomas. 'Pliz tell me the way to ze Railway Museum?' she said. The group stopped. Thomas explained. 'And where is ze Museum Gardens?'

'Just here,' Thomas pointed and smiled. The others were growing impatient. The girl thanked Thomas with a dazzling smile and followed them into the Gardens.

They walked in past St Mary's Lodge where Bruce Exelby had had his flat, without glancing up.

The following day was the inquest.

10

Make room! Be alive! And let me gang
What makes here all this madding throng?
Hie you all hence! High might you hang,
  Right with a rope.

The Lokk Smyths' Play

The room was packed.

Reporters had come up from London, having discovered from their experience of the press conferences that they could be in York in two hours by train and that once there it was only ten minutes' walk to practically anywhere in the town centre. They had looked around them at the crowds of tourists, the warm sun on the ancient city walls, the tree canopy over the dappled Museum Gardens and along the river, and found that there was life north of Watford, and that it was good.

Outside the court room was a maze of little spaces and passages, with several small rooms used by magistrates, each furnished with a carafe of water, a glass, and a blotter. The reporters were jamming the court room itself. Most of the cast had come along to the court, as had production staff, wardrobe, property, and front-of-house staff. Apart from those actually being called as witnesses most of them had not been able to get into the hearing. The result was that, together with a few members of the public, they were all milling about, passing on bits of information either correct or erroneous.

It was easy enough for anyone to come in off the street, walk up the stairs, and lose themselves in that maze of small spaces . . .

The coroner took his place and the police began to produce their series of witnesses to the events of that night.

God was first – and recounted once again the events he had gone over so often.

Isaiah was next. He had been on stage, in Limbo, ready to join the conversation between Adam and Eve. Symeon, John the Baptist, and Moyses were waiting to walk forward and join in, each in turn. When Exelby climbed on to the stage Isaiah was about to speak. Exelby had stumbled past him, looking pale. Yes, the director had seemed to say something to him. It had sounded like a question, but he had only caught the last word of it. That was 'Father?' Yes, he was sure of it. Then the director had stumbled on and collapsed on to the stage. From then on he knew nothing more than anyone else.

After taking the evidence of Adam, Eve, Symeon, John the Baptist, and Moyses, the Coroner turned to Belzebub, Satan, and the little Devils.

They had been waiting in a group at Hell's Mouth, made like the mouth of a beast, with flames and dry-ice smoke. Where they were standing was rather dark. They burst out of it one by one a little later in the play, ran up the slope on to the stage, and there had a conversation with one another before the dramatic appearance of Jesus in the arch above. Only one of the Devils had been asked to appear at the inquest, to speak for all of them. He was the first on stage so he had been at the front of the group.

No, the play had not progressed far enough for him to come on stage. He had seen the director stumble across and fall, nothing else. After the police took charge they told the Devils they could go home, so they went back to the St Olave's parish room to change. Well, not straight away. Yes, they had stopped to talk to the Angels, who were waiting ready for the Mercers' Play, Doomsday. No, they hadn't realized the director was dead. To be honest they thought he was drunk and that it was all a bit amusing.

Then Sergeant Diamond gave his evidence, and next the coroner called the pathologist.

The death had been from a wound from a narrow-bladed knife of stiletto pattern, six to seven inches long. Yes, the knife produced by the police could have dealt the wound. The instrument had entered the chest wall at the level of the nipple on the left side and very slightly to the rear. It had passed through the left lung and made small punctures in both the left branch of the pulmonary artery and the aorta. These had caused bleeding into the left lung (from the pulmonary artery) and into the pleural cavity (from the aorta). This aortal bleeding had caused the collapse of the lung.

The victim would have experienced little pain at first. After fifteen to twenty seconds the loss of blood would lead to a rapid fall in the blood pressure, with shock, pallor, dizziness. About forty seconds after the blow he would begin to experience pain from the build-up of pressure in his left chest.

'My picture of what happened,' said the pathologist, 'is that he realized he had been attacked and might need help, that he climbed the ladder as the quickest way of reaching other people. By the time he stumbled past Isaiah he was dizzy and his breathing was becoming laboured; blood would be rising in his throat, making it difficult for him to speak more than a word or two. By the time he reached the position where he fell down he would be fainting. The sergeant tells us the pulse was rapid and weak.'

'Is it not surprising,' said the coroner, 'that death did not take place within a few seconds?'

'The punctures in the arteries were small. I would say very small. Made virtually with the tip of a narrow knife. Had they been larger wounds death would have taken place in seconds.'

'Is it not surprising,' asked the Coroner, 'that the wound did not bleed externally?'

'When a fine blade is withdrawn the puncture closes up. There was only a small stain of blood on the left side of the deceased's shirt, about an inch across.'

'If medical care had been available more quickly could Mr Exelby's life have been saved?'

'Impossible. He could not have survived a punctured aorta. Even in an intensive care unit. The blood loss is so rapid. Death from anoxia to the brain takes place within a couple of minutes.'

'Just over a couple of minutes in this case. Does that alter your diagnosis?'

'Not at all. The police tell me they have reconstructed his movements and timed them at two and a quarter minutes to two and a half. Bleeding in this case would be relatively slow. I stress, *relatively*.'

'Your postmortem revealed the wound?'

'It did. Also that the left side of the chest was full of clotted blood, with the lung completely collapsed.'

'Thank you.'

The police produced the weapon. It was six and a half inches long. It bore a trace of the victim's blood, which had been matched to his blood group. No fingerprints. No threads of fabric. Nothing else to aid them. The whole weapon had an antique and theatrical look. The presence of the initials B.E. on the handle was not mentioned.

It was in the press of people that Jane Bugg fainted.

'Give her some air,' commanded Sally Vause. 'Go and get some water to throw over her, somebody – there's some on the magistrates' tables. Be quick. Move back, everyone.' Clare, Susan Brown the assistant director, Velvet Smith the assistant wardrobe mistress, and Betty, Sandra, and Mrs Moore, members of MRS and of the Crowd, all went in search of water.

No one could move back. It was as much as they could do to make room for the six water-seekers to squeeze out.

'She isn't coming to at all. Anyone got a newspaper to fan her with? Lord, she is a lump. I can hardly shift her. Put some chairs together and let's lie her on those. She'll be better than on the floor where folks will tread on her. Why is there never a first-aider about when you want one?'

Several of the cast, not caring whether or not Jane was trampled on but rallying to a certain extent to one of their number, heaved and strained to get her on to a line of hard upright chairs, where she lay uncomfortably, beginning to open her eyes and look around her. Clare brought a carafe of water. Sally administered it, by splashing it over Jane's face. Mrs Moore came with a bucketful, marked 'Fire'.

'Push her head in it,' someone suggestly helpfully.

Velvet arrived a long time later with another carafe, and,

finding it unwanted, drank some of the contents herself.

It was in the maze of small rooms and odd corridors, outside the courtroom, in a little empty room, that Tom, trying to find his way to a window for a breath of air, came across Sydney Absolom.

'You don't do yourself any good hanging about, Syd,' he said sternly.

'You don't understand, Tom.' Absolom grabbed Thomas by the lapel and hung on to him. 'I know who did it. I've been putting it all together in my head.'

Tom gently released Syd's grip on his jacket. It wasn't so much that he minded, but the jacket was linen, the only formal thing he could bear wearing on such a day as this, and it creased badly – even under a thin dry hand like Absolom's. Then he looked around. It seemed they were alone.

'You must go to the police. They'll find out quickly enough if you're right. Tell them what and who you suspect.'

'But they suspect *me*, Tom! How can I talk to them? They don't believe a word I say.'

'How can you be so sure that you know? What information have you got that the police haven't?'

'I've got better than information. I've got the knowledge of this city and its people over sixty-five years. The other day the way someone was talking got me thinking, and I've remembered a lot of things – hidden things, Tom, that nearly everyone has forgotten, and when I say everyone, hardly anyone knew in the first place. Those few that did have an inkling have forgotten. I'd forgotten. But now I've remembered, and it's as plain as a pikestaff who's done it. You can't beat local knowledge. You think you know the city, Tom, but you've been here no time at all. You haven't shared in its miseries and triumphs, pleasures and pains like I have.'

'This is serious, Syd. You must go to the police.'

'Let me tell *you*. I don't want to go to the police. Let me tell you and you can decide then what the best action is for us to take.'

'You should have gone before, as soon as it came to you. Go now.'

'Don't start telling me what to do.'

'Syd, don't be touchy. I'm only thinking of what's best. You may be right and you may be wrong but the police are the people to deal with it. Don't worry. Don't bother your head about it. Keep calm. Stay away from the plays. Be sensible, Syd. Go and have a cup of tea, then tell the police all about it. Now *go*, there's a good chap.'

Tom paused, remembering his recurrent feeling of an evil undercurrent, hatred, assassination, death, murder. It all still seemed incredible. But he had just been inside that hot courtroom, testifying; Exelby had gone for ever; the evil was still at large. 'I don't see what good it will do to tell me.'

'It matters, Tom. To both of us.'

'You mean . . . you mean it's someone we know . . . it's practically bound to be, really, isn't it? Bound to be someone in the plays, or connected with them, I should think.'

'Someone you see every day at present, Tom.'

Tom shivered.

'Again, old chap, it's bound to be, isn't it? I expect I'm cowardly – I don't want to know who you suspect. You are probably wrong. That would bias me against that person and it wouldn't be fair. I'd rather the police sorted it out. You're playing with fire.'

Thomas didn't want to say that he had, nagging away at him, the feeling that he himself knew something significant – which when it once came floating up into his consciousness, would unlock the riddle – he thought. He didn't want muddling up by anyone else's half-baked theories. He wanted to keep his mind clear for that thought to surface. It was hot and he was feeling fed up with his old friend Absolom.

'Go home, Syd,' he said again. 'I must get out of here for a breath of air. I think I'll go for a beer. Come if you want to.'

Without waiting to see if his friend was following him, Tom shouldered his way through the neighbouring room, which was packed, and through the tight knot of people at the head of the stairs. He clattered down the flight and out into the street, where a wave of dry hot air hit him. It might not be possible to fry an egg on the pavement but he thought it would have poached one lightly, if anyone had wanted to try.

Rapidly he turned left and found his way down the nearest street to the river. Once near the water there was cooler air, and he walked along to the pub at the end of King's Staith for a beer. Expecting Sydney to be following along behind him, in spite of his own brusqueness, he was surprised not to find him there when he looked round. Tom shrugged his shoulders and went in for his pint, then brought it out into the open and sat at one of the tables near the river. The place might not be perfect – it was overcrowded, and noisy with a hundred kids. But no one in sight was connected with the mystery plays, there was not a single policeman, and he didn't know a soul.

'Hello there,' said Linda. She took the seat opposite him, and Susan and Paul sat one on either side. 'What's a nice neighbour like you doing in a place like this?'

'I could ask you that.' He grinned with an effort. 'Can I treat you to anything?'

'We've got ours, thanks.' The barman had followed her out with a tray.

'I see you've got rid of that collar, Paul,' Thomas said to the boy.

'Didn't need that thing.'

'He's quite all right now. Probably we were a little over-cautious. I thought you were testifying today, Thomas?' said Linda, with a 'now-mind-your-manners' look at Paul.

'I've done my bit. Came out for a breath of air and a change. It will be over soon, I should think. I'll go back in five minutes and see what's happening.'

The police worked out afterwards that it must have been in the time of excitement just before the verdict was announced that Sydney Absolom fell from one of the second floor windows of the building, and split his skull on the pavement below.

People in Clifford Street on a hot June day in a festival week are mostly tourists on their way to and from the Castle Museum. Hardly any of them seemed to have even noticed the building housing the magistrates' courts on the other side of the street.

Some of them had noticed the sudden downward movement, as Sydney fell, out of the corner of their eyes, and turned their heads quickly enough to see the full impact of his head with the pavement. One of these people was immediately sick into the gutter.

The policeman on duty in the street, strolling up and down in his shirtsleeves, heard a shout and turned, running the few yards to where the man had smacked down. It was due to the policeman's presence of mind that the witnesses stayed where they were and didn't go rushing off to have a nice cup of tea and try to forget all about it. He yelled to them across the street, and those who thought they had seen what happened stayed where they were until another policeman arrived and took brief statements and their names and addresses.

The fact of seeing Absolom fall caused their imagination to conjure up earlier pictures of him standing at the window then leaning out, dangerously.

'Old men are daft, leaning out like that in the sun. Must have turned dizzy,' one of them said to his neighbour in the crowd. He was a burly, beer-bellied man with a small boy clinging on to his hand. The small boy was holding an ice-cream cornet in his free hand and licking it.

'I saw someone push 'im,' the small boy announced to all and sundry, not very clearly because of two missing front teeth and a mouthful of ice-cream. The roar of the traffic helped to drown his words, which made their way up to his father's ears as an irritating buzz.

'Shut up, Zen, or I'll thump yer,' said his father.

'I saw someone.'

'You didn't see nuthin'. Eat your ice-cream and shut up.'

A policeman approached. 'Did you see the accident, sir?'

'No,' said the man with the beer-belly.

'Thank you, sir. We won't detain you, then.'

The man and his child walked off in the direction of the Castle Museum.

'I saw someone push 'im, Dad.'

'You behave yourself or I'll tell your mam of you.'

The only witness to the crime was dragged off, protesting. To make it worse the ice-cream fell off the top of his cornet and landed irretrievably in the dust.

At the end of the hearing came the verdict.

Murder by person or persons unknown.

The door from the courtroom opened with difficulty, what with the people outside who wanted to get in and the people from inside who wanted to get out. The word spread, round the gradually opening door. The hearing was over, pending further inquiries. Murder by person or persons unknown. The words spread through the knots and groups of people in that maze of anterooms and corridors, among people who had not yet heard of the further death, outside.

There were no other witnesses. No one had noticed Sydney's presence at the court except Thomas Churchyard, and just when he might have been useful in keeping his friend company and preventing the fall, he must have been drinking beer, sitting in the sun on King's Staith and talking to Linda and the children, and assuming that Syd had gone home.

Everyone still in the magistrates' court building was detained there until they had given their names and addresses and had been questioned briefly by the police, which made them all hot and cross. No one had seen anything; it was obviously an accident; they were all very sorry about it and a little sickened by the details, but what good did it do keeping them here like this?

At last they were released, and by then time was very short before the evening performance. The cast and the backstage and front-of-house teams had to eat, rest, wash and change, and somehow arrive in time at the Museum Gardens.

'I suppose it was an accident,' said Bob Southwell thoughtfully.

'I've been in contact by phone with his doctor and he says the old chap had all kinds of things wrong with him and a fit of dizziness wouldn't surprise him at all, though he hadn't actually complained of it.'

'Good thinking. Thanks. Fix up the inquest, will you, Smart? We'll need a coroner's officer.'

'It will be very straightforward, sir. I could fit it in.'

'Right. Notify his relatives, and all that. I want a copy for myself of the list of people present in the magistrates' court and in the whole building at the time.'

Detective Inspector Smart nodded and went out of the

incident post.

When Exelby was murdered Southwell had never had time to do any real detective work himself – the administration of his suddenly increased staff had fully occupied him. Now that the dust had settled he found his mind dwelling on the case.

It was the following afternoon that James Jester, who had asked to see the detective chief inspector, came into the murder room at the police station.

'How's the research going on, then?' asked Bob.

'Steadily, sir. Just found something interesting.'

The young detective was holding a piece of paper.

'Yes? What?'

Jester handed the paper over, saying as he did so, 'In an old theatrical periodical, sir.'

Bob looked at the photocopied photograph and its surrounding letterpress silently. It showed a young – a very young – Bruce Exelby, in Elizabethan costume. His profile was turned to the camera in the approved manner, and the paragraph underneath was headed, 'Promising young actor's debut as Hamlet.'

'I may be unusually stupid,' Bob said at last, 'but the significance of this escapes me.'

'But don't you see, sir? At his belt!'

Bob saw at once. The stiletto-type dagger thrust casually through the actor's belt was identical to the one which had more recently been thrust into his body. Holding the photocopy at an angle and peering at it closely, Bob thought he could pick out the slight gleam of the silver inlaid dots on the haft which spelt B.E. Certainly the whole elaborate shape was very familiar. James Jester shyly produced a magnifying glass and Bob looked through it. It didn't really help much but he did feel even more convinced that the tiny gleam was from the inlaid letters. He retuned the magnifying glass with an amused look.

'Do you always carry one of those?'

'Stamps are my hobby, sir.'

'I think you're right, Jester. That looks like our dagger. Which proves it was his own. When was this picture taken? I seem to remember that he wasn't an actor for long.'

'He wasn't, sir. It was taken here in York, at the Theatre Royal. He acted Hamlet while he was in the Rep – the resident repertory company.'

'So he had it when he was in York twenty years ago, but his secretary assures us she had never seen it among his possessions at his flat. Suggestive, eh?'

'Yes, sir.'

'It might be as well to check all the later photographs you can before we jump to any conclusions.'

'Yes, sir.'

'Like, if he left the dagger behind in York – it was here all the time – and he came back to join it . . .'

'I'll do some more checking, sir.'

'I've remembered something,' Bob Southwell said. 'It might be anything or nothing. My next-door neighbour once told me that in his pet society (he's a great one for these voluntary organizations) only three members had been born in York. He's on holiday and will probably be in his garden at this time of day. Just have a trip out and ask him to tell you how long each member of his society have lived in the city – to the best of his knowledge. The three who were born here might be of no significance if some of the others have been here for over twenty years . . . assuming Exelby's former residence in the city is of any relevance . . . Just take down what Mr Churchyard can tell you from memory, we can check out more detail later.'

Jester came back within the hour with a list. The three who had been born in York were Sydney Absolom, Sally Vause, and Velvet Smith. Thomas himself had lived in the place eleven years; George Grindal he believed about five; Mr and Mrs Moore had retired to the city a couple of years before; the newsletter editor was married to an official in a bank who moved their executive staff regularly, and so had probably only been resident a few years; the university student was a bird of passage; and Betty and Sandra Tweddle had come from the Malton area when they opened their flower shop, which event Tom Churchyard remembered, so that must be less than eleven years ago.

'Right, Jester.' Bob Southwell looked pleased, and thoughtful. 'Now fetch me that list of people present in the magistrates' courts building yesterday.'

All of MRS had been, at one time or another – for Tom had left before the name-taking – except George Grindal, who had more urgent matters to attend to in the shape of saving someone from their urge to end it all.

There was really no need for Thomas to be involved any further in the affairs of his old friend Sydney Absolom. He was depressed and blaming himself enough without any addition to his mood. But the next day a telephone call involved him – a call from Sydney's sister, Mrs Baines, who had travelled from Wilberfoss where she was living out a retired widowhood. She wanted his help in clearing things up, and Thomas could not refuse her.

Once more he arrived at the neat little house in the inner suburbs, and walked up the concrete path from the gate, the concrete marked out to imitate crazy paving. Mrs Baines opened the door to him. She was wearing a hat, and in the next few days when Thomas saw quite a lot of her he never saw her without one, so he could not have said whether the puffs of white hair which were so characteristic of Sydney were also sported by his sister. A few grey-white curls around the edge of the hat made him think they might be, and he looked rather wistfully at them.

She shook his hand firmly, and insisted that he drank a cup of tea. At least that had not changed. It was just as thick and dark as in Sydney's time, and served in the same cup with rampant roses. It seemed strange that the cup should still be there when its owner was lying in the mortuary.

'He never had dizzy spells,' was Mrs Baines's opening fusillade.

'He didn't mention them to me, no.'

'Because he didn't have them. I know what he had.' Mrs Baines embarked on a recital of Sydney's physical ailments, concluding: 'But he didn't have dizzy spells. Marvellous on heights our Sydney was. I've seen him walking on our roof many a time. He used to like getting up there when father checked it over once a year. He always cleaned out the gutters and did the bedroom windows. Loved being up a ladder, our

Sydney did.'

'That doesn't mean he would never have dizzy spells, Mrs Baines. He was getting older, you know.'

'He were two years younger than me.' Mrs Baines was very positive in her tones whatever she said. 'And look at me! I'm all right!'

'But you've just been telling me how many things he had wrong with him.'

'Yes. But nothing *serious*.'

'What are you trying to tell me?'

'That someone pushed our Sydney. He would never have fallen out of a window on his own. But if he'd been looking out, someone could have pushed him.'

'We all get old, Mrs Baines, and old people on very hot days do tend to get dizzy.' Tom had the feeling that he was going round and round in this argument just as he had on occasions with Sydney.

'He was murdered,' Mrs Baines stated impressively.

'You had better tell the police what you think.' This was familiar too. Tom shuddered.

The inquest was held quickly on Sydney Absolom. The medical evidence was clear on the cause of death. There seemed to be no basis for a verdict of anything except accidental death. There was very little evidence of any kind. The hearing was soon over, the funeral soon arranged, and Thomas stood at the graveside of his old friend.

But it was not only in Mrs Baines's mind that a doubt remained. Thomas, talking to Bob Southwell in their back gardens, mentioned not only her conviction that her brother was particularly good with heights, but also his own conversation with the dead man, in which he had tried to persuade Sydney to tell his suspicions to the police.

'It was all very vague,' he explained. 'I'm afraid I wouldn't listen.'

'We all regret something, after a death,' Bob said with sympathy. 'Errors of commission and omission. The only positive thing we can say is that it makes it look very doubtful that he was the murderer of Exelby.'

'I've always been sure that he was not.'

'And off the record I agree with you. Apart from anything else, Smart went to see Mrs Baines – it is part of the coroner's officer's duties to contact the relatives and do all he can. She told him that Absolom thought he had discovered the murderer – so you were not the only one he confided in.'

'Yes, I know he had told Mrs Baines.'

'You didn't say so to me.'

'Well . . . I didn't think it significant . . .'

'It is very significant, Tom. The fact that you were not the only person he confided in is very significant.'

'You would expect him to tell his sister, if he saw her – they didn't meet that often, but they were close.'

'And she would have known the people he knew, twenty years ago or longer.'

'Yes, she would have.'

'So he may have told her more than he told you, in a crowded building when you were being rather impatient with him.'

'Yes.'

'Absolom, because of his long residence in the city, had special knowledge, and he had used it to make a deduction. That means that the person he believed to be the murderer had most likely also lived here twenty years ago, when Exelby was a young actor at the Theatre Royal. It was something that Absolom remembered from those days which, he felt, gave a motive.'

'I see that; but I did tell you he thought he knew who did it.'

'But as well as telling you, he also told his sister. He may have told a hundred people. He may have told the person he suspected, perhaps in order to get them to own up.'

'He said it was someone I knew well, and saw every day.'

'Who do you see every day?'

'I see Jane Bugg for one, and often wish I didn't. She's a clerical assistant in our office.'

'Jane Bugg told me that Syd committed suicide by leaping from the window, because he really had murdered Exelby.'

'Always helpful, our Jane,' said Tom bitterly. 'She's like that at work. Always sure she knows best, and she's usually wrong. I don't know why they keep her, except that she puts on a good front and bluffs her way out of everything.'

'So you think she did the murder?'

'No, I don't. It doesn't seem in character, somehow.'

'She did faint – wouldn't that be a sign of guilt?'

'Are you postulating that Syd was murdered also? She couldn't have done that while she was fainting.'

'Just before?'

'I don't know,' said Tom wearily.

But Bob knew that Jane had been in a small room with several other people just before she fainted, and if anyone was responsible for Sydney's fall it was unlikely to be her, and the reason for her faint was more probably heat than guilt. It was fairly certain that she had been unconscious when the accident occurred. He moved on to another tack.

'Is there anyone else you see every day?'

'Now I come to think of it, Sydney said "every day at present". That's different to normal days.'

'Mrs Baines told Smart that Syd had known one of MRS long before, that the person was embezzling money from the firm they both worked for, and that he let her – yes, it was a her – know that he knew, to stop the proceedings; but he didn't give her away to the bosses, because she did stop doing it.'

'That could only be . . .'

'Velvet Smith?'

'Either Velvet or Sally Vause. But Velvet is our treasurer and absolutely spot on, and Sally was head of an important office dealing with money all the time.'

'Smart put the same point to Mrs Baines.'

'And?'

'Apparently she said, "Other times, other manners."'

'A bit of embezzling in youth is hardly the same as murder in middle age . . .'

'True. It probably is of no significance whatever, only telling us that we should have approached Mr Absolom from quite a different angle, and quizzed him in a friendly way over his memories.'

'Is that what you've been doing to me? "Quizzing in a friendly way"? I feel as if I'd been put through the third degree,'

Tom said ruefully, looking over the shrubs.

'I'm sorry, Tom. But I am a policeman, as well as a friend, and you want me to find the murderer as much as I want to find him. And stop worrying about your friend Sydney – you aren't responsible for his death.'

'Did Mrs Baines tell you who exactly it was Syd suspected?'

'No. In the end he turned coy and didn't name the name.'

Tom went off comforted, but Bob found himself brooding on the conversation. Was Absolom's death a second murder? As the days went by he became gradually convinced – by something within himself rather than by evidence – that it was.

11

Now see I sign of solace clear,
A glorious gleam to make us glad.
The Saddlers' Play

Once more Thomas Churchyard and Poison Peters were sitting on the grass in the Museum Gardens. Tom had been to Miller's Yard on Gillygate, and bought filled rolls of wholemeal bread and a few other things for their lunch. Tourists and peacocks strolled about the Gardens.

In their protective coloration of casual clothes (including Poison's 'Erik Blood-Axe Rules OK' T-shirt) they went unnoticed. Poison swigged quite openly from his bottle of Malvern water. Talking quietly, they felt as secure from scrutiny as they would have done in Poison's caravan, and the dappled grass, the rose beds, the varied trees, the general atmosphere of holiday, relaxed them much more than being shut in a small space.

They could even forget the presence of Poison's protective detective, who sat at a little distance with his eyes scanning the crowd for assassins. The only ones he saw were the peacocks, who now and then attacked those tourists who were eating buns, with the idea of getting their share.

One of them came up to Poison, who threw him some scraps of bread. The peacock gobbled them down then shrieked for more, opening its unlovely mouth and emitting a noise like a furious tom cat.

'They won't even spread their tails for it,' commented Tom. 'Food just for shouting. Maybe that's what I get, food for shouting.'

'I think they're rather ugly birds, dragging their worn-out tattered feathers behind them, and look at those scaly legs.'

For a while they watched the peacock silently, until it stalked off.

'Tell me,' said Tom, 'What made the difference? You told us once about how terrified you were at the idea of playing the part. What made the difference? How did you come to realize how to tackle the job?' As he asked he felt uncomfortably that these were the very kind of questions the media people asked Poison and how sick he must be of it.

'It was funny.' Poison was gazing upward into the blue air over the trees. 'I was in a fix. We had a party to celebrate my casting, did I tell you that? Bruce Exelby threw it. Showbiz people, you know, and press, all the shower. Champers, caviare, congrats, the works. Finished at two in the morning. I was legless by then.'

'On spring water?'

'Potent stuff, yeah? Anyway they sent for the hire car I use in London and carried me down and put me into it. I always have the same driver. He knows my habits. They keep him on contract for me and I pay through the nose. He drove me home, I changed, then he took me down by the river. I wanted a walk, think things out, see?'

'Still worried?'

'Yeah. So I went on one of my night prowls you don't approve of.'

'In present circumstances it's dangerous,' said Tom under his breath.

'Usually it helps. But this time I was just as miserable and shit-scared as ever. Then I dropped into this caff, after I'd walked for a bit, early morning; and I mean caff – a right dump – down and outs go there – and sat down at the same table as this old geezer. Dog collar. Ugly sort of bloke. Looked as if someone had squashed his face in. Not the sort you gaze at with joy, know what I mean?'

'What was he doing in a place like that? Dog collar? Was he one of the down and outs?'

'No, not him. You do get vicars in them sort of places sometimes.'

'Go on.'

'We started talking. D'ya know, he had a beautiful voice. It was strange, coming out of that ugly mug. The sort of voice that doesn't operate in single notes. The sounds are more like chords. Know what I mean?'

'I think so. I'm not as musical as you of course.'

'Huh!' Poison was diverted from his topic for a minute. 'What about all that egg-head stuff on disc, then?'

'That's for listening. What I mean is – that's my hobby or one of them – music's your craft. The ways of looking at sounds are different.'

'Yep.' In a second, Poison had comprehended, agreed, filed away all the subtleties of the remark, and returned to the previous discussion. 'Like I said, we started talking. Somehow I found myself telling him about it – asking his advice if you like, though not in as many words. I told him all sorts of things, come to think of it, that I've never told anybody else. He was that kind of man. If I hadn't met him then I might have chucked the whole thing in.'

'He helped?'

'Right. Just read Luke, he said. Read the Gospel of St Luke and try to feel it, to imagine it, to take it into yourself. That's all the preparation you need do now. Leave the rest until the time comes. Then when he got up to go he stood and looked down at me a minute, then put his hand on my sleeve, friendly-like. "God bless the work," he said. Boy, he was an ugly bastard.'

'Sounds like George.' Thomas was thoughtful.

'You what?'

'It sounds to me as though you met one of our Canons from the Minster, George Grindal. You've described him very well.'

'You mean you know him? He lives here in York?'

'I think he's your man. He lives here, but he's away a lot, various work he does. He's away now. He's a member of my society, MRS. It's typical of him to be in a sleazy caff for down-and-outs in the middle of the night in London. And he was present when we were discussing your appointment, and never said a word – and he knew you, and how you felt, all the time.'

'I thought all you MRS people were in the plays? I've never

seen him.'

'No. He is involved, we're all involved. But what he does is advise on the text if they need someone who knows the original and can read it. Exelby wanted a few changes and George helped sort them out so that they were authentic. But that was before you arrived.'

'I'd like to meet him again,' said Poison. 'To tell him it all worked out. And to thank him. I said to myself over and over, "Just read Luke."'

'Oh, it worked out all right. It certainly worked out.'

Worked out it had.

The plays were the biggest success ever (though on one level or another, someone said that of every production). As the time went by and the cast stood on the edge of their third week, the success took them and the whole city, lifting them high above normal life and expectations, producing one of those idyllic periods of seven days when life is transcended. And this, even though the shadow of the unsolved murder still hung over them.

'PETERS TRIUMPHANT' screamed the headlines and the placards propped up next to the street-corner newspaper sellers, by the Guildhall, in Exhibition Square, and in Rougier Street.

'EXELBY'S CASTING VINDICATED.'

'POP STAR WINS THROUGH.'

'MYSTERIES BREAK ALL RECORDS.'

The week began – as good weeks do – with Sunday, and the Sunday papers, and Thomas Churchyard read the *Sunday Times* over breakfast. He always had bacon and egg for breakfast on Sunday. When he got to the play reviews he was startled to see large photographs of the mystery-play production all over the top of the page. It was obvious that their fame had spread country-wide. Whether or not because the attention of the national press had been caught by the murder Thomas did not wait to find out. He wanted to share this with someone, and while he had been cooking he had noticed that Linda was out in the back garden next door. Remembering that he had shaved, reassured that he was tidy enough to be seen, he dashed out of his back door.

'Look at this!' he exclaimed. 'Fame at last!'

Linda was planting out annuals from a polystyrene punnet. The children had erected a tent on the lawn (which under their onslaught was rapidly turning into grass) and were both inside it, visible only as an occasional limb projecting under the canvas. Linda rocked back on her heels and looked up at Thomas.

'That looks good,' she said. 'Read it to me.'

As Thomas read Linda got to her feet and stood listening, trowel in hand.

'"The quality of the York mystery plays is superb this year,"' he read. '"The evocative and surpassingly beautiful set, part modern reconstruction and part ancient ruins, and the quality of the open-air setting in perfect weather, would certainly help any production; but this production needs no help. It would function in a village hall. Bruce Exelby's swan song – as it unfortunately has turned out to be – is a crown worthy of his previous career. The costumes"' – and here he had a long paragraph to read, discussing the design of the costumes, which Tom found tedious, but Linda looked interested – '"and now, first in importance, we turn to the acting. Against all predictions Mr Poison Peters has proved that he is an actor of outstanding quality. His rendering of the role of Christ, one of the most difficult in the theatre, is such as we are not likely to see again for a long while. Anyone privileged to be present at one of the performances is likely to remember it for the rest of their lives as an outstanding theatrical and religious event. As the only professional actor in a cast of amateurs he might have been badly supported, but such is not the case. Thomas Churchyard as God" . . . er . . . humph . . . yes . . .' Thomas stopped reading abruptly.

'Go on,' said Linda.

'There's a bit here might interest you,' said Thomas. 'Clare has got a good write-up for her Virgin Mary.'

'Never mind the Virgin Mary,' said Linda. 'What does it say about God?'

Thomas pretended he hadn't heard her. '"The sheep gave a remarkable air of verisimilitude,"' he read. '"Contrary to reports that their discipline had caused trouble to the production, their behaviour was impeccable."'

'Blow the sheep,' said Linda, and, catching him unawares, twitched the newspaper from his hand, and moved further away quickly so that he couldn't easily snatch it back again.

'It's an honour to get a write-up in the *Sunday Times*. Now let's see. "Thomas Churchyard as God was also outstanding. He is a fine and impressive actor and no professional could have brought out more dignity and presence. The human foibles so touchingly represented by the Crowd contrasted splendidly with the acting of Christ and God, who were well supported by Michael, Gabriel, and the cast of Angels." Well! There's glory for you!'

'Quite,' said Tom. 'I hadn't actually read that bit or I don't think I would have rushed out here with it like that.' He felt embarrassed, exhilarated and excited.

Linda smiled mischievously at him. 'Go on. Enjoy your fame. Why not? We all get knocked enough in this world. Let's have a sherry to celebrate. Stay there. Don't you dare go away.'

Tom rather liked being ordered about by Linda. He stood obediently where he was while she darted off. The sun shone, and the children in the green cool of the tent were playing a card game. Their high voices raised in dispute enhanced rather than spoiled the special atmosphere of a sleepy sunny Sunday morning. He decided that it was pleasant to have this young family next door to him. Not that they were that young. He thought Bob Southwell was about his own age, but Linda was a few years younger. He couldn't imagine Mrs Spartan who used to live there commanding him to stay still while she brought sherry out into the garden.

'By the way, where's Bob?' he asked, as Linda reappeared with a tray, bottle, and glasses.

'Working and worrying as usual over your wretched murder,' she said. 'I was hoping he might arrive to join us. Perhaps he will. He went in to the murder room early and promised to be back in an hour. It's two hours already so he's about due. I brought three glasses.'

'Mum! Can we have some? Mum!'

'No you jolly well can't. You can go and get the lemonade

bottle and some biscuits and picnic in the tent.'

'Oh great!' There was a stampede from the tent followed before Linda had finished pouring sherry by a boisterous return and a dive into the low ark of canvas. 'Can we eat our dinner in here as well, Mum? Mum!'

'Perhaps,' answered Linda. 'Look, Tom, will you do something for me?'

'Yes, what?'

'Bob's getting all worked up over this case. Can you do anything to help him unwind?'

Tom did not know what to say at first. 'Isn't he used to things like this investigation?' he asked tentatively.

'Yes, of course he is up to a point. But – it might surprise you to know that policemen are people – they can still find murder investigation upsetting – when one human being hates another enough to inflict this kind of violence. And apart from anything like that, Bob's just been promoted – new area – changed houses – he can't move for media people – there are plenty of strains in the situation.'

'I can see there must be . . . journalists have been after me too, asking questions and wanting interviews . . . I wonder what I can do . . . Does he fish? I've got a good collection of records of classical music – any good? Does he play chess?'

'Oh, Tom. Don't you ever do just ordinary things? Like going to the pub?'

'Of course I do. This is very excellent sherry, Mrs Southwell. Your good health.'

'Here's Bob. Darling, come and join us. We're celebrating a super write-up of the plays in the *Sunday Times*.'

As Bob came towards them with his light stride Tom found himself agreeing with Linda that there was an appearance of strain around the eyes and mouth. But Bob kept all weariness out of his voice as he reached for a glass.

'How civilized! Sherry in the garden on Sunday morning.'

'Let's be even more civilized,' Tom answered, 'and go for a pint before Sunday lunch. You haven't made the acquaintance of our local yet.'

'You mean I'll have to come and haul you out when the Yorkshire puddings are ready?' cried Linda in mock horror.

'Do you think anything could make me late for my Yorkshires?' teased Bob, but Linda knew only too well that a good many things could come between him and proper nourishment at regular times, so she only pouted in reply, grateful that Tom had responded so quickly to her request.

Bob and Tom went to the Greyhound. In the dark cluttered interior no one turned round to look at them or jumped at them with a tape recorder. There was an atmosphere of busy relaxation. They leaned on the bar. 'Two pints of bitter please,' Tom said. 'OK for you, Bob? It's real ale.'

'Great.'

The landlady greeted Thomas as an old friend. He joked with her over the bar counter. After the beer was served they moved over to a small table where they could catch a glimpse of the green outside and a couple of tethered horses.

'You a regular here?' asked Bob, visibly relaxing.

'He's been all sorts,' put in the landlady, who had followed them over so that she could wipe a table which had just been left empty. 'Helped me behind the bar – chucked people out –'

'You haven't, have you, Thomas?'

'If Tom chucks someone out they stay chucked out,' confirmed the landlady.

Tom buried his nose modestly in his beer.

'She makes the best onion sandwiches in York,' he confided to Bob. 'A friend of mine – he's often in here, too, but I can't see him today – is fond of onion sandwiches and has got her trained.'

'I don't think I'll go in for them; Linda might object.'

'Oh well, this pal of mine isn't married.'

'About this murder –' said Bob.

'Don't you ever think of anything else?'

'Not until it's sorted out, no. Some extra Crowd costumes were made, weren't they? Task force used them. Couldn't anyone who wanted to murder Exelby have got hold of one and mingled with the Crowd?'

'Yes, I suppose that's possible. But the wardrobe people would have noticed, surely.'

'There are a lot in the cast . . .'

'It's possible. Now, let's have a game of dominoes.'

Bob agreed, thinking to himself that the Crowd did not wear gloves, and if the chance of a Devil's costume had come up, that would have been even better. Then he really did relax, and played dominoes.

One of the strange things about his role, Poison found, was that fans, when they managed to get through to him, did not want to sleep with him but to ask his advice on their problems.

He seemed to be expected to know everything and be able to help them on everything. It was humbling. The look in the eyes which beseeched help did not make him puffed up but brought home to him how little he or anyone could mitigate human suffering. Those people whose small problems filled their sky seemed just as much in need of help as those whose problems were so immense that only God himself could have made any difference to them.

Poison did his best. It was a small best, for he had no power to alleviate anyone's troubles. But to himself, as so often before in the last few weeks, he said, 'Read Luke,' and something out of his reading might come into his head and give some comfort to the other person.

Tom had told him that George Grindal had returned to York and was looking forward to meeting Poison again; and they went together to the Minster.

As they entered at the west door a young Scandinavian tourist came rushing up to them. She was blonde, dressed in a pure pale-yellow dress drawn in round her narrow waist, and Tom braced himself to tell her the way to somewhere. But for once she took no notice of him. Her blue eyes were all for Poison Peters.

'Will you write on ze book?' she asked, and, without drawing breath, went on, 'And the such a funny name, is it fish?'

'Is what fish?' asked Peters.

'Zis Poisson. Is the French for fish, yes?'

'Poisson is the French for fish. But my name's Poison, gedit?' he answered, but she obviously did not understand him. He sighed elaborately and took the paper she held out, which was a programme for the mystery plays. Thomas handed him a ballpoint.

'I've written "Poisson" now, with her saying it,' Peters remarked to Tom. But he turned back to the paper, lifted the pen and on the programme's white border drew the outline of a simple fish, with a sudden concentration, as though it was a symbolic act.

Returning the programme to the girl, he gave her a radiant smile; catching up with Tom, he looked as though freed from a burden; his back was straight and tall; he moved smoothly as though swimming. Tom looked at him out of the corner of his eye, but Poison was rapt and silent. The vast sacred cool creaminess of the long airy vaulted space absorbed them. The presence of many other visitors did not disturb them. They moved slowly up the length of the nave aisle.

As they came level with the choir Julia Bransby came rapidly across their path, looking bright and alive.

'What are you doing here?' asked Tom.

'Oh, hello, Tom, congrats on the success! I've just been having a look at an altar frontal. They wanted to discuss conservation. Thank goodness people are getting more conscious all the time about the need to preserve things. There's the most smashing stuff here. My favourite's relatively modern though – an embroidered hanging from the Versailles of Marie Antoinette. Incongruous, perhaps, but so lovely. Found like so many of the beautiful textiles in the Minster by Dean Milner White. This altar frontal I've just been to see isn't nearly so glamorous. But interesting, of course.'

She paused for breath and smiled at Peters.

'We've come to see George Grindal.'

'But I've just left him! He's gone to the vestment room I think.'

They went back with her to the low arched door, where she parted from them, Thomas following her with his eyes.

'Does she always talk ten to the dozen like that?'

'Not usually. She's rather quiet as a rule, but something's excited her.'

'Fancy her, do you?' asked Poison.

'I do rather.'

Thomas knocked lightly, then opened the door. George had his back to them, and was putting an ancient rose-red

Portuguese cope, half as old as time, away in the wide drawers.

'Look – I'll leave you,' Tom said suddenly. 'You don't need me. I'll dash after Julia and ask her if she's time to have a coffee with me in the Dean Court. You'll know where to find us for the next half hour. If not, I'll see you tonight.'

'Right.'

Poison went in alone to meet George Grindal again. The detective stood outside the closed door. The two voices in conversation were very faintly audible through its thickness. The man could distinguish no words until half an hour later when the door swung open again.

'There's someone who would like to meet you,' George said as the two of them emerged from the vestment room. 'Are you free for the next hour?'

'Yes.' Poison looked serene. For George he was willing to do a great deal.

'I'll just ring and see if it's convenient. If so we'll go now.'

A few minutes later they were picked up (complete with detective) from the west door of the Minster by a long black limousine.

'So pleased to have the chance to meet you, Mr Peters,' said a tall elderly man coming forward to take his hands. 'In our Christian work it is not often we have the assistance of someone like yourself. Your influence with young people – I may say, with people of all ages, in your role as Christ – is now doing great good.'

For once Poison was speechless. The dwelling had an overwhelming aura of graciousness and sanctity. He had never been in a palace before, even a relatively small one, nor spoken with one of the heads of the Church. He longed to look round the room – gaining a better picture to remember of vast oil paintings and polished dark wood, and windows looking out on to lawns and flowers. But he could not break away from the force-field generated by the archbishop.

'Thank you, your Grace,' he said at last.

'Do sit,' the tall man released Poison's hands and sat down himself in a comfortable chair. Poison sat near him, George Grindal taking a place nearer the door.

'Tell me, Mr Peters, what has given you this spiritual power which you are exerting so well?'

'I feel as if I'm only trying – not achieving –'

'You are achieving. Yes indeed. Have you always been a believer?'

'Well, no, your Grace. My mother was, but she died when I was six. My stepmother doesn't believe in anything much, nor does my dad. But –' and the pop star was emboldened by the other's close attention. If he was ever to speak of these things, it must be now. 'I think the worship of God is basic in mankind. If you hear about the earliest men, they revered something and worshipped something. It is necessary for men to do that. It's in us, somehow. There's another thing. Even the worst of men knows right from wrong. If they chose to do wrong they know they are doing it. This difference of right from wrong isn't taught to us necessarily, it's in us. 'I don't go to church. But I can't help feeling that there's something somewhere that's good, and that I want to look up to, and noticing that however bad people are, they know that they're being bad – they know there's a difference. Yeah?'

'Yes. It's taken some of our best thinkers a lifetime to see that as clearly as you have done, Mr Peters.'

They talked for some time. At last, venturing on remonstrance: 'Then tell me . . . why do you do wrong things in your life? It does worry me that you, thinking as you do, should ever set a bad example to our young people.'

'Well it's what they expect, see – it's not really like that, your Grace.'

'You don't take drugs?'

'No way.'

'But don't you think it harms all these young women – groupies, don't you call them – to encourage them to be promiscuous – ?'

Poison went dull red. 'I'm not that keen on them, actually . . .'

The archbishop hastily dropped the subject. He showed Poison round the gardens, drowsy in the summer sun and yet alive with the sound of bees, and they parted at the end of half an hour the best of friends.

'Do you know,' the archbishop said thoughtfully some time

afterwards, when talking this encounter over with George Grindal, 'I am tempted to believe that boy is, as they used to say, ha-ha, er, a' – here he looked embarrassed – 'well, a "clene maiden"? It may seem incredible to you but it was borne in upon me that he was altogether a remarkably pure young man . . . quite impossible of course, don't you think?'

It was an hour after leaving the Minster that the long limousine deposited Poison, George and detective back in the centre of York.

It had been quite involuntary that first time, when in giving his autograph, Poison had written Poisson and added the fish; having done it once, he did it again; and then one day, instead of a signature, he drew only the sign of the fish.

He looked at it in surprise and thought that he ought to try to get more sleep. Every night he had been keeping vigil, praying for help and guidance, and by degrees the vigils had been getting longer. If his body was starting to play tricks on him he had better try for eight hours. He was sustained by adrenalin, upheld by ecstasy.

Bob Southwell had returned to the statements which had been collected so painstakingly by his briefly enlarged team in the few heady days straight after the murder of Bruce Exelby. He had had them all printed out by the computer; the printouts had all extraneous matter cut away so that they read simply and clearly. He thought he had hit on a discrepancy.

'Jester,' he shouted.

'Yes, sir?'

'Do you remember how many Devils there are in the mystery plays?'

'There doesn't seem to be a set number, sir, but this time they appointed seven, only one got the sack if you recall, sir, and so there are six.'

'I certainly thought so. I have six dots for them, here on my plan on the stage – waiting outside the mouth of Hell in the darkness before bursting through the dry-ice smoke and up the slope.'

'That's right, sir.'

'But here we have a statement – from one of the Task Force, no less – that when Sergeant Diamond thought Exelby had been taken ill, and told him to "get that lot out of here," he sent the seven little Devils home. I've looked through all the other statements. Lots of them mention the Devils, but it is only David Longman who gives a number.'

'In the heat of the moment would he pause to count?'

'Counting is an odd thing, Jester. Do you ever play a game which involves dice?'

'I have done, sir.'

'And when you shake out the dice, do you count every spot?'

'No.'

'No – because they form a pattern, and you notice the pattern. You don't mistake three dots for four dots, even without counting.'

'But the devils wouldn't be standing in regular rows, or anything like that.'

'True, and it was growing dark. But people instinctively recognize a pattern, and, I think, if things are odd or even. Get a message out to that member of Task Force and ask him to come in, now, this minute.'

Bob busied himself with some sheets of scrap paper and one or two felt-tip pens.

'They looked just like they always had,' the man from Task Force said later. 'Just a group of lads in red and black, with those helmets on. Really weird. You could almost believe they were devils.'

'Perhaps one of them was.'

The policeman looked at his superior with a doubtful expression. Was he going round the twist? Did he mean that a real devil from Hell was among the group in costume?

'Many people in the outer office, Longman?' asked Southwell conversationally.

'About six, sir.'

'How many steps on your staircase at home?'

'Twelve.' By now Longman was convinced his superior was going crackers.

'How many miles on the clock in your car?'

'8,645.'

'New, is it?'

'New last year, sir.'

Southwell took the sheets of paper he had been doodling on. 'Now look at this, Longman. I'm going to show you these quickly and I want you to tell me how many dots there are without actually going, "one, two, three". Don't pause for thought.'

They were all irregular groups of dots. Like a teacher with flash-cards and a small child, Bob showed them to Dave Longman. The man from Task Force smartly spoke out numbers, quickly and without thinking, as he had been instructed. He had to be quick to keep pace as Bob Southwell rapidly changed the sheets.

'Well, Jester?' asked Bob when he had been through them all twice.

Jester had been ticking off the numbers as Longman spoke them. Southwell had written a list in advance, in the order in which he intended to show them.

'They are all right, sir, bar one.'

The one Dave had got wrong was a group of twelve; with all the lesser numbers he had been spot on.

'Now you try, Jester. Longman, write down what he says.'

James Jester was not as accurate as David Longman, but got the majority right.

Bob Southwell drew in a long breath. 'Dave, you're one of those people who can't help noticing the numbers of things in your environment. Lads, let's celebrate. Fetch your coffee in here and we'll add something medicinal. Just this once. I think we've cracked it.'

'You mean . . .'

'There was a Devil too many.'

Walking quietly along the narrow lane called Almery, Southwell came in sight of the low one-storeyed St Olave's parish room, scene of many a romp, what with bring-and-buys and charity book sales and Sunday School Christmas parties and auctions by reputable auction houses, and the wardrobe of the mystery plays.

He found a place where the wall not too far away took a step backward into somebody's garden, making a little dog-leg of itself, and drew in there, resting unobtrusively. For a while he watched the random comings and goings of cast and wardrobe and property staff. At last the activity died down. Then he left his convenient niche and went up to the wooden door and pushed it open.

'Anybody at home?' he called genially.

'Hello, detective chief inspector,' said Sally Vause.

'Mind if I come in?'

'Please do. Although I'm just off. All packed up for the night.'

Sally was alone, and looking tired.

'Just thought I'd have a look round.'

The costumes hung neatly around the space. Bob drifted about, touching one here and there, with no apparent purpose. At last he came to the row of seven Devils' costumes, each with its helmet mask in front of it on the floor.

'Do they each have their own?' he asked.

'Yes. We started by making seven basic costumes, but when the boys actually came, we altered them a little to fit.'

'Bit small for me!'

Sally thought the detective chief inspector very witty.

'My son Paul would love to try one on,' he said. 'I don't suppose I could borrow one, just overnight?'

'Well . . .'

'There's one you aren't using, isn't there? The boy who played that silly practical joke?'

'Oh, that's the biggest.' Sally pointed to it, at the end of the row. 'We had to let that out a bit instead of taking it in. Yes, you could borrow that one overnight with pleasure, as long as I get it back first thing tomorrow. It might be wanted as a spare if one of the others gets torn or something. I don't know how we've managed so far without any accidents of that kind.'

'What time will you be here?'

'I open up at ten. Silly really, I needn't until tea-time. But it's amazing how often there's a job. And I'm retired, so why not be here in case I'm needed?'

'Why not, indeed.'

Southwell had, as she was talking, lifted up first one and then another of the arms of the Devil costumes. In the dim light she could not be sure what he was doing – he seemed to be almost stroking the fabric of the hand coverings. It was surprising that a man should take such an interest – women often handled the costumes for the sheer pleasure of touching them, but men usually pretended to be above such things.

'This is the spare, then?' He had lifted down the one she had indicated and was rolling it up carefully.

Sally would rather have rolled it up herself, but she did not protest.

'Goodnight – and many thanks. You will have made one little boy very happy.'

But Bob Southwell did not drive off towards home. His car was parked conveniently near the parish room, on the car park which stretched over the place where once several little streets of terrace houses had been home to hundreds of people. His wheels were on tarmac over what had been Bean Street.

Instead he started up his engine and, the Devil costume on the front seat beside him, drove back to the police station and to the murder room.

Once inside he unrolled the costume, and once again ran his fingers expertly over the glove ends to the arms. The tips of the fabric gloves were decorated by talons carefully made by props, but he ignored those. His sensitive finger ends were exploring the smooth dark red fabric between the base of the thumb and the first knuckle area of the first finger, of the right-hand glove. Even in the strong unwavering light of his own work room there was nothing to see, but fingertips are incredibly sensitive, and his had sensed a thickening and stiffening of the fabric in one tiny area.

The station was quiet; it was by now late at night. Most of his own team had gone home.

'It will have to wait until morning,' thought Bob. 'No, dammit. I'm not willing to wait.'

To a determined police officer there are places where, with a little coaxing, even at midnight someone will look under a microscope at a little scrap of fabric – half an inch by one eighth – where something is stiff which ought to be soft.

'Blood,' said the pathologist, who had just got home from a party when the phone rang, and who had welcomed a little more excitement before bed. They were in his laboratory at the hospital.

'Whose blood?'

'Can't tell you that. Only the blood group. Hang on . . . a rare group,' he said at last. 'Very unusual indeed. A2B Rhesus Negative NN.'

Bob had not realized until then that he was holding his breath.

He clenched his hand round an imaginary dagger, and struck out in front of him, then in dumb show indicated the area of his hand between the base of the thumb and the first joint of the index finger.

'Yes.'

'Not much doubt of it?'

'I should say none. This is a blood group for only one in fifty thousand people, and it is Bruce Exelby's blood group.'

12

When I was sick and sorriest,
You came not nigh, for I was poor.
The Mercers' Play

It was not until the plays were in their third and most triumphant week that, on waking at two in the morning, Thomas Churchyard remembered the small but significant point which had struck him as incongruous as he stood looking down from the steps of Heaven on to the alert, stirring cast of the mystery plays waiting among the graves of St Olave's.

He had been dreaming about the scene. His first thought on waking was that he really mustn't let the affair get on top of him. Dreaming about it was just ridiculous. The vision was still in his mind, more real than the bedside lamp, the darkness of the summer night outside the curtains, the book which lay ready for wakefulness on his bedside table.

Once he had remembered, the solution was obvious, but it took him a while to work it out. And then sorrow washed over him in a great wave. He could see How. He could see Who. He could not see Why.

The obvious thing to do at two in the morning was to go back to sleep, and first thing in the morning to walk next door and tell Bob Southwell all about it. And that was precisely what he felt he could not do.

Sleep, of course, turned out to be impossible. All that happened when he lay down and drew the light covers up to his chin was that the thing made itself more and more clear to him as it revolved round and round unceasingly in his head.

As for going to Bob Southwell . . . that was what he ought to do. Ought, perhaps, to ring him now, waking him from whatever slumbers he was having, with an apparently unsolvable murder on his hands and extra staff no longer at his disposal. That was what he had told Sydney Absolom to do, go to the police. That was what Sydney Absolom had never had time to do. Before he got there he had tipped out of a window . . . or been pushed . . . that suddenly looked even more likely . . . 'And I can't go either', thought Tom.

'Even if I put myself in danger by not picking up the phone now, this minute, and ringing Bob?

'Even if . . .

'Why? That's what I can't understand.

'If I go to Bob Southwell and tell him what I now believe I put another human being on the spot without giving them any opportunity to consider; perhaps to repent, perhaps to give themselves up to the police because they realize that what they've done is wrong, morally wrong, that they have imperilled their mortal soul by taking the life of another – perhaps two other – human beings.

'If I go to Bob Southwell I am playing God with someone else's life.

'Am I entitled to do that, to take that power, as if they were a rag doll with no self-determination? Who am I, to go to Bob and point the finger, to say, this person is guilty, arrest them, try them for murder?

'Have I no loyalty towards this person? Yes, I have.

'What happens if I tell them themselves, what I suspect? Discuss it with them? Try to make them see that their only course is to go to the police themselves . . . or to take their own life . . . would they do that? Would that not compound the sin, rather than cleanse it? Would that be any better than a long prison sentence or a lifetime in a mental institution?

'Confession is good for the soul,' thought Thomas.

He was sometimes emotional and religious in the night like this. During the day he was a mightily efficient engineer with a degree in electronics and a section of an important department to run. But in the still watches of the night primeval Thomas emerged, doubting, fearful, reliant on the ideas first instilled in him at his mother's knee, influenced by the thoughts and principles of the medieval period he loved so much. He could think now only in large, grand ideas, of responsibility and restitution, of immortal souls, of sin and death.

He lay there and struggled with the inside of his brain as the rest of the summer night passed away and the early dawn came, and still returned to the one dominating thought; I cannot play God with another's life.

The Thomas who at last thought it was late enough to get up and begin the day was a more straightforward man. This was a Thomas who did not beat about the bush, and if he had a task to do went ahead and did it.

He did go to see Bob Southwell, as soon as he thought it reasonable. He went to the back door and Linda opened it. He could see through the utility room and into the kitchen where the children were eating boiled eggs.

'Oh, I'm sorry, Tom,' said Linda. 'Bob's already left. He's living and sleeping this case at the moment. If he isn't down there he's sitting thinking about it. He couldn't settle this morning. Some new idea seems to have hit him late last night – he wasn't in until the early hours – so he's gone down to fiddle with that computer.'

'I think I know who did it. I'll go to see him,' said Tom. He was intending to, of course. But he could not get away from the idea that to do so was unfairly to influence another's destiny. Who was Thomas Churchyard to give a person up to justice? What right had he to point the finger? And was he sure? He had gone to see Bob and Bob was not there. Was this chance, or an omen? a pointer? an augury? Was this a signpost to what he ought to do?

He looked vague and withdrawn as he nodded at Linda and walked away. She closed the door again faintly puzzled and a little worried.

It was a lovely June morning and although heat was promised for later, at present it was warm enough to be pleasant and not too hot. Thomas decided to walk. Twenty minutes or so to think about what he was doing would not be a bad thing.

He walked from Clifton along Bootham. He turned left into Gillygate – called after St Giles – and passed its varied buildings. It was recovering from planning blight, and all the little interesting projects which had found a cheap home there would gradually give way, he supposed, to the rampant materialism and money-making bustle of the other shopping streets.

At present it was still an interesting place, narrow-pavemented, leading to a large car park where coaches disembarked their passengers who then walked in long bunches into the tourist areas of the city. Thomas had to step off the kerb, risking his life under the wheels of the fuming lorries, or squeeze himself into doorways three separate times to avoid such phalanxes of determined tourists.

Portland Street is a short road leading to the playing fields of Bootham School. Having trees and grass at the end of the cul-de-sac and a few small trees and shrubs in the minute front gardens saves it from being totally arid. On that June morning parked cars and motorbikes, the sound of a transistor, raucous purple paint on one tall flat-fronted house and posters in the window of another gave the place a slightly rakish modern air, superimposed on its basically Edwardian style.

Tom knocked on a door and after a few seconds it was answered by Velvet Smith, neatly and tidily dressed as always, and nondescript as ever. She looked surprised to see him.

'There was something I wanted to ask you about,' he said awkwardly.

'Well, come in, Thomas. Is it too early for coffee?'

Her rather blank dark eyes did not show surprise, although he had never been to her house before, and although it was barely nine o'clock in the morning. 'Is something wrong about the plays?'

'No, it's not that . . . A coffee would be welcome.'

'Come in.'

He stood in the entrance hall. A flight of steps carpeted in a vigorously patterned Axminster rose straight in front of him. To the right were two doors, obviously to front and back rooms. A passage running alongside the stairs led to the kitchen door. The floor of the entrance and passage was of encaustic tiles in an elaborate pattern. The woodwork was all massive and moulded, grained and varnished dark brown.

Tom was a little taken aback. Although some things were

modern, the feel of the house was of a previous generation. It had a strong presence; it was borne in upon him that it was like a lodging house; it had that impersonal, predatory feel.

Velvet, after some apparent hesitation about which room to use, led him into the dining room, at the back. Sure enough, there were three tables – two of them gatelegs, folded and standing against the wall – and about a dozen chairs. On the walls were photographs of actors and actresses, many of them signed.

She watched him as his glance swept the room, and smiled sardonically.

'I didn't realize,' he said.

'You didn't realize?'

'Presumably,' said Tom with an effort, 'these are people you knew?'

'Yes. My parents ran a lodging hosue, mainly for theatricals. This area was noted for it. Have you been in York so long and didn't know that? The whole cast of a visiting company could be accommodated along here somewhere, and a good few of the regular repertory company as well.'

'It must have been interesting.'

'It was darned hard work. Theatrical landladies are often joked about. It wasn't much of a joke being one. Interesting, yes, compared to other kinds of lodging houses. But with lots of disadvantages.'

Tom felt acutely disinclined for coffee, but he had accepted the offer, and so he sat down when Velvet indicated a chair. The window looked on to a narrow back yard, which had been made brighter by containers planted with flowers. He thought he could smell old odours of boiled cabbage, soot, and furniture polish.

Velvet brought a tray with two cups. She poured hot milk and coffee from the matching jugs.

Tom had been thinking a good many things. Such as: perhaps a longing for the stage had imbued Mrs Smith, and made her choose theatrical lodgers; such as: he had never noticed before the practised competence with which Velvet served drinks. Most women he knew served drinks competently so he had not realized that she had a different air altogether when doing it –

the air of someone who has done such things in a service capacity; such as: her involvement with acting and the stage had continued with MRS and with the mystery plays. Tom did not know how to approach the subject which had brought him.

'Did you know Bruce Exelby when he was a young actor, then?' he said at last.

She seemed as if she was never going to answer. A strange expression crossed the face he thought he knew well. 'Yes, I did know him,' she said at last.

He sipped his coffee and looked at her. Velvet was plain; there was no getting away from it. She was also inexpressive. Her thoughts did not show themselves on her face. It was a pale, pudgy face, neither fat nor thin, but lacking in tone. Her dull darkish hair was short and close to her head. Her eyes were dark, about the same rather nondescript colour as her hair. Her nose was so ordinary that it defied him to find any other adjective to describe it.

'I never remember you talking to him on the set, Velvet,' he said at last, trying to keep his voice normal. 'I don't remember that at all.'

'He never showed me a flicker of recognition.'

'Did he ever lodge with you?'

'Oh yes. All the time. It was a second home to him. He lived with us all the time he was in York – two years.'

'He must have forgotten.' Tom did not like to say 'Perhaps you've changed,' but she seemed to pick up his thought.

'Oh! I was always unobtrusive and insignificant.'

'I wouldn't say that, Velvet.'

'You would, because I am. I'm not insulted. Believe me, it can be very useful.'

Useful, in doing things without being noticed. Tom sipped again at his coffee. It was hot. Even in his elevated and agonized state he appreciated good coffee. And hers had come out of the same jug, and she had drunk quite a lot of it.

'Being small can be useful too, I expect,' he said. 'Small enough to wear a costume made for a large child.'

She looked at him steadily.

'I wonder what you are getting at, Tom. I wonder why you came here.'

'I have guessed something about the murder.'

'Why didn't you go straight to the police with your guesses? Why come to me?'

'It may sound silly. Because if I had accused – a certain somebody – I would have been manipulating another person's life without their being aware of it. If I go to the police it will be with your knowledge.'

'*My* knowledge? . . .' She sat very straight, and looked intently at him. 'And what will you tell them, Tom?'

Tom felt very cold. This was what he had come to do, yet now he felt afraid – not afraid of Velvet, but afraid of making himself look a fool. Such a basic, human fear. How many good and right actions have not been carried out because someone was afraid of looking a fool? Afraid that his night-time deductions were wrong. Afraid of coming out with the accusation, 'You killed.'

'I will tell them,' he said at last, 'that I believe that late on the night of the last dress rehearsal, while Sally Vause came round to see a bit of the production, or maybe just to chat to friends, as she did most evenings, you put on the costume of the little Devil who'd been thrown out of the production for that bit of criminal stupidity with the willow branch – that you ran along in the growing darkness to the Museum Gardens – that you went in under the stage and found Exelby for a moment alone – that you stabbed him – that after stabbing him you ran and joined the other Devils in the smoke and flames of Hell's Mouth – and when they were sent away after Exelby died, you ran ahead of them – probably even on that night they stopped to make wailing noises to scare the Angels, or just to speak to them, to tell them what had happened – and that you had taken off the costume by the time they and Sally Vause returned to St Olave's parish room.'

Velvet was very still. It seemed as if inwardly she was concentrating all her forces into a still centre. Her voice, when it came, was still, stone still, and deadly as that of a snake.

'All very clever,' she said. 'And what led you to this brilliant conclusion?'

'I saw you,' said Tom miserably. She became even tenser and more still. 'I saw you run from near the Etty monument, across the grass, and round the end of the wall to join the other Devils.'

'Where were you?'

'On the scaffolding.'

'And you saw a Devil run across and thought it was me dressed as a Devil? What made you think that? For the rest is all taradiddle and supposition, Tom.'

'A woman doesn't run like a boy,' said Tom miserably. 'Her hips rotate more, even if she is small and slim. It was not a boy's run. It was the run of a woman. It was your run, Velvet. I haven't seen you run but the more I think of it the more convinced I am.'

'So you think I am a murderess.'

'I don't want to think that. You and I are friends, as well as colleagues in MRS . . . I thought all the members of MRS were my friends. But . . . the Etty monument is only a few yards from the place under the stage where Exelby was stabbed. The time was right. You had every opportunity for doing what I have described – you are in charge of the costumes when Sally is not there. No one can be recognized once they have those frightful devil costumes and masks on.'

'Don't give me any friendship stuff, Thomas. You're on the point of – as you think – shopping me to the police with this story. I can't understand why you didn't do just that, instead of coming to me first. I might have a stiletto handy. You've never noticed me in MRS, so don't pretend you have. I was just useful, as I have been all my life.'

'Very useful,' responded Tom, in hearty but assumed approbation.

'Why did you come here accusing me?'

'I thought you could only have done it out of some sort of misery. It didn't seem understandable. I wanted to give you the chance to go to the police yourself. It would be better.'

'Oh yes,' her eyes seemed to bore straight through him. 'Oh yes. I did it,' said Velvet slowly. 'You have guessed correctly, dear Thomas. I did it.'

He could hardly speak. At last: 'But why?'

'For revenge. One will do a great deal for revenge.'

'What harm had Exelby done you?'

'Oh, that!' Her eyelids fell over those normally inexpressive dark eyes. 'It seems long ago now. It was a burning grievance for so many years, urgent. And now the wrong is avenged it is receding. I could start a new life now. I could start to really live for the first time. But for you and your friendly neighbourhood policeman, that Southwell, Thomas. But for you.'

'Was it you he wronged?' Tom felt odd using such a Victorian-sounding phrase. He was thinking the conventional thing – that Bruce had made her fall in love with him and then jilted her; perhaps there had even been a child.

'Oh no!' Her lids went up and she looked at him intently now. 'I was as insignificant to him as I am to you. He didn't trifle with my affections, if that's what you're thinking. Oh no.'

Tom just sat and looked at her. He had never envisaged any scene like this. She was playing with the spoon in her coffee cup, turning it over and over with a small metallic irritating sound.

'Oh no, I don't matter.'

'Of course you matter! . . .' Tom heard himself again being over-hearty.

'He ruined my parents' lives, Tom. It is as simple as that. I revenged them. It is over now.'

'Tell me?'

'All big talk, he was, about the productions he was going to do which would make such a lot of profit. He carried my mother away on a tide of talk, and persuaded my father to give him a large loan. Then he went off and got this great production off the ground, inspired, produced and directed by himself.'

'I remember he made his name with the musical, *Pink Nocturne*. It did tremendously well.'

'It was a great success. Not so great on the balance sheet, because the production costs were so colossal. It broke even, made a small profit. It was Bruce Exelby's springboard into the big time, and he never looked back.'

'And your father got his loan back? With interest I hope.'

'My father got nothing. Bruce had promised us the earth – we were to be at the first night of the show – he would let us have the money back within six months – he would never forget our kindness – we would always be his closest friends and our home his second home. When at last my father asked for the money – he didn't ask for a long time – Bruce told him that he had understood the money to be a gift, not a loan. He never returned a penny.'

'But couldn't your father . . .'

'Have sued him? There was nothing in writing. That money was every penny he had, Tom. All his savings after a lifetime working for the railway. He had been planning to retire the next year. His health was poor and he was tired. It's no picnic working full time and then in the evening helping your wife to run a boarding house.'

'Legal action?'

'He took legal advice and there was nothing he could do. He'd even raised a mortgage on this house to help Bruce. He'd been taken for everything he'd got by a con man, who was now leading the glittering life. Bruce just kept on repeating that it had been a gift, and it was his word against my father's.'

'What happened?'

'Well, I still live here, you see, so you know we pulled through – I did, at least. Instead of retiring my father worked until the week he died. I had to watch him getting greyer and greyer, thinner and thinner. I left school at fifteen and worked, daytime, evenings, weekends. Mother ran this place on a shoestring. That didn't make her the most popular landlady in the street. We scrimped, ourselves. We didn't know what it was to have new clothes or go on holiday. Day in, day out we struggled to keep our heads above water. Week by week we counted every penny. Dad and I walked to work. Mother gave up using the laundry and did all the washing herself at home. We sold everything we could from the house – everything the guests didn't see went.'

'Why didn't you ask him for the money back?'

'Oh, we did. Many and many a time, until we got a solicitor's letter threatening action if we didn't stop bothering the great director. He didn't know us, didn't want to know us, didn't know what we were talking about, owed us nothing. I remember the words. They are burned into my brain as they were into my father's. I took Bruce Exelby's life to avenge my father. As I drove the knife home, I said, "That's for my father."'

'How could you, Velvet?'

'Quite easily, believe me. It corrodes you inside, a long hatred. I felt nothing but satisfaction as I used his own knife on him.'

'His own knife?'

'Yes. He gave it to us as a keepsake after the York production of Hamlet. It has hung for many years on the wall of my bedroom. I have looked at it every night before going to sleep, and every morning on waking. It was about the only thing we didn't sell. I would never have sold it. It was a focus for my hatred. Now it has gone, all there is is a mark on the wallpaper, a mark the shape of the dagger.'

Thomas suddenly realized he was still holding the cup from which he had drunk coffee. His fingers had clenched so tightly round the fragile handle that when he settled the cup carefully into the depression on the saucer, and relaxed his hold, the handle fell in pieces.

He had in the last few minutes felt profoundly sorry for her and her family, and that he too might have longed to take revenge. Then his feelings changed. Theatrical landladies were not soft touches as a rule. Surely her father should have had more sense than to make an unsecured loan. Had they brought on this loss themselves, by coming forward like lambs eager to be fleeced? Surely the lawyers could have done something – surely Exelby could have been shamed into paying the debt . . .

'I can't stay here, Velvet. I must get out into the air.'

'You're not going, Thomas. You came here and brought this up, you can't go just like that. Sit still and listen. The past counts, you see, Thomas,' she said. 'You've always got your eyes fixed either on the present with your work or on the medieval past. You forget that there are other pasts, nearer than the Middle Ages. They matter too. You've come to live in York and think it very pretty and imagine yourself back in time. There's a lot of living you ignore by doing that.'

He stood up. Somehow it did not occur to him at that moment that he himself was in any personal danger. He looked down at her.

'Didn't you realize that revenge is in other hands than yours?

"Vengeance is mine, said the Lord."'

'Revenge was mine and it was sweet. Sit down, Thomas. Here's another cup. We'll both drink some more coffee. We have things to talk about.'

Thomas realized that he was shaking. It must be useless arguing with a self-confessed murderess. But he had to try to make her see, and to gain time to think. His voice became forceful.

'I can't seem to bring it home to you, Velvet. The really terrible thing is "looking at evil and calling it good, looking at good and calling it evil". You committed an evil act – how else can one describe murder? – and you call it good. It was not good. You were not right to take vengeance. If what Exelby did was terrible, what you did was more terrible – to yourself.'

'It was the greatest satisfaction of my life. I thrust in his own knife, up to the hilt. I avenged.'

'At what cost?'

'I don't care what cost.'

'At what cost to yourself? All these years you have allowed this hatred and desire for revenge to eat you away inside. You have been a walking whited sepulchre.'

She looked at him and laughed in a way that chilled his blood.

'You are getting biblical with a vengeance, Tom. It's all this God business. All right, I'm eaten away inside. That man ruined two people I loved. I'm not capable of love any more, only of hate. You think because I was in your silly little society that I am a mate, a pal, a friend did you say? Not me. I joined because Exelby was going to direct the mystery plays, and I knew that Sally Vause would almost certainly be in charge of costume, and it struck me as a useful society to be in to get to the position to do what I did. Sorry, Tom. You are an altruist, aren't you? What a sucker!'

'Right from the start . . .?'

'Yes. I joined MRS the week the director's appointment was announced, last year.'

'The opportunity might not have occurred.'

'Opportunities are made. That was my last night with the real chance of action – he was going away the next day after the first performance, and I did not dare leave it to the last. I would have preferred it to be on the first night of the production, with all the audience in front.'

'That would have ruined the production completely . . . Could you work among everyone for months – and feel nothing of the comradeship, the community feeling?'

She snapped her fingers. 'That for your community feeling. There's only one way to get what you want in life and that's to take the matter into your own hands and do it yourself. Bruce Exelby taught me a good deal. He taught me to hate and to be strong. And to seize opportunities, and improvise. And if you're thinking of Sydney Absolom, yes . . . his death was not an accident. I did it to him too, because he told you he had found out who killed Exelby and was going to tell the police. I was coming into the room looking for a water carafe and overheard him talking, so I stood behind the door and waited. You left without noticing me, Tom. I told you that it is useful, being insignificant. That was an impulse, I'm afraid. Although I was really rather pleased with my improvisation and its success. Stupid Syd! Why did he have to stick his nose in?'

'Because he was being accused.'

'Rubbish! He wouldn't have harmed a fly. Anyone with half an eye could see that. Anyway – he's just between you and me. The coroner's verdict on him was accidental death. If an old man leans out of a high window on a scorching day he's asking for a dizzy spell.'

'You're not even sorry?'

'Yes, I am. I'm sorry about Sydney. I liked him and up till then he'd never done me any harm.'

Thomas was feeling very sick. The last thing he wanted was Velvet's coffee yet he seemed to have no alternative but to drink more. She had replaced the broken cup and was lifting the two jugs. Twin streams came down into first her own cup and then his. He realized that it was going to be difficult to get away.

'I want you to make your mind up what to do,' he said. 'Are you going to tell the police yourself?'

'No fear.'

'I will give you twenty-four hours to make up your mind on a course of action.'

'No need. My course of action has been determined by you this morning. I can't stay here now. I shall pack and go abroad before the police can stop me.'

'I can't let you do that, Velvet,' he said gravely.

'And how are you going to stop me?'

'By force if necessary. But I'd rather it was with an appeal to your conscience. Tell a jury what you've told me and you should get off lightly. Not that I'm condoning anything – that's just the way it will probably be.'

'I have no conscience, Tom. If you are going to stand in the way you will have to be number three.'

Poison was having an interview with his agent and road manager. They had both come north to take him over when the last night of the plays released him.

'I gotta have a bit of time off,' he told them. 'No way am I going on tour again just yet.'

'Just some recording sessions, boyo,' said the agent. 'That's all you got lined up for the next month. Then we start thinking about a tour of America – the big one. Unless of course you want to stay in this acting lark. There's an offer in from the RSC of a straight part if you want it, a lead, starring role.'

'I dunno.'

'Doesn't pay like singing does,' put in the road manager.

'Too right, but it's up to you, boyo.'

'Look, I wanna give my next tour a new slant. I've got ideas for some new songs.'

'Sounds good.'

'I wanna work up some ideas on the theme of reconciliation.'

'Of what, boyo?'

'Reconciliation, and the redeeming power of love.'

'You going all religious, mate? Cliff Richard does all right with that. Might work out.'

'Dammit, I'm not!'

'Calm down.'

Poison threw himself on to the checked counterpane of the caravan bed, and gazed at the ceiling.

'Just wait, wilya?' he said. 'Wait until I've had time to get my ideas into shape. I need a lot of hours in the studio with a session man on drums, maybe. There's music running through my head, words. I've gotta have time to work them out. Then we'll give them a try on the next tour.'

'And if they're a frost?'

'Then too bad. They would have to go.'

'Well . . . OK, if you realize that . . .'

'I realize that.'

'And what do I say to the RSC?'

'Tell them not now. One day I might want to act again, but not right now.'

'OK.'

'Now beat it, you two. Go feed the ducks. I've got things to do. I want to see a mate of mine.'

Bob Southwell had arrived at the end of a long piece of patient reasoning and deduction. He was sure he had the person, the opportunity, and the method by which that opportunity had been utilized, though motive was still obscure. He got up from the computer desk with a long-drawn-out sigh of tired satisfaction. The girl computer operator appeared in the doorway with a cup of coffee.

'Nine twenty-five, sir,' she said. 'You aren't supposed to look at that thing for more than two hours without a break. Bad for the eyes. Please move away from the machine while you drink this, it ruins them if you spill coffee on them. Accidentally, of course,' she added hastily.

'I haven't been using it solidly,' Southwell sounded quite mild.

'No, sir. If you'll excuse me saying so, you've been sitting gazing at the screen while you were thinking more than you've been using it.'

'I've hardly used it all. The work's been going on in my mind.'

'It would still fit in better with police regulations for computer users if you came over here and drank this coffee, sir.'

She thought that Bob Southwell was like a carving knife, thin, bright, keen, and liable to cut, to be treated with respect. He came over to the side desk quite amiably and drank the coffee. Before he had finished it, there was a knock at the door and a constable came in.

'Someone asking urgently for you, sir.'

'Who is it?'

'Mr Poison Peters.'

Bob looked irritated. At this juncture, he could do without the pop star, whom he had never liked anyway.

'He's very insistent that it's urgent. Seems to think someone's in danger.'

'Let him in.'

'Yes?' he said shortly.

'D'ya know where Tom Churchyard is?' asked Poison, in a breath.

'At home still at this time, I should think.'

'Well he isn't. And before he left he went to your house and asked for you, said he'd made deductions and wanted to tell you who done it. Isn't that what that other bloke said – the one that fell out of the window? That he knew who it was and was going to tell the fuzz?'

'That's right,' said Bob, putting down the empty coffee cup and rising to his feet. 'If Tom's come to the same conclusion as me and decided to confront her with it instead of coming to me . . .'

'That's exactly what I've been thinking. It must be a woman. A woman who's been brooding on some injury for a long time, and gone bitter and twisted inside. And Tom would feel all chivalrous, and not want to shop her to the fuzz.'

Bob regarded Poison in amazement. He gave him credit for unexpected powers of logical thought. 'And there aren't many women who had the opportunity. What time did he go to my house?'

Policeman and pop star looked at one another.

'About twenty to nine. D'ya know where she lives?'

'Yes. Come on.' Not for a second did Bob think of standing on protocol and making Poison stay behind.

On his rapid stride through the police station Bob collected two of his staff and outside they embarked in two cars, Bob and Poison in the first and the two detectives in the other.

They put the sirens on and screamed through the streets.

Within the cars no one spoke. They turned up Portland Street and drew up with a protest of brakes.

'He's a big bloke,' Poison said as they jumped out, 'and she's small.'

'Doesn't follow that he'd win, if she staged a physical attack,' retorted Bob. 'Find your way round the back,' he said to the two detectives, and directed them with a gesture. Ringing the doorbell madly he waited – one second – two seconds – three seconds –

He tried the handle at the same time. The door was held by a small Yale lock. Poison expected to see him put his shoulder to the door like they do in films. Instead Bob moved over to the sash window in the front bay. It was open just a crack at the bottom. With a strong clasp-knife blade he levered it up. As soon as the window was six inches above the sill he put his leg into the room, and then shoved the window sharply upward.

'No time to stand on ceremony,' he said. Poison followed. They burst hastily but fairly quietly into the front hallway – then into the dining room, for the open door of the kitchen showed that to be empty – and without a word Southwell, grabbing her from the back, pinioned Velvet Smith's arms behind her.

Thomas Churchyard was standing there as if frozen.

The two detectives had managed to get in through the back yard and the unlocked back door. Holding her carefully as though she might sting, Bob handed Velvet Smith over to them.

'I arrest you, Velvet Smith, for the murder of Bruce Exelby and suspected murder of Sydney Absolom . . . . Take her down to the station, you two. Charge her. Watch her like a hawk.'

Velvet's face was that of a fury. 'You said you hadn't told them,' she hissed at Thomas. 'You said no one knew where you were.'

'I didn't tell them.'

'We can sometimes work things out for ourselves, Miss Smith,' said Bob sarcastically.

Velvet was taken out of the room. He turned to Thomas. 'What the hell do you think you're doing?'

Tom drew himself up, and looked rueful.

Poison came forward.

'If it hadn't been for your friend here you'd have been a

goner, if she'd had her way,' Bob said. 'If he hadn't come to me when he did I might have been another hour or two – might even have decided to wait for the end of the mystery play production – after all it's nearly over. Has she hurt you in any way?' Bob seemed to realize that he was not being very sympathetic.

'Physically, you mean? No. What could she have done to me?' asked Thomas, still rigid with the shock of the recent conversation. 'I'm twice her size.'

'So what?' Bob was reminded painfully of his little daughter's unintentional physical victory over his athletic son. 'I wouldn't put it past her to hurt you. You seem to forget what she's already done. If she's studied self-defence,' Bob added sharply, 'a hard kick on your kneecap would have had you writhing on the floor. Then she could have done a good bit of damage with ammonia which she probably has in the kitchen, or a kettle of hot water, or anything else which was handy.'

'Then she'd have finished up with a big corpse to dispose of, which would not have been very sensible of her. No. She hadn't got started on the kneecaps. She's hurt me enough other ways. I didn't know anyone could look so evil, or that anyone close to me was so treacherous. I can't get over it, the horror of the way she is.'

'There's no doubt no rational woman would have attacked you. I wouldn't care to tackle you myself. But she's not rational any more, Tom.'

'Come on,' Poison looked at Thomas keenly. 'Come and have a cup of tea.'

'I think I've drunk enough for one morning.' Thomas produced a nervous laugh.

'Well come and have something. A Marmite sandwich.'

'I'll be glad to get out of this place. What an atmosphere! Thick with hatred.'

'I want you at the station for a statement, but have your sandwich first and a natter if you want.'

'No. I'll come and get it over with.'

'I'll come with you,' said Poison.

Poison settled into the back of the car as if police cars were his favourite mode of transport. Together he and Tom went into an interview room, and for a minute they were alone.

'Look Tom, this isn't the time or the place,' said Poison, 'but I'd like you to use my real name. It's John. There aren't many people I ask to do that.'

He looked very young and very serious.

Thomas smiled at him. 'You're a pal, John,' he said and they shook hands formally.

Bob Southwell came into the room. 'We'll take your statements now.'

'How is Velvet? I feel responsible for all this. She is our treasurer in MRS.'

'Your responsibility is over now if you ever had any. Detecting, and taking care of a criminal, is part of my profession, Tom. It seems to have been your accidental vocation, but that's over. Now, the statement . . .'

There was a crowd at York station, but there were no banners. Tom, Clare the Virgin Mary, Lucifer, and a few others, were at the front and a miscellaneous collection of York citizens at the back. The train was due to leave for London in five minutes.

A long car drew up, and Poison got out, taking care not to damage the spikes of his pale hair. The crowd broke into a cheer, one fan screamed and sobbed, and he smiled at them out of a pale face with rouged lips, batted his long mascara-ed eyelashes over the vivid golden brown eyes, and spread his arms wide as if to embrace them all, thin bony hands combing the air. The midsummer sun struck lightning out of his silver jacket and lost its beams in the blackness of his soft shirt with the embroidered five-pointed star across the breast. A solitary cameraman stepped forward and flashed a light bulb. The reporter from the *Yorkshire Post* asked a last question.

'Yeah,' said Poison. 'I love your beautiful city, yeah.'

SILVER LAKE COLLEGE LIBRARY
658.022
W9-DBK-090
3 9319 00049 6819

How To Start A Family Business & Make It Work

Also by Jerome Goldstein:
In Business for Yourself

How To Start A Family Business & Make It Work

JEROME GOLDSTEIN

M. EVANS AND COMPANY, INC.
NEW YORK

Library of Congress Cataloging in Publication Data

Goldstein, Jerome, 1931-
How to start a family business and make it work.

Bibliography: p.
Includes index.
1. New business enterprises. 2. Small business.
I. Title.
HD62.5.G654 1984 658'.022 84-3995

ISBN 0-87131-435-5

M. Evans and Company, Inc.
216 East 49 Street
New York, New York 10017
Design by Lauren Dong
Manufactured in the United States of America
9 8 7 6 5 4 3 2 1

To Ina, Rill, Nora, and Alison.

Acknowledgments

My special thanks to editor Maureen Heffernan of M. Evans for her encouragement and insights in shaping the final manuscript.

Many entrepreneurial researchers and family business counselors, whose knowledge and experience have aided owners to succeed in a family enterprise, are mentioned throughout this book. Their expertise has helped me to better understand the intricacies of what it takes to manage both the founding of a business and the sustaining of family relationships. These persons include Albert Shapero of Ohio State University, Peter Davis of the Wharton Applied Research Center, Neil Churchill and Richard Peiser of Southern Methodist University, Grant Calder of the University of Utah, Kathleen Wiseman of Working Systems, and Steven D. Popell, management consultant.

Contents

How To Start A Family Business & Make It Work

Introduction

FOUR OUT OF every five Americans are reported to take a dismal view of the state of family life, present and future. According to a 1983 survey of mostly college-educated adults with a median family income of $33,500, many believe that family life is in trouble—deep, deep trouble with even gloomier times ahead. To turn things around, some experts call desperately for a renewal of old-fashioned values: closeness, a willingness to work together, responsibility toward family and humankind.

But how do we effect such a monumental turnaround? What steps can we take in an age when the term *nuclear* is more frequently associated with warfare than with the close-knit family, when the symbol of mobility has changed from the jet to the space capsule, when knowledge is communicated via the personal computer screen instead of person to person?

Into this prevalent gloom about the malaise of the family enters a counterforce that has its roots in economics as well as kinship. At an accelerating pace, this movement is attracting members in both cities and rural areas throughout the United States. It's healthy for families monetarily and personally. It's the ever-stronger presence of the new family business.

About 3 million small businesses started last year. With an estimated 16 million businesses of all kinds in the United States, start-ups are responsible for a 20 percent growth rate. The vast majority of these new enterprises—somewhere between 60 and 90 percent—can be classified as family businesses. Launched by a husband and wife, brothers or sisters, parents and children, or any combination thereof, these businesses represent the most vital, optimistic socioeconomic activity reported today. These are mergers forged not on Wall Street or in Washington, but around the kitchen table.

What explains this renewed popularity that the family business is enjoying? What are people seeking? Is it more money? More security? More satisfaction? Greater control of how to spend most of their time and with whom to spend it?

And what does it take to succeed in a family business? How can you tell if you've got the right temperament and the necessary talents? What is there to be learned from the families who have succeeded . . . as well as from those who have decided to close up shop? How do you strike the right balance between family goals and business needs? What's it like to work with family members, and how can you avoid "too much togetherness"? How can you perform the dual roles of spouse/partner or parent/boss without conflict or confusion? What happens when you put the responsibility of economic survival directly upon the family unit?

Just as with raising children, the challenges of raising a family business are ever-changing, reflecting both your family's stage of development and the personal dynamics within it.

In the six years since my wife, my daughters, and I started our own publishing firm, we've been in the midst of the family business movement. *In Business*, the magazine we have created, is written for people in new and growing businesses. We've interviewed hundreds of family members who have made the decision to start out as we did. In each case, it's evident that the entrepreneurial spirit has united with family ties to create the launch.

Sometimes businesses seem to be the result of careful plotting and logical planning. Some seem to spring forth out of long-felt desires; while still others are the result of what academic researchers call an "entrepreneurial event," perhaps the laying off or firing of one family member. The motives for starting a family business do vary (often among members who are responsible for the launch). Still, I've invariably noted common themes, common goals, and shared philosophies and attitudes.

PERSONAL SATISFACTION

One reason for starting up a family business is the simple goal of getting more fun out of life. Why spend so much time commuting, waiting in airports, dealing often with people you really can't tolerate, playing at office politics—and then complaining for hours about what you've been forced to put up with?

Larry Kuivanen had been a disillusioned weapons designer before he made an unequivocal about-face. These days, Larry and his wife, Robin, design wooden toys and furniture for children. "I'm promoting smiles instead of guns now," Larry says as he explains the origins of Just Wood Manufacturing Company in Pawcatuck, Connecticut. He's put his talent for designing to work to create rocking horses, kids' chairs, wagons, blocks, and trains. Larry and Robin started working in the basement of their home seven years ago. Robin had never worked with wood before. With a little encouragement, however, she mastered the equipment, giving Larry time to get out and sell.

TAKING CONTROL

Who decides how you, your spouse, and your children make a living? Is it a corporation whose sole activity and purpose is to generate ever-increasing profits for its shareholders? If you happen to be one of the persons who own stock in that corporation, it's difficult to fault that objective, since it most likely was your reason for investing in that company in the first place. But as an employee, you can't expect tremendous control over how you spend your time on the job.

Al Shapero, a management professor at Ohio State University and a leading international authority on small business, has the following to say about entrepreneurs:

> They are the most obvious example of people who have taken apparent control of their own lives. I have studied entrepreneurs in Brazil and northern Italy, black entrepreneurs in South Africa, entrepreneurs with Ph.D.'s in Texas, and a full spectrum of entrepreneurs in Columbus, Ohio. To study them for any length of time is to gain the illusion that the world is divided into two categories of people: those who act as if they have free will, and all the rest.

The spouses, the parents, and the siblings who are nurturing their own businesses today are clearly declaring their intent to take control. As Shapero has found in his research, their chief motivation is independence, not money.

I left a job as executive vice-president that brought me an income of more than $100,000 a year. It's debatable at this point whether that kind of money will come as salary from our business: wildly optimistic earnings statements come only from publishers who wish to impress financial analysts. But, as Shapero describes us, the big payoff is knowing that we can direct events.

FAMILY TOGETHERNESS

It may sound a bit corny, but if a family has looked forward to vacationing together, to playing as the children are growing up, and to seeking out new experiences together, then why not take a crack at working together?

My wife, my daughters, and I have forged a new and richer relationship by working together to start one magazine completely from scratch while reshaping another existing magazine. The process of putting the parent-child relationship aside and learning to deal with each other as comanagers has created its tensions. But the rewards of making a joint decision, testing its practicality, and watching some work and others flop have been significant. And we wouldn't have come to know them at all, if we had all led separate work lives.

STATUS

I recall a conversation I had in 1978 with an executive of a New York–based foundation in which he bemoaned the low status associated with a small family business. "Every parent," he told me, "wants a child to work for an IBM or a General Motors. To remain in the old mom-and-pop store or to start a new business is a sign of weakness, a retreat from the real world of corporate action. Status, security, and big money go with a Fortune 500 job." Attitudes about employment status have changed drastically since he spoke these words to me, and I doubt that his observations were quite valid even then. The many shake-ups, layoffs, and million-dollar losses that have plagued top corporations have shown that size does not protect a company or its workers from economic ups and downs. Bankruptcies can hit the huge as well as the tiny, and lately the "fat and lazy" big corporations have been hardest hit.

Job status today does not emanate from a national brand-name company the way it did some years ago. Then if your company logo could be seen on network TV, you shared in the notoriety. Your college degree had obviously gotten you somewhere. Friends and acquaintances would automatically assume that you conducted major business deals on the golf course, and your mother could drop your employer's name with pride to your aunts and uncles. Little or no status went with starting up your own business, unless you took pleasure in being classified as a dropout.

Not anymore! Today, certainly fueled in part by the declining fortunes of major corporations, the ex-corporate leaders who start again on their own are credited with vision and vigor. The examples swirl around us, with profiles appearing almost daily in local and national publications and interviews on radio and TV talk shows. Everyone seems to stop to listen when an entrepreneur begins the tale of how he or she got started.

Even the most sophisticated business people are eager to hear and to admire. A friend of ours who a short time ago got his kicks by eating at Lutece on trips to New York City now delights in talking with the owners of a new bistro. The highlight of his trip to Vermont was a stay at an inn run by a former executive of a high-tech firm on Boston's Route 128.

As a family publishing company, we have gotten our share of recognition for having created a national magazine for independent, innovative individuals. Last year, the International Council for Small Business named the magazine its Publication of the Year with these words:

> *In Business* has succeeded in serving those thousands of persons who need inspiration and direction in meeting their compelling desire to become independent owners of small businesses. *In Business* has provided a clear and honest dialogue combined with insight and references. It is a special magazine for those who yearn for personal growth with dignity, but at a pace and style tailored by and for each individual.

Nothing tops the brief glow of national recognition when your business is discovered by a reporter or interviewer. After a newspaper article appeared on their *Goodfellow Catalog of Wonderful Things*, Christopher Weills and Sarah Saterlee, who had spent two years compiling the book, were contacted by "Good Morning, America." After the morning TV program aired, Chris wrote us: "For all of five minutes, Sarah and I basked in national glory. The experience was heady: chauffeured limos picked us up and deposited us around the town. Our airline tickets to and from California were paid for, as was our hotel. We *loved* it. Now it's back to the reality of overdue bills and missed deadlines. (What else is new!)"

Status—it goes with the young, growing family business.

FLEXIBILITY IN TIME AND LOCATION

No punch clocks are needed in the family-run businesses we know so well. The reason is that the people involved are working all the time; even meals provide a time to review decisions and plan ahead. But the other side of the coin is that most jobs can be arranged around personal priorities. Last year, for example, the July marriage of our managing editor, our middle daughter, coincided with the closing date for the September-October issue of *In Business*. So much for closing dates. Our entire managerial and editorial team had set up its own production schedule to arrange the backyard wedding, and because of particularly deft juggling of personal and business commitments, the wedding went off fine, Nora and Jon took off for a two-week honeymoon, the tent went up and down on schedule . . . and subscribers received their September-October issue only two days late.

When we started out six years ago, my wife suggested we call the company the Closed-for-Summer Press, take off for Vermont in mid-June, and stay there until September. We haven't quite managed that, but this year we did decide to buy land along the Vermont lakefront and gradually transfer summer activities up there. We do so much work via the telephone and at the typewriter that it seems feasible. Again, flexibility in management and work patterns can be built in to satisfy the family and the business.

WOMEN AND FAMILY BUSINESS

Historically, writes social scientist and management expert Peter F. Drucker in the *Wall Street Journal* column "Speaking of Business," women always participated in the labor force at the same rate as men; women and men alike worked from the time they were able until they dropped.

> Neither farm nor craftsman's shop can be run alone by either man or woman; both require a couple. And,

> until recently, all but a tiny fraction of the human race made its living on the farm or in the craftsman's shop. . . . By 1914, it had become the mark of the "self-respecting working man" that "his woman" need not work for wages. And by 1950, it was commonly assumed that most women would stop working with marriage and surely when the first child was about to arrive. Until perhaps as late as 20 years ago, "female emancipation" largely meant freeing women from the necessity of taking a paying job. Now, all this is considered reactionary and discriminatory. And for women under 50, regardless of their marital status and almost regardless of whether they have children, the labor force participation rate is again equal to that of men.

The family business movement is definitely linked to the return of women into the labor force.

The pages of *In Business* magazine have regularly profiled women entrepreneurs, and often their prime motive has been the ability to fulfill their career aspirations while being flexible enough to work at home when necessary, often from a home office.

"The 1970s were the decade of women entering management, and the 1980s are turning out to be the decade of the woman entrepreneur," says Carolyn Doppelt Gray of the United States Small Business Administration (SBA). According to SBA statistics, the number of self-employed women reached 2.3 million in 1982, up 35 percent from 1.7 million in 1977, while the number of self-employed men increased only 12 percent in the five years. Businesses owned by women currently account for more than $40 billion in annual sales.

A *Wall Street Journal* article notes that formerly a few women became prominent as entrepreneurs in female-oriented fields such as cosmetics and apparel "but rarely in mainstream industries. That is changing, as women are becoming owners of companies in construction, electrical contracting, moving and storage, finance, automotive supply and computer manufacturing and software."

Women business owners seem to be faring well, according to all the information we've been able to gather. Our own surveys of *In Business* readers show the success rate of male- and female-owned businesses is exactly the same, and all our success figures are far higher than the usual SBA numbers, which indicate a 50 percent failure rate in the first five years after launch. These statistics agree with a report from a counseling service in New York City that serves women business owners. Their numbers indicate that out of 800 women entrepreneurs who have graduated from the organization's program, only four have entered bankruptcy proceedings.

MONEY

I'm constantly telling people not to have unrealistic goals about financial rewards from starting a family business. In my experience, the payoff in dollars comes gradually. Growth in sales and employees does not equate to big profits for the owners. The big problem with expecting large profits too soon is that it leads to disappointment over bottom-line results when you actually may be building a base for financial success.

But the first five years or so are usually tough in the family business. They were for us and for everyone else we know. Although sales grow, economies of scale don't take effect, so margins only gradually improve. And sales are not generally large enough to allow six-figure salaries for the owners. All these cautions about early payoffs and realistic attitudes should not diminish expectations of long-range financial rewards. For most of us, they will come, and it's always satisfying to read about owners of family businesses who are cashing in on their effort.

An example: Andrew Kay raised the capital to launch the Kaypro Corporation by putting his family's real estate holdings up as collateral. The company, based in Solana Beach, California, sells a line of portable microcomputers with 80-column display and a variety of software packages. Besides Andrew and his father, Kay family members in the business include wife Mary (corporate secretary), two sons (both vice-presidents), two daughters, a son-in-law, and brother. Each is a stockholder and works full-time or part-time for Kaypro.

By summer 1983, the company's sales had reached the $12 million mark. In an article describing Kaypro's public offering, *Fortune* magazine had this to say: "If investors buy five million shares at the $15 to $18 price pegged by Prudential-Bache, Kay, 64, will instantly reap at least $9 million. The remaining shares owned by Kay and his family, including those of his 87-year-old father who still comes into the plant at five in the morning to putter around, could be worth almost $500 million."

The most dramatic numbers—the million-dollar-plus rewards to founders, spouses, and children—come as a result of rising stock values. A recent analysis of $100 million-and-up winners in the 1983 bull market by *Fortune* editors revealed that entrepreneurs and their heirs rather than portfolio investors made the really big stock market fortunes.

SECURITY

If you have the confidence that accompanies the sense of taking control, then you've got to include a *sense of security* for yourself and family that goes with running your own business.

No personnel director will hand you a pink slip on a Friday afternoon. No superior will suddenly tell you that you must move to Houston and take over the office there if you want to stay with the company. While there are tough, often unpleasant decisions to make and jobs to do, the process of deciding on those moves includes you. That's a security you cannot enjoy when a layer of middle managers or company officers decides your fate. In the family business, your security is what you create. And that's all you can expect anywhere.

Not being forced to relocate in order to keep one's job is an important aspect of the security that accompanies a family business. The no-move feature has assumed great importance in recent years. During the footloose 1950s and 1960s, 20 percent of the U.S. population changed location each year. Since then the percentage has fallen to below 17 percent and is continuing to decline.

TRADITION

When I asked my nephew why he stepped into the retail clothing store in upstate New York, he practically started doing Tevye's routine from *Fiddler on the Roof*. "I'm the third generation, and the Matthews store has become a tradition in this town," he told me. And tradition is indeed a very important motivation for the increasing numbers of young people who follow in their grandparents' footsteps.

Manhattan's Garment District on Seventh Avenue offers many examples of the power of tradition in the family business—and so do the specialty food shops on Ninth Avenue. According to the *New York Times*, there's a "new generation of young, educated men and women who now want to take their places in companies begun years before by enterprising, immigrant grandparents." Typical of the trend is 23-year-old Fred Hazan, who has a bachelor's degree in computer science and works for Lloyd's Sportswear Company. The firm was founded by his grandfather when he was 24, a few years after he arrived in the United States from a small village in Greece. The history of how his grandfather managed to learn the trade by working for a few cents an hour and then borrowing some money from a textile manufacturer is "an inspiration" to young Fred. "He was my age. He did a pretty amazing thing. I'd like to do the same myself." For the 77-year-old patriarch and founder Freddie Hazan, his sons are "a blessing. . . . A family feels great pride when a son or grandson enters the company."

Describing other situations in the Garment District, the *New York Times* mentioned Anne Dee Goldin, 30 years old, who became senior vice-president at Goldin-Feldman International after her father's heart attack. "It's in my blood," she explains. "I come from a long line of furriers. My father, his father, my mother's father, and both her brothers are furriers. I am very proud of my family." She also notes the changes that have taken place in only the last few years. An earlier generation—those between 35 and 45—which includes her brother and sister, pursued other careers. "Our parents encouraged us to be doctors or lawyers," says Anne Goldin. "During the 60's, it wasn't fashionable to join a family company. It's my generation that is coming back into the businesses."

Often, the family business is built upon a production tradition that goes back for generations. Journalist Gene Logsdon tells us about Robert Picking's copper shop in Bucyrus, Ohio. "Robert is only 100 years old," Gene says,

> and last I heard is still going strong. He has about six guys working for him, mostly young, mostly craft conscious, if not bona fide craftsmen. Picking makes

copper kettles, coal scuttles, tympanies, and a few other copper items, *exactly* the way his grandfather made them in 1874 in the same shop with the same tools. And they are booked ahead three years in orders. You would not believe this shop. Walking in there is like walking into the last century, only it is not a fakey museum, but the real thing. It's a lovely place. Some of the sawhorses—work vises—the men sit at while beating (planishing) the copper kettles to make them strong have deep, deep grooves worn in them where knees of a century of workers have rubbed. The place just sends me into raptures.

COMEDY

Often you see a sign in a small business that reads, "This is a nonprofit company—we didn't mean to be, but that's how things are." I prefer to substitute the word *zany* for nonprofit. Just about every young and growing family-run company I know can properly use the term. It goes with the turf. The role-playing can be straight out of a comedy routine. Wherever you go, you find situations that have the ingredients of a hilarious TV series.

In Athens, Greece, we came across Stavros Mellissinos, a poet-sandalmaker whose shop in the ancient Plaka is probably the only place in the world where you can listen to a modern Omar Khayyám and have your feet shod simultaneously. Fortunately, a brother-in-law keeps sandal production up when poetry creation moves into high gear.

And when controversy flares in the family business, watch out! If you can't yell at your spouse, who can you yell at, right? Unlike the executive suites of corporate America, everything is out in the open.

TOGETHERNESS

If there's one thing you can count on in a family business, it's togetherness. A lot of it! The constancy of companionship can be taxing at times, but it does guarantee against loneliness! And loneliness has been cited as a major cause of entrepreneurial stress.

In a study of 450 entrepreneurs, David Gumpert and David Boyd found that at least once a week, 55 to 65 percent of the respondents had back problems, indigestion, insomnia, or headaches. The group felt it was the price they had to pay to succeed. Stress is the cost of success, and a leading cause of stress for the individual entrepreneur is loneliness. Not so with family entrepreneurs who are immersed in their business. They may still have trouble getting away from it all, but they won't be lonely.

MBA EQUIVALENT: BLOSSOMING OUT–BUILDING CONFIDENCE

Every member of a family business quickly gets into a position of responsibility. There is much to do with few people to do the doing. There's no choice but to make a decision and then see that it gets carried out. Particularly in areas such as marketing and financial management, the on-the-job duties of solving cash-flow problems, long- and short-range, provide an educational opportunity that may in fact be superior to a formal master's of business administration (MBA) program.

Fran Henry, who spent two years away from her consulting firm, Enterprise Associates, to earn an MBA at Harvard Business School, believes that the real wisdom in developing a successful business must come from personal experiences. An MBA, in her opinion, is valuable in providing "a sense of breadth in approaching a problem . . . in learning how to read balance sheets and income statements, how to understand the production processes, but—it doesn't give any wisdom. Wisdom only comes from your personal experience. . . . Business school doesn't do anything to make you a good decision maker."

Our business manager and marketing director, Rill Ann Goldstein—who is our oldest daughter—may yet decide that she wants a full-fledged MBA degree from a leading business school. In the meantime, she's learned a tremendous amount about what it takes to get a new business up and running. That knowledge will always be transferable to another company, even if—horrors—it's not family-owned.

FUN

Call it enjoyment or whatever. Fun is closely akin to satisfaction and why the family business makes sense. There's no room for martyrdom in a successfully run family business. No individual member can feel that he or she is carrying the full burden of the business. That ain't fun—and without fun, the effort won't continue.

As mentioned earlier, a family business hangs together on a number of levels. Never are all levels operating equally well. The beginning is the simplest; that's when family members come to the enterprise with the most enthusiasm and the freshest attitudes. Yet the beginning is the hardest time financially. Little money, small staff, and many jobs that have to be done. Sure there are priorities to be met and there are fires to be put out, but despite all the work, there's only one place to go—and that's up. So make sure that you and your family start a business that you like, one that involves creation of something you believe in and have a talent for. There is no way you will like everything about the business. What's important is that the overall environment and the key activities fit your family.

This book is written for those of you who may someday see a family business in your future or who are about to enter one, as well as for those of you who are in the midst of a family firm right now. I hope it will bring you useful insights into what is involved: how to plan, how to follow through, and how to make the most of the experience.

I have not attempted to provide you with a one-stop encyclopedic text on everything you need to know about managing the family business. You'll find scores of excellent reference books on specific topics at the library or bookstore, and I've included a Family Business Resource Directory in the appendix that will lead you to sources of specific information. What I have tried to do is to lay out guiding principles for each stage of your family business cycle, to explain what is new and different about today's growing movement to family-owned enterprise, and to show what you can learn from others and what you have to work out for yourself.

1

Is a Family Business for You?

THE MOST IMPORTANT question to ask yourself *before* plunging into the entrepreneurial world is this: *Is a family business right for us?*

The specific idea—the product or service you're about to create—is second in importance to that key question and all the factors related to it.

There's no better topic of cocktail party conversation than that of "making it on your own." We've all heard about the great little French restaurant: "All you need is a love of cooking, some highly praised recipes, and a subscription to *Gourmet* magazine, right?" Or the country inn in Vermont: "It's perfect. We love to ski, and then there's the income from the maple syrup." Or perhaps it's an absolutely sensational potato peeler discovered in France that will be the basis of a mail-order enterprise that will outdistance Williams-Sonoma. Invariably, the conversation generates an overpowering momentum that follows what I call the "EEK" pattern.

Escape: No more 9-to-5 hassle . . . an end to office politics . . . no more commuting. Kathy and Bob (and the kids) will escape to a world of their own, independent of the traumas of corporate life.

Easy: The scenario is all laid out. If it's a restaurant, the superior food, tasteful decoration, and intimate atmosphere will fill tables nightly. The chef has been selected; the rave reviews will get the word out. Mimi Sheraton will fly in from New York. It's like duck soup (which will be served on Wednesdays).

Killing: The area needs a restaurant like this. There's never anyplace to go to eat anymore. Or if it's a mail-order business, there are millions of lists with names and addresses of people dying to buy a potato peeler that works. What we're making now is peanuts compared with the big bucks that will come inside those thousands of envelopes. And we can rent a post office box for less than $50.

As conversations at parties go, the topic of starting a business rates higher than most. Anyone thinking about starting a family business should take every chance to discuss the idea and get feedback. The danger comes when casual feedback is interpreted as market research, business planning, capital formation, or expert counseling.

Since our family is so deeply involved in publishing a magazine about new and growing small businesses, we are constantly hearing from people who tell us their plans. Sometimes the conversation ends after a few minutes, sometimes it continues for hours. However long the discussion, I try to home in on the three Es—Experience, Energy, and Expectations.

EXPERIENCE

How much experience do you and your family have in the business area you're considering? Does that experience equip you to produce a quality product or service?

It is by no means necessary for an entire family to be veterans in running a restaurant, for example; but at least one member should know the details of managing a commercial kitchen, buying food wholesale, or running a dining room. When I press the point about experience, the counterargument is often made that such experience can be bought, for example, that a manager with expertise in the kitchen and dining room can be hired. But a prime characteristic of most successful start-up family businesses I know is that the family members hold the critical posts. The reason for this arrangement is that there simply are not sufficient revenues in the early stages to pay the salaries of experienced persons. Remember, we're talking about running a family business—not investing in a business that will be run by nonfamily members.

Usually, experience, no matter how broad, does not mean expertise in every facet of the business. But it should mean that enough knowledge exists within the family to handle the majority of day-to-day operations. And it also means that at least one family member will be able to tell when it's time to bring in an outside consultant, or when someone is steering you onto shaky ground. In other words, you should have enough experience not to make more than your share of dumb mistakes.

ENERGY

By energy, I'm talking about human effort by the family members who will be running the business. There's no substitute for this kind of energy expenditure, which must be both mental and physical. It's not easy to think smart, but you have to. And you also will be amazed at how much time it physically takes to get necessary tasks performed.

Because of the human effort required, I continually stress to people who talk to us about their proposed family business how crucial it is to make certain that the business they're starting is one they *like,* even *love.* If it's an information-oriented business, you'd better not resent wading through piles of notes or magazine clippings and organizing them into some communicable form. If it's a restaurant or inn, you'd better like dealing with people, shopping carefully, and cleaning up, as well as cooking and skiing.

EXPECTATIONS

Expectations can cut both ways. From the financial side, you need to be optimistic about profits you'll eventually generate. You can't be wishy-washy about the dollar investments you're personally making, and you certainly can't be negative when it comes to raising money from relatives and friends, not to mention when speaking with the loan officer at your bank.

But you've got to be realistic—and this continually comes up in conversations I have. If you've made—or allowed yourself to be conned into making—profit projections that are too high, two major problems will invariably occur.

First, you'll get discouraged too early when you don't meet those profit projections. You'll think your idea is a lousy one, that you've failed, or that someone else in the family has failed, and you'll close up before you've had a chance to develop the business properly.

Second, high profit forecasts will only follow from high revenues, and high revenues early in the game only come from costly promotion and sales efforts, such as advertising, salespersons on the road, and direct mail. For a start-up to get on that kind of sales merry-go-round, it means major capital expenditures—which usually means major borrowing. At today's finance charges for borrowed money, the high cost of an early sales or advertising campaign will put your business under tremendous pressure to produce quick results. Sometimes a business does, and we all know about the marvelous success stories that sound like dreams. But new family businesses should not depend on someone else's get-rich-quick stories. That's why realistic expectations are better than great ones.

There's another E—in fact two more Es—that will help you decide if a family business is right for you. It's the "Entrepreneurial Event." I first heard the term used by researcher Al Shapero of Ohio State University at a conference attended by business school professors who were studying the characteristics that make entrepreneurs and why these individuals do the things they do. While others discussed such personal characteristics as a propensity for risk taking or high achievement (more on this later), Al Shapero homed in on the event. In his analysis, what makes the right start-up time for a man or woman has much to do with what has happened (suddenly) to that person. A refugee from Vietnam landing in the United States may have few options other than to make it on his or her own. Someone who has lost his job may very well be about to experience an "entrepreneurial event," as in the case of Liz and Nick Thomas.

For years, the Thomases were the hit of social gatherings of friends and family. Just imagine a mustard recipe handed down for generations that could be traced back to the czar's court in Moscow. Friends who would often receive a jar of mustard as a holiday gift invariably suggested that the Thomases sell it. However, until a financial planning service that Nick cofounded didn't work out, no serious effort was made to develop a mustard business. But without income, and with four young children to support, the Thomases decided to go for broke with the secret recipe.

Their case study illustrates how to parlay some special expertise bit by bit into a full-fledged enterprise that took them, in 13 months, from a completely manual setup in their kitchen to a mechanized 1,300-square-foot plant. "We had just enough money (about $200) to make two cases of mustard," Nick recalls. "It took all the powdered mustard the local grocery stores stocked to put us into business." The Thomases targeted a few local gourmet food shops as the initial market. On their first sales outing in December 1981, they convinced the owner of a cheese shop to taste the mustard. One taste on a piece of cheese and she was sold. The owner and her partner ordered two cases—and the inventory was wiped out!

That method of production and marketing—making batches at home and selling via the tasting method to food shops within a 100-mile radius of Philadelphia—carried the Thomases through their first few months in business. Money from the first 2 cases enabled them to buy 6 cases of jars (24 to a case) and so on. Liz remembers the early days when they had to invent a device to get the mustard into the bottles, because "using spoons just took too long."

Liz and Nick won't deny the role of luck and coincidence in their fairly trauma-free start-up. But enthusiasm and willingness to talk about what they were doing enabled them to meet some helpful people early on. At a cocktail party, for example, the vice-president of a major food manufacturing company overheard Nick expressing his fears about the effects of mustard gas. It turned out that the executive knew a lot about spice companies, and he shared his expertise. A few minutes later, a representative of a mixer company heard them describe how they were making the mustard by hand. His advice led to the purchase of their first mixing machine.

The most memorable experience to date was trying to convince Murray Klein, president of Zabar's, a prestigious gourmet food emporium in New York City, to carry the mustard, called Chalif Mustard. The reception was less than enthusiastic, but Nick's hounding persuaded Mr. Klein to allow a taste test. When the Chalif gang arrived in company T-shirts ready to sell, Klein had forgotten his promise. He finally agreed, however, to let the Thomases set up. They bought some cheese and crackers and got to work. Despite heavy rain, 26 cases of Chalif Hot 'N' Sweet were sold in three hours. Klein was impressed, and by afternoon's end, a shelf was being cleared for the mustard. Now Zabar's sells 5 to 10 cases a week.

Another early marketing technique was to have Liz's cousin go into gourmet food shops in New York and ask if they carried Chalif Mustard. "If the vendor didn't have it, she would rant and rave about how good it was, and how much it shocked her that they didn't carry it," says Liz. "About a week later, Nick would make a sales call on that shop—and the owner usually would try a case or two." Chalif Mustard is now in 182 retail locations in 20 states. The Thomases also work through distributors and a national food broker. "Word of mouth is getting our product around to people. For example, Chalif Mustard is in an herb shop in California, as well as a shop in Mississippi, and they contacted us after learning about the mustard from store owners in other parts of the country."

Nick also credits sales success to his experience selling insurance. "I was taught to expect 10 nos before getting a yes."

TRUST

In addition to experience, expectations, and energy, *trust* is a key factor in launching a family enterprise. You need to have a fairly good knowledge of how family members operate in a work setting and confidence in their ability to function well in their jobs and carry their own weight.

Prato, Italy, a thirteenth-century city west of Florence, is a center for designing and producing high-fashion clothing that is sold in boutiques around the world. The output comes from some 10,000 individual firms, each employing a few workers. These companies perceive their small size to be a major advantage: "In our business as soon as you become too big, your costs go up," says one firm's owner. "The best size is one that lets the owner control all the processes and that keeps all operations within the range of his eyes." And from another: "We can move very rapidly with the market, while big firms can't change easily."

But the key ingredient is trust. In most of the small firms, fathers, sons, and other relatives work together, bound by a powerful sense of personal loyalty. "The idea," a political science professor explained to a *Wall Street Journal* reporter, "is to trust only your family. Consider everyone else a potential enemy." That's a bit extreme, but it does convey the spirit of "In family we trust."

Thirty-two-year-old Steve Gentile and his brother, Mac, started a screen-printing business in Arlington, Virginia, in 1974. In the past ten years, two more brothers and one sister have joined the firm—and now his father is thinking about joining the business when he retires as an insurance agent. Steve talks about trust as a key factor to consider in launching a family enterprise. "When my sister told me she'd like to join us, I can't say I was overwhelmed by her qualifications. She was my kid sister—a good kid, sure." But Steve soon became impressed by her sound, competent selling style. She's now in charge of sales and, predicts Steve, "will do a great job."

The Gentiles' experience is an important one. Who did a favor for whom when the kid sister was hired? Was the older brother going out of his way to make room for someone the firm didn't really need? Or was the sister ready to pitch in and fill a void that existed? The one thing that will wreck relationships in a family business is for some to think they're being a martyr, that they're doing someone else a favor by joining the business or staying part of it. The situation is equally unworkable when a family member thinks that he or she is "carrying" a parent or child and that the firm would function far better without that person.

In our case, as in that of the Gentiles, we've found just the opposite to be true. No way could we have built up two national magazines with a circulation of more than 70,000 if our daughters had not taken charge of key areas from the outset. They saw a new publishing company as a way to learn about the magazine business—at minimum wages. It was an exciting challenge to learn on the job.

With my 25 years of magazine publishing experience, I could offer advice, critique promotion copy, suggest story ideas, mumble something about subscription fulfillment. But it was up to our daughters to make sure that ideas were carried out, phone calls were made, and contacts were followed up. In the five years since we started the company, I don't remember any of us talking about "favors" or a "free ride."

It's often amusing to me how often executives who have grown up in the corporate world, plowing through the maze of middle-management boxes, picture the family business as some kind of depository for lazy relatives of all kinds. 'Taint so—at least in our experience or from what we hear from others who are deeply committed to a family business.

I hope the pages that follow will help you gain a clear understanding of what it's like to be involved on a day-to-day basis in a new and growing family business, the nitty-gritty as well as the romanticism of creating a new enterprise that will sink or swim strictly upon your efforts. There's no magic and no secret formulas. There are real difficulties that you must face and overcome.

But, as this book will show, we have yet to meet anyone—whether a financial success, someone barely surviving, or a "failure"—who regrets having made the effort to launch a family business.

DO YOU HAVE THE RIGHT TEMPERAMENT?

Conventional wisdom portrays the entrepreneur as a taker of risks, but Al Shapero asks, "Is someone a risk taker if he or she does not perceive the risk?" Shapero points out that the great majority of entrepreneurs he has interviewed told him they do not perceive much risk in starting their companies. Theirs is not the mentality of the cool and bloodless analyst who calculates the odds that a certain venture will sink or swim. Shapero finds, instead, a person who believes that chances of success turn upon his or her personal intelligence, creativity, dedication, and persistence.

As for temperament, Shapero reports that persons who launch the kinds of family businesses we're describing have distinct characteristics. They tolerate ambiguity far more easily than do corporate managers; they deal more easily with the messy world we inhabit; they survive without assurance of next week's schedule or next month's paycheck. "Unlike corporate managers," Shapero explains, "entrepreneurs do not believe that powerful others control their lives. They know that they may fail, but not because other people decide they aren't good enough. The record is rich with the stories of entrepreneurs who have failed more than once, but who have treated failure as a learning experience and picked themselves up to start again."

Entrepreneurs are optimistic. We think the future can be good, and there's no accountant who can tell us otherwise. Our family accountant told us four years after we had started that we'd have been better off financially —with the high interest yield then—to have put the money into certificates of deposit. But, two years later, the returns on CDs are way down and our profits are up.

People in a family business seldom do the conventional market research that is considered the be-all by most of the pundits in the business world. We're concerned with what we have to create or publish, what advice to give, what widget to make. We're sure of the quality of whatever our effort will yield, and we know there should be a need for it. So much for market research.

With that kind of attitude, it's tough for a pessimistic accountant to make much impact. Again taking The JG Press as an example, had we sought advice before starting, we probably would have been told not to begin at all, since we were obviously undercapitalized and didn't know how to reach the market. "Each new company," states Shapero, "is someone's (or some family's) personal commitment to the future, an act little affected by averages and probabilities." In his analysis, entrepreneurs are not born, *they become*. Their characteristics are not genetically determined or fixed forever in their earliest years. Experience makes them what they are.

Academic researchers have studied the characteristics that go into the making of a successful entrepreneur. Professor Neil Churchill of the Southern Methodist University's Caruth Institute of Owner-Managed Business prepared an amalgamation of characteristics compiled by several different authorities. Here is Churchill's representative list of characteristics that he deems critical to an individual's successful translation of an idea into a going enterprise, taken from his paper "Entrepreneurs and their Enterprises: A Stage Model":

1. *Good health, personal energy, and drive:* These three qualities are necessary for long hours of self-paced and business-driven effort.
2. *Need for (and belief in) internal direction:* The entrepreneur believes in his or her own freedom to choose goals and initiate actions. Entrepreneurial researchers are fond of the term *internal locus of control,* referring to the conviction that one's own actions, not external events, determine the success or failure of the enterprise. Because of this, and their self-confidence, these people seek out situations in which they can take the initiative and have personal impact on the results. This also leads them to *build* a business instead of just making their money and getting out.
3. *Self-confidence:* Entrepreneurs are ebulliently confident in their ability to succeed as long as they are in control; if they lose control, their constructive participation diminishes. To know that they are maintaining control, they require and use a high degree of feedback information on the organization's progress and on the performance of comparable entities.

4. *Never-ending sense of urgency:* When building an enterprise, entrepreneurs thrive on action and achievement. Inactivity makes them uneasy. They are not competing against external measures but against self-imposed expectations—often to exceed their best achievement to date.

5. *Comprehensive awareness:* They possess the ability to keep goals clearly in mind and to see the effects of individual actions both on the details of the business and on its long-range goals.

6. *Realism:* These individuals usually accept things and deal with them the way they are. This sense of realism, coupled with self-confidence and emotional stability, permits them to learn from their failures and to persist in difficult times.

7. *Superior conceptual ability:* Not troubled by apparent ambiguity, uncertainty, or disorder, they are persistent problem solvers and easily and quickly switch (even without consulting others) to alternative ways of achieving goals when the present program is unproductive.

8. *Low need for status:* Entrepreneurs are not precluded from seeking advice and data or saying "I don't know," and obtaining help for their business. Their need for status is satisfied by achievement rather than by external symbols such as office decor and automobiles. Money is used as a measure of performance rather than an end in itself.

9. *Moderate propensity for risk taking:* In other words, an attraction to *challenges* but to neither high- nor low-risk situations. They want the odds to be interesting but not overwhelming; they act after assessing risk and convincing themselves that little risk remains. Yet an outsider would say that they are playing for high stakes—"bet your business."

While Professor Churchill has compiled characteristics for *individual* entrepreneurs, the list applies as well to *family* entrepreneurs. Each member of the family will not exhibit strength in each of the traits noted; still, we find that in most cases the critical levels are satisfied. The trick is to make sure that the person who shows strength in any particular characteristic performs the function that makes the best use of his or her strong point.

DIARY OF A START-UP

What is it like in the beginning when you and your family go out on the limb with a family business? What might you expect when the sign first goes up on the door, or when you actually open up a bank account and get checks printed with the company name?

Everyone should keep a diary of start-up time. Here's a sampling of ours, which will give you a better idea of how it feels to make the transition from a salaried office job to a family-run operation.

DAY 1 THROUGH 7

No need to bother with a dress code in case you wondered. Hold off on the suit, high heels, etc., for another month or so. The JG Press opened up with two rooms on the second floor of an old Victorian home off Main Street. Real estate office on first floor. Architect's office on our floor. Second floor features porch and bathroom, but the drawback is that everything has to be carried up. Phones are installed; post office box is rented. Letterheads and envelopes are printed, but color is off. First decision: use up off-color stationery instead of dumping.

Phone calls are from friends who wish us well . . . and some from printing and paper salespeople who wish us well and ask for orders. Much to do to get settled, so no one minds lack of phone calls or mail activity. Arranging furniture and deciding on the location of file cabinets is more than enough to keep staff of four busy.

Don't mind transition from previous job with company employing 500 people and grossing $65 million in annual sales. Relief from barrage of questions that didn't really need answers, people controversies, staff meetings, memos, etc. Actually quite a shift—going from executive vice-president in charge of editing and publishing magazine with million-plus circulation to editing and publishing magazine with 1,500-plus circulation. (This magazine, previously published by Rodale under the name *Compost Science*, dealt with waste recycling by municipalities and industries. I had obtained publication rights from Rodale by assuming its liabilities to subscribers.)

Oh well, have to start somewhere. And besides, I'm president, Ina is vice-president, and Rill is secretary. Better make sure that we go to see lawyer next week to make sure all forms are in order. Starting out as a sole proprietorship. Plan to shift to subchapter S corporation. (Incorporating will give us added liability protection with same personal tax advantages.) Check with accountant about bookkeeping procedures. Our expertise is in publishing, not taxes or finance.

Remember to take out trash, which is easier than carrying cartons upstairs and lets us avoid tripping over boxes all the time. Put $10,000 in company bank account. First checks drawn.

Day 30

Amazing how quickly the first month in the life of The JG Press has gone. Office routine is down pretty well. Milly Lalik, the only nonfamily company staff member (who left previous company when I did), continues as executive secretary, office manager, receptionist, and head of reader service. Since the *New York Times* is only delivered to places getting more than 10 copies, Milly picks up paper at local newsstand. She also gets mail on the way in.

During first month, we make plans to expand circulation of *Compost Science*. The magazine had always been money loser for Rodale, which had been okay since its other publications, *Organic Gardening* and *Prevention*, were big profit makers. We decide to raise price, change name to something less specialized. We also plan a national conference to take place in four months. I go ahead with my first book.

Major effort will be to launch an entirely new magazine on turning personal interest/talent into business. Titles we're tossing around include *Alternative Jobs and Skills, New Age Entrepreneur, Alternative Business.* Begin to do rough budgets, talk to list brokers, publishing friends. Definitely will wait until daughter Nora graduates from college in June to launch the magazine. Rill is taking on the roles of business manager and marketing manager; Ina reviews editorial, handles subscriptions.

We buy small refrigerator for office.

Day 60

Review first two months. Major observation: with just a few of us and relatively few promotion dollars available, we can't make things happen in a hurry. We're coming up with ideas that seem valid and have written fairly decent advertisements to generate subscriptions, but everything takes a long time. We're working with free-lance copywriters and artists—have to accommodate their schedules since most are moonlighting. Have come to the realization that we can't get impatient, especially when developing a new magazine.

At this point, editorial theme for new publication, still tentatively called *Alternative Jobs and Skills,* focuses on a current business trend. New career opportunities are developing and new college courses are being offered in such fields as engineering, agriculture, pest management, waste recycling, community development, and journalism. The publication will serve as a consistent guide, advocate, and cheering squad for finding a particular employer and gaining the knowledge, experience, and skills needed in alternative approaches. Heavy emphasis will be on developing your own business in these areas. There will be profiles of people who are working in such areas; we will encourage participation by readers willing to share information. Economic relevance of certain trends I've been personally involved with for a long time will be stressed.

Check with attorney specializing in publications. Approve agreement giving us publication rights to *Compost Science*; begin "search" process prior to selecting new name for magazine to make sure it's acceptable to trademark office.

Begin writing book on integrated pest management. Working title is *Despraying America: How to Reduce Pesticide Use on Farms and in Cities.* Alison (youngest daughter, a high school junior) joins Ina in the subscription and bookkeeping departments.

In a few weeks, landlord promises to paint adjoining room—we're expanding already. Will have one room for each of our circuses.

Still have little sales—not much to sell, and not much promotion activity.

Have published two issues—bimonthly—of *Compost Science/Land Utilization.* National conference on waste recycling in Omaha is all set. Total sales for first three months have come to $25,000. Put an additional $20,000 in The JG Press account.

Nora graduated from college last month. After a couple of weeks painting house of friend's parent in Vermont, she's joined us full-time as managing editor.

New publication is taking shape. Ina comes up with name while we're playing tennis: *In Business*. Finally decided after giving speech at University of Massachusetts that careers is not topic of magazine. Entrepreneurial spirit is. Decide to focus on small business start-ups and growing business. Everybody's excited—feel we're on right track.

Hire person to sell advertising space in *Compost Science*—and *In Business* (when published). Person is young man with strong back—can carry two cartons to my one as he bounds up stairs. (He even bounds up attic stairs.) Transition from being only male employee to one of two is also an easy one.

Number of decisions to make increases as new magazine takes shape.

We try to analyze the market. Who will our readers be and how will we reach them? What's our competition? What mailing lists are available? Who are the logical advertising prospects? Are we mostly for persons already in business . . . or those who plan to be? Or both?

Editorial development—what's the right combination of how-to and profiles? How sophisticated should we (and can we) be? Can we line up writers to develop national coverage? What about graphics?

Financing—we finesse as much as possible. We know we're undercapitalized, especially since the pros say we need $3 to $5 million. We scoff—say their computer model isn't ours. Work with copywriters to develop direct-mail subscription package. Prepare budget based on 10,000 print run, six issues a year.

One Year

The troops are getting restless. One year since we started, and we're three months late getting out first issue of new magazine. Also begin to realize how few people care that magazine is late. There always seems to be another decision to make: should we use same typesetter as other magazine? What about typeface and design? Have rejected several different logos. And all of us hate the decision making that goes into finalizing the direct-mail subscription package. And all the quotes from printers are much higher than we had forecast. Never expected a free lunch, but does it have to be so costly? Accountant happily tells me that business tax loss will reduce personal income tax for last year. Cheers!

Copier breaks down. Oh, well, it worked for a year. Need a new IBM Selectric. Rill gets estimates from a subscription service bureau.

I remain optimistic. Everybody knows I'm always optimistic, so nobody pays much attention. We still have another two months at least before first issue of *In Business* will be out. We're beginning to pay price of smallness. Everything takes longer when there are so few of us to carry out these great ideas we come up with. Last thing anyone feels like hearing about right now is "I've got this great idea . . ." But we still come up with these great ideas—which generally means that we have to write or phone still another person.

Actually, it's probably a good thing we can't move any faster than we have at this stage. It's too easy to waste money before an idea is refined enough to go into the manufacturing or publishing stage. It's frustrating to have to wait, but it's also a lot cheaper.

We know—at least we should know—that we've accomplished a great deal in a year, but we know even more surely that there's still so much to do if the new magazine is to succeed. For the first time, we talk about getting outside investors—giving up some control of the company—so that we can hire more staff, plan bigger subscription promotion mailings, and get more copies out on the newsstands. We believe the magazine is a winner, but the slow pace is starting to gnaw at everyone.

By focusing so much energy and money on *In Business* (without even having an issue to show anyone), we've been letting the other projects slide. We had hoped to have 5,000 subscribers to *Compost Science* by year-end, and we only have 3,500. But we've been contacted by the head of a nonprofit organization funded by the Rockefeller Foundation who is interested in making *In Business* the official magazine of the organization. It would mean the sale of 5,000 copies of the premier issue of *In Business*. So the news ain't all bad! Actually, we've done okay. We didn't expect big sales for our first year; the total was $63,000. With any luck at all, our forecasts show that next year's sales will triple.

Probably the biggest gain is the experience and knowledge each of us has acquired in the past 12 months. I had over 25 years' experience in magazine publishing, but it's a fresh and invigorating kind of know-how you get when starting up from scratch. All of us—despite the growing impatience at our slow pace—are knowledgeable in the jobs that need to get done, ready to tackle any new project, and ready to keep asking questions.

We're one year old. We have not become one of those new businesses that get listed as a failure before 12 months are up—and we're still very enthusiastic. Now if we were only profitable and if our loyal staff would stop putting half-filled coffee cups into the garbage cans . . . I don't mind emptying the trash baskets, but I hate to put my hands into soggy paper.

2
How to Choose Your Business

HERE ARE BRIEF descriptions of services and products that have been—and are continuing to be—the foundations of new and growing family businesses. The list, along with the capsule profiles of people running these enterprises, is designed to serve as an idea generator—one that will provide the basis for family discussion. The idea at prelaunch stage is to match up your own background, abilities, finances, and interests with an emerging business opportunity.

The enterprise chosen, as mentioned elsewhere, should be rewarding. Sure it needs to be profitable, but whatever it involves, the involvement should be exciting and fun. The best choice should reflect your talent. "We like sales, the magazine publishing industry, and New Hampshire," says Chris Smith of InterMarketing Associates. So he began a firm that sells advertising space in a few special-interest magazines. He and his partner now live in New Hampshire and, from their office nearby, make their sales by telephone, by direct mail, and through trade shows.

How good is your idea—how viable and profitable? Only time will tell, but there are steps you can take to help you judge. First, talk over your idea with others in that business, not only those who like you and want you to succeed, but also the most experienced and objective businesspersons you can find. The harder-nosed your listeners, the better!

Put a test ad for your new product or service idea in a local newspaper or specialized magazine, and see if you get inquiries. (If you're selling items, it's a good idea to have a few samples of the product on hand, to back up the ad.) You can also take those samples and offer them for sale through an existing outlet.

As part of your effort to evaluate a new business idea, it's worth the investment to seek out a professional small-business counselor—someone who thoroughly understands what you and your family hope to accomplish, but who also has the professional experience and training to listen and advise. For this professional help, you'll probably have to pay a few hundred dollars—a relatively small expenditure that will be well rewarded.

Fran Worden Henry of Enterprise Associates is often sought out by business owners-to-be. In her view, "these people generally have a good service or product that they want to provide at a reasonable price. They have phenomenal knowledge about their product or service, and are terrifically excited about launching their business. But while they may know everything there is to know about their 'thing,' they may not know the broad market. They have a strong sense that it will sell, but that is all they have. They come to us because they realize that unless they get some other kind of input, they run the risk of setting out in the wrong direction."

Below are examples of interesting opportunities in growing fields.

MAIL ORDER

According to Cecil Hoge, author of *Mail Order Know-How* and a veteran of mail-order advertising who is still active in running Harrison Hoge Industries with his wife and son, one of the chief advantages of selling items by mail is that it allows you to operate at any size or pace you choose. You don't need large offices or staff, and you can gradually build up your base of customers. Hoge's main line of products is inflatable boats and accessories. His company's present mailing list includes some 250,000 names; catalogs are mailed out to these six times a year. Mail-order sales are running several million dollars a year.

In mail order, perhaps more than in most other business areas, you can learn a great deal from watching what other firms are doing and from not being afraid to ask questions of the pros. "The know-how we've gained has given us a good life," Hoge comments. "My wife and I live on Long Island Sound, minutes from the factory, as do my son and daughter-in-law. Every day I walk an hour on the beach, and my wife gardens. We sell things we're proud of in a way we're proud of." He stresses that to be successful, mail-order businesses must be run with the most scrupulous honesty, not only for its own sake but also for the sake of longevity. A frantic pursuit for Mercedes cars and Monte Carlo condos can put you in an early grave, or even earlier jail. "Ethics came to mail order because it proved good business. Anyone could go into it and lie and cheat. But to survive, a company needed repeat business, and that meant customer satisfaction. Winning trust and holding it were the keys to survival."

Hoge offers this 10-point checklist to new or would-be mail-order entrepreneurs:

1. Investigate mail order gradually. Don't rush. Look at mail-order ads in publications, on TV, and in the direct mail you receive.

2. Write down your job experience, hobbies, sports, interests—any activity you're good at. Select the one you can best imagine turning into a career.

3. In that area, write down any idea for a new item or how to improve one that exists. Select your best idea. Research that field further. Develop and try to perfect your business idea.

4. If you're creative, practical, and have a feel for money, go it alone. If you're a dreamer, team up with a doer. If you're more practical than creative, find a creative partner.

5. Limit your objective. Specialize in a product (or catalog). Avoid commitments for merchandise, components, molds, dies, employees—any overhead, initially.

6. Keep studying mail order.

7. Try writing an ad yourself. Specify the advantages of your product in the headline. Tell how to order or inquire. Be clear, complete, brief. A space ad as small as one inch will work; so will a classified ad. Simple black-and-white brochures, even typewritten and photocopied, may do to start. Avoid advertising production costs.

8. Substitute time and persuasiveness for money and risk when possible. Seek free write-ups in local publications directing orders to you.

9. Advertise with one small ad, once. Try one specialized publication, appropriate to your product, in which mail-order ads repeat. Sell your product for cash, at several times your cost.

10. Give up on that particular product if the test ad fails, but don't give up on mail order. Set aside a sum you're willing to lose monthly or annually as if you were spending it on a hobby. Keep testing new ads or new items. When you hit on one that gets good response, run your ad elsewhere—cautiously.

NATURAL FOODS RESTAURANTS

"I see the interest in natural foods carrying straight through the 1980s," says 37-year-old Terry Dalton, founder and owner of the Unicorn, a combination restaurant, bakery, and food store in Miami, Florida. Just four years old, the Unicorn had sales of $2.5 million in 1983. Adds Dalton: "With the steady demand for restaurants that serve nutritious foods in a tasteful and professional manner, a restaurant should be successful wherever it is."

Restaurants have traditionally been popular family enterprises, but too many would-be owners are convinced that all they need is a liquor license, a nifty name, and a clever decor to operate profitably. "It's a universal misunderstanding," say Jim Breen and Bill Sanderson, founders of Restaurant Development Associates in California. "The personal nature of the business, the direct contact with the public, and the opportunity for self-expression and creativity make restaurants appealing to many people who dream of opening a business." The consultants caution that the restaurant business tends to be capital-intensive, so you need a theme and a projected image to capture a steady clientele. They believe that an emphasis on quality natural foods can help you carve out a successful niche.

HEALTH FOOD

Deep Roots Trading Company of Lewisburg, Pennsylvania, grew out of the natural food store operated by Ellen and Roger Spivack. "As a way to add income, we began to grow fresh salad sprouts, caring for them in a kitchen behind the shop. The sprout business took off, in supermarkets as well as restaurants."

As natural foods move into supermarkets and the kitchen cupboard, tofu and other soybean products have gained increasing popularity. Three of the more successful firms, Legume, Soyfoods Unlimited, and the American Miso Company, are family operations run by husbands and wives who are working to make their products household names. Gary and Chandri Barat of Legume, for example, expect to become "the Dannons or Perriers of the tofu industry," while Valerie Robertson of Soyfoods Unlimited, who currently ships some 2,700 pounds of frozen tempeh burgers to New England each month, plans to go nationwide with 10 times more distribution.

JUICE STANDS

Bob and Georgia Groth make and sell all-natural fruit shakes at their Flying Fruit Fantasy stand in Baltimore's Harborplace. Their business began as the result of a sideline. "I was running a restaurant/bar in 1978 in Washington and knew I wanted to get into something else," says Bob. "We began by setting up a booth to sell fruit shakes at a fair on Capitol Hill. People lined up from the start."

Success at weekend fairs with the blended fruit shake led them to invest $10,000 to buy and convert an old mail truck into a mobile stand. They decided to set up in Harborplace's pedestrian mall, where traffic is great and impulse food buying commonplace. Sales have progressed so well that the Groths are now selling franchises, offering a package of a fully equipped stand, ingredients, and location in a high-traffic mall.

SPECIALTY FOODS

As interest in quality foods reawakens, new openings in the marketplace have been filled by specialty companies. Some—like Chalif Mustard—are recent arrivals. Others have been family operated for generations. All show an unswerving commitment to quality. For example, the Sterzing Food Company of Burlington, Iowa, makes thick, nongreasy potato chips. The John Lasser Company in Chicago makes old-fashioned soda pop. There's the Straub Brewery in St. Marys, Pennsylvania, turning out an all-natural beer, and Rowinsky's Cheesecake is popular in Cambridge, Massachusetts.

Bob Davis of Wahoo Wieners in Wahoo, Nebraska, thinks fledgling small business owners in this field who buy an established business with a good name are making a smart move, even if it's more expensive than starting on one's own. He estimates that between 10 and 20 percent of the purchase price of the O.K. Market (makers of Wahoo Wieners) was "blue sky"—the good reputation, customer loyalty, and good feeling the firm generated under its original owners.

Other examples of quality regional food companies include Homespun, a two-year-old condiments company in Washington, D.C. Homespun was born in 1981, when Jane Becker, a real estate broker, decided that the recession made the cranberry chutney she gave as Christmas presents more salable than homes. She began Homespun with $2,000 of her own and $25,000 she borrowed from friends in amounts from $1,000 to $10,000. Forty-eight-year-old Brookie Durkin of Winslow, Arizona, began making homemade lollipops for her teenage son to sell at school for a little extra spending money. One thing led to another, and the Licker Company came into existence. Now, Mrs. Durkin and 10 part-time helpers turn out 19,000 lollipops each week.

GOURMET FOOD DISTRIBUTOR

In 1981, Hope and Mark Klayman of Southampton, Pennsylvania, had no idea that a gourmet food distributorship was in their future. Two years later, Hope's Specialty Foods is building a nationwide network of distributors.

While dining for the first time at Joe's Restaurant in Reading, Pennsylvania, famous for its mushroom-based cuisine, Hope and Mark struck up a conversation with the owner. He told the Klaymans of his attempts to market Joe's Mushroom Soup. Hope, listening intently, boldly offered to distribute Joe's product. Pleased by her enthusiasm, the owner gave Hope some soups to take home for taste testing. The next week, Hope ventured into a cheese shop. "Have you ever heard of Joe's Restaurant?" she asked. "I'm distributing his soups." The shop owner was familiar with Joe's soups and ordered a case. Hope Klayman was in business.

An initial sales strategy was devised with the help of phone books and road maps. "Find all the cheese shops and sell 'em" was the motto. Within two weeks, she had orders from 20 stores. "I became the thermos lady," says Hope. "Everywhere I went I had a hot jug of soup—no one got away without tasting."

Because she was the master distributor for Joe's Products, Hope could set the prices, order quantities, and sell just about anywhere she wanted. "My problem was that I didn't know what percentage of the sale I needed as commission to cover costs and finance growth," she says. "My first figure, 19 percent, was a naive estimate, but I learned quickly. Now, it's usually set around 30 percent."

The initial investment of $240 went toward opening a checking account, ordering invoices, setting up files, and buying maps. The biggest expense, however, was fueling the family car for sales trips and deliveries. Hope was able to get a $7,000 loan from a local credit union, which was used to finance the purchase of a large van. The next step was to expand the product line.

Mustard filled the bill perfectly, and two gourmet brands she chose became best-sellers. The number of delivery routes increased rapidly from one to 13. Products were being sold to gourmet and specialty food outlets, cheese shops, independent groceries, health food stores, a bakery, and even a bookstore!

It became quite clear that help was needed with deliveries and bookkeeping to allow Hope to spend more time selling and developing a more diverse product line. Mark Klayman joined his wife, taking over 80 percent of the deliveries. He hired a full-time secretary/bookkeeper and built a network of sales reps that now stretches from Hawaii to Detroit to Atlanta and back to Pennsylvania. Reps work on a 10 percent commission for initial sales and 5 percent on subsequent reorders.

Efforts to build the business are paying off. Specialty food manufacturers now approach Hope to sell their products. The number of accounts has grown to 247, and the company represents 324 products, including sauces, spices, French cider, jelly beans, and honey from New Zealand. Hope is the distributor for 24 manufacturers and a broker for 5 manufacturers. Inadequate storage space was a stumbling block to growth, until Mark's father rented them space in his pizza company's warehouse in Philadelphia. Hope can now offer faster delivery and can easily transport foreign products to storage.

Steady growth and low operating costs combined with

a flexible sales approach—Hope won't turn a small order down—have led to a dramatic increase in sales. During the first four months of 1982, for example, $27,500 of food was sold; in 1983, sales reached $65,000 by late April. The company broke even in December 1982, netting $36,000 in sales. "Realistically, $200,000 is our sales goal for 1983," says Hope, "giving us a gross profit of $50,000. That's a real good start."

SPORTING GOODS CONSIGNMENT SHOP

Sports Again in San Rafael, California, is a consignment shop for buying and selling used sporting goods and accessories. Inventory ranges from bicycles, badminton sets, and boxing gloves, to kayaking, windsurfing, and weight-lifting equipment. According to co-owner Liv Diaz, a store like hers can bring in sales of $7,000 to $10,000 a month.

"We started out with about $3,000," says Liv, "and we did a lot of work. To build our initial inventory, we went to garage sales, flea markets, and anywhere else we could find used equipment. It would have cost a lot more to start if we hadn't done so much of the work ourselves."

Since the store was stocked, however, the owners haven't had to go out on buying trips. Instead, people bring in their used equipment, which is sold on consignment. Sports Again has about 550 consignees, and goods are sold on a straight percentage of 50/50. The percentage on items over $150 is 70/30, 70 percent going to the consignee. "It helps to bring more expensive items into the store," says Liv.

"To set a price, we first ask the consignee how much they paid for it," she says. "We also watch the ads very closely to see what the stores are selling the items for, and we keep a stack of catalogs from stores and manufacturers to see what the original cost was. The price is based also on how popular the item is and on its condition."

To get new inventory as well as to attract customers, Sports Again does a lot of advertising in newspapers and sometimes on the radio. In addition, fliers are distributed at colleges and throughout the community. "We have no trouble getting goods to sell," says Liv. "The advertising brings in new inventory and new customers. Most of the goods are sold on consignment, although sometimes we do buy items outright. If someone is moving, for example, and doesn't want to bother with consignment, we might buy their equipment."

INNKEEPERS

"It's amazing how many of our guests have a deep desire to run an inn themselves," says Margaret Lobenstine, who operates Wildwood Inn with her husband in Ware, Massachusetts. The Lobenstines have operated a bed-and-breakfast inn for five years, having sold their house in California and used the money to buy and renovate a Victorian home with five bedrooms and three baths on the second floor. The Lobenstines live on the third floor.

On a larger scale, Tom and Betsy Guido operate Chester Inn in Chester, Vermont. The Guidos actually run a three-in-one operation: a gourmet restaurant on the inn's first floor, a renovated bar and lounge, plus 31 rooms that can accommodate up to 70 guests. According to Jim Howard, the broker who arranged the sale of the inn to the Guidos, prospective buyers need to have on hand enough funds to cover down payments of 25 to

40 percent of the purchase price plus working capital of between $10,000 and $25,000. To assess market values of country inns, Howard uses the rule-of-thumb that an inn will sell for about $20,000 per guest room. "This sort of place," he adds, "will typically earn a minimum of $16,000 per year per room in room income, equivalent or double that figure in food income, and 50 percent of that figure in bar income."

HOME CONSTRUCTION

In Little Rock, Arkansas, Bill Bland and his family have set up a low-overhead home construction company with heavy emphasis on passive solar systems. In January 1982, he began construction on his first subdivision of eight houses. He also started designing a second subdivision of 60 units. The selling price of the houses averages less than $40,000 for between 960 and 1,080 square feet of living space—which is small—plus carport and a large deck. Down payments average $3,000, and monthly payments range from $350 to $500. Purchasers can immediately take advantage of solar tax credits of up to $4,000 on each house. Not all standard appliances, such as stove and refrigerator, are provided with the house. Bland's houses are designed to be extremely energy-efficient, allowing for solar gain in winter and shade in summer. Because of the energy-saving features of these houses, the cost of heating and cooling them is approximately half that of neighboring homes.

Bland operates with virtually no overhead and is not encumbered by a stock of unsold houses. His wife does the books, his son-in-law is the construction superintendent, and his daughter, a realtor, attends to the details of selling.

NEWSLETTER PUBLISHING

If you have access to specialized information that has a defined audience, you may want to consider starting a newsletter. With the proliferation of word processors, there has been a corresponding increase in the number of newsletters, and it's now estimated that more than 5,000 newsletters are published in the United States. Just about every trade area, from crafts to plumbing, has its own. The more commercial the field, the higher the price of the subscription. Many such newsletters are published out of a home office.

Six years ago, Ritchie Lowry took over the management of his family trust funds. The amount of money he manages is substantial—more than seven figures—and he's been determined from the outset to invest it in ways that are socially responsible. He will not, for example, buy stocks from companies manufacturing weapons and nuclear armaments. He gives high priority to companies in the pollution control field. In his words, "I search for good money."

In April 1982, Lowry, along with his son Peter and daughter-in-law Susan, started a publishing business and a monthly eight-page newsletter called *Good Money*. It was started with an original capitalization of $25,000, and the Lowrys figure that they will break even when subscriptions reach between 1,000 and 1,500. As of October 1983, business was booming. Revenues have been increasing steadily and recently have risen 70 percent. With renewals starting next month, profitability should be just around the corner.

Newsletters are also the core of a one-stop publication shop in Pasadena called Newsletter Specialists.

Founded by Jim Laris and Marjorie Wood, it offers custom newsletter design and other kinds of business writing. The partners will also design brochures, write copy, and arrange for typesetting and art. "The business didn't require a lot of investment because we didn't buy any equipment besides typewriters and a paste-up table," says Laris.

FREE-LANCE WRITING

According to Richard Margolis, a free-lancer for many years, the trick to this business is "to hold one's convictions dear, along with one's standards of excellence, even if compelled to sell one's talents cheap." He further notes: "The beginning writer's professional assets are likely to be restricted to a ream of recycled paper (speckled), an old typewriter (the *r* sticks), and one or two dubious connections in the publishing world."

One outfit we know in Washington, D.C., provides news coverage on a continuing free-lance basis to city magazines across the country. Ideally, the stories will also provide the basis for other assignments, so the work leads to additional income. In fact, that is the real essence of successful free-lancing: trying to use the same material more than once for articles in noncompeting publications and eventually even in a book.

TROUT RAISING

Ten years ago, Fern Wood Mitchell and his wife became part of a new aquaculture industry when they set up a trout farm called Shenandoah Fisheries in Lacey Spring, Virginia. The fish eggs are purchased from a company outside Tacoma, Washington. They arrive in less than a week's time, neatly packed in insulated containers. Mitchell puts the eggs in glass tanks, similar to fish aquariums, in the basement of his house. The eggs hatch and eventually are forced up and out into a holding tank by a jet of water. There they pause, tens of thousands of baby trout swimming together in huge dark masses, awaiting transfer into one of three smaller (12-foot) pools outside. As they grow, the trout are moved from pool to larger pool until, 14 to 16 months later, they are harvested. The trout are taken from the water with great care and are carefully dressed to preserve head and tail. Mitchell's part-time staff of neighborhood women proceed to cut out the back and all attendant bones with surgical skill. The day after harvesting, the fish are dispatched by truck to 30 or 40 of the finest restaurants in Washington, D.C.

Mitchell took a calculated chance when he launched the business 10 years ago. "I got an old beat-up pickup truck, put a few trout on ice in the back, and visited a dozen or so chefs in the best restaurants in D.C.," he remembers. "All of them were getting trout through various wholesalers. Some were able to get a few trout direct from Virginia and Pennsylvania. But most were coming in from Idaho."

Today Mitchell sells over 100,000 trout a year at between $2.50 and $3 a pound; almost all the fish go to restaurants. The average size is 13 inches and 12 to 16 ounces. He never advertises. The chefs tell other chefs, and the orders just pile up. Mitchell grosses $200,000 a year, and can't fill all his orders. He believes the volume could be doubled easily. Mitchell began the business with $100,000 in savings, and he cautions against trying to make it without considerable funds. He believes the business can be launched with as little as $40,000.

SUPPLYING RENOVATORS

Donna and Claude Jeanloz have built up a mail-order business, a magazine, and most recently, four retail stores—all from the experience of restoring two homes of their own. Their company, located in Miller's Falls, Massachusetts, specializes in hard-to-find fixtures, hardware, and ornaments, such as wooden toilet seats, porcelain knobs, and lamps. Explains Claude: "I concentrate on Renovator's Supply. Donna is in charge of the magazine (*Victorian Homes*). We both hope we're spending enough time with the children." Annual company sales from all their activities are well over $5 million. "It might sound trite, but it's the American Dream," says 34-year-old Claude. "We had high hopes and we were well prepared."

When Claude says that they were prepared to go into business back in 1978, he's referring to both expertise and capital. "If we'd had to borrow money to get started, we never would have made it," believes Claude. The couple had $50,000 profit from the sale of one home, and they invested this in their first, 36-page black-and-white catalog, which listed over 300 out-of-the-ordinary items. In the fall of 1978, this brochure was mailed to 27,000 prospects gleaned from *Old House Journal*'s mailing list. Though the couple had absolutely no experience in direct-mail sales, Claude had worked for seven years as an independent management consultant for big firms around the country. "I'd been setting up manufacturing plants for other people," remembers Claude. "I just decided to try it for myself."

Working from their kitchen table, the Jeanlozes had a slow start. "We discovered afterward that January is the best month for mail order, not October," recalls

Donna. Gross sales were $38,000 in 1978. Then all hell broke loose. Brass switch plates started selling like hotcakes, and word about Renovator's Supply began to spread not only among individual homeowners, but also among contractors, designers, and restaurant and hotel owners. A second catalog, issued in April 1979, paid for its printing costs by that summer, and 1979 gross sales topped $250,000. It quickly became evident that customer records could no longer be kept in shoeboxes, and in December 1979, a computer was installed in the Jeanlozes' bedroom.

In 1980, they moved the business down the road into a spacious and slightly dilapidated old Ford dealership in the center of Miller's Falls. With the help of 24 employees, Donna and Claude issued two-color catalogs in 1980 to nearly 300,000 customers and grossed an astounding $1.2 million in sales. In 1981 and 1982 growth continued to defy predictions, with three catalogs mailed to nearly 6 million names and three shifts of employees working around the clock to process an average of 1,000 orders per day.

MICROCOMPUTER SOFTWARE STORES

Software stores are appearing all over, but there's room for more. Computer dealers often don't know a lot about software, because they sell only the packages that come with the equipment. Also, a number of good programs are available from "cottage programmers," people who write and produce software out of their homes. Quality control, guarantees, customer education and support, and a few computers in the store for demonstration use are what you need to do well. Market your software through local computer user clubs, at trade shows, and in newspaper ads. Consider selling through mail-order ads in computer magazines. Hold seminars at the store to attract customers. Find a few reputable software publishing houses that produce consistent, quality products. Some franchises are available.

COMPUTER SOFTWARE

If you like to write computer software, you have several choices: independent contracting with computer software houses, selling directly by mail, or doing custom work for owners of small business computers. Start-up requires a computer, some blank disks, and enough money for small classified or space ads. Advertise in any one of the many computer publications. One pitfall: people violating your copyright and making copies of software for friends.

EMPLOYMENT SERVICE

Matching clients with a variety of needs to a reliable work force can be lucrative. One California woman we know turned her $12,000 investment into well over $70,000 in just a few years. Existing companies provide workers to perform a variety of duties, including housecleaning, serving at parties, baby-sitting, chauffeuring, lawn care, sewing, chair recaning, and much more. Contract arrangements, fee schedules, and information sheets help to organize the business. Initial advertising is necessary.

ENERGY STORES

In the late 1970s, stores selling energy-saving/generating devices were speculated to be a high-growth industry of the 1980s. Retail outlets opened up all over the place, selling insulation, auditing services, low-flow shower heads, wood stoves, thermal shades, and passive and active solar devices. But homeowners weren't quite ready and the market quickly peaked and bottomed out. But these stores are beginning to come back; most are starting out more slowly, taking pains to educate consumers by holding free seminars, giving demonstrations, and selling small-ticket items to persuade customers of the advantages of using these devices.

TYPESETTING

Start by renting time off-hours on another company's equipment. Sell to specialized markets at first—new businesses, colleges, and nonprofit groups that don't have a lot of money to spend on publications. Charge less than regular typesetters. Once you've grown a little, you can buy or lease equipment. Also, explore typesetting by telecommunication, receiving copy via a phone line. This makes you available to a larger market and allows at-home start-up for some.

HOME HEALTH CARE

The number of elderly will increase rapidly in the next 20 years, along with the cost of health care. Many older people may not be able to afford or need to go to a nursing home or may only need assistance temporarily. A Virginia woman who recently went into the home health care business started out with 3 employees and one client; now she has 110 employees and a client list of 2,000. Her staff includes RNs and LPNs, as well as employees hired to stay with patients or run errands. The business is labor-intensive, and owner and employees are on constant call. A computer can help to keep track of clients and employees as well as cash flow.

CRAFTS

Potters, weavers, sculptors, painters, and basket makers have one problem in common—selling what they make. In most cases, many years have gone into developing the skill, but little or no time went into learning the business. Craftspeople often start by selling their pieces at crafts fairs. (American Craft Enterprises in Rhinebeck, New York, is the biggest sponsor.) But what about selling crafts retail? Here are some ways to go about it:

1. Start out by selling on consignment or selling your "bread and butter" items wholesale to galleries and gift shops. Get your name known.
2. Consider joining in with other craftspeople to open one large shop. Split the rent, advertise cooperatively, and hire a manager. Hold exhibits and show openings on a regular basis to attract customers and publicity. Be sure to have plenty of open space and good lighting for displays. Build up a mailing list so invitations can be sent out. Organize a crafts fair once a year to find new artists or other products to sell.

BOOKSTORES

Independent bookstores have to be creative to survive these days. Their markets are being chipped away by national book chains and discount booksellers. Effective in-store displays, active advertising, thorough customer services, promotional events such as author parties, and in some cases, specialization can help. Consider a combination bookstore-café or a bookstore that sells cards, posters, records, art prints, and games. Secondhand and remaindered books—replenished regularly—may help to draw a steady flow of customers.

OLD-FASHIONED GENERAL STORE

The "country" general store (it can be in an urban area) appeals to many shoppers' sense of nostalgia. Pick a theme, preferably one that picks up on local customs. Pennsylvania Dutch quilts, handmade brooms, and regional specialty food are good examples of items that fit with a theme. Start small, stocking lots of inventory in one or two rooms. Expanding too quickly can sap cash flow. An electronic cash register helps keep track of inventory. Try to get local and regional publicity; also advertise. If necessary, run specials to get people into your store.

BAKERY

Building a several-million-dollar business on a cheesecake recipe isn't impossible. But succeeding in a big way with a bakery takes consistent quality, fine ingredients, upscale prices, and a combination wholesale and retail business. Start small, baking at home and selling your breads, cakes, pies, and pastries to caterers, grocery stores, restaurants, and individuals. Build a following and then open a retail store. Maintain quality. Once you've established your name in the marketplace, you can do wholesale business on a large scale to food stores and specialty shops.

3

Spouses as Partners... and Other Combinations

IN THE COURSE of gathering information for this book, I've come across businesses made up of just about every possible combination of family members: husband-wife (most common), closely followed by parent-child (or parents-children), brother-brother, sister-sister, and on and on.

No single combination seems to work automatically or fail predictably. The ones that work best are characterized by a respect for one another's personal strengths and effort, a comfortable feeling when in one another's presence, a commitment to make the business succeed, and a sense of proportion. These people don't become obsessed with the work that needs to be done or feel that they're martyrs. At least, they don't consider themselves martyrs for long periods of time. No one should have to work with a martyr or live with one either, for that matter.

Some general pointers about combinations:

1. Don't go into business with a brother, father, sister, mother, or even aunt or uncle if you wouldn't be

willing to spend part of a vacation with that person. In other words, if you can't stand his or her personality, forget the whole deal. I don't care how much money that relative has available to invest or how great she or he is at selling. If someone grates on you when you're relaxed, working with that person under stress will make both of your lives miserable.

2. Don't tell yourself that you're doing someone else a favor by joining the business. Either it's a good opportunity and worth the gamble to you and the others involved or you might as well stay where you are. If you do stay where you are, by the way, just don't complain in front of the family about the misery of your present job.

3. Don't think your (fill in relationship) can do the impossible. If that person is inexperienced, he or she will have to grow into the job. Always be realistic in your performance expectations.

4. Don't be supersensitive. Some of the best-run husband-and-wife businesses I know are those in which one can call the other an airhead—when deserved, of course—without the other taking undue offense. I prefer that such endearments not be uttered in front of the staff, but it's been known to happen, and we all survive.

Our neighbors, Rose and Rudy Ackerman, work together as partners. Before going ahead with the idea, they wondered if they could take their work home without creating more turmoil than their artistic personalities could handle. As far as we can tell from our observation point across the street, all is working out fine. In Rudy's opinion, to run a business with your spouse "you have to have an awfully strong marriage to begin with." Adds Rose: "We've always served as each other's sounding board. We make most decisions together; each of us listens to the input of the other person. Our arguments are incessant—they can be very loud arguments. But they're over minor things, day-to-day things. I can't think of anything major that we've argued about. We've had growing pains working together. I wanted to take on more authority, but I didn't know how to do it. Then Rudy would ask me to do things that I wasn't yet trained to do. But I've learned them. And we've always worked together, as a team."

Dr. Margaret Baker, a Philadelphia psychologist who specializes in counseling career couples, believes that when families work together, they often create an ambivalent atmosphere of competition, togetherness, smothering, support, role confusion, and family pride. From research and her own experience working with her husband, Dr. Baker has concluded that running a business together is easiest when both partners establish what they each want from the endeavor and agree on the means to pursue their individual goals. As reported by Rebecca Christian in *In Business* magazine, Dr. Baker stresses, "It's very important that the marriage has reached a stage where both spouses are perfectly comfortable in it and believe they are growing together. Each person must have a true sense of self and must be willing to let the other be stimulated by other people and other things. The spouses should have learned to handle their own competitiveness with each other. Otherwise, the work place can become a battlefield for working out difficulties that should have been resolved earlier."

Maintaining other interests and letting each other go when necessary are two talents Dr. Baker believes a couple needs when working together. She observes: "Most people don't make a conscious decision to work together. The opportunity evolves and they say: 'Why not?' They really should discuss ahead of time whether they are going to maintain a strict businesslike relationship at work or whether an informal style would suit them better. After they try it for a while, they should reevaluate the rules."

The matter of ego cannot be ignored. In an ideal world, all family members would devote themselves to the cause with equal fervor, and the total success of the effort would be reward and gratification enough. But in the real world, title and status mean a lot to a lot of people. If you're the macho type who imagines that everybody will call you a wimp if you're ever seen taking orders from your wife, then going into business together could bring trouble.

Maybe because of the way The JG Press started out, I think it's important that the relatives start out *together* in the business and genuinely feel the sense of accomplishment and participation in what they've accomplished. This feeling—the knowledge that you've built something out of nothing—can help all the partners weather many stormy times.

When a business is established and a son or daughter is about to join, it's also critical that he or she be given an opportunity to develop that sense of accomplishment. One local business we know seems to show a knack for putting the newest family member into the least important area of the business. Whether that person succeeds or fails at a project doesn't matter much, and so he or she invariably loses interest—and the confidence of people he or she is one day supposed to be leading.

A survey conducted by Chemical Bank of 1,000 small-business owners showed that, though the owners are proud of what they've created and would do it all over again. they would rather see their children working somewhere else, preferably in larger corporations. While Chemical Bank has a large public relations firm doing its research, I still think their findings don't reflect the current trend.

Far more indicative of what's happening is the decision by sons and daughters to enter their parents' professions or firms. Part of the trend is based on sheer economics, not only the renewed respectability of family businesses. According to one psychiatrist at the Cornell Medical Center, "Now Dad's or Mom's job starts to look better. You might expect all sorts of neurotic stuff going on about being unable to leave the home and to establish roots of one's own. But I think most new family businesses are fairly free of that." Says one 20-year-old undergraduate who plans to join her father's practice after graduation from dental school: "Of course, I have to think whether I am going to be able to finance my own office. But, for the time being, I can be doing something that I enjoy and can help my father, who works so hard and who is an extremely gifted individual."

Working for a parent usually increases the child's respect for the parent's knowledge in her or his chosen field. For example, a son who had just become a partner in his father's store said, "Whatever I learned about retailing in college and in other stores was nothing to what I learned from him."

Besides questions of trust, opportunity, and talent, children and parents who are thinking of joining forces should consider the matter of rebellion. Is a child who still has to prove himself or herself, who needs to test his or her own independence, ready to "come home" to the business? It's far better to have the matter of youthful rebellion worked out *before* involvement with the family business. That's another reason why perceptive parents prefer that a son or daughter obtain some outside job experience first. Says a New York psychiatrist: "In many traditional family businesses, children are expected to come into the firm at the beginning of their careers, the exact moment when they have started to break away and become independent. All of a sudden, they have to take orders from Mom and Dad once again. The ones who pull it off most successfully have already been away to college or have worked a year at another job and know they can stand on their own two feet. Then it's not degrading to take orders from your family."

Some families fear that competition within the business will lead to a certain amount of tension, or even downright nastiness. Billie Kotlowitz, a family therapist in Manhattan, says that when a daughter enters the business, it may cause problems in the mother-daughter relationship. "Young girls very often don't want to do what their mothers have done—social work or teaching. They want to be the lawyer or doctor that their father is. My fear is that the mother will be cut out. Fathers and daughters will have lots in common, but perhaps the mother won't be able to discuss professional matters with them."

In my experience, therapist Kotlowitz can relax. What I see happening is just the opposite. In fact, the mother often serves as the keystone in both family and business. A *keystone* is defined as "something on which associated things depend for support." Architecturally, the keystone is the wedge-shaped piece at the crown of an arch that locks the other pieces in place. In many of the family businesses I know, including ours, the mother is the unifying link between the family as family unit and the family as business.

For a doctoral thesis at Harvard Business School, John Davis surveyed 89 father-and-son pairs who worked together and found that simmering conflicts typically flare up when sons are in their mid-to-late thirties and fathers are in their sixties. At that point, he found, sons need to assert themselves by taking risks—perhaps introducing new products or expanding into new regions—while fathers want to protect their retirement security by keeping the business on a steady course.

When it looks as though parent and child are headed for this kind of impasse, Davis recommends that the younger generation study what took place in the early days of the business—the routes the founder took to develop and build it. If the sons and daughters can find new ventures that are consistent with what was done earlier—instead of setting off along any trendy path—they are much more likely to win the cooperation of the founder. At the same time, the founding generation should try to recall the excitement they felt when the business was new, and recognize that their children need opportunities to get that same exciting sense of exploring uncharted ground.

WHEN IN-LAWS COME ABOARD

For many businesses, the coming aboard of in-laws complicates harmonious decision making. A son-in-law who joins a slowly growing firm may want (and need) more remuneration and may therefore push for ways to increase sales more rapidly. At the same time, the son-in-law may have the skills to bring about those sales that were lacking until he arrived. The new surge may be just what the business needs, but it may disturb the serenity of pre-in-law days.

Professor Calder of the University of Utah notes that as long as the members of the family are single, family loyalty permeates the organization; the business belongs to "the family," and the group shares a mutual pride and interest in the endeavor. But when members marry and their spouses attempt to enter the inner circles, the in-laws may not share the perspective of the children of the family who have seen the business grow, often under hardship. These spouses often feel that the business forms a wedge between them and their partners. They may have different spending and saving habits or may disagree with family members' views about the importance of the family business, family relations, and leisure time. Such differences inevitably lead to conflict and have repercussions in the business itself.

WHEN CHILDREN ARE BOSSES

With increasing frequency children are employing their parents. "From 9 to 5, I'm Barbara," explains 52-year-old Barbara Moses who performs administrative duties for her daughter, Rebecca, a New York fashion designer. "After that, I'm Mom." So begins an article in the *New York Times* on parents who work for their children. When a mother is employed by her child, the ability to separate the personal matters from the professional matters is the key to maintaining a good relationship between them. According to psychologist Marilyn Machlowitz, interviewed in the article, it is important not to let a family member's judgments interfere with one's sense of worth and competence. "Does the mother feel this is an act of charity or that she's on the payroll for tax purposes?" How well you handle your mother's criticism on the job is also important, Dr. Machlowitz says, adding: "Is your reaction to it a throwback to being five years old and spilling your milk?"

As explained in the *New York Times*, Barbara Moses went to work for her daughter after 18 years as an executive secretary for a number of companies. "My mother has all the beliefs I had," notes Rebecca Moses. "The business became hers as much as mine. When we were just starting, we worked out of my loft. We'd start at 7:00 in the morning and do absolutely everything ourselves. My mother would come in and wake me up, and we'd pull the garments, write out tickets by hand, pack and seal the boxes, and invoice. She'd be there until 9:00 or 10:00 every night." Now Rebecca Moses has more employees but Barbara Moses still comes in at 7:00 and makes coffee. However, she now has her desk in the reception area of the company's new Seventh Avenue quarters.

MULTIGENERATIONAL BUSINESSES

With what seems to be a new appreciation of family tradition, more and more grandchildren are entering businesses begun by their grandparents decades before. These grandchildren—who are often in their mid-twenties—eagerly take on menial training jobs and look ahead to the time when they too can have an executive suite of their own. Their backgrounds are far different from those of their grandparents: they come with backgrounds in anthropology, English literature, and computer science. Included in this group are granddaughters, who are often the first women to join previously male-managed firms. In the words of an MIT professor, there has been a "mystique of the male in family companies, a feeling that the son is the natural follower. Daughters are a very recently emerging pattern."

At the Anglo Fabrics Company in New York's Garment District, five of 89-year-old founder Leo Honig's grandsons are at present on the payroll, with two more expected to join after they graduate from college. "I can't say that there's nothing else in my life that's worth doing, but I'm comfortable here," says 33-year-old grandson Tom Honig, who hopes that his 3-year-old son will someday join the company. "If you're brought up a certain way, entering the family business seems natural. I think I would like Ruben to have his first working experiences here."

One of the most heart-warming stories about multi-generational family businesses that I've seen was a recent report on New York City's ethnic food shops, such as the oldest Italian cheese store in the United States. (It's appropriately located on Grand Street in Little Italy.)

"For New York families like the Allevas, the Anagnostous and Fables, the Kurowyckys and the Weisses," begins the *New York Times* article,

> a store, *their* store, is a living organism requiring, more often demanding, a constant nourishment that only they as families can provide with the labors of their hands and heads. Their lives are their stores, their stores their lives.
>
> Families such as these, whose lineages are European and for whom nothing is more important than tradition and family continuity, are not uncommon in this city of immigrants. And though there are likely more of them who run food shops here than in other American cities, their number appears to be dwindling as children grow up, are educated and elect to leave the family businesses for other ways of life. But this is not true of all of them.

With that prologue, writer Fred Ferretti launches into a description of the kinds of people we continually encounter while gathering information for *In Business* magazine. Robert Alleva, a college graduate who had worked as a medical technologist, says that he "always had in the back of his mind to come back" to the 92-year-old store. "I'd like to keep it going, I guess forever."

Seventy-two-year-old Erast Kurowycky, a Ukrainian who survived Soviet and Nazi takeovers, emigrated to America and set up a meat business on New York City's Lower East Side, which his son and his grandson have since joined. "I do not often admit it, but I am proud and I am happy. It is a good trade," says Erast.

And for 13-year-old Paul Fable, who helps his father at his bakery making and selling phyllo, the reason why he does what he does is simple and straightforward: "It's the family. I have the experience. My life will go on, and I know I have someplace to go."

At Paprikas Weiss, on Second Avenue near 81st Street, Edward Weiss, his wife, and his mother are in the store founded by his grandfather in the early 1900s. Judi, 23, now a student at Harvard's Graduate School of Education, is in charge of the Hungarian food shop's publicity. Her brother, Peter, 26, at Harvard's Graduate School of Business, plans to manage the store's growing mail-order business when he graduates. According to Ferretti, Edward Weiss wanted to create "a little part of the best part of what the immigrants left behind in Europe." And, adds his wife, Renee: "My husband and I wanted them here, everybody." And evidently the children want to be there very much, Harvard degrees and all.

4
Early Testing and Planning

THE TIME TO make certain that you are not creating an impossible monster is *before* your business is actually launched—when it's in the planning stage. Don't set goals that immediately put overwhelming strains on all involved. Don't assume that everyone else will be willing to make the same time and energy commitment that you are prepared to make.

When you set about making the important decisions, such as location, job responsibilities, market niche, and sales and financial goals, make them in a style that's comfortable and familiar to the family. If you haven't been dictatorial before, don't think the business gives you a right to become the Great Dictator—even if your livelihood depends upon it.

BUSINESS PLAN

Just about every business counselor I've ever met advises one and all to spend weeks—even months—developing a business plan on paper before spending dollars on starting the business. This advice, of course, certainly makes sense. The only trouble is that most family businesses I know—ours included—were created without an official-looking document that bankers or accountants would deem worthy of being termed a business plan. Nevertheless, all of the owners I'm referring to are quite lucid about goals and strategies (although a bit fuzzy about some particulars).

To begin the process of early planning, describe your proposed venture in narrative form, as if you were writing a letter to a friend. Describe the product or service your business will offer, who the prime customers will be, what kind of competition you foresee, and the equipment, staff, and promotion that will be needed. Once the narrative is complete, then the elements can be converted into a set of financial figures that should give you a fairly clear indication of how much money is needed and the income you can reasonably expect.

Do a five-year projection of your costs and income and then raise as many "what if" questions as you can think of. (For example: What if I cut the product's cost by 65 cents or raised its price by $1.10? What if I did both?) Figure out how these variables would affect your projections. You can now get answers to such "what if" questions as fast as you can pose them by using a microcomputer equipped with a Visicalc or similar "electronic spread-sheet" program.

The more experienced you are as a family in the particular business area you are entering, the more shortcuts you can take in the planning process. The more unfamiliar you are with your chosen field and market, the more formal your business plan should be.

Many agencies and institutions—such as the Small Business Administration, state commerce departments, local Chambers of Commerce, and Small Business Development Centers—have excellent publications available on how to prepare a business plan. The University of New Hampshire, for example, has developed Business Planning Worksheets, which serve as a step-by-step guide. The planning outline for financial data explains that you should calculate the following:

A. Sources and applications of funding
B. Capital equipment list
C. Balance sheet
D. Breakeven analysis
E. Pro-forma income projections (profit and loss statements)—three-year summary. Detail by month for first year; detail by quarter, second and third year.
F. Pro-forma cash flow
(again, three-year summary as above)

Craig Seymour, who directs the University of New Hampshire's technical assistance program for small businesses, says that this is the time (when you're doing the business plan) to ask the critical question: "Is the estimated sales volume large enough to support the two (or more of you), pay the rent, cover the overhead, carry a reasonable inventory, and return a profit?"

For some would-be entrepreneurs, the challenge of planning is sufficient reason to stay at a 9-to-5 salaried job. Being confronted with so many questions and so many variables quickly becomes overwhelming. But as you get into the process, assuming you're genuinely committed to the specific nature of your proposed business, you'll learn to make the best (that is, the most honest) estimates. Prepare for many frustrating hours with a calculator, pencil, and pad. Forecasting income and expenses is difficult, even when you have a track record of five or more years. Pre-start-ups must do a lot of educated guessing.

Chapter 5, "Financing the Family Business," will shed

more light, I hope, on that aspect of planning your family business. Right now, I'll take a look at such questions as market research, ownership, and choosing the right location.

WHO WILL BE YOUR CUSTOMERS?

Ideally, it would be great if you could do a market test *before* you take the plunge. Whether you'll be selling an item of clothing, gourmet food, computer software, or even a magazine, you'd know far more if customers could examine the product and buy—or not buy—at the price you establish. But that kind of market research is mostly limited to the huge companies who can select a city or region, run their ads, and carefully examine consumer reaction before making a full-scale go–no-go decision. For you, such an approach is not an option.

Let's assume that you believe your product is good because you *personally* like it. If it's software, you know from shopping, researching at the library, and interviewing professionals in the field that there's nothing like it on the market. If it's a category of clothing, your personal experiences have convinced you of the demand. Throughout this book there are stories of people who have started a business by acting on a need they perceived first in themselves. I firmly believe in *starting* with that premise. But don't make the mistake of assuming that a market exists *only* because your personal and mental attitudes indicate that it should. The more organized you are in gathering data about the market you target, the better will be your chances for success.

For objective information, identify the trade association and publications serving the industry that your proposed business will join—no matter how provisionally. Read as much as you can about trends, sales figures for products, and their average prices. Call the executive director of the associations, the editors of the publications; identify people in the industry who might offer you constructive information on getting started. Send out questionnaires if appropriate.

The more you act like an investigative reporter, the more useful the data you'll gather. (You may even gain some initial customers.) Don't be afraid to ask questions or show your ignorance if, indeed, you're unfamiliar with aspects of the new business area. In my experience, the veterans of an industry are proud of their field and their knowledge and are willing to help others get off to a good start. It's the people with limited knowledge who tend to hide the fact by being disagreeable when someone asks them questions. The same approach works when seeking answers from local businesspeople. Assuming you'll identify beforehand—and then omit—someone who may feel that you'll become a direct competitor, you can expect that local businesspeople will answer your questions accurately and helpfully. When pertinent, census information will help. Reference librarians can point you to the closest available sources for regional or national demographic data.

While confidence is one of the qualities you'll need *after* launching your business, this is the time to be aware of what one leading authority on entrepreneurship calls the "built-in conflict between hobbies and successful venturing." According to Karl Vesper of the University of Washington and author of *New Venture Strategies*, "Hobbies are things that people are willing to do at their own expense, which puts a strong downward pressure on profits." A common problem with hobbyist-entrepreneurs, says Vesper, is that they tend to start their companies to provide something they would like to have themselves, taking it for granted that many others would like the same thing and can therefore be expected to buy from the new company. "Then it turns out that the desire was not widespread at all," says Vesper, "and zero sales result." You must be aware that customers will not automatically gather round to buy your new product when it is first announced, regardless of how much you like it. You'll have to make a major marketing effort—and your early research must show you whom to go after first with your limited advertising promotion budget.

AN EXAMPLE OF A MARKETING PLAN

To illustrate the methodology of doing a marketing plan as part of an overall business planning effort, Craig Seymour of the University of New Hampshire offers this illustrative case history:

Marilyn and Martha believed there was a need for a quality children's clothing store in their town, since none existed and they often found themselves driving over 20 miles to buy clothes for their own children. They were well aware of the need for sound business planning and undertook the writing of a business plan.

Data Collection

Marilyn and Martha began to collect the necessary data. They started by estimating the market potential for their idea. Using sources found at the local library, they were able to determine the number of families living within a 20-mile radius of their town and the average number of children by major age group in those families. They calculated the average annual family expenditures for children's clothing from trade data obtained from a cooperative retailer. Multiplying this number by the number of families gave them an estimate of the total potential sales for their market area.

Market Penetration

The next task involved estimating their (yet to be built) store's market penetration—what part of the total market they could conservatively expect to sell. They started by looking very carefully at the competition within their market area as well as competitors located outside but which drew purchasers from within. A list of *all* stores that sold children's clothing was compiled and divided into major categories by price, quality, and style. After analyzing this information and talking to other retailers and potential customers, Marilyn and Martha estimated that they could probably account for 5 to 10 percent of the total market.

Calculating Breakeven

The next critical question was: "Is the estimated sales volume large enough to support the two of us and a staff, pay the rent, cover the overhead, carry a reasonable inventory, and return a profit?" To find out, they went to their local banker who told them that *on the average*, gross profit (sales less cost of goods sold) should run about 40 percent of sales for a store of the type they envisioned. To calculate their *breakeven*, or the level of sales needed to just cover all fixed and variable expenses, they divided their estimated fixed expenses such as rent, salaries, advertising, insurance, heat, and so on by the 40 percent figure.

In this way the two women verified their belief that their business was feasible from a financial as well as a market perspective.

OWNERSHIP

Members of my own family have never been sticklers for formality when dealing with each other. So far, we seem to be following a similar informal pattern with ownership of the business. Our firm, The JG Press, is incorporated in the state of Pennsylvania. We started out as a sole proprietorship, but incorporated for the added liability protection. The stockholders in our corporation are Ina and myself. Our will specifies that our estate—which includes the shares of The JG Press—be divided up equally among our three daughters. One of these days we plan to begin distributing shares, possibly at the next annual meeting of the board of directors, which takes place around the dining room table. The ownership arrangement seems to work all right for us, at least at this point in our lives and in the development of the company. As the years go by, we definitely plan to review the fairness of the present arrangement.

Whether at start-up or somewhere down the line, every business should have a formal agreement, especially when the ownership is shared by relatives. Most experienced persons will urge that the agreement be in writing, although it can be legally binding even if unwritten. Any lawyer or accountant will be eager to tell you any number of horror stories about situations in which formal agreements were not drawn up and trouble followed. While two or more people can put up equal amounts of cash, it often happens that two years down the line, equal amounts of personal effort are no longer being made. I can think of the case of two brothers who bought their father's farm in Kentucky. For one, it was an 18-hour-a-day job; for the other, it was an investment.

No provision had been made for salary. After three years of very strained relations, the full-time farmer arranged to buy out his brother's interest. Harmony has since been restored.

Many states have adopted a uniform partnership act which defines a partnership as "an association of two or more persons to carry on as co-owners of a business for profit." A more inclusive definition, based upon the historical development of partnerships, is that a partnership is a contract, expressed or implied, between two or more competent persons to place their money, effects, labor, or skill into a business and to divide the profits and bear the losses in certain proportions.

A partnership in a family or nonfamily enterprise does not necessarily mean equal investment, remuneration, authority, or effort by all partners. But however the arrangement is understood, it should be specified in the agreement. One veteran observer has said how amazed she is to see that while most people do specify details about financial investment and division of profits, a large number never clarify just who is going to do what. The formal agreement should go a long way toward preventing problems. From what I've observed, the most serious problems arise not when the business is struggling to survive and grow. Rather, it's when the money starts rolling in, and there's much to divvy up. That's when the ornery situations develop. Someone is bound to want more . . . or, more frequently, will claim that someone else is reaping a windfall "even though I (we) did all the sacrificing when the going was so tough."

So spell it out, and relax—until you hit the big time!

Recently, a series of newspaper headlines has called attention to several flourishing family businesses whose heirs have tried to break up the multimillion-dollar corporations. In some cases, the founding parents created the problem along with the profits when they gave equal shares of voting stock in the corporation to all their children as a sign of their equal love for them. The problem with this kind of equality surfaces when children who don't work for the company on a day-to-day basis seek current dividends at the expense of future growth and vote their shares that way at directors' meetings. Many experts think it makes much more sense for the voting stock to go to the children who manage the business and the nonvoting stock (or other family assets) to be assigned to heirs who are not active in the business.

THE RIGHT LOCATION

With some businesses—mail order, for example—location doesn't really matter. As long as you have easy access to a post office, you can be just about anywhere. But some businesses need to be near heavy traffic and clearly visible from the road. Others need access to a specialized labor pool. Hence the right location can be critical.

Small-business consultants Patricia and Gregory Kishel (authors of several books on managing new enterprises) have prepared a checklist to help you evaluate a particular community or site when searching for the right location. The following material is from *How to Start, Run, and Stay In Business,* published by John Wiley & Sons:

1. Is there a need for your product or service? The first rule of marketing is "find a need and fill it." Unless your product or service can be profitably transported to other communities, it's essential that your business be able to fill a need in the community in which it's located. If not, a change must be made—either in your business or its location.

2. How many customers are there? Is the number

of potential customers large enough to justify locating your business in the community? The closer you are to your main market, the easier it will be to serve it.

3. How strong is the competition? What strategy can you use to set yourself apart from your competitors? If yours is to be the first such business in the community, why haven't others already located there? Perhaps there is some drawback to your chosen location that you have overlooked.

4. Is the community prosperous enough to support your business? To determine the community's level of prosperity, take a close look at its economic structure.

5. What is the community's growth potential? Are people moving into the community or leaving it? Some positive indicators of growth are land development projects, the presence of major businesses, well-kept homes and storefronts, active citizen groups, and adequate public services.

6. What kinds of people live there? In addition to the size of the community's population, you should be concerned with its makeup. Is the average age 52 or 22? How much does a typical worker earn? What percentage of the community is married? Single? Divorced? What's the average number of children per household? This type of demographic information can be obtained from local census tracts and Chambers of Commerce. For an even more complete profile of the local residents, you might examine their life-styles as well. What do they like to do? Read? Ski? Sew? Garden? Are they politically conservative or liberal? This kind of "psychographic" data can be obtained through questionnaires, interviews, and your own observations.

7. Are there any restrictions on your type of business? Each neighborhood has its own unique restrictions, instituted to either promote or discourage different types of businesses. By finding out what these are ahead

of time, you can avoid unpleasant surprises later. Otherwise, you could end up unable to obtain a business license, expand your facilities, receive deliveries, or maintain certain hours of operation. Check with the zoning officer at city hall.

8. Will your suppliers have access to you? Unless your suppliers have ready access to you, you could find yourself paying premium shipping costs or unable to obtain necessary shipments. This, of course, has a bearing on the products and services you provide and the prices you charge for them.

9. Will the local labor force meet your needs? The more specialized or technical your work tasks, the greater the difficulty in finding the right people. As for wages, these vary in accordance with each community's standard of living. Before settling on a location, make sure the labor force is both adequate and affordable.

10. Do you like the community? Just as relying on personal preferences alone can be disastrous, so can ignoring them altogether. The location that is right for your business must also be right for you. Regardless of your answers to the first nine questions, if you can't say yes to this one, keep looking.

Major streets are perfect for restaurants, real estate offices, dry cleaners, copy centers, and other businesses dependent on automobile traffic for sales. Assess the surrounding businesses and the desirability of the neighborhood, not to mention the availability of parking.

Shopping centers, with their lures of abundant parking and a variety of stores and services within walking distance of one another, have the edge when it comes to attracting customers. Businesses that cater not only to working people but also to nonworking adults and teenagers can benefit the most. Among these are clothing and shoe stores, fabric shops, record stores, book and gift stores, restaurants, and snack stands. Rents, however, tend to be high.

Downtown business districts are particularly well suited to businesses that cater to office workers. Those businesses most likely to flourish downtown include restaurants, bars, clothing and shoe stores, barber shops, and travel agencies. More and more cities are in the process of revitalizing neglected downtown locations—turning formerly vacant warehouse or factory space into inviting collections of shops. These could be excellent spots for your business.

Side streets, though less traveled and frequently out of the way, offer lower rents. Businesses not dependent on high traffic flow for sales, such as nursery schools, plumbers, and seamstress and tailor shops, may have the best chances of succeeding. Finally, industrial locations, designed and zoned for manufacturers and industrial suppliers, offer flexible, spacious work spaces and generally lower rents. Nonindustrial businesses, such as mail-order houses, can take advantage of these sites.

Now let's get into the ever-perplexing problem of financing your family business start-up.

5
Financing the Family Business

WHO'S IN CHARGE OF THE LIFE PRESERVER?

THIS IS A tough area—setting a limit on how much you're willing to risk on building a profitable family business. And, in case I haven't got the point across before, it *is a risk*. Any new venture is a risk, and the chance you take is definitely greater when several—or all—family breadwinners get their dough from the same oven.

When we started the business in 1978, I was not conscious of our taking a big risk. It was a logical move for me personally—having just left a company I had been with for 25 years in which I had enjoyed great independence. It was like reliving the excitement of building up a new company, only this time we worked with our own money. Less than two years out of college, Rill had what she considered to be a mediocre job—certainly not a career position. And Nora was still a senior in college. Who needed a life preserver? I had owned 2 percent of the stock in the publishing company I was leaving, and the agreement was that I had to sell back the stock when I left. So there was more than enough to start a publishing company without worrying about financial life preservers.

Well, it's amazing how many $25,000 investments you can make in putting together a family publishing operation. At this point, we are able to grow from present earnings, but in the publishing business—as in any other—there are no guarantees that subscription and advertising income will stay ahead of expenses.

Right now, Nora is the only one who has someone to bring home the bacon independent of The JG Press—and we're all rooting for her husband, Jon Clark. But of course, we're still overwhelmingly confident about the future financial performance of our company. (In fact, we may yet entice Jon to come aboard.)

If you tend to worry about financial matters, then you'd better realize that you'll live with financial insecurity for the first few years after start-up. But I would guess that if you are a worrier, then you're worried right now about the life preserver that your present employer provides. Security is an elusive goal in these times, and I opt for a homemade preserver.

FINANCING THE START-UP

How much money *should* you have to start a business? "More than you estimate," says one expert. "You must have the extra margin for the unexpected. Remember, after you start, you can't get money if you need it. Insufficient capital is the number one reason for the high rate of early failures." There's much evidence to justify those words of fiscal advice. Lack of capital has traditionally been viewed as a major cause of failure in the early years of a new business with good reason—just about every start-up is undercapitalized. That's why we believe so strongly in something we call the *One-tenth Financing Principle.* Our theory is to recognize the implications of having only 10 percent of the finances available and then turn that recognition into a strength. There are two steps to implementing the principle:

Step One: Research the field you are planning to enter. Get as much information from recognized experts in that field as you can about "accepted" industry costs —employees, managers, rental space, and equipment. Attend seminars, if necessary, and read the trade publications; talk to people in closely related businesses. From this data, calculate an average dollar figure that is considered to be needed to launch and sustain the start-up. Then *divide that number by 10.*

Step Two: Research your own financial reserves. How much do you and your family have available in savings? What, if any, sources of income can you expect to continue *outside* of those dollars from your proposed business? And a key question: While every new venture must be perceived as a risk, how much of your available capital are you prepared to invest without being excessively worried or plagued with self-doubt in the early stages? Think long and hard, and write down a dollar amount you're willing to invest.

Now compare the figure in Step One with that in Step Two. If they're fairly close, you're in decent fiscal shape according to the One-tenth Principle.

Before we launched *In Business,* we did a great deal of "intuitive analysis" and a modest amount of objective research. The latter effort included several talks with publishing pros, who are used to making start-up decisions based upon computer models that can calculate seemingly endless varieties of "what ifs." We were more comfortable relying on our 25 years of experience in magazine publishing, an experience that told us if we had something worth while to publish, there would be people wanting to read it. While we knew that magazine publishing is a relatively capital-intensive industry, we didn't believe that meant we needed up to $2 million to start. The One-tenth Principle has worked for us.

One key message of the One-tenth Principle is that insufficient capital at start-up time can be more of an advantage than a disadvantage. It forces extreme caution before committing advertising dollars to chase an elusive market . . . or to build an expensive staff and house them in expensive quarters before the arrival of a finely tuned, readily salable product or service.

Another implication is that while capital need only be one-tenth, commitment must be 10 times. It takes a tremendous amount of human effort—often an entire family's—to shift decimal points in your capital structure.

Experience is worth tens of thousands of dollars to you—leading to shortcuts that reduce expenses in production, marketing, and employees. If your suppliers know you and respect your knowledge, the more likely you'll be extended credit as your business begins and grows.

AVOIDING THE "DEEP HOLE"

How do you go about establishing a business that grosses $500,000 a year, without digging yourselves into a deep hole that takes years to climb out of . . . and that creates all kinds of pressures as you and your family learn the ropes?

The answer is: slowly and steadily. Always look for the openings in the marketplace, and hustle to get there. Successful business owners learn how to hustle in their own ways. It doesn't mean using high-pressure tactics, but it does mean using your available capital wisely and imaginatively. Most of all, it means that you don't carry on as if you had to bet everything on the last race, so that you can go back to the track in the morning.

We'll be hitting the $500,000 sales mark this year. Surprisingly, our most profitable publication is our small circulation magazine *BioCycle*. In five years, our paid circulation has grown to include about 4,000 professionals who care a great deal about garbage, sludge, and manure. Small as that number may be by some standards, these consulting engineers, public works officials, treatment plant managers, and waste makers are mighty influential in deciding what cities and industries do with their rejected materials. In the past few years, we have been holding seminars and conferences, publishing books, and in general, carving out a special niche in this extremely narrow market. The result is that our financial returns from this part of our communications efforts are bright.

But before we realized that we should put more of our financial resources into the *BioCycle* area, we were devoting about 80 percent of our resources to our other magazine, *In Business*, which has far more room for expansion and growth. But the problem is that to capture that growth, we'd need much more capital. We did not want to borrow money from the bank, and we didn't want venture capital. So now we've slowed the growth rate for *In Business*, put more money into the *BioCycle* area, and use the returns to build up both areas gradually.

The point is that you don't need to borrow large amounts of money, which would most likely come from yourself, your relatives, or your friends (*not* from a bank). You especially don't need to borrow it to reach a preplanned income level that you probably set unrealistically high. Too often, I meet people who toss around big figures as part of their business plan, and too often the high amount includes the cost of an unnecessarily expensive office, impressive furniture, and more staff than they need at first. Get your experience without borrowing heavily. Your hot idea will stay hot enough while you're learning how to reach the market.

LEARNING FROM OTHERS

Talking with other business owners will inevitably result in learning about effective, innovative financing techniques—and give you the confidence to adapt them to your specific situation. In an article in *In Business* for example, Herb Kierulff, a professor at Seattle Pacific University and a management consultant to small firms, relates this account:

> I have a client, Ralph Brice of the PowderHawk Company, who has just received a patent on a new device. Ralph explained that this device permits skiers to convert their downhill skis and bindings into back country climbing skis that work as well as snowshoes on uphill terrain. They can be reconverted to their original mode in less than five minutes when the climber has reached his or her destination and is ready to ski down.
>
> Ralph had made a few of these for demonstration purposes, but lacked the expensive dies and manufacturing facilities needed to produce his product. His solution: find a small manufacturing firm with these capabilities and a person who likes to ski. Considerable research brought him into contact with a local computerized tool and die shop whose owner is an Austrian-born alpine skier. One demonstration was enough to convince the man that the PowderHawk was a product worth backing. Not only will he

make the dies, he will also manufacture the product and give the PowderHawk Company 30-day credit. My client is now examining other innovative methods to pull him one step further.

In Glen Echo, Maryland, near Washington, D.C., Ken Diffenderfer recently opened the Fishermen's Marketing Company, after selling fish from a truck for three years. To lessen the gamble of opening a retail store in today's economy, and to raise some capital, Diffenderfer did the following, reports the *Washington Post.*

> He sent a letter to his regular roadside customers offering a 10 percent lifetime discount on seafood in return for a $100 investment in his fish market. "Seafood with interest" is what he called it. . . . The response was so great, with more capital offered than needed to open the store, that potential investors were scaled back to a waiting list, said Diffenderfer.
>
> He estimates the 70 investors who did pitch in will earn a $156 annual return on their $100 gamble if they make what he considers the typical weekly purchase of $30 worth of seafood, then discounted 10 percent. A full refund of the original investment may be obtained at any time, he said, and there are 40 would-be investors waiting in the wings.

Diffenderfer admits that the discounts may make it more difficult to earn a profit, but he says, "we're profitable so far."

FRIENDLY RISK CAPITAL

In an article in *In Business,* Nora Goldstein wrote about William Wetzel of the University of New Hampshire, who has done considerable research into the field of "friendly money"—the pool of seed capital potentially available from local investors who are interested in your venture for reasons beyond those of traditional venture capitalists.

To illustrate how to go about raising $50,000 to $100,000 in seed capital, Wetzel first stresses that you should understand what seed capital is. He defines it first as *risk* capital, coming from investors (yourselves and others) who are "financially and psychologically prepared to face the possibility of losing everything in return for the possibility of substantial rewards, primarily financial but also partly psychological." He also describes it as *creative* capital—rewarded only when the venture that is created is worth more than it cost. It is also *patient* money since 5 to 10 years can pass before a venture develops real economic muscle.

With the nature of seed capital clearly defined, Wetzel then offers this advice on finding potential investors—individuals of means with an interest in seed capital situations:

Since seed capital investors typically maintain close contact with ventures they finance, the first place to look is close to home, within 100 miles and preferably within 50 miles. Let's assume that within a 50-mile radius of your venture, there is a population of 200,000 people. Based on national statistics, it is likely that within that group there are 500 or more millionaires and probably 2,000 people with a net worth of at least half a million. Ninety percent of them are probably inexperienced and uninterested in "risk capital" investments. But that still leaves a group of 50 to 200 people who are both experienced and interested in backing competent entrepreneurs with creative ideas. These potential investors typically learn of investment opportunities through an informal network of friends, business associates, and financial professionals, including commercial bankers, investment bankers, attorneys, and accountants. Tapping into that informal network is objective number one in your search for seed capital.

The overriding concern of all seed capital investors is the competence of the entrepreneur involved. Therefore, ask yourself two questions: (1) Who knows you well enough to assess your management and entrepreneurial talent? and (2) Of those who know you well enough to evaluate your ability, who is most likely to provide an entrée into the investor network? The answer to question 2 will probably include your banker, accountant, attorney, and even better, local entrepreneurs who have succeeded in raising and managing risk capital.

Present your venture plan in detail and in writing to these potential contacts. Ask for their critique of your venture and their help in reaching investors. If you and your plan don't make sense to them, you will soon find out and save yourself much wasted time. If you and your plan do make sense you are on your way; finding a credible reference is a giant first step in locating and interesting an investor. Writing an effective business plan is an art, so if you need assistance, get it from a local accountant or small-business consultant.

Ted Harwood, an entrepreneur who found some "friendly money," cites his experience with an industrialist who committed $10,000 to help Ted produce a family board game called *Capital Gains*. "There are pools of unworried and unhurried capital (UUC) lying around for the resourceful entrepreneur," declares Harwood, "although tapping into one of these pools is not something to count on when planning the venture." Here are a few of Ted Harwood's recommendations for locating some UUC of your own:

Is there anything about your venture that makes it

worth while to launch for reasons other than simple return on investment? If it's a "life-style" venture, you might find an investor who feels it should be funded because it would be in the public interest. A board game with a political or social message is an example of a product with this kind of appeal. Or you might find an investor who fervently believes that, by golly, the public should be exposed to your product and the naysayers be damned! In short, you may find people willing to subsidize some ventures because they don't think the traditional capital markets should be the only arbiter of the worthiness of a particular venture.

Finding friendly and unhurried risk capital is definitely a long shot, but many family business start-ups have a quality about them that makes them extra-attractive to the kinds of investors described here. Don't hinge all your plans on finding such a person, but at the same time, don't rule out the possibility.

TAKING THE EQUITY ROUTE

"It's unusual for a business both new and small to do a public stock offering to raise start-up capital. But we didn't want to saddle Pond Hill Homes with debt, so we chose the equity route," explains Harold Williams, chairman of the board of Pond Hill Homes, Ltd., a company that provides complete building packages for homeowners and builders, founded by the Institute on Man and Science in Rensselaerville, New York. "We also wanted people who didn't have a lot of money to be able to invest, and the Regulation A offering was the best vehicle for that purpose." Six months after the offering began, almost 125,000 shares of stock were sold at $5 a share, bringing in $625,000.

Equity investments come in many forms. For brand-new companies, the most common form is risk capital from individuals—sophisticated investors—who can afford the risk and need tax write-offs. If the business succeeds, they are usually rewarded with a large return on investment for their willingness to provide seed money.

But in forming Pond Hill Homes, the institute did not want to appeal to the sophisticated investor alone. "We decided on a public stock offering for several reasons," notes Williams. "We wanted people with $5 or $10 to be able to buy stock. We also wanted the company to be publicly accountable—to customers, stockholders, and to the community and public at large."

Pond Hill Homes stock was offered under Regulation A of the Securities Act. Regulation A is a conditional exemption from registration for certain public offerings, not exceeding $1.5 million in any 12-month period. An offering statement, consisting of a notification, offering circular, and exhibits, must be filed with the Securities and Exchange Commission's (SEC) office in the region in which the company's principal business activities are conducted. The SEC in its pamphlet "Q&A: Small Business and the SEC" explains that although Regulation A is technically an exemption from the registration requirements of the Securities Act, it is often referred to as a "short form" of registration. That is because the offering circular, which is similar in content to a prospectus, must be supplied to each purchaser, and the securities issued are freely traded in an aftermarket.

Only material approved by the SEC can be shown to potential investors. A company is not allowed to trot out specific information that the SEC hasn't approved. In addition to meeting the federal SEC guidelines, a company doing a public stock offering must file with every state in which it wants to sell stock. State securities laws and filing fees vary.

FINDING BUYERS

In a traditional public stock offering, an underwriter is used to find buyers, usually selling to its own clients. The commission for selling the stock is negotiable. Two basic formats are used to work with a company offering stock, best effort and commitment. Best effort means that underwriters will do "their best" to sell stock, but have made no binding commitment to do so. On a commitment basis, the underwriter knows exactly where it will sell the stock, and he or she usually takes a very few days to sell it once it's issued. Best effort deals take more time, because the market isn't as certain.

In the case of Pond Hill Homes, the Institute on Man and Science worked with an underwriter in Albany, New York, on a best effort basis. "No underwriter would have touched Pond Hill on a commitment basis," says Williams. "In our case, we sent the underwriter a lot of clients, having contacted potential buyers ourselves. When working out an arrangement with an underwriter, be sure to take your own selling efforts into account and negotiate a lower commission rate."

In a Regulation A stock offering, Williams suggests that owners consider the possibility of serving as their own underwriter. "Your ability to do so depends on the degree of risk, and whether or not an underwriter is needed to identify buyers," says Williams. An underwriter may not be needed in every case.

For example, an ongoing business may decide it will raise working capital by going public only if its customers want to go public with it. The owner could send out a letter to the customers, asking if they would be interested in buying stock, and if so, how much they might be interested in buying at what price. Then an offering circular could be written, describing what the money will be used for, and how much is going to be raised. By not using an underwriter, there is less dilution. Many small businesses have a loyal following, and a public stock offering allows the business to tap that.

Small-business owners can be effective at presenting their company to investors. "The owner or founder probably does the best job of defining what the business is, and what values and beliefs are driving it," says Williams. "In a start-up, there are no earnings figures, so potential stockholders want to know more about the company's rationale. The founder can get that idea across better than anyone else can."

On the other hand, be cautious about selling stock yourself. "You begin to feel personally as well as professionally responsible for the success of a person's investment," says Williams. "That's where an underwriter can act as a buffer."

SECOND STAGE FINANCING

In the early stages of a business start-up, the key challenge is to generate sufficient cash to break even and to hang tough with the limited capital available from personal sources. At this stage, growth usually comes from cash flow, and most often, growth is modest. At the second stage, the company has carved out a market niche and opportunities for rapid growth are evident. But it's equally evident that to take advantage of these opportunities, more capital is required. At this moment in the life of the business, commercial bank loans, SBA guaranteed loans and the like become a logical option.

Likely sources you'll want to explore include:

Commercial Finance Companies

Generally regarded as the place to go when you are almost but not quite bankable, commercial finance companies lend against specific assets such as inventory or (sometimes) equipment, but most often accounts receivable. They are less concerned about overall financial condition than banks, since they sharply focus on the availability of uncollateralized assets in the above categories. The principal disadvantage of their financing is that it is expensive—generally at least several percentage points higher than bank financing.

Commercial Banks

Generally considered the "lender of first resort" by small-business persons, commercial banks are also often much misunderstood. They are not early-stage investors or even risk lenders. What they are to a small-business person is a relatively attractively priced source of collateralized expansion or working capital. Their loans can be short-term or intermediate, but they are almost always more than fully secured and require personal guarantees from the firm's principal(s). Longer-term loans can be available to small businesses from commercial banks, usually in conjunction with Small Business Administration (SBA) or Farmers Home Administration partial guarantees. Many banks prefer to stay away from these programs, but those that do participate in them are often willing to make riskier loans through them than they would otherwise.

Public Agency Financing

The sources of possible federal or state agency financing are numerous and ever-changing. Headed by the SBA, Economic Development Administration, Farmers

Home Administration, and state development authorities, capital from this group can take the form of direct loans, loan guarantees, or even, in isolated cases, outright grants. Funding of such programs is in many cases inconsistent, however. The only way to determine all potential sources and their liquidity is to call around at the time you are seeking the capital. Whatever you do, check to see that funds are expected to be available before filling out lengthy application forms.

PREPARING A LOAN REQUEST

Most family businesses will have to get started on capital that doesn't come through bank loans. But as your business reaches a second stage of growth, then financing is more available from a bank. When it comes to borrowing money from a bank, the family business is in no worse a plight than any other small-business start-up venture. The main caution I would make is to try to impress the loan officer with your professionalism not with what a nice family you have. The bottom line is ability to pay back the loan, not the high regard you have for each other.

With that caution, try to find a loan officer at a bank who knows something about the business you're in or about to start, as well as something about you and your background. The loan officer should know what it's like to run a small company—the risks, opportunities, and understandable cash binds.

Steven Popell, a management consultant who has worked with many small businesses in California, recently set forth these points to guide persons seeking bank loans:

Make sure that the loan officer you choose earns your respect and confidence in the first interview. First impressions tend to be accurate in banking relations. Your loan officer should give clear evidence that he or she will receive bad news in a thoughtful and mature manner and will not just push the panic button. An impulsive move by a panicky loan officer at just the wrong time could jeopardize the very existence of your company.

The bank in question should be large enough to grow with your company. Some of the smaller banks will frequently be more creative and aggressive than the larger ones in their pursuit of your business. Also you can switch your account with relative ease to a larger bank when the time comes, as long as your company is successful. If you plan to do business with a large bank at any location other than its headquarters office, deal with one of that bank's major commercial (business loan) branches.

Choose your bank and loan officer at least one full year before you ask for funds. During the pre-loan-request period, keep your loan officer fully informed of your company's progress. A quarterly lunch and presentation of a financial statement should be the minimum of informative contact. Include the bad news along with the good. Get your loan officer used to your problems, as well as your brilliant successes. It will give him or her a greater feeling of confidence that you can weather storms and surprises—a feeling that will be to your benefit when you ask for money, and throughout the term of the loan.

Your loan office (and you as well) should be thoroughly familiar with your company's financial status and recent performance. The officer will be looking at four elements with utmost care:

1. Your company's financial status (both short- and long-term) as indicated by the balance sheet
2. Your company's ability to repay, as indicated by

your most recent income statements and your projections of future profits and cash flow

3. The reasonableness of the business use of the loan proceeds—both in terms of the likely *return on investment* and the matchup between short- or long-term needs

4. Perhaps most important of all, the quality of management

Bankers love financial ratios. If the numbers on the balance sheet accurately reflect assets and liabilities, certain key financial ratios can give a clear indication of the company's short- and long-term financial condition and, more important, its credit worthiness.

One important indicator of a business's short-term financial condition is the *current ratio*—the relationship between current assets and current liabilities. Another is the *quick ratio*—the relationship between quick assets and current liabilities. *Current assets* represent cash and those assets that can reasonably be expected to turn into cash within one year. *Quick assets* represent cash and those assets that can reasonably be expected to turn into cash within 90 days. *Current liabilities* are those liabilities that must be paid within one year.

The reason that these two ratios are important is that they indicate the company's ability to discharge those obligations that will come due for payment within the next 12 months (current liabilities). If a company has a current ratio of less than 1.0, then its short-term financial health is doubtful. If this ratio is 2:1 or better, and the cash account is reasonably healthy, the company will probably not experience a short-term financial bind. If the quick assets described above can meet these criteria (a quick ratio of 1.0 or better), this says that quick assets are sufficient to handle all current liabilities. With anything much less than .5, one begins to worry about a cash bind in the offing, possibly because of too heavy an investment in inventory or, perhaps, a dip in sales.

The key indicator for long-term financial condition and borrowing capacity is the ratio of equity to long-term debt. If there is more equity than debt, then there is generally long-term borrowing capacity, assuming other factors indicate the company's ability to repay. A 2:1 relationship is desirable.

A loan officer will not loan money to any individual or company without a definable source of repayment. Even loans collateralized by tangible assets (such as equipment) must pass the test of ability to repay. Collateral will frequently cover only a portion of a bank's loss, and it is, after all, management's utilization of the collateral—and not the collateral itself—which provides the income from which debt service cash is generated.

The surest indicator of ability to repay is the *income statement,* also referred to as the *profit and loss statement,* or P&L. In the absence of a major event (not the loan itself) that effectively changes the very kind of company you have, a history of P&Ls going back at least three years will be among the most important financial information you will submit with your loan application.

Pretax profit ("bottom line") will receive immediate and lasting consideration. If you are able to achieve profits of at least 10 percent of net sales, you will very likely impress your loan officer. If your profit margin is much less than 10 percent, or if your company is unprofitable, you had better be prepared to give sensible explanations of why your past results are not relevant for predicting future performance.

With the historical profit performance firmly in mind, your loan officer will probably turn full attention to your projections of future profits and cash flow. Projections represent your most tangible statement as to your ability to repay the loan. They must, above all, be realistic. If your projections differ significantly from historical performance (without adequate justification), they will hinder, not help, your loan application by damaging your credibility.

Since projections represent a view of the future, they are necessarily based on assumptions, and it is these assumptions that must be able to withstand close scrutiny. What makes you say that your sales are going to increase by 30 percent per year for five years? On what grounds do you claim that your gross profit will increase from its historical level of 35 percent to 50 percent in just 12 months? How can you possibly expect to double your sales without increasing your overhead? If your answers to questions like these are vague or incredible, you'll probably have to find another bank.

Your loan officer will look at the use of the funds for which you are applying from at least two standpoints: first, the likely *return on investment* and, second, the matchup between the kind of loan you are requesting and the use to which you are putting it. The key question in all this is, What will the company be able to do with this money that it could not do without it, and as a result, what new profits will it generate? Once again we are talking about the reasonableness of your assumptions and the credibility of your figures.

If you are requesting a working capital credit line, without which your company's growth will be sorely restricted, then your return on investment will come from the profits earned on the additional sales. Investment in capital equipment or plant can pay off through increased sales or by allowing you to reduce your *cost of goods sold* (and increase your gross profit). How you go about calculating return on investment is far less important than the reasonableness of your assumptions underlying the calculation. Anything from a simple payback method to sophisticated discounted cash flows is acceptable. If anything, be wary of oversophistication at the small company level.

The extent to which your loan request properly matches the type of loan with the use of funds will demonstrate to your loan officer how much you understand the fundamentals of financial management. The prevailing rule is to use short-term financing (an annually reviewed accounts receivable line, for example) for short-term needs (working capital). Long-term financing (a term loan for a fixed number of years) is for long-term needs (say, equipment or property purchases). The logic behind this rule goes back to the ability to repay.

6
Family Business Life Cycles

WHAT COURSE CAN you expect your business to take once it's off the ground? As director of the Caruth Institute of Owner-Managed Business at Southern Methodist University, Neil Churchill has had much opportunity to observe the maze through which small companies must weave. Professor Churchill identifies five stages: existence, survival, success, take-off, and resource maturity. In an article published in the *Harvard Business Review*, Churchill and his colleague Virginia Lewis describe each stage.

THE FIVE STAGES

STAGE I: EXISTENCE

In Stage I, the main problems of the business are obtaining customers and delivering the product or service contracted for. Key questions include: Can we get enough customers, deliver products, and provide services well enough to become a viable business? Can we expand to a much broader sales base? Do we have enough money to cover the considerable cash demands of this start-up phase?

At this stage, say the authors, the organization is simple with the strategy being to remain alive. "The owner *is* the business; he or she performs all the important tasks, and is the major supplier of energy and direction."

Stage II: Survival

Having demonstrated some ability to get customers and satisfy them, the key problem shifts from "mere existence to the relationship between revenues and expenses."

Stage II, write the authors, is: "Can we, at a minimum, generate enough cash flow to stay in business and to finance growth to a size that is sufficiently large, given our industry and market niche, to earn an economic return on our assets and labor?" Organization remains simple, with managers carrying out rather well-defined orders of the owner. Formal planning is, at best, cash forecasting. The overwhelming hazard of Stage II is that it can seem to go on indefinitely, earning marginal returns on invested time and capital—until patience or strength run out. Observe Churchill and Lewis: "The 'mom and pop' stores are in this category, as are manufacturing businesses that cannot get their product or process sold as planned."

Stage III: Success

Ah, how sweet it is! Now the questions get even more complex, as does the organization. Should the owner exploit his or her company's accomplishments and expand—or keep the company stable and profitable, providing a base for alternative activities by the owner? If an owner opts for going fishing, or becoming mayor, or even launching a new business, the substage here will be Disengagement (III-D). If the decision is for Growth, (III-G), then the owner takes the cash and the company's borrowing power and risks it all in financing that growth.

"Many companies continue for long periods in the Success-Disengagement substage. The product-market niche of some does not permit growth; this is true of many service businesses in small or medium-sized, slowly growing communities and for franchise holders with limited territories. Other owners actually choose this route," note the authors. "If the company can continue to adapt to environmental changes, it can continue as is, be sold or merged at a profit, or subsequently be stimulated into growth."

In the Success-Growth substage, it's critical that the basic strength of the business remains profitable to keep churning out cash, while managers are developed and hired. If the III-G strategy works, the company heads for IV. If it doesn't work, there's always III-D. "If not, retrenchment to the survival stage may be possible prior to bankruptcy or a distress sale," they note.

Stage IV: Take-off

Since the problems shift here to growing rapidly and financing that growth rate, the questions shift to *delegation* and *cash.* Will the delegation be accomplished effectively or will the owner have to abdicate? Can the owner tolerate a high debt-equity ratio and a cash flow that is not eroded by inadequate expense controls? Say the authors: "The owner and the business have become reasonably separate, yet the company is still dominated by both the owner's presence and stock control. This is a pivotal period in a company's life. If the owner rises to the challenges of a growing company, both financially and managerially, it can become a big business. If not, it can usually be sold—at a profit—provided the owner recognizes his or her limitations soon enough." Often the entrepreneur who founded the company and brought it to the success stage is replaced either voluntarily or involuntarily by the company's investors or creditors."

Stage V: Resource Maturity

At this point, the authors say, the company has arrived. Advantages of size, financial resources, and management talent have been achieved. All it has to do is preserve its entrepreneurial spirit. But, warn Churchill and Lewis, if it does not, the company may cross into yet another stage—*ossification.* When that happens, its "resource maturity" may make it prey to rapidly growing competitors who are in the middle of Stages I through IV.

While Professor Churchill's description holds true for small businesses in general, there are a number of management problems unique to family-run businesses. How a family handles these will determine whether the business moves through the five stages gracefully or with undue friction.

FAMILY GOALS AND BUSINESS GOALS

One of the key characteristics that distinguish the family business from the nonfamily business is the relationship between the personal goals of the people who run it and the goals of the business.

In the case of the nonfamily business, employees are paid a salary to serve company aims. Company needs come first and foremost; the personal needs of the staff are not the business's main concern. But in a family business, the reverse is true. The business must succeed commercially, but its real *raison d'être* is to further the needs, wants, and purposes of the family members who run it: their need for income, achievement, security, a pleasant working environment, an opportunity for creative self-expression. The challenge facing any family that takes the plunge is threefold: to make the business successful as a business, to be able to pursue simultaneously the two potentially conflicting sets of goals, and to keep the family working together happily. These three aims will affect every major decision you make, as well as all future planning you do.

For example,a primary goal for many husband-and-wife businesses is to provide a place of employment and career training for the next generation. But when a son or daughter is named sales director, how will that choice affect the business's ability to reach a certain projected volume of sales? "Often, because of this kind of situation, family businesses are not as profitable as they could be," says one consultant, "but terrific sales might not be the main purpose of the business. A hotshot salesperson might increase income, but at what price to the stability of the family organization?"

Keeping family and business purposes on track together involves three main steps. First, articulate your goals at the beginning. These are what will motivate the individual members of the firm. Figure out together your large, long-term goals and your more specific short-term ones. Then, rank them in order of priority. Examples of larger goals might be to employ family members, to allow flexibility in how you spend your time, to get or give on-the-job training, to see if a great idea is workable as a business, to see if your family can make an independent business fly, to make yourselves a fortune. Examples of short-term goals are to reach a certain level of sales within a specified period of time or to fulfill projections in the original business plan.

Second, agree on the means the staff will use to meet these goals. Third, periodically step back and look at yourselves and the business to see if you're still on course. Is your current situation pretty much what you envisioned when you were first planning the launch? Does the business seem to be "running away with" the family? Are family problems and conflicts dragging at the company? One partner of a husband-wife sales consulting firm in Atlanta measures his enterprise against one strict rule: "The business must be fun, and as long as we enjoy it we will continue. If it stops being fun, we will sell."

At The JG Press, this three-step routine is familiar. The key approach is to be able to talk about the "sticky" issues with everyone else. Some can't be resolved immediately, but so far we've been able to stay on a path consistent with our original aims. I will not claim that the path is consistently smooth—far from it—but the direction remains the same. In the opinion of my wife and myself, we have managed to provide interesting jobs —sometimes excessively time-consuming jobs—for ourselves and our children. We've been flexible enough in organizational structure to set up an out-of-town editorial office, when it became clear that Nora and her husband, Jon, would settle in Washington, D.C. We've been able to assign critical management positions to our children and watch them grow in knowledge and ability to run a publishing company.

How much these decisions have influenced our potential profitability is tough to tell. In my opinion, there is no way we would have come this far with two national magazines on the financing we had available without the effort of our daughters. They have taken responsibilities that would have cost the company three or four times as much if filled by a nonfamily member. Would an "outsider" have performed more efficiently? I don't know—but I feel the owners of The JG Press answered that question when we first opened up. We feel we have the right spirit and drive—and these are the guts of a successful family business.

Corroboration of this attitude comes from the Wharton Applied Research Center at the University of Pennsylvania. Studies there indicate that many of this country's largest, most successful firms were built on values, attitudes, and approaches commonly found in well-run family businesses.

In his article "Family Business: Perspectives on Change," publisher in the *Wharton Annual*, director Peter Davis says, "there are certain attitudinal things, motivational things that family businesses can handle and handle well. Their values are human values. . . . People can relate to them. And so family businesses can ultimately motivate people and be successful.

"And," continues Davis, "the family business can take the long-term perspective. In fact, it *must* take the long-term perspective. That's interesting because there is a criticism that American businesses are too shortsighted. The family business can't do that. The beat of time for a family business is a generation. It's not a year."

This long-term outlook is characteristic of all the family-business owners we know. The bottom line is how well things stay together as long as the family wants to work together, and that attitude is opposite to the hired manager's obsession wih big, quick profits that keep absentee owners happy.

"Far from being amateurish, family-owned businesses have several advantages over their counterparts. Because of a commitment to continuity through future generations," says Davis, "they've always had an interest in long-range planning and investment, as opposed to the quarter-by-quarter focus of public firms. Also, because of the close relationships within top management, such firms can make far speedier decisions and provide a more humane, familylike working environment for the entire company."

NONFAMILY EMPLOYEES

Building and maintaining a competent staff is critical to the growth of a family business. It is also one of the most difficult problems to solve. How do you get an "outsider" to feel at home in a family environment on a day-in, day-out basis, an environment that mixes personal and business matters constantly? How can a valued staff person be on the "inside" when so many decisions are made during informal family gatherings in the evening or during the weekend?

We've been lucky in having found nonfamily employees who perform admirably despite the distractions, who for the most part appreciate the informality of our working environment. Still, even at our magazine, the division between family and nonfamily members is evident and understandable.

Professor Grant Calder of the University of Utah studied the issues affecting nonfamily managers of 40 small manufacturing firms. In a report in *Business Horizons*, Calder identified the difficulties family-business owners encounter in getting capable management people to join their firms. Here are what he sees as rather significant obstacles:

Many capable people fear domination by family members; they also fear insecurity if capital reserves dry up or control changes. They recognize the fact that family members expect them to assume great responsibility and to work long hours, yet often nonfamily managers can expect to be compensated only as employees, not as owners.

Employees must be adaptable to the environment of the family business and its location—and such persons are usually difficult to find. A person who has worked in a large corporation usually has trouble in the close quarters of a small family business where clerical assistance is scarce, where coffee breaks are unscheduled, and where they're constantly in the middle of family matters. Salaries are rarely comparable to those paid by large corporations down the street, so other inducements must be attractive. Frequently, says Calder, the future of the manager in a small family business, insofar as promotions and security are concerned, is not as bright as it would be in a larger firm.

The fear of becoming involved in a company ridden with family conflicts may deter outsiders from joining. They may also be uncomfortable with the uncertainty that always exists in the family firm itself—the problems of management succession and continuity. Finally, the responsibilities placed upon the management of a small family business are so extensive and varied that relatively few people can really qualify for the positions.

Calder is in no way pessimistic about the ability of the small family business to address staffing needs and come up with solutions. To illustrate, he recounts this anecdote:

The Frank Company, manufacturer of leather products, has experienced little difficulty in obtaining competent junior management personnel to supplement the family members. This is true despite the fact that it has been operated for many generations as a family-controlled partnership, and family members have always held the top management positions. For many years, this company has recognized its dependence upon its employees and has developed favorable relationships with them. Although junior executives recognize that they will not be eligible for any of the top managerial positions, they are content to work for the company because of the cordial employer-employee relationships. The employees are afforded latitude in their work and in arranging vacations, and a pleasant informality exists between workers and owners.

By the way, it's my own strong belief that owners of family businesses should not be defensive about benefits or the work environment they provide to employees. It's my conviction that we have a better overall record than far larger public corporations. A 1983 survey of 18,000 executives by Opinion Research Corporation of Princeton, New Jersey, tends to confirm my belief. According to the survey, which compared current attitudes toward work in a group of middle managers to those of a similar group 10 years ago, white-collar staffers are losing respect for their firms and for top management. Here are some of the findings:

- In 1983, only 45 percent of managers surveyed rated top supervisors' ability highly; in 1973, 70 percent did.
- Now, 45 percent see opportunities for advancement; then, 55 percent did.
- Now, 60 percent rate their firm as a good place to work; then, 80 percent did.

If the small family business is to thrive, it is essential to give nonfamily personnel clearly defined responsibilities and to reward them for carrying out those responsibilities. To make a policy of limiting delegation of authority to family members only sets up unnecessary barriers to success. In the early stages of the business, the lack of delegation to nonfamily employees results from the simple fact that there's not enough money available to afford to pay competent outsiders. The temptation to watch out for is to keep on "doing it all yourselves," even after the start-up and survival stages are over.

Based upon his study of the 40 small family manufacturing firms, Calder listed these as the most effective techniques for motivating nonfamily managers:

- Giving recognition to the individual that provides him or her with a feeling of importance and a sense of belonging to the organization
- Guarding against family friction and undue family interference
- Creating security through pensions, retirement programs, fringe benefits, and long-term management planning
- Establishing and preserving congenial working relationships. Contented management is generally efficient management.
- Encouraging and stimulating employees by showing appreciation for their efforts and accomplishment
- Delegating authority and responsibility so that management can have the satisfaction of a justified pride in accomplishment
- Providing adequate compensation based on the efforts and contributions of the individual, whether he or she is a family or nonfamily member
- Permitting employees to purchase equity securities in the company

MANAGING GROWING PAINS

Every successful small firm, whether it's launched by family, friends, or even enemies, eventually faces the problems of growth and expansion. Researchers often refer to the moment of truth that arrives when the family business makes the transition from the entrepreneurial stage to the administrative stage.

The family business frequently reaches this turning point during the changeover from the first generation to the next, "a transition which many family businesses do not survive," observes Richard Peiser of the Cox School of Business at Southern Methodist University. He notes that a successful transition is most easily made when family life cycles and business life cycles coincide.

As the original owners of a family business age, Peiser writes in an article in *Business Horizons*, their needs and goals tend to change. As the first generation becomes more conservative, seeking to hold on to what has been gained, the second generation is ready to branch out and prove itself. Differences between founder and firm often come about later in the life of the business, after it has achieved a measure of success. "The problem can appear in several forms," he notes. "The founder's interests may move in directions away from the firm, and what is best for the founder may cease to be what is best for the firm. At this point, many nonfamily businesses move in the direction of professional management."

The symptoms of life-cycle crisis are fairly easy to identify. Unusual difficulties and delays in decision making are particularly unhealthy signs. When you begin to notice that simple decisions take an inordinate amount of time or that family members are consistently pulling in opposite directions, it's time to look for remedies. A useful first step in correcting the situation is to set up a system of delineating responsibility and accountability, one that closely and clearly identifies success or failure with each individual. To accomplish this effectively, and to maintain the growth pattern of the business, Peiser suggests the following:

1. Make all family members aware of current projects, and set short-term performance goals for each member. These objectives should be measurable, time bound, specific, and realistic. "This is not a rigid system of management by objective," says Peiser, "but rather a simple attempt to involve the key decision makers in the process of defining and evaluating performance."

2. Focus the family upon itself in both an affective and rational manner. Back away from the nitty-gritty problems, and remember that you're all part of a family, not just a commercial enterprise.

3. Make strategic plans. Every family business must identify and address the critical issues of the future: how the current strategy holds up, acceptable alternatives, what new skills are needed, and the effect of new strategies on the job and career of each family member.

7

Improving Your Marketing and Selling Performance

THE DIRECTNESS AND simplicity of the marketing approaches of many successful family businesses are most impressive. You won't find many of them conducting high-powered market research studies. Most rely on a gut feeling that quality will sell.

Probably the single most important rule of marketing for the family business is to *target* the special niche your product or service fits best, and then concentrate your promotional effort to reach that targeted group.

In your initial enthusiasm, it's easy to fall into the trap of thinking that almost *anybody can* be your customer. Unfortunately, unless you focus your efforts, the likely result is that almost *nobody will* be your customer. Don't think that population trends, environmental concerns, baby booms, or whatever will make your product a national bestseller. Train yourself as a marketer to think in terms of specifics, of fractions, of tiny segments. There's no way you will have an advertising budget large enough to achieve mass marketing success. So instead think small, or more accurately, think clearly and do everything you can to sell to that tiny segment. Once you have a solid customer base, you can build up to other and larger markets. But without that initial customer base, you'll find yourself going in circles, always searching for the magic button that will bring in loads of those mysterious customers . . . if only you knew where they were.

To the true professionals in the field, marketing concentrates on satisfying the needs of the buyer through the product. There's a potential paradox often at this point, since many new family businesses I know start with the founders and their commitment to the product that they create. The marketing challenge then is to match up customer satisfaction with the founders' perception of product value.

In the early stages of a new product's life, it is critical to do as much market research as possible to pinpoint your best prospects. Do everything you can to identify key characteristics of your best customers and aim your marketing efforts to their specific needs. In some cases, the key characteristics can be *demographic* (age, sex, income); *geographic* (Sun Belt, urban, rural); *psychographic* (personality traits, political tendencies); or *consumer-behavioral* (magazine reader, mail-order buyer).

To come up with the answers, you can try personal interviews, mail surveys, questionnaires to existing customers. Try to learn as much as you can about who buys (or will buy), why they buy, and how they rate your product.

It makes no difference what the nature of your business is; sound principles of marketing must be implemented. Whether you're dealing with gourmet foods or hand-crafted clothing—or even something as potentially noxious as city sewage sludge—you'll find that to succeed in the marketplace, you not only have to provide a quality product or service, but you must also keep in close contact with the customer base you serve.

"Successful businesses must be *customer-oriented,* not product-oriented," stresses consultant Fran Henry. It's important to get into the customers' shoes and look at your business from their viewpoint. As we interview successful owners of growing family businesses throughout the United States, we're continually seeing how personal insights into the value of what they offer are made clear to customers.

Ann Buscho, who in 1982 started a company called Sprouts, in San Rafael, California, is typical of many. Her market research was highly personal. Her infant daughter was allergic to the synthetic fibers that went into nearly every piece of baby clothing Ann could find. So she started making 100 percent cotton children's wear. Soon, friends were asking her if they could buy similar clothing for their children. Before she knew it, Sprouts had become a flourishing business selling to specialty shops all over the country.

Pat Sherwood and Elizabeth Bertani were homemakers and part-time students at a northern California college when they discovered their shared interest in cooking a few years ago. Today, they are at the helm of The Parsley Patch Pure Spice Company, which anticipates million-dollar sales in 1984. The Patch began with an all-purpose salt substitute that Elizabeth had developed to liven up the low-fat, low-salt cooking she adopted after her husband's heart attack. By April 1982, the company had a wholesale line of seven seasoning blends: French, Italian, Mexican, Curry, Oriental, Winter Spice, and All-Purpose. The products were developed with the help of 100 taste testers including friends, restaurant cooks, vegetarians, even people unenthusiastic about herbs.

When The Parsley Patch began in 1981, Elizabeth

and Pat expected, at the most, strong country-wide sales by the end of that year. But within a month, they had national customers. This was due in large part to their taking the new product to the Gourmet Products Show in San Francisco, where they found sales reps clamoring to sell the blends. The gourmet market was the initial sales target; the partners had a product line that, they believed, held a special appeal for sophisticated tastes. Prices were higher than those of other mixed seasonings because of premium ingredients and expensive packaging (glass jars with cork tops). Early accounts included stores like Liberty House, Marshall Field's, and Macy's of northern California.

But because Parsley Patch blends are salt-free and made from quality ingredients with no fillers or preservatives, Pat and Elizabeth planned from the start to move into the health food market. This campaign began in 1982. They brought down prices with cheaper packaging: attractive cardboard boxes with cellophane refill bags. By the end of 1982, The Patch had 13 health food distributors (including two in Canada), with especially good distribution in California and Washington.

Sales for 1982 increased 237 percent over the seven-month 1981 sales. The product line was sold directly to stores, as well as through specialty and health food distributors in all 50 states.

The goal for 1983 was to widen sales further. "We are moving into the grocery chains—initially the specialty, dietetic, and health food sections," Elizabeth explains. "Although our prices will be higher than those of well-known brands, we have become more price competitive by shifting to the standard spice jars, which are smaller and cheaper than either our previous jars or our cardboard packaging. In addition, no one else offers a complete line of natural blends that covers all the different categories of ethnic cooking," says Elizabeth.

In just about every case, *quality* is the key to marketing success—to finding the right niche for the small, specialized business. Even large companies are finding that "quality is hot," notes *In Business* columnist Carter Henderson, who adds, "Companies that have never given it a second thought are now spending thousands of dollars a day to study the subject with America's leading quality consultants."

Jim Howard, head of Country Business Services—a firm specializing in providing support to new business owners—agrees that quality is paramount. "The new market will be a quality rather than a quantity market," Howard stresses. "Businesses will do better to focus on top quality rather than bottom price. Not only will this attract a real (if not usually recognized) growth market, it is also lots more fun."

Reaching the people who are your best customers without spending a fortune in advertising is the marketing challenge we all assume when we launch our business . . . and grow with it. It's fun . . . when it works out, but frustrating when it doesn't, especially when your ad budget is extremely small. That's when hustle and innovation must prevent frustration and doldrums.

Enthusiasm and confidence go along with hustle and chutzpah. And, as Liz Thomas notes, paying attention to packaging pays off. "In our case, there are lots of mustards out there, and they all look the same—packaged either in earth-tone crocks or with earth-tone labels. Our bottles display the Romanov eagle. The blue-and-white color scheme isn't complicated, yet it attracts attention. My brother designed the logo, and it was his idea to include a tag, attached to the bottle, describing the history of Chalif Mustard. We also supply recipe sheets to retailers, although they don't always display them with our product. At taste tests, we wear Chalif T-shirts and aprons—everyone notices us."

But most important, the Thomases' enthusiasm about

their mustard is a major contributor to sales. For example, it helped them cultivate new accounts at the Fancy Food and Confection Show held in New York last June. Sharing a booth with their broker, Liz and Nick went prepared to watch, learn, and show the mustard. But it didn't take them long to get caught up in the action. "We didn't know it, but the other exhibitors were taking bets on when we were going to run out of steam," says Liz. "We came away with 120 new accounts, and quite a bit of media attention." Nick describes their experiences at the trade show as an important test of Chalif Mustard's ability to compete. "We left feeling there was no reason to doubt the quality of our product," he says.

Clever packaging and a good ad helped Tom and Mary Lynn Thompson sell croissants as gifts. From their Allentown, Pennsylvania, bakery, they sold croissants to three local restaurants, packaged them as executive gifts for Prudential-Bache in Philadelphia, and advertised them in the local paper, offering a special Christmas gift of home-delivered croissants in fireside baskets. "Sales increased exponentially with the ad," says Tom. "Mary Lynn and I delivered dozens of baskets ourselves. The feedback was tremendous." The success of the Christmas basket encouraged the Thompsons to go full-time with their new product. The result was C'est Croissant, started in the fall of 1982. A box of 12 croissants with three jars of fancy preserves, a tea towel, and a gift card sells for $15; a dozen butter and almond croissants are $10. The boxes are shipped UPS and arrive within three to five days after packaging.

GOOD REPUTATION IS A MUST

In Charlotte, North Carolina, Mary and Walter Knox started a video production company in June 1979, operating out of their home with rented equipment. According-ing to industry reports, corporate video is a $1.5 billion industry with more than 3,000 companies. Walter Knox told reporter Beatrice Quirk that their Video Production Company of America had gross billings of slightly under $1 million in 1982 and that the company has been profitable since its beginning.

According to the Knoxes, the key to their success has been a good reputation. Most of their competitors are larger companies such as TV stations, production outfits, or large video firms with more capital. The Video Production Company of America still gets clients through making bids, direct mailings, sales calls, and advertising, but over half its business comes through word of mouth. "Every time we finish a project, it goes out in the field where people see it, and the word gets out about us," says Mary. "Reputation is all in this business, and a bad reputation can be fatal."

Although word of mouth is important, Mary, who handles the firm's marketing, still puts great effort into selling her firm and the concept of using video as a communications tool. Prospective clients are shown that video is a viable option compared to print and that it can do more than print, works better than slides, and is cheaper than film. Video is unique in that it literally sells itself. On sales calls, Mary uses a 10-minute video presentation of clips from previous commercials and corporate projects to show prospective clients what The Video Production Company of America can do.

MIGHTY PLAIN, BUT MIGHTY GOOD

One of our favorite marketing examples is supplied by an old store not too far from Waco, Texas—a store called Western Fair in Lott. We heard about the store from a neighbor in Pennsylvania who grew up in Waco and said people come from all over to shop there for hats, jeans, shirts . . . and, of course, boots.

"The town of Lott has only a few hundred residents," writes Nita Sue Kent in *In Business*,

> and a main street so decrepit it could be a movie set. From the sidewalk, there is no sign of any enormous clothing store, only a block of brick store fronts, with a jumble of signs that proclaim Tony Lama, Justin, or Acme boots, Levi, Wrangler, and Bluebell jeans. The entrance to Western Fair is reassuringly plain. Inside the single door is a wooden booth with four cash registers.
>
> Once, when the judge (founder Rolla Will Hailey) wanted to remodel the Fair, Mrs. Hailey insisted that the front entrance remain much as it had always been—the door to a country store. And that is what the Fair is today—a country store that has made it big. High quality and the hardheaded realistic approach of a small-town merchant has made it worth while for thousands to drive hours to shop there.

MARKET RESEARCH

Whether your family has been operating the business for 50 years or 50 days, you need to be constantly getting answers about potential and actual customers. The way to get the answers is through market research. However, many owners figure that such research must involve high costs, lengthy questionnaires, and complex mathematics. It's not true, says Alan Andreasen, University of Illinois marketing professor. Writing in the *Harvard Business Review*, he points out that reliable information to improve marketing decisions can be obtained simply and cheaply.

"Managers can obtain marketing data simply by

carefully observing (customer) behavior. Retailers have found pedestrian and vehicle traffic counts to be invaluable in assessing the success of competitors' new products or services and in evaluating new outlet locations. . . . What distinguishes marketing research from casual observation or a 'feel' for the market is careful specification of the needed observations, systematic observation, observation at random times and places, and careful recording and analysis of results."

Surveys can be done inexpensively and effectively. When prospective customers are few, usually the best and easiest way to learn their reactions is through talking with them directly. If many and scattered, use printed survey forms. These can be either inserted in packages or mailed to random samplings regularly

The objective is to closely monitor the needs and desires of your customers. Chances are people are interested in your product for a number of different reasons. You may be dealing with several different segments and separate market areas. Your challenge is to blend your product line so you serve each area well, and all highly effectively.

Demographic data such as age, education levels, and family patterns of customers cannot be ignored. Much information is available through such sources as the Census Bureau, State Data Centers, computer service bureaus, and trade associations. Always analyze data on your present customer list. For example, Professor Andreasen advises inspecting zip code data of existing charge customers to learn about geographic dispersion and travel patterns of customers. "When supplemented by census data, it can indicate income, education, and other household characteristics of these customers." Research, he says, need not be intimidating. It can play an important role in effective management and marketing success.

8
Staying Healthy

MANY PERSONS WONDER if being together with your family seven days and seven nights a week will jeopardize sanity as well as smooth business operation. After five years, I really don't regard too much togetherness to be a problem, but then again, there are those who question my sensitivity.

Since Nora works out of our Washington, D.C., editorial office, it's definitely not a problem for her. If there's been a problem for the rest of us, it's too much of business, not too much of us.

We do manage to get away for vacations and extended trips. In a few days, for example, Ina and I will be leaving for Naples, Italy. On this particular trip, we'll be attending a waste recycling conference at the University of Naples where I'm scheduled to give a talk. But we will be away for two weeks, and that certainly helps to alleviate any tensions resulting from constant togetherness. Whenever there's a good reason to take a trip, whether for pleasure or business (or a combination), it usually can be done. That's part of the flexibility that belongs to a family business. It's also a way to keep irritability under control.

Also beware of the weekend trap. I get sloppy with time. So it's Saturday, so what? Let's all meet at the office and take our time getting the next issue assembled. There's even beer in the refrigerator. That kind of weekend togetherness is an easy habit for the family business to fall into. It's okay on a now-and-then basis, but the trick is to keep it from becoming routine. Working seven days a week with your kin will surely lead to early burn-out.

I really don't mind going to the office for a few hours on Saturday, especially when the weather is lousy. And I've been known to spend a few hours there on Sunday as well. In the beginning, Rill and Nora followed the same routine. It seemed to be the only way to keep up with projects. Ina compounded the problem. She's a night person and is perfectly willing to come in during the late afternoon and stay until midnight. Nora was the first one to put definite limits on regular weekend work. Of course, to accomplish the feat, she got married and moved to Washington. If she gets behind at deadline time, she's as bad as anyone. Still, she's probably been the most disciplined about pacing her work during the Monday-to-Friday workweek and leading her own life apart from the business.

Rill has the widest range of responsibilities of us all, so she always has a project to finish . . . or to start. In the past two years, she's become the most organized about preparing reports, recommending a decision *on paper*, and summarizing monthly results. She's even learned how to avoid coming in every weekend.

The absence of scheduled meetings may be one result of overtogetherness. That could be good or bad depending upon your attitude toward formal meetings. In my previous employment, I came to the conclusion that a sound, substantial decision was never made at a company meeting.

But it is true that so much dialogue takes place informally—while walking to the office, during meals, even in shouting matches across the office—that we can't be absolutely certain that all information is sufficiently transmitted to the people who need it.

KEEPING FIT

Fifty-year-old Gene Logsdon closes his office door at 4:00 P.M., meets his wife and son, and drives to the ball field ten minutes away. There he turns into a combination George Steinbrenner (instead of the Yankees, the team he "owns" is the Upper Sandusky Country Rovers) and a George Brett (he also plays third base).

The routine of leaving early for the softball diamond happens two or three times a week from June through September—plus weekends when tournaments are scheduled. For the fun of making it all happen—of bringing together 15 players between the ages of 15 and 50—full-time free-lancer Logsdon spends about $1,000 a year, which takes care of uniforms, entry fees, and beer when his team wins. (They buy him beer when they lose.)

"I love it, and so does the team," says Logsdon, who left a top editorial position with the Philadelphia-based *Farm Journal* to work out of a home office on his Ohio farm. All of his seven sisters and brothers live within 10 miles of where they grew up. Logsdon finds softball so much fun that he has become an enthusiastic director of the Ohio Branch of the Amateur Softball Association—despite his long abhorrence of anything bureaucratic. This past season, the Country Rovers—the name of Gene's column in several publications—came in second in the county and won about half the tournaments.

Logsdon is typical of many small family-business owners who like what they do so much that they have to work just as hard to build the breaks into their routines.

For many men and women, athletics plays a big role in breaking up a heavy-duty routine. I lean to tennis, having had trouble since childhood hitting a ball out of the infield. If you're part of a small business, whatever you do for fun—as well as for improving your mental and physical health—can be absolutely critical. According to a study recently completed, 55 to 65 percent of 450 entrepreneurs surveyed suffer at least once a week from back problems, insomnia, headaches, and indigestion. One-third of the respondents have one or more of the symptoms at least twice a week, and more than one-third have chest pains once a week. I hasten to point out that the business owners who were surveyed were not specifically *family* business heads. Most companies had from 25 to 99 employees, sales of $1 to $2 million, and pretax profit margins of 4 percent to 7 percent of sales. The persons with problems complained that their spouses and families didn't understand their business troubles. These individuals hesitated to take time off for vacations, were frustrated and disappointed with work relationships, and tended to block out the symptoms of their high-stress levels.

A family business, if nothing else, leads to an understanding of what the problems are and what jobs have to be done. But the need to get away, to get some physical exercise, and to do what is necessary to reduce stress is no less pressing in a family firm than in one run by a single entrepreneur or corporation CEO.

The entire subject of *keeping fit* is so vital that we've had a regular column on this topic in our magazine for the past two years. The department is written by Charles Kuntzleman and Dan Runyon of Fitness Finders, a

Michigan firm that specializes in developing company fitness programs. Recognizing how most owners do not schedule specific time to exercise, they worked out ways to be an "exercise sneak"—to build physical activity into your work routine. They also stress that we all should engage in aerobic exercises such as walking, swimming, biking, running, and cross-country skiing. Besides burning up extra calories and fat, these activities also improve overall muscle strength and endurance. Most important, these exercises help take care of your most important muscle—your heart. Twenty to 30 minutes of walking, running, bicycling, swimming, or cross-country skiing three to four times a week will do wonders for this all-important muscle.

Kuntzleman and Runyon urge all to never sit for more than an hour and a half without getting up and moving around for five or ten minutes. Try to schedule the day so that every hour or so, you get up to do such things as filing, delivering messages, or talking with your spouse, parent, or child.

9

Choosing a Successor

After the struggles to survive and grow, the greatest single issue facing the family firm may well be *succession*. The academics who have studied family businesses invariably dwell on the complications of transferring power from one generation to another, especially if the company has grown to considerable size. Usually the articles in journals such as the *Harvard Business Review* begin with references to how tough it is to remove the reins from the old founder's hands. For example, in the July-August 1976 *Harvard Business Review*, Louis B. Barnes and Simon A. Hershon observed the following:

> The transition problem affects both family and nonfamily members. Brokers and bankers, professional managers, employees, competitors, outside directors, wives, friends, and potential stock investors all have more than passing interest as a company moves from one generation to the next. Some of these transitions seem orderly. Most, however, do not. Management becomes racked with strife and indecision. Sons, heirs, key employees, and directors resign in protest. Families are torn with conflict. The president-

father is deposed. Buyers who want to merge with or acquire the business change their minds. And often the company dies or becomes stagnant.

Needless to say, as one who might now be described as a 52-year-old president-father, I was more than a bit aroused by the future prospects described by Barnes and Hershon. And here I had always envisioned tender loving care from those daughters. Evidently the frequency of those accounts and the attendant pain from power struggles upset both Barnes and Hershon, since they decided to make a formal research inquiry into "what happens as a family business or, more accurately, a family *and* its business grow and develop over generations. Specifically, what happens in the family and company between those periods when one generation or another is clearly in control but both are 'around'? In addition, how do some managements go through or hurdle the family transition without impeding company growth? And can or must family and company transitions be kept separate?"

The first conclusion reached by the authors is that too many commentators on family business overemphasize the need for professional management as a solution. "It is apparent," they say, "that families do stay in their businesses, and that the businesses stay in the family. There is something more deeply rooted in transfers of power than impersonal business interests. The human tradition of passing on heritage, possessions, and name from one generation to the next leads both parents and children to seek continuity in the family business."

When transitions are well managed, all perspectives are addressed as sensitively as possible. Barnes and Hershon cite four different perspectives:

1. Family managers (inside the family and inside the business)

2. The employees (older employees wanting rewards for loyalty and security, while younger ones wanting opportunities for growth)

3. The relatives (family members not in active management)

4. The outsiders (competitors, suppliers, customers, etc.)

Their studies showed that quite often a mother was a behind-the-scenes influence.

> Time after time we saw cases in which an entrepreneur's wife played an important role in bridging the growing gap between father and sons. . . . It also happened that an entrepreneur's widow would step in as a peacemaker for the younger generation. But when it came to helping make both transitions occur, the wife was more important than the widow. . . . She would help or persuade her husband to look toward the (children's) future instead of his own past. In effect, she provided a relative's outside-the-business perspective. Such outside perspectives turned out to be crucial in transition management, because they helped to heal and avoid the wounds of family conflict.

Barnes and Hershon conclude that the founder or even the founder's children, as they get older, must consciously make the decision that, even though they will die, the company will live. And at some point, a critical network of family managers, employees, relatives, and outsiders must begin to focus upon the duality of both family and business transitions. In their opinion, the talks should begin at least seven to eight years before the president is supposed to retire. "Even though the specific plans may change," they believe, "the important assumptions behind those plans will not. . . . In effect, a successful family transition can mean a new beginning for the company."

As director of the Wharton Applied Research Center at the University of Pennsylvania, Peter Davis has had many chances to explore the issue of succession with members of family-held corporations who have attended workshops sponsored by the center. The workshops are attended by sons, daughters, grandchildren, nephews, and nieces who are faced with decisions about their participation in the family business.

"Succession represents more than a shift of power—it represents a symbolic demise of the founder and can spill over into the way the founder sees his or her role in the family," Davis says. "It's not uncommon to see an entrepreneur playing one child against the other to keep each in line and postpone the succession issue.

"There's no single formula for successful succession. Sometimes a contract is worked out years in advance; sometimes the founder stays on formally as a consultant. The most important advice is for the founder and the children to develop a working relationship that succeeds on a day-to-day basis, one that shifts from competition to cooperation," Davis adds.

Davis sees several steps to accomplish this:

- The clear delineation of business roles for all family members, with appropriate business training for family members who need it
- Recognition of personal development needs

Aging entrepreneurs are frequently oblivious to their children's psychological needs, especially during the "critical" age of the thirties. Davis points to a statement by Stanley Marcus of Nieman-Marcus: "Probably the single greatest disappointment in my business career was the failure of my father, on his own initiative, to name me as president prior to my fortieth birthday."

Children must also recognize their parents' needs for closure and development of mentoring roles.

To illustrate the nightmare that can occur in a family business, Davis recounts the tale of how Edsel Ford was named Henry's chosen successor in the 1930s in name but not in substance. In the ensuing years, serious mistakes were made, and by 1946, Ford was losing $10 million a month. By not giving up control and establishing a successor whom he supported, Henry Ford almost destroyed what he had founded.

"When the transition is badly managed, a relationship exists at the very pinnacle of the enterprise that is emotional, uncomfortable, and destructive," Davis writes. "The relationship becomes the focal issue among those with responsibility for providing leadership in the business. Attention turns inward to the concerns and behavior of family and management. There is no energy left for moving the company forward, for creating new programs and initiatives necessary to take advantage of tomorrow's opportunities. The business begins to fail, uncontrollably."

Davis explains that the case of Edsel Ford dramatizes the power of "a dimension of the human condition which we have been attempting to design out of management and the conduct of business for a hundred years—the dimension of emotional involvement." But as we know, in the family-owned businesses, emotional relationships are built in. They are there because the family members bring them in along with their talents, finances, and sweat.

Involvement is a particular characteristic of most founders of small businesses, and that means pride of ownership. That trait also tends to create an ambivalence to the qualities of the son or daughter who is chosen to be successor, explains Dr. Matilde Salganicoff, a clinical psychologist who has specialized in family business problems. "A conflict develops between the creator and the second generation," she says. "Consider the fact that every step forward a child makes in learning the business is a sign of your own mortality . . . that you are one day closer to stepping aside." As a result, she relates in her article "The Family Business: Who Really Profits?", the original founder may resist setting up a fair arrangement with the successor, even though he or she has chosen the successor.

Both Dr. Salganicoff and Davis emphasize the need for planning to make a smooth transition. Ideally, alternate situations can be created that give the founder a continuing, but noninterfering role. Dr. Davis also points out the importance of company heads' giving their children—while in their thirties—enough authority and challenge. "If that reluctance to hand over power is there, the children may feel frustrated by it. . . . As a general rule, it behooves family businesses to try to create conditions whereby the next generation can take over at a productive time of their lives. And the problem is that this means the outgoing generation not only has to avoid late retirement, it often must take early retirement."

RIVALRY

In a 1971 article in the *Harvard Business Review*, Harry Levinson listed the "conflicts that plague family businesses." It's a laundry list of horror tales replete with fictional anecdotes. "The fundamental psychological conflict in family businesses is *rivalry*," Levinson wrote, "compounded by feelings of guilt, when more than one family member is involved. The rivalry may be felt by the founder—even though no relatives are in the business—when he unconsciously senses (justifiably or not) that subordinates are threatening to remove him from his center of power."

Rivalry comes in all manner of relationships. Levinson lists father-son rivalry—father has great difficulty giving up his baby, his mistress, since the business is an extension of himself and his source of social power. Woe to the son (or daughter) who seeks his place in the sun. According to Levinson, the father does not want his son to win at whatever goal he seeks for the business, since victory would displace him from his summit position. "These conflicting emotions cause the father to behave inexplicably in a contradictory manner, leading those close to him to think that while on the one hand he wants the business to succeed, on the other hand he is determined to make it fail," Levinson predicts.

Levinson's anecdotes are replete with such utterances as "Why don't you let me grow up!" and "He's destroying the business." But I wish he had at least one or two examples of fathers and mothers who managed to give up authority without excessive trauma.

One example that I'm thoroughly familiar with involves an imaginative entrepreneur who loved to run with his latest brainstorm and leave the business end to his son and his son's management team. The father had a tremendous ego—so tremendous that his latest creation satisfied it, and he didn't mind that major decisions about the primary business were carried out without his close supervision. When the father suddenly died, a seasoned second-generation management team was well in place and the business continued to thrive.

Incidentally, as Levinson pointed out, financial success does not spare the scion from criticism. "If he takes over a successful enterprise, and even if he makes it much more successful than anyone could have imagined, nevertheless the onlookers stimulate his feelings of inadequacy. They say, 'What did you expect? After all, look what he started with.' " Sons and daughters who move into the top spot in their family business must be prepared to hear such petty remarks. They're most often uttered by relatives or "friends" who need someone to talk about when they get together. Usually the remarks are made by people who don't know the complexities of your business and who aren't capable of understanding them. So why worry?

Looking at sibling-sibling conflict, Levinson stressed that brothers and sisters should

> see that in their relationship they recapitulate ancient rivalries, and should perceive clearly the psychological posture each assumes toward the other. . . . Since there is love and hate in all relationships, theirs cannot, by definition, be pure. They should not feel guilty about their anger with each other, but they do need to talk it out. Having done that, they then must consider how they can divide the tasks in the organization so that each will have a chance to acquire and demonstrate competence and work in a complementary relationship with the other.
>
> . . . If the brothers still cannot resolve their conflicts, then it becomes necessary to seek professional aid. If this does not help, they should consider being in separate organizations. In such a case, the big problem is the guilt feelings which the departing brother is likely to have for deserting the other and the family business.
>
> . . . Where there is conflict, or inadequately rationalized territories, members of the family should move up and out of operations as quickly as possible into policy positions. Such movement recognizes the reality of ownership but does not confuse ownership with management.

10
If You Need Outside Help

I'VE ALWAYS HAD an ambivalent attitude toward professional consultants, similar to the way I feel about medical doctors. The worst thing, I believe, is to run a business (or yourself) in a way that leads you to be dependent upon outside professionals. Yet, if you are in a hole or if you're ill, there's nothing more helpful than knowing you have the phone number of someone you trust.

When a family business starts out, it's necessary to build on your own strengths and insights. The more your growth strategy permits you to build up your know-how and confidence, the better your chances for success. I can't think of any family business that founded its operations on the expertise of a big-name consultant. But I can think of several family-owned firms that turned themselves into a hodgepodge of trendy marketing fiefdoms by following the advice of the "best industry experts." In each case, what was once a unified, manageable whole became a fractionalized entity pitting one VP against another over whose bottom line was rosier.

With that caveat out of the way, it's wrong for any family business to think all available wisdom resides within its own family sages. Whether it's a tricky management question or a computerization technique, if you see it as a problem area, then it pays to find the right consultant.

"When a family business is in trouble, it can be really messy," says Wharton's Peter Davis. "A family business in trouble is like a whirlpool, sucking everyone in—even the outside consultants who are hired to solve the problems." Davis knows only too well how complex the problems can be, having served as a consultant to a firm that eventually turned over the company reins to him when no successor in the family could be peacefully named. Knowing that a consultant loses power when "sucked into the personality issue," Davis gradually disengaged himself as president, arranged for an outside manager to be brought in, and remained as a member of the board of directors. The company has continued to thrive in a much-improved atmosphere, and the experience led Davis and his colleagues at Wharton to develop a *coaching model* when asked to be consultants to family businesses. Their basic message is that family members have to work out their own problems, with consultants primarily serving as resources to help develop the best game plan.

Aside from identifying outside specialists in marketing, organization, or finance, you may want to establish an in-house advisory board composed of outsiders. I'd recommend not setting up such an advisory board until after you're out of the survival stage—until you have established a market niche and have a profitable operation. It's not that you don't need advice when you're struggling, it's simply that you have few options and outsiders may just drive you up a wall with advice you're not ready to follow. Once you enter the success phase, that's when you will be facing choices about expanding markets and product line. And that's when a more formal advisory board can help.

Harold Fox, a Ball State University professor, describes such boards as typically meeting two to four times per year and functioning somewhat like a working board of directors. He calls them a *quasi board.* Unlike an official board of directors, which represents the stockholders and is formally accountable to external and internal parties, an *advisory council* (or *quasi board*) is appointed by the owners and has no legal obligations to others. "Ironically," notes Dr. Fox, "this lack of official status is the basis for a quasi board's efficacy. Top managers can unload their burdens without trepidation. After frank discussions, a practical course of action emerges that benefits from the panel's expertise and detachment." Here is his description of a typical board:

1. There are three to five outside members. Larger panels can become unwieldy; smaller ones lack diversity of expertise and temperament.
2. Likely candidates include business acquaintances and former schoolmates.
3. Pragmatic thinkers offering board experience in business management and in-depth familiarity with at least one major business function are suitable.
4. Knowledge of the principal's business is not necessary; it could inhibit original contribution.

Leon Danco and Don Jonovic of The Center for Family Business in Cleveland have written an entire book on *Outside Directors in the Family Owned Business.* They categorically say that "every president needs others to help him do his job, people with whom he can be open and honest, people whom he can respect and who respect him, and people who, he feels, are committed to his dream." The authors make the point that the future is mostly the successors' business and the board serves an important function with that point in mind. It's not a question of taking sides, but the board forces the company to make long-range plans. "Since a successor-management is going to be managing the company in the future," write Danco and Jonovic, "the sooner that future is defined and work starts on making it happen, the sooner the successors will know there is a future, and that somebody besides the successors believes in it." The board will most likely see that a succession plan is prepared, no matter how tentatively. Finally, it will help to defuse and arbitrate potential disagreements.

We haven't set up a board of directors, quasi or other, but we have helped to create a small-magazine publishers' association that meets once or twice a year to share information and experiences. I find this group helps us by giving us the opportunity to hear opinions from knowledgeable persons in the magazine business. We also learn about consultants who have been particularly helpful to other publishers.

Conclusion

WHY NOT, IF a family likes to spend a lot of time together, why not go for broke? Live the way you want to live, do the kind of work you like to do, locate where all of you (at least a majority) want to live, and maybe, maybe become what is referred to as economically upscale.

If this book hasn't convinced you, it has convinced me. No apologies . . . yet! We've bought the lakefront property in Vermont. There's an acre—plenty of space to have an office out back for Ina and myself. Better yet, an office connected by an enclosed breezeway, so we don't have to shovel snow to get to the typewriter or (perhaps soon) a word processor and personal computer. As many of our kids who want to relocate there are welcome, but we suspect Boston, Hartford, or Albany might be as close as they'll get full-time. With our kind of publishing company, we can easily work together in geographically separate locations. I imagine they'll certainly want to visit in swimming weather and skiing weather and in the fall foliage season. But in winter, we'll probably spend a month or two down South—or maybe even here in Pennsylvania, so we don't lose touch completely with old friends.

Why not—it's been a pleasant if steady grind to get our magazines as far as we've gotten them. At the moment this is being written, January 1984, we have a print run of 63,000 for *In Business,* 7,000 for *BioCycle,* and 1,200 for *Sideline Business.* It's taken us since January 1978 to get this far, and we're proud of every step we've made.

A family business can bring all the problems that have been mentioned in these pages. So can just about any job you'll have working anywhere. But unlike any job, a family business brings you the joy of continuing as a family entity. Best of luck and a warm welcome if you decide to join the fun.

Appendix: The Family Business Resource Directory

Federal Government Resources

- Directory of State Small Business Programs, 1980 Edition
  Small Business Administration
  Washington, DC 20416

  State-by-state breakdown of loan, procurement, technical assistance programs, and more.

- Federal Trade Commission
  Washington, DC 20580

  Write for listing of regulations affecting your industry, e.g., textiles, packaging.

- House Small Business Committee
  2361 Rayburn House Office Building
  Washington, DC 20515

  Official legislators on small business issues.

- Internal Revenue Service
  Washington, DC 20224

  Free tax handbooks plus free seminars. Write for local listings.

- International Trade Administration
  Business Counseling Section
  Office of Export Development, Room 4009
  Department of Commerce
  Washington, DC 20230

  Export assistance.

- Minority Business Development Agency
  Public Affairs Office
  Department of Commerce
  14th and Constitution, NW
  Washington, DC 20230

  Many regional and local offices. Technical assistance and financing for minority-owned businesses. Publishes free bimonthly *Access*, with new laws, resources, and profiles.

- National Science Foundation
  Small Business Innovation Office
  1800 G Street NW
  Washington, DC 20550

  Research grants, patent assistance, workshops, reports.

- National Technical Information Service
  Department of Commerce
  5285 Port Royal Road
  Springfield, VA 22161

  R&D arm of federal government. Write for report catalog.

- Patent and Trademark Office
  Department of Commerce
  Washington, DC 20231

  Free booklets on patents and inventions.

- Register of Copyrights
  Library of Congress
  Washington, DC 20540

  Free information on copyrights.

- Security and Exchange Commission
  Office of Small Business Policy
  500 N. Capitol Street
  Washington, DC 20549

  Rules and regulations for public or private stock offerings. Write for free pamphlet, "Q&A: Small Business and SEC."

- Senate Small Business Committee
  424 Russell Office Building
  Washington, DC 20510

  Legislative committee for overall small-business issues.

- Small Business Administration
  1441 L Street NW
  Washington, DC 20416

  Main government agency for small business. Offices include Advocacy, Procurement, Lending, Technical Management Assistance, Publications.

STATE, REGIONAL, AND LOCAL RESOURCES

- Small Business Council
  Chamber of Commerce
  (Contact local office; see phone directory.)

Often offers seminars and special events for small businesses. Usually offers referral service.

- Small Business Management Program
  Community College (See phone directory.)

  Courses in managing start-up. Can act as liaison to area Small Business Development Center.

- Small Business Center
  State Department of Commerce
  State Capitol

  Local state senator or representative office will have address. Generally provides booklets on company formation, handling paperwork, etc.

- County Economic Development Center
  (Office will be located in your county seat.)

  List of special incentives for new business development; small-business loan fund; seminars, etc.

Associations, Support Groups

- American Women's Economic Development Corporation
  1270 Avenue of the Americas
  New York, NY 10020

  Courses and counseling for women entrepreneurs.

- Small Business Development Center
  Small Business Administration
  1441 L Street NW
  Washington, DC 20416

  Sixteen university-based technical assistance centers. Workshops, counseling.

- University Business Development Centers
  Small Business Administration
  1441 L Street NW
  Washington, DC 20416

  University-based technical assistance.

- National Venture Capital Association
  2030 M Street NW, Suite 403
  Washington, DC 20036

  Trade association for venture capital professionals.

- Small Business Foundation of America
  69 Hickory Drive
  Waltham, MA 02154

  Gives and receives research grants, conducts seminars, does regional and federal advocacy.

- Women Working at Home
  145 N. Ninth Avenue
  Highland Park, NJ 08904

  Researches women working at home. Published *Home-Based Business Guide and Directory* ($14.20), $25 membership.

- American Association of Small Research Companies
  8794 West Chester Pike
  Upper Darby, PA 19082

  Matches up small R&D companies with potential large contractors by organizing conferences.

- Center for Family Business
  University Services Institute
  PO Box 24268
  Cleveland, OH 44124

  Membership organization for family-owned businesses. Seminars, newsletter, books.

- National Association of Small Business Investment Companies
  618 Washington Building
  Washington, DC 20005

  Trade association for SBA-licensed venture capital investment companies. Newsletter on venture capital.

- National Association of Women Business Owners
  2000 P Street NW
  Washington, DC 20036

  Has many local chapters to assist women entrepreneurs. Newsletter, workshops, lobbies.

- National Association of Women in Commerce
  1333 Howe Avenue, Suite 210
  Sacramento, CA 95825

  Membership association for women in career planning or business start-ups. Workshops.

- National Federation of Independent Business
  150 W. 20th Avenue
  San Mateo, CA 94403

  Small-business association with over 600,000 members; strong Washington lobby with Washington office.

- National Small Business Association
  1604 K Street NW
  Washington, DC 20006

  Membership association, lobbying group. Procurement search service, newsletters.

- National Association for the Self-Employed
  PO Box 612067—Commonwealth Plaza
  Dallas, TX 75234

- National Family Business Council
  8600 West Bryn Mawr Avenue
  Chicago, IL 60621

Magazines and Newsletters

- *In Business*
  Box 323
  Emmaus, PA 18049

  Bimonthly magazine ($18 per year). Directed to owners of small-scale firms, as well as persons interested in starting. Regular coverage of family-owned businesses, including profiles.

- *The Family in Business*
  5862 Mayfield Road
  PO Box 24268
  Cleveland, OH 44124

  Monthly newsletter of the Center for Family Business and sent to members. Includes interviews and management advice.

- *Sideline Business*
  The JG Press, Inc.
  Box 351
  Emmaus, PA 18049

  Monthly newsletter ($30 per year), by *In Business* editors on starting a part-time business to gain experience, create extra income. Includes profiles, brief sketches, and management how-to.

Readings on Family Business

Barnes, L. and Hershon, S. "Transferring Power in the Family Business." *Harvard Business Review*, July-August 1976.

Barry, B. "The Development of Organization Structure in the Family Firm." *Journal of General Management* 3, No. 3 (1975).

Calder, G. "The Peculiar Problems of a Family Business." *Business Horizons* 4 (1961): 93–102.

Danco, A. *Inside the Family Business.* Cleveland: The Center for Family Business, 1980.

Davis, P., and Stern, D. "Adaptation, Survival, and Growth of the Family Business: An Integrated Systems Perspective." *Human Relations,* 1980.

Kinkead, G. "Family Business Is a Passion Play." *Fortune,* June 30, 1980.

Levinson, H. "Conflicts That Plague Family Businesses." *Harvard Business Review,* March-April 1971, 40–48.

Levinson, R. "Making Your Family Business More Profitable." *University of Michigan Business Review,* May 1975, 24–29.

Machlowitz, M. *Workaholics.* Reading, Mass.: Addison-Wesley, 1980.

Moch, L. P., ed., *Essays on the Family and Historical Change.* Texas: Texas A&M University Press, 1983.

Organizational Dynamics, Summer 1983. A special issue that included such articles as "Managing Continuity in the Family-Owned Business"; "Realizing the Potential of the Family Business"; "The Family and the Firm: A Coevolutionary Perspective." (The quarterly journal is published by the American Management Association.)

Topolnicki, D. M. "Family Firms Can Leave the Feuds Behind." *Money,* July 1983.

Vesper, K. *New Venture Strategies.* Englewood Cliffs, N.J.: Prentice-Hall, 1981.

Index